MISTER
ROMANCE

LEISA RAYVEN

D0108256

This is a work of fiction. All of the characters, organizations, and events that are portrayed in this novel are either products of the author's imagination or are used fictitiously.

MISTER ROMANCE - Copyright @2017 by Leisa Rayven.

WWW. LEISARAYVEN.COM

First edition: April 2017

Cover design: Regina Wamba, MaeIDesign
Cover photograph: Deposit Photos
Formatting: CP Smith

ISBN 978-0-9953847-2-9

*This book is for everyone who's ever felt
ignored and invisible.
Please know that I see you,
and you're beautiful, and incredible,
and more priceless than you'll ever know.*

MISTER
ROMANCE

One

The Man, The Legend

When I hear the term *Mister Romance* drop from my sweet-but-naive baby-sister's mouth, I'm convinced she's been duped into believing yet another urban legend. Asha's sitting at the breakfast bar in our small Brooklyn apartment, looking way too put together for six a.m. on a Monday morning.

I stop filling the coffeemaker and turn to her. "You're telling me that women hire a man to make their romantic fantasies come to life? Come on, Ash. There's no way that's a thing."

"It's true!" she insists. "Joanna was dishing the dirt in the break room at work. He sets up all these amazing scenarios. You know the tropes: damaged billionaire, sexy bad boy, devoted best friend, hottie contractor. He has this whole range of characters that don't usually exist outside of romance novels, and the word is he blows his clients' minds. Joanna overheard a whole bunch of women talking about him last weekend at some thousand-dollar-a-ticket charity event."

I make a scoffing noise and go back to making coffee. "What the hell was *Joanna the secretary* doing at that kind of event?"

"Her cousin is related to some obscure Latvian royalty or something. The crown prince's limo broke down on the way in from the airport, so Joanna was invited at the last minute to take his ticket."

I give my sister my best deadpan look. "Latvian royalty. Of course. Makes perfect sense."

My sister is a junior editor at one of New York's oldest publishing houses, and even though I haven't met all her coworkers, the ones I have met are definitely on the strange side of quirky.

"Isn't Joanna a compulsive liar?" I ask.

"Well, yeah, she tells some tall tales, but that doesn't mean she doesn't know stuff. One of the women talking about the über-stud claimed that a date with him cured her depression. Another said he saved her marriage, because until he showed her how sensual she could be, she'd forgotten how much she enjoyed sex. This whole gaggle of women thinks he's their romantic savior. White-hot Jesus, or whatever."

I shake my head and watch as coffee dribbles through the filter. Always the more imaginative out of the two of us, Asha has inherited all my mother's blind optimism but zero common sense.

"So what you're telling me," I say, as I pour two cups of fresh Joe, "is that this mythical man-beast about whom *Pants-On-Fire* Joanna was raving, is some kind of ... what? Superhero gigolo?"

"He's an *escort,*" Asha clarifies.

"Isn't that just a fancy label for man-whore?"

"No. He doesn't have sex with his clients."

I pass her a cup of coffee. "You just told me he did."

"No," she says as she defiles her mug of hand-roasted Columbian blend with four sugars, "I said he makes their *romantic* fantasies come to life."

"And that doesn't include sex?"

"No."

"Doesn't sound very romantic. A guy who won't sleep with me? I can get that for free."

Asha adds cream to her coffee and lets out an exasperated sigh. She does that a lot with me. My relentless cynicism wears on her hopeless-romantic sensibilities. Always has.

One time when I was eight and she was six, I was arguing with Mom about the non-existence of Santa. Asha got so upset she went through my *Peter Pan* coloring book and drew devil horns on everyone, even Nana the dog.

Horrible little monster.

To get back at her, I threw a whole bunch of glitter on her bedroom floor while she slept. When she woke and asked what happened, I told her Tinkerbell was so angry about her defacing Peter, she'd exploded with rage. Asha cried for a full half hour before Mom could convince her I was joking.

Needless to say, my little sister never defaced any of my property again.

"Would you ever actually pay for sex?" she asks with a contemplative expression as I load some bread into the toaster.

I think about it for a second. "It would have to be epic bangage to be worth my hard-earned cash."

"How epic are we talking?"

"Three orgasms, guaranteed. Maybe four."

She smiles. "There's no way you're getting those kinds of results with someone you don't know."

What she really means is *someone you don't love*. She thinks that the best sex happens with people who truly care about each other. It's one of the reasons she avoids one-night stands and harbors disdain for me having so many.

"If you didn't know the guy," she says with her usual condescension, "there's no way you'd be able to relax enough to pop multiple times."

I shrug. "I think you underestimate my ability to allow relative strangers to provide me with pleasure."

"Oh, come on. You can't tell me you *always* come."

"Most of the time, I do."

She looks at me in disbelief, and I can't deny I'm fudging the truth a little. God knows, the last few men I've slept with have never heard about the existence of a clitoris. Or proper cunnilingus technique. Each one of them had about as much oral finesse as a bloodhound in a sausage factory.

"Don't you ever want more?" Asha asks wistfully.

I laugh. "More, what? Dick?"

"More ... everything." She sighs. "A partner. Lover. Friend. Protector. Cheerleader. A *real* man in your life."

"As opposed to all of the imaginary men in my bedroom?"

"Eden, you know what I mean."

"Of course I do. I just don't believe I need a man to complete me. I'm quite happy how I am."

She rolls her eyes and sips her coffee. No matter how many times we have this discussion, she just can't comprehend me not wanting to be in a relationship or saving my body until I find *the one*. The poor baby hasn't dated enough to know that 'the one' doesn't exist. The entire concept is the greatest fraud in human history.

Mind you, she's no virgin. She had a serious boyfriend in high school who she thought was the keeper of the Holy Grail, right up until he tripped and fell dick-first into her former best friend on prom night. It completely upended her five-year plan to marry Jeremy after college and become the youngest senior editor ever at a New York publishing house. Even though that last part is still possible, I'm not unhappy about her tossing Jeremy and living the single life with me. Asha is by far the best roommate I've ever had, even if she does give me constant grief about my love life.

I'm smearing peanut butter on my toast when she takes a mouthful of cornflakes and points at me with her spoon. "One day you'll meet a guy who will change your mind about men, and when that happens I'm going to laugh, and gloat, and probably make a laughy-gloaty YouTube video to commemorate the occasion."

"Doubtful."

"Definitely." As she says it, some milk and cornflake shrapnel spray from her mouth onto the counter.

"Stop talking and eat. Besides, you're wasting your breath. I'm happy doing my thing."

Asha swallows and wipes her mouth. "Which is what? Having substandard sex with a rotating roster of losers?"

"At least I'm getting laid."

"Badly. My bedroom is next to yours. Do you think I don't hear things? Call me old-fashioned, but it's supposed to be *at least* seven minutes in heaven. Not three."

"Yeah, but sex is kind of like pizza; even when it's bad, it's good." I crunch down on my toast and give her a smile.

She scoffs and pulls a book from her bag, before holding it open on the counter and starting to read. Unsurprisingly, it's a romance novel. I shake my head. As if she needs more fuel for her unrealistically romantic fire.

I'm taking my last bite of toast and washing it down with coffee when my bedroom door opens, and a shirtless man emerges.

Speaking of underwhelming sexual partners.

"Hey." The half-naked man rubs his hair and saunters over in low-slung jeans. Then he leans in and gives me an awkward kiss on the cheek.

God, I hate the morning after.

"Uh, hi," I say. "Want some coffee?"

"Sure." He leans up against the counter as I pour an extra cup and hand it to him. Asha stares at me, then at him, then back at me.

"Oh," I said. "Sorry. This is my sister, Asha. Ash, this is ..." *Shit. What's his name?* "Tim?"

"Tony," he corrects.

"Sorry. Tony."

"Hey, there." Tim/Tony waves at Asha and gives her an appraising look; the kind most men give my sister. If the two of us sit at a bar together, it's Asha who always gets approached first. With her killer curves and crimson lips, she looks like a pinup girl, while I look like the pinup girl's efficient-but-plain personal assistant.

Tony shoots me a quick glance, and I can tell he's thinking he hooked up with the wrong sister. His *douche-osity* comes as no surprise. Apparently, I have a type.

What he doesn't know is that my sister hardly ever hooks up, so he's lucky he got any at all.

Asha gives him a weak smile. "Hey."

Tony was the bad decision I made last night after Asha left me at our local watering hole, The Tar Bar, so she could go home and read. I've warned her before that I'm not to be trusted on my own after drinking tequila. It's like I'm an iPhone, and tequila turns all my permissions to ON.

"So, Tony," Asha says with more than a touch of disapproval. "Shouldn't you be heading off to work?"

Tony chuckles. Yeah, 'cause he looks like he has a job. "Band practice doesn't start until one."

Asha gives him what I've come to recognize as her *judgey* smile. The thing about having a workaholic single mother is that she instilled a kickass work ethic into me and my sister, and if someone has even a whiff of slacker about them, they immediately get demerits from the Tate sisters. Not enough demerits for me not to sleep with them, but still ...

"So great to see you have goals," Asha says, with a pinched expression. And as Tony seems about to engage her in conversation, she studiously turns her back on him and sticks her nose in her book.

Tony must get the hint, because he puts down his coffee cup and retreats to the bedroom. A few minutes later, he reappears, fully dressed.

"Well, see 'ya. Thanks." I walk him to the front door and open it. He turns to me and says, "So ... uh ... did you want to give me your number, or ...?"

Why do men always feel the need to ask that? It's clear as day this guy has zero intention of calling me, and yet he still blurts it out like he's afraid if he doesn't, I'll cling to his leg until he agrees to get my digits tattooed onto his ass.

"No, I'm good," I say.

The relief on his face is almost comical. "Okay, then. Cool. See 'ya 'round."

I close the door and head back into the kitchen.

Asha studies me as I clean up. I ignore her.

"Eden –"

"Don't want to hear it."

"You could do so much better."

"Asha, stop."

"You *deserve* so much better."

"Do I?"

She slaps her book down on the counter. "Of course you do! You could get an *amazing* man if you just put in a little effort."

I recognize her subtle dig at my lack of style. Every day I wear the same thing: jeans, boots, t-shirt, and some sort of jacket, usually leather. Ash, on the other hand has more flair than a whole salon of hairdressers. She has a way of turning her thrift-store clothing into cutting-edge fashion that looks way more expensive than it is. Also, even though we both have our mom's fiery red hair, I'm content to let mine hang to my shoulders and embrace the natural curl, while Asha keeps hers short, funky, and dead straight. It goes perfectly with her horn-rimmed glasses that are more for show than actual vision correction.

She's a quintessential hipster, and I'm the opposite of hip. Asha often tells me that I'm so unhip, it's a wonder my butt doesn't fall off.

Oh, did I forget to mention she's an insufferable smart-ass?

"Edie, all I'm saying is that you don't have to resort to banging the *King of the Potheads* to get sex. There's a better quality of man out there. You just need to have slightly higher standards than *breathing* and *has a penis*."

"Hey, that's not fair. I also insist on him having all of his own teeth and less than five felony charges."

"Wow. I had no idea you were so fussy."

I smile while taking her empty coffee cup to the sink to wash it. As much as I love her, men is one topic upon which my darling sister and I will never agree.

"You should at least do a story on him," Asha says as she shoves her book into her bag and grabs some fruit from the bowl on the bench.

I look over at her. "Who? Slacker pot-head Tim?"

"*Tony.* And God, no. I'm talking about Mister Romance. It'd make a great feature, right?"

I write for *Pulse*, a news and entertainment website with more than five-million subscribers. But even though I graduated top of my class in journalism from NYU, my boss has me doing inane click-bait pieces that make me ashamed to own a functioning brain. There are titles like, *YOU WON'T BELIEVE WHAT KIM KARDASHIAN IS DOING WITH HER BUTT NOW!* and *10 SIGNS YOUR CAT IS TRYING TO KILL YOU! NUMBER 3 WILL CHILL YOUR BLOOD!*

I'm waiting for the day I put my four years of investigative journalism training to use, but with how inflexible my boss is about giving staff new opportunities, I have no idea when that will be.

I finish with the cleaning up and wipe down the sink. "Ash, I'm almost one-hundred percent sure that Joanna was screwing with you about that whole Mister Romance story. But even if he does exist, I'm never going to be given a real news feature if I suggest something that's meaningless fluff."

She loads the plates into the dishwasher. "Then make it not meaningless. The guy has the city's social elite in a frenzy, even when he doesn't sleep with them. What's he providing to these rich housewives of NYC that their million-dollar lifestyles and powerful husbands aren't? That's the big question. And if you figure out the answer, it's going to be one hell of a story." She closes the dishwasher and kisses me on the cheek. "Just think about it, okay? See you tonight."

After she leaves, I think about what she said. I can't deny that her idea intrigues me. All I need is one solid story to pull me out of the mire of banality in which I currently find myself. One big break that will prove to my pig-headed boss that I have more to offer than mindless drivel. A good-looking conman fleecing Park Avenue's finest out of their Botox allowance could do the trick.

With fresh energy, I grab my laptop and Google *Mister Romance*. Apart from several million hits for books and websites with the word romance in the title, there's nothing that looks remotely like what Johanna described. I scour page after page, looking for even the slightest clue that he really exists, but after an hour I still have nothing.

I shut my laptop and rub my eyes, hating myself for wasting time chasing a lead from Joanna the compulsive liar. Good God, I think I'm catching my sister's hopeless gullibility.

How mortifying.

With a grunt of frustration, I pack my computer into its case, grab my purse, and head toward the subway station. Looks like I'm off to another week of intellect-destroying, morally-vacuous meme generation after all.

Oh, joy.

Two

A Dick Says What?

I'm banging my forehead against my desk and groaning quietly when a shaggy head of light brown hair appears over the top of my cubicle. Hazel eyes follow, and the rest of my friend Toby's face appears.

"Tate, what the fuck are you doing?"

"Punishing myself."

"Why?"

"Because after the festering pile of bullshit I just submitted, I need to pay."

Toby sighs and walks around into my poor excuse for an office space. As usual, he looks like Gulliver visiting the town of Lilliput.

Toby was one of my first friends when I began at *Pulse*, partly because we shared a warped sense of humor, and partly because we were cubicle neighbors. He's one of the few reasons this job hasn't driven me insane. A self-confessed geek, he writes the technical features. The best way to describe him is that he looks like a Green Bay Packer who wandered into a cardigan store by mistake and emerged looking like Shaggy from *Scooby-Doo*, if Shaggy were six-five and on steroids.

Now, he stands behind me and lifts my head away from the desk with his giant hands. "Okay, that's enough."

"You don't understand."

He comes around to sit in the other chair. "I do. You've inflicted the most heinous dickfungus from the dark side of your brain onto the unsuspecting interwebs. What else is new? It can't be that bad."

"It can. It is."

"Show me."

I sit up and slap at my mouse listlessly, until my latest three posts open on the screen.

Toby leans forward to study them. The first heading reads, *THE SECRET SHOCKING PICTURES THE GOVERNMENT DOESN'T WANT YOU TO SEE!*

He looks at me. "Let me guess. Fake alien autopsy?"

"Yep."

"Lame. And old."

"Yep."

He clicks on the next post. It's a video. *PEOPLE WHO DON'T LIKE SPICY FOOD TRY SPICY FOOD! SEE THE HILARIOUS RESULTS!*

He narrows his eyes. "You filmed this?"

"Yep."

"Tell me it's not those three dweebs from accounting who have zero personality but are up for anything if a pretty girl asks."

"Okay, I won't tell you it's the Three Doh-migos."

"But it is them, right?"

"Yep."

He sighs and goes back to the screen where the third article screams, *THESE ARE THE WORST SERIAL KILLERS IN THE HISTORY OF THE WORLD! TAKE OUR QUIZ AND SEE WHICH ONE YOU ARE!*

When I put my head back down on the desk, he doesn't stop

me. "See?"

"Okay, no. It's not your best work. I mean, it's like you're not even trying to destroy innocent folks' productivity by enticing them to click on crap."

"My heart's not in it."

"You heart doesn't have to be. Just the greedy, selfish part of you that likes having money for food and rent."

I sit up and push my hair out of my face. "That's easy for you to say. You get to write about tech stuff and video games things you love."

"Yeah, but I wrote my fair share of click-bait crap before Derek moved me into the IT core."

"I was the editor of the *Washington Square News*, Tobes. I won the Hearst Award, for God's sake."

"I know. And you were down to the final two for a junior reporter's job after you interned at the *New York Times*, yadda yadda yadda. But none of that means squat these days. The sad truth is, you can't throw a cronut in New York without hitting an unemployed journalist, and a lot of them are just as qualified. You have to face the reality that your journalism degree is as useless as an ejector seat on a helicopter. The job market is like a war zone right now, but at least the pay here is above average."

"So what do you suggest? That I keep doing a job I hate? Or quit to find my dream job and risk being unemployed and homeless?"

"I dunno, Tate. You need something to make Derek sit up and take notice of you. Are you working on any features to show him?"

"Actually, yes." I sit up and grab my notebook. "Scam parking tickets are showing up all over New York. The fines look real, but the bank account listed for payment isn't on file with the city. Some con artist is raking in the cash."

Toby nods. "Not bad, but hardly Watergate. What else do you have?"

"Uh ..." I look down my list. "There's a renegade street artist who spray paints huge penises on potholes, so the city is forced to fill them or risk offending passersby?"

Toby chuckles. "I like his style, but again, hardly enough for a full feature."

"Okay." I scan my sparse list of story ideas. Already, I know it's a waste of time. If there were something here that was meaty enough to impress Derek, I'd have walked my ass into his office by now and suggested it. This is all dime-and-nickel stuff, when what I need is solid gold.

I put down the notebook and look up at Toby. "I have nothing."

He gives me a condescending pat on the shoulder. "Well, that's your problem, Tate. You need *something* to get somewhere."

I'm in the middle of flipping him the bird when "Bootylicious" blares out of my phone. Toby immediately sits up a little straighter. He knows it's Asha's ringtone, and he's had a crush on her ever since they first met. Whenever she's around he's like a giant Labrador being told he's going for walkies.

I give Toby an apologetic look, and he heads back into his own cubicle as I answer. "Hey, Ash. What's up."

"He's real."

"Who?"

"*Mister Romance.* Joanna was talking to her cousin about him this morning, and the cousin was horrified Joanna had been eavesdropping. She said that everything about hottie-escort is super-secret. The only way you can get to him is through an introduction from an existing client. It's like some hot-dude lending system."

"Okay, that's interesting. Is Joanna's cousin a client?"

"No. But she knows someone who is. Hold onto your boobs."

She pauses for dramatic effect. "It's Marla Massey."

I suck in a breath. "As in the wife of *Senator* Massey? The ex-televangelist who holds up his Betty Homemaker spouse as the blueprint for all good wives? Are you serious?"

"Deadly. Seems while the good congressman is in Washington, his devoted wife has a sexy playmate. Can you imagine what would happen if this turns out to be true?"

Goosebumps break out over my arms as I register how big this story could be. If I do this right, it could give me the career I've always dreamed of. Screw *Pulse*. I could have my pick of jobs from any number of top-tier media companies.

"So, what do I have to do?" I ask. "Become friendly enough with Mrs. Massey that she introduces me to her professional boyfriend? Seems kind of impossible."

"Yeah, unless you suddenly morph into a mega-rich housewife who enjoys art galleries and Bible study, you don't exactly move in the same circles. But whatever you do, be careful. She's not even going to talk to you if she knows you're a reporter."

Asha is right. I have to be clever about this, or my one-and-only lead will go up in a puff of Chanel-scented smoke.

"Okay, so how do these women contact this escort? Phone number? Email? Giant penis beacon in the clouds?"

Asha lowers her voice. "Joanna says that if someone is deemed discreet enough to become a client, the woman referring her will forward a special questionnaire. Once it's completed, it's sealed in an envelope, along with a thousand dollars in cash, and delivered it to a P.O. box in Williamsburg."

I almost fall off my chair. "A *thousand* dollars?! That's what this guy charges for a date?"

Toby appears over the top of the partition and whispers, "What the fuck are you talking about?"

I wave him away and grip my phone tighter.

"No," Asha says. "A date costs *five* thousand. It takes a grand for him to even consider taking you on as a client."

"Jesus! I don't care how good-looking he is, there's no way *any* man is worth that kind of money."

"Well, apparently, these ladies think *he* is."

I lean back in my chair and grip my desk. "Do you have the address of this P.O. box?"

"Yes, I'll text it to you. But it's no good unless you can dig up the questionnaire. Joanna's cousin doesn't have one, and even if she did, I doubt she'd give it to us."

"Would Marla Massey have one?"

"Probably. But how would you get it without asking her?"

I look at Toby, who's still frowning at me and trying to figure out what the hell I'm talking about. "I'll work something out. Thanks for the info, Ash."

"No problem. It's for my own benefit as well. God knows, if I have to hear you complaining about your job one more time I'm going to cut my ears off."

I smile. "Such a supportive sister. Toby says hi, by the way."

"Uh huh. Byeeeee!"

After we sign off, Toby asks, "So, how is she?"

"Still not interested, I'm afraid."

He shakes his head. "Doesn't she understand how much awesome she's missing out on?"

"Clearly not, but I promise to put in a good word for you if you help me with this story."

"I had a feeling that was coming. Tell me more."

As I fill him in on all the details surrounding Mister Romance, Toby becomes more and more animated.

"Eden, this could be huge. Especially if more of his clients turn out to be as high profile as Marla Massey."

"Exactly."

"So what do you need from me?"

I give him a pleading smile. "I need you to hack into Marla Massey's email account and find a client questionnaire."

Toby's expression darkens. "You're kidding me."

"Not even a little."

This is a sensitive area for Toby. The only reason I know he freelances as a hacktivist in his spare time is because he confided in me one night when we were super drunk. Until now, I haven't let on that I remembered, but hey ... desperate times and all that.

"She's a *congressman's wife*," Toby says.

"I know, but I don't see any other way."

"It's not like she won't have some kickass cyber-security protecting her stuff. I mean, come on."

"Are you saying you can't do it?"

He lets out a short laugh. "Don't be ridiculous. I'm just making sure you know how much of a legend I am before I crack her system like an egg."

"Noted."

He nods. "And you'd also better tell your sister that I'm a beast in the sack or something similar for this to be worth my while."

"Done. Completely fictional accounts of your sexual prowess coming right up."

"TATE!"

I look around as I hear my name bellowed from the doorway of my boss's office. *Pulse's* editor-in-chief, and general all-purpose ass-kicker Derek Fife, might be considered attractive if he didn't have the personality of a particularly nasty dose of The Clap.

He scowls at me and hitches his thumb toward the door. "My office. Now." Without waiting for my response, he heads back to his desk.

"Nice knowing you," Toby says as he disappears. We both know that Derek's tone means someone's getting their ass handed to them, and it looks like it's going to be me.

I stand and take a deep breath before pulling back my shoulders and striding into his office.

When I stop in front of his desk, he says, "Shut the door and take a seat." He doesn't even look up from his tablet.

After I close the door and sit in the chair opposite him, Derek continues to swipe at something on his screen, his brows furrowed.

"Tate, do you know why *Pulse* has such a diverse range of divisions?"

"To capture a large variety of readers?"

"Exactly. And why do you think we use click-bait articles every day in addition to real news?"

"Because you're hoping to draw in readers with trash and get them to stay for the good stuff?"

"No. It's because the click-bait crap generates massive amounts of revenue that helps pay for everything else, including your salary." He looks up at me, his expression hard. "Do you think that you're earning your salary right now with the content you're providing?"

I clasp my hands in my lap. "Uh ... well –"

He holds up his tablet to show one of my articles from a few days ago. *THIS WOMAN BENT OVER TO PICK UP A PENNY. YOU WON'T BELIEVE WHAT HAPPENS NEXT!*

He raises his eyebrows.

I swallow nervously. "Uh ... so you didn't like that one?"

"*Nothing* happened next. She picked up the penny and continued on her way. It's a complete non-story."

"Yeah, I was going for irony."

He swipes and shows me another. *THE BIGGEST COLLECTION*

OF GIANT COCKS YOU'VE EVER SEEN!

I nod. "Yes, but you see –"

"What were the images of, Tate?"

I sigh. "They were pictures of roosters."

"And not even *giant* roosters. Regular, *average-sized* roosters. The comments section was like a fucking Thunderdome of anonymous hate." He leans forward and lowers his voice. "You see, the *Great Unwashed of the Internet* considers every click precious, and if you waste the valuable three seconds they were planning on using to 'pray' for sick children by liking Facebook posts, or signing whatever-the-fuck useless petition is going around and make them look at pictures of non-pornographic feathery livestock, they are merciless in expressing their anger."

"I know."

He throws the tablet onto his desk. "And yet you continue to post content that I could get from my ten-year-old nephew randomly mashing a keyboard with his head."

"Derek, you see it's just that –"

"You're terrible at your job?"

"I can't deny that I perhaps don't have the flair for these types of posts –"

"Massive understatement."

"But if you just give me a chance to write something more substantial, I promise you won't be disappointed. Let me prove myself to you."

He leans back in his chair and crosses his arms. "You know the rules, Tate. You don't get a crack at a feature until you –"

"Pay your dues in the mines. Yeah, I know. But I have a lead on something that could be really big."

He narrows his eyes. "What lead?"

"There's an escort here in New York called Mister Romance."

"Jesus Christ." He rubs his eyes. "Mister Romance?

Seriously?"

"Wait. Hear me out."

"You have ten seconds to convince me."

I sit forward and become more animated. "His clients are the elite of New York's society ladies. So far, I know of at least one congressman's wife who pays for his services, and I have no doubt that if I dig deeper, I'll find a slew of well-connected women on his client list. Possibly celebrities, too. Actors, rock stars ..."

Derek stares at me for a few seconds, silent and unblinking. "He fucks these women for money?"

"No. He dates them."

"What the hell does that mean?"

"I'm not sure, but even without the sex, think about the implications. At *five-thousand dollars* per date, this guy is swindling romantically bored women out of *huge* amounts of cash. The scandal would be epic."

He leans forward. "You have reliable sources on this?"

"Only secondhand right now, but I've just come into some information that could lead to a goldmine. And because we're in on it early, we could secure an exclusive scoop for *Pulse*."

That gets Derek's attention. He steeples his fingers in front of his mouth. "Exclusive is good. Our advertisers like exclusive."

I put my hands on his desk. "Then let me run with it. If it doesn't pan out, I promise to devote myself mind, heart, body, and soul to creating the most irresistible click-bait known to man. I will find glorious portraits of the most massive roosters on the planet. *But,* if I land this story–"

"Here we go."

"I want a permanent spot at the features desk. And a raise."

Derek chuckles, but not in a cute way. More in a *you've deflated my rage boner, and I resent you for it* way.

"You have some balls on you, Tate," he says. "I call you in here to fire you, and now you're making me seriously consider giving you a *promotion*?"

I give him my most determined expression. "I'm a reporter, Derek, and a damn good one. Let me report. At least give me a shot to show you what I'm capable of. I won't let you down."

He thinks about it for few seconds while he taps a forefinger against his lips. Then he says, "Okay. One shot. Follow this thread down the rabbit hole and see where it leads. Keep me up to date on your progress."

"Will do." I mentally give myself a high-five. "Oh, and one more thing – I need a thousand dollars in cash."

He picks up his tablet again. "And I need a self-blowing dick. Guess we'll both have to live with disappointment."

"I need the money to buy a meet-up with this guy," I explain. "He won't talk to me if I say I'm a reporter. I need to pose as a client. A *wealthy* client. If he takes me on, I'll need another four thousand bucks to buy a date with him."

Derek's face crumbles in confusion. "The fuck?! What the hell does this guy do to these women that's worth five grand?"

"That's what I'm going to find out."

He reluctantly turns to his computer and taps out an email. "Tell me this isn't some excuse to get your rocks off on the company dime."

I roll my eyes. "Derek, please. As if I need to pay a man to go out with me."

He scowls before sending off his email. "Go see Emily in finance. She'll have the cash waiting. But you'd better give me a decent return on my investment."

"I will."

"Good. Now get the fuck out of my office." He pulls on his wireless headphones and cranks up the volume of something that can only be described as angry white-guy thrash.

"You're such a piece of shit," I mutter under my breath.

He looks at me sharply and slides the headphones back from his ears. "What was that?"

I give him my sweetest smile. "I said this story will be a hit." Without waiting for a reaction, I turn and leave, grateful to have staved off the executioner's axe, at least for a while.

CR

By the time I get back to my desk, Toby is in my chair, hunched over my computer and typing furiously.

I'm about to inquire about his progress when he says, "Don't ask. There's no traceable IP at the Massey's home address, which means they either don't have internet – which is unlikely – or they're off the grid. But don't worry. I'm gaining remote access to her phone, and just as soon as I get into her email folder, I'll be able to ... Oh."

"Oh?"

"Oh."

I lean over his shoulder to see what he's looking at, but the screen is just a big bunch of code. "Please translate, 'Oh' for me, Tobes. Is it good news or bad news?"

"Both. She's using an email account that's totally different from her public one. Maybe this is how she hides her activities from her husband." He laughs and looks over his shoulder. "Goodwife69 is her handle. Ironic." He goes back to tapping keys. "Okay, secret and possibly filthy emails – come to Poppa."

He works for a few more minutes, and then a blue progress bar appears on the screen. He stands and gestures for me to take the chair. "Done. Wait for that to download, and you'll have a duplicate of her entire email account. If the questionnaire exists, my guess is it'll be in there."

I hug his arm. "You rock my world, Tobes. You really do."

He shrugs as color blooms in his cheeks. "That's what all the ladies say. Just remember, if the feds come knocking, you did all of this by yourself, and you don't know me. Now, is it okay if I get back to my own work?"

"If you must, but I'm taking you to lunch later to say thank you."

"Deal."

After he leaves, I sit and nibble at a stray cuticle on my forefinger while the progress bar fills up. When it's done, I make myself comfortable as the dashboard of Marla Massey's email account opens on the screen in glorious color.

"Okay, Mrs. Massey. Let's see what we can find."

I'm aware that what I'm doing is highly illegal, not to mention immoral, but this story is my ticket to a better life, so I suck up my hesitation and dive in. Even so, I remind myself to only search for emails related to her boyfriend. If Marla has other dark secrets, they're not my concern.

I type *Mister Romance* into the search bar. Predictably, nothing comes up. With what I've heard about this guy living in some sort of ghost universe, I didn't really expect it to be as easy as that, but a girl can always hope.

Next I try *gigolo, manwhore,* and *escort.* I come across some promotional emails regarding romance books, but that's it. In fact, from what I can tell, most of her inbox is filled with receipts for online purchases and subscriptions. Maybe Marla opened this account to hide that she has a compulsive shopping problem. She wouldn't be the first to do that.

After a few more minutes of scanning the inbox, I'm starting to think Toby was wrong about clandestine communication, but then a subject line catches my eye: *Thank you for thoroughbred referral*. I click on the email and scan the content.

> *Dear M,*
> *Thank you so much for recommending that magnificent thoroughbred from the Mason Richard stables. Gorgeous creature! It's been a long time since I've had the pleasure of spending time with such a magnificent beast. You have my gratitude, my friend. I feel ten years younger.*
> *C x*

It's from someone called CJ872.

I read it again. Mason Richard stables ... M.R. Could that be our elusive Mister Romance? It's a stretch, but I don't think it's a coincidence that the praise could equally describe a horse or a man. Perhaps the ladies talk in code to protect his anonymity.

I'm about to do a more exhaustive search when my phone blares with *Only the Good Die Young* by Billy Joel. I cringe when I see *UR LOVING GRANDMA!!!* on the screen. I never should have allowed her to program in her own number and ringtone.

I'm not in mood to talk to Gran, or Nannabeth as she prefers to be called. Without fail she'll ask about my love life, and when I fail to provide confirmation that I'm seeing an amazing man who's *serious* about settling down, she'll go on a well-intentioned rant about how I should want to find *that special someone* as soon as possible, because, "let's face it, muffin, you're not getting any younger."

I sigh and reject the call. I feel bad for doing it, because I love Nannabeth dearly, but fending off her constant relationship pressure is draining, and right now I don't have the energy.

To relieve my guilt, I shoot her off a text.

<Hey, Nan! Sorry, can't talk right now. Piles of work. But I'll come see you bright and early on Saturday, ok? Love you!>

A few seconds later, I get a reply.

<Dnt wrk 2 hard!!!!! Luv U!!!!>

I laugh. Whatever letters she saves by forgoing vowels and correct grammar is made redundant by her love of excessive exclamation points.

Duty done, I turn off my phone and go back to the emails. Now that I know what I'm looking for, I type *thoroughbred* into the search bar. Several other emails show up, all about a gorgeous stallion courtesy of Mason Richards, and the language used cements my suspicion that the stallion is Mister Romance. After a few more minutes, I find an attachment on one of the emails, and when I open it, I let out a squeal of triumph when I see it's the elusive questionnaire.

Toby's head pops up. "Success? Or do you have the hiccups?"

"Success," I say with a grin. "I found the questionnaire."

"Hell yes! Now, we're cooking with gas."

I hit print, and as page after page spits out into the document tray, I feel like Sherlock Holmes on the scent of a new, intriguing case. The buzz of anticipation in my stomach tells me the game is most definitely afoot.

Three

Private Eyes

I squint through the viewfinder of my camera and adjust the focus on the man walking into the Pack N' Ship. The plate glass windows allow me a great view of the interior of the building, and I hold my breath as I wait to see if he collects mail from box number 621.

He doesn't.

Dammit.

I've logged over fifty people coming in and out of the building in the past four days, but there's been no sign of anyone collecting mail from Mister Romance's box. It's convenient that there's a cafe right next door, so I can survey the area in relative comfort, but still ... I was expecting to find something out by now, if not hear from the man himself. God knows I spent enough time filling out his required questionnaire; the damn thing was twelve pages long. It seems our industrious escort wants to know everything about his clients, from boyfriends during high school and college, to favorite movies, music, and books. There was even a personality test. Why on earth he needs all that information is beyond me. Surely, all a fantasy boyfriend needs to know is what women want from him. And yet, nowhere did he ask about my romantic fantasies. What's that all about? Does he just choose the fantasies for which he owns the costumes?

Apart from using a fake name, I was truthful while answering the questions. I figure that when he takes me on a 'date' it will be easier to remember the truth than lies, and I'd hate to lose his confidence over factual inconsistencies. Of course, I had to pretend I was way more financially blessed than I am. Can't have him knowing I grew up dirt poor while Mom worked two jobs. It wouldn't really fit with my society lady cover.

I'm tracking another dead-end package picker-upper when a shadow falls over me. I look up to see my waiter.

"Oh, hi. Perfect timing. Could I get another espresso?" I'm on my seventh for the day. I may be a little wired.

"Sure," he says as he hands over a thick envelope. "And a guy asked me to give you this."

Puzzled, I take the envelope and look inside. It contains my thousand dollars in cash, along with a typewritten note on thick paper:

Dear Ms. White,
Thank you for your inquiry, but I'm afraid I'm unable to take you on as a client at this time.
Please accept my sincerest apologies.
Warmest regards,
M.R.

I look around the cafe then turn to the waiter. "Who gave you this?"

He shrugs. "Some guy. Tall. Dark glasses."

"Where did he go?"

He points down the street. "That way. But you won't catch him. He slipped me a twenty to wait fifteen minutes before passing it. He's long gone."

I lean back in my chair and sigh.

Dammit! This is not how I saw my master plan going down.

How the hell did he know I was here? More importantly, what the heck do I do now?

"You still want that coffee?" the waiter asks.

"No. Just the check, please."

"You got it."

As he leaves, I rub my eyes. There must be another way to play this. I just need to think of it.

I call Toby and tell him about the new development.

"Well, crap," he says. "That sucks."

"Exactly."

"What's the next step?"

"Can you find out who the box is registered to? Maybe I can track him down that way."

He sighs. "More crime? My God, lady, you're a bad influence." I hear rapid key tapping in the background.

"But you're doing it anyway?"

"Eh. It brightens my otherwise dull day. Stretching my hacking muscles is always kind of exciting."

"Will this take long?"

"Maybe. Some of these private companies have more security than others. I'll call you when I have it."

"Cool. Thank you, Tobes."

I hang up and examine the note once more. He signed it M.R. Seriously? He even refers to himself as Mister Romance? Man, that's cheesy.

I write up some notes while waiting for Toby to call me back.

Why is M.R. so paranoid? Is he just concerned about protecting his clients? Or himself?

Why did he reject me? And how did he know I was here today, watching for him? I assume he's onto me, but how?

My phone buzzes with a text from Toby:

<This is going to take an hour or so. Multi-stage firewall. Chillax for a while, so I can work my magic.>

The waiter deposits my check, and I throw down some cash before shoving my computer into my bag and checking my watch. It's only 3pm. Might as well head to the gym while I'm waiting.

I grab my stuff and head toward the subway.

I need to do something to work off all of this caffeine in my system, or I'll start bouncing off the walls.

CR

Led Zeppelin blasts through my ear buds as my feet pound the rubber of the treadmill. Even though sweat is streaming down my face and my lungs are burning, this is the part of my workout I like the best. My adrenal glands have switched into overdrive, and the resulting rush is making me feel more than a bit high.

Ahhh, yes, come to me, sweet endorphins.

At this time of the afternoon, the gym is mostly empty. It hasn't yet been inundated with the after-work rush of image-obsessed princesses and muscle-bound posers, and that's just how I like it. I tend to stick to the treadmill and stair climber, but I hate waiting for machines, and I especially dislike navigating around the Lycra-clad mating rituals that happen when this place is packed.

Overall, I don't approve of the gym as a pickup place. When I'm here, I want to feel free to be my worst self. That way, after I shower and put on makeup, I can pretend to be my best self. Trying to impress someone when I'm still in my caterpillar phase isn't my idea of a good time.

Having said that, I'm all for perving on prime pieces of gym meat, and there's a perfect specimen a few feet away. In fact, the only other person in this part of the gym is the dark-haired hottie running on the treadmill two over. I'd seen him here earlier in the week, and I ogled him then, too. His arms are lovely. Thick and defined. Lightly tanned skin. Muscular chest and legs. And the way his dark hair flops over his forehead as he runs is sexy as hell.

As I head into my cooldown, I sneak glances at him. The way he moves is both graceful and incredibly masculine, and I find the combination mesmerizing. I could watch him all day.

Just as I'm thinking that, he glances over and catches me staring. I immediately look away. He's not allowed to notice me right now. Not when I'm sweating from every pore and smell like landfill.

On my arm, my phone buzzes with a call. I keep jogging as I answer.

"Tobes! Hey." *Okay, talking and running while trying to breathe is a challenge.* "What do you have?"

There's a small pause before Toby says, "Uh ... is this a good time?"

"Yeah. I'm just at the gym. Why?"

"Oh. Okay, it's just there was heavy breathing and grunting, and I thought ... well, never mind. So, the P.O. box is registered to Reggie Baker of Greenpoint, Brooklyn. I'll text you his address."

"Could this Reggie could be our guy?"

"Sure. If this Mister Romance is a sixty-year-old retired teacher."

I shake my head. "Yeah, that's unlikely. Does Reggie have a family? Any sons in their twenties?"

I hear keys tapping in the background. "Nope. Reggie and his wife have two daughters, Priscilla and Daisy, both in their thirties."

I lower the speed on the treadmill until I've slowed to a fast walk. "Well, that doesn't give me much to go on, my friend."

"I know. Sorry. It would have been nice if the box had led straight to our guy."

"But of course it doesn't. That would be too easy. Thanks anyway, Tobes."

"No problem. I'll text the address details anyway. Let me know if you need anything else."

I sign off and pull my phone from the case on my arm. This story is going nowhere fast, so unless I want to lose my only lead, I guess I'll have to wrap things up here and head over to pay Mr. Reginald Baker a visit. Perhaps speaking to him will yield some results.

I shut down the treadmill and turn to step off it, but due to some weird superpower in human legs that takes over after running in one spot for a while, I launch off the rubber belt with way too much momentum to stay upright. With the girliest squeal that's ever come out of me, I flail and drop my phone. But just as I'm preparing to faceplant into the concrete floor, strong arms close around me and pull me against a hot, hard body.

"Whoa, there. Ye alright?" Warm male voice. Thick Irish accent. Smooth skin pressing against me as large hands set me back on my feet.

I look up at my rescuer to find my hot, dark-haired treadmill neighbor looking down at me with concern. Of course I do. Because it's not bad enough he had to witness my uncoordinated pratfall, he's also doomed to experience my workout stench and gross perspiration pressed against his beautiful, muscled body.

"Shit, sorry," I say. Embarrassed, I pull back to step out of his arms. "Thanks for the save."

I expect to see him wipe his hands on his shorts, because honestly, I'm kind of slimy. But he doesn't.

Instead, he retrieves my phone from the floor and gives it a quick examination for damage. "No problem. I did the same thing the other day. It's a good thing I was the only one here at the time, so no one witnessed me sprawl on the floor like a baby giraffe."

"I'm sorry I missed that."

"You should be. If you'd captured it on camera, you could have made me an internet sensation. How dare you deprive me my fifteen minutes of public humiliation?" Every time he says 'you' it sounds like 'yeh', and all of his 'r's have a slight roll to them, which is sexy as hell. To make matters worse, when he hands my phone back, I get a jolt when my fingers brush his.

Oh, God, no. Being attracted to a guy like him isn't a good idea. My instincts are telling me to withdraw and retreat, but my eyeballs overrule them, so I stay where I am and smile instead. "Well, now I'm really sorry."

He gives me a satisfied nod. "You're forgiven. On the upside, I get to make a first impression that's not based on you laughing your ass off, so there's that."

I push at the thick clumps of hair that have escaped my pony tail and are now clinging to my cheeks like seaweed. "Well, yeah. There's nothing worse than embarrassing yourself in front of total strangers, right? That's the worst."

He lets out a low chuckle, and man, if I thought he was sexy when he was running with floppy hair, then the lopsided, appraising grin he's now giving me is off the charts.

"Actually, I found you falling at my feet quite charming. You didn't need to go to so much trouble to get my attention, I assure you, but I'm not complaining."

Jesus, his accent is killing me. Not to mention those sparkling green eyes. The high cheekbones. Those luscious, curvy lips.

I need to get out of here. And yet, I continue to babble. "What can I say? Some girls like to attract men with good looks and a great personality. I prefer to showcase my extreme clumsiness. I think it's an underrated way of appealing to the opposite sex."

He nods, and I don't miss the way he gives my face and body a quick but thorough assessment. "You might be onto something there. I do find you incredibly appealing right now. So, does this tactic work for guys, too? I mean, if I took a tumble down the stairs, would it convince you to let me take you out for a drink later tonight?"

I wince. "Oh, no. You can't go straight to the stair falling. That's a rookie mistake. You'll kill yourself. Start with something small, like tripping over your own feet. Or running into a pole. I might make it look easy, but there's a big difference between being adorably clumsy and unattractively unconscious. You have to know your limits."

He nods seriously. "Ah, I see. This is the exactly type of wisdom I need. Not only are you saving me from humiliating self-harm, you also managed to ignore my request for a drink without making me feel like a total loser, which is impressive."

I grab my towel off the treadmill and pat my face. I didn't mean to ignore his request. It just took me by surprise. Usually when men approach me, it's in a bar after they've had a few. Or, if I've had a few, I'll let them know I'm interested by inserting my tongue into their mouth.

Men who look like this fine Irish specimen don't usually notice me, especially at this gym. In my experience, the super-hot guys don't go for the Plain Janes with angular frames and modest B-cups who work out in baggy T-shirts and non-designer leggings. They prefer the silicon-enhanced Playboy Bunnies who somehow exit the spin classes with perfect hair and makeup intact.

It's not that I think I'm unattractive; I know I can make myself look good. But considering my face currently resembles a particularly angry hemorrhoid, I doubt my post-workout appearance is showing me in my best light.

"Thanks," I say, "But I try not to go out with men who've been entranced by my clumsiness. It's not fair to them. I mean, the moment I put on heels and try to walk across the room, you'll be ruined for all other women forever. You're young. You have your whole romantic life ahead of you. I'm turning you down because I care." *And because it's weird being asked out by someone as beautiful as you.*

He drops his head. "Wow, clumsy *and* selfless? You've already ruined me."

Then he hits me with those dazzling green eyes, and without meaning to, I find myself staring back.

"I'm Kieran, by the way. And you are?"

Without thinking about it, I take his hand. It's warm and rough, and completely envelops mine. "Eden. Tate."

"Nice to meet you, Eden."

"Likewise, Kieran." He steps a little closer as he squeezes my hand gently. The result is that my whole body floods with vicious tingles.

The reaction is so strong and unexpected, I have to step back and take a breath.

Good God, what is it with this man? I haven't been this attracted to anyone since ... actually, I can't remember having this kind of reaction before. I usually go for guys who are good-looking but not extraordinary. This guy is definitely extraordinary. Attractive in ways I've never really thought about. This is exactly the kind of connection I try to avoid.

Feeling flustered and more than a little out of my depth, I turn back to the treadmill and grab my water bottle out of the holder.

"Well, nice to meet you, Kieran. And thanks for saving me from a broken nose."

"You're leaving?"

"Yeah. Gotta work to pay the bills."

"Well, maybe I'll see you around? I'm here most days." He seems so hopeful, I have a pang of regret.

"Yeah, maybe. Bye."

He smiles as I pass, and again I get a flutter in my stomach that puts me on guard. I'm used to feeling vaguely attracted to men, not whatever the hell he's making me feel. It's unexpected and disturbing, and I try to shake it off as I head into the shower.

I'm not someone who experiences these meet-cute situations. They're for leading-lady types, and that's not me. If I were in a movie, someone like my sister would be the romantic lead, while I'd end up playing the smart-ass friend who has no trouble getting laid, but is more interested in men as an extreme sport than life partner.

As I finish showering and get dressed, I try to put Kieran out of my mind.

The brutal truth is, it doesn't matter how hot and sexy he is, if he's taking an interest in me, then it's a safe bet he's some version of asshole-in-disguise. And as much as I don't mind sleeping with assholes, going on dates with them isn't my idea of a good time.

Assholes make you feel things then disappear. They make you think you're the center of their world and one day decide you're not. Right now, I should be focused on getting my career out of the toilet, not investing in probable heartbreak.

I grab my gear and head to the door, and even when I see Kieran in my peripheral vision and feel his eyes on me, I don't look at him.

Time to go to work.

CR

I look up at the giant, filthy building in front of me and dial Toby's number.

"'Sup?"

"You sure that address you sent me is right?"

"Yeah, why?"

"It's not a house. It's a warehouse, and an abandoned one at that, complete with boarded-up windows and graffiti." A homeless guy sitting on a set of stairs a short distance away tips his whiskey bottle at me and gives me a toothless smile. "The whole nine yards of derelict chic."

"Huh. Well, that's the only address I could find. Want me to do get some background on Reggie Baker?"

"Sure. Couldn't hurt. Can you also find out what you can about this building? Previous owners ... any tenants of record. Then could you email me when you're done?"

"You got it. Oh, and just letting you know ..." He lowers his voice to a whisper. "Derek has been sniffing around, asking me what you're up to."

"What did you tell him?"

"That you're on the verge of cracking the story wide open. He didn't seem convinced. He wants you to come in tomorrow morning to give him an update in person."

"Great. Can't wait to tell him I have nothing more than he already knows."

"Well, then, you might want to make something up, because the monthly revenue figures came in yesterday, and he's been in full mega-dick mode since. Don't give him an excuse to nuke you."

"Thanks for the warning, Tobes. I'll do my best."

After we sign off, I walk around to the other side of the

building, searching for a way in, or better still, something I can use as a clue to find my quarry. All I uncover is that the warehouse is enormous and looks like it hasn't been used in a long time. The one sign of life is a back entrance up a short set of stairs where there's an eye-catching mural depicting a huge black-and-white face. On the door next to it are the words, *Abandon hope, all ye who enter here.*

I climb the stairs and try the door handle. Of course, it's locked, but among the grays of the mural I spot a shiny high-tech number pad.

Hmmm ... interesting.

The flashy technology is out of place, considering the rest of the building looks like it's straight out of the depression.

I get the feeling I'm being watched, but when I check the alley, there's no one around. Except, of course, for the giant mural man beside me, who's more than a little creepy.

I turn back to the keypad. For shits and giggles, I enter my birth date. Unsurprisingly, the door lets out an annoyed buzz and declines to open.

After jamming some more buttons, I work out that if I hit the numbers in a certain sequence, the tones play *Uptown Funk.*

I'm in the middle of figuring out what other songs I can make up when my phone rings so loudly, I nearly jump out of my skin.

I answer without even checking the screen. "Tobes?"

A deep, male voice who's definitely not Toby, says, "Please stop pressing random numbers. Any more wrong attempts will release the hounds, and I can't be bothered cleaning up the mess when they get a hold of you."

"What the hell?" A quick look at my screen reveals a number I don't recognize. "Who is this?"

"You know who it is. You've been looking for me."

Oh, my God. It can't be. "Uh ... Mister Romance?"

I hear a huff of frustration. "Christ, could you not call me that stupid name? It conjures up an image of a two-bit magician with a top hat and button-hole carnation. Or worse, me on the front cover of a book, all flowing hair and naked chest."

The mental image of a Fabio-esque dude makes me smile. I assume my mysterious caller actually looks like those cover models on romance novels and not Danny DeVito. I mean, I doubt women would spend their money on a DeVito lothario, but you never know. Everyone has their kink.

"It's not funny," the voice says, and even if he's as ugly as a bag of rocks, he could make a fortune just dirty talking to women. That voice is sinful as hell.

I clear my throat. "So, what should I call you?"

"If I had my way, nothing. But considering your refusal to take my subtle hint to leave me alone after I gave you back your money, you can call me Max. And shall I call you Bianca White? Or Eden Tate? Which do you prefer?"

On my application, I'd called myself Bianca White. How the hell did he found out my real name?

Prone as I am to nervous fiddling, I once again bring up my finger to the keypad.

"I told you not to touch that," he says, voice tinged with frustration.

I look up, but can't see a camera. Then, I whip around and examine the wide alley. Shadows flash as people hurry past the mouth of it on their way home, but none of them stop.

"Where are you?" I ask, feeling more nervous every second. The sun's going down, and the widening shadows do nothing to make me feel safer.

"Good question. Where do you think I am?"

I turn the other way. There's a dark figure standing a dozen yards away, staring at me. He's backlit, so I can't make out any features, but I immediately reach into my purse and bring out my can of mace.

"Okay, that's creepy as hell." I grip my phone tighter. "Is this your Bruce Wayne impersonation? Because honestly, I've seen better."

"If you don't want strange men to confront you in dark alleys, Miss Tate, I'd suggest you stay out of them."

"Wise words. If I try to leave, will you let me go?"

"You believe I'd hurt you? I'm insulted. Do you think I'm some kind of thug?"

"Of course not. I'm sure you're a perfectly nice psychopath. But FYI, if you take a single step toward me right now, I'll scream so loudly they'll hear me back in Manhattan."

A low chuckle comes through the phone. "As intrigued as I am to witness the full extent of your vocal range, calm down. There's nothing to be afraid of." The dark figure turns away, and a loud belch echoes off the walls of the alley. "That's Charlie, the local wino. He's harmless. Well, he could probably talk your ears off about what a bitch his ex-wife is, but other than that, he wouldn't hurt a fly."

I look around again, searching for another man, maybe crouching behind the line of dumpsters. "How are you seeing this? Are you here?"

"Look up to your right." I glance up. Set back into the wall and camouflaged by the mural is a tiny security camera. "Smile, Miss Tate. You triggered my security system when you tampered with the keypad. I'm watching you on a live feed through my phone."

"So, you're not here?"

"No."

"Pity. I'd very much like to slap you for scaring the crap out of me."

"Actually, Charlie scared you. But by all means, go slap him. I think he'd be into that."

My heart's still beating double-time, and I lean against back against the door. "Do you get your thrills teasing innocent women? Or is it just me?"

"Innocent, Miss Tate? Is that how you'd describe yourself? At your request, your friend Toby has been engaged in all kinds of illegal activities over the past week. And now, here you are, trespassing on private property. If I wasn't such a gentleman, I'd have already called the cops, but I'm giving you one more chance to do the right thing and walk away."

"How did you find out who I am?"

"Your friend isn't the only one with computer skills. Do you honestly think I don't vet all my potential clients? I'm disappointed you made it so easy. I would have expected the woman who successfully infiltrated a secret society on her college campus to create a more resilient cover story. It was like you weren't even trying."

That stings. I was trying. I chose the name of a girl with whom I went to high school, who's now married to one of the heads of Wall Street's most prestigious brokerage firms. We weren't friends, but we looked enough alike that we were often mistaken for sisters; unlike me and my real sister. Anyone Googling Bianca White would find a rich socialite with my approximate features and money to burn. How the hell did he get from her to me?

"Okay," I say, "so my cover is blown. What now?"

"Nothing. You get the hell off my property and forget you ever heard about me."

I laugh. "Yeah, that's not gonna happen. You may have delayed me finding out who you are, but I'm a firm believer in the theory that a determined drop of water can wear down a mountain."

"And in this scenario, you're the water, and my identity is the mountain?"

"Bingo."

"That still doesn't give you a story. Even if you track me down and expose my entire client base, there's no story without testimonials from my clients or an interview with me. And I'm here to tell you, the ladies who use my services will never talk to you. Neither will I. What's the point of continuing to pursue this?"

"What can I say? I hate mysteries. Always have. And you, Max, are one giant mystery wrapped in an enigma. At the very least, I need to figure out your celebrity client list."

He goes silent for a moment then says, "Why?"

That takes me by surprise. "What do you mean?"

"I mean, why do you have to figure it out? I'm offering something to women that makes them happy. We're all consenting adults. No one is getting hurt, so why ruin that? If you expose my clients, all you're going to do is cause pain and misery to people who don't deserve it, as well as depriving me of my only source of income."

"Am I expected to feel sorry for you and your super-rich clients? Drop the story out of sympathy?"

"That would be nice."

"Not going to happen."

He lets out an exasperated sigh. "You know you're infuriating, right?"

"Yes. I also know that when I set my sights on something, I tend to achieve it, so you'd might as well grant me an interview and save us both a lot of time and effort."

"Honestly, Miss Tate, I'm not that interesting. Your readers would be bored."

"A man who brings women's fantasies to life? I know at least half of the world's population would find that fascinating. Including me."

I can almost hear him grinding his teeth. I'm a little appalled by how much pleasure I'm deriving from pushing his buttons. He may think he knows women, but he doesn't know me, and I'm going to take him down, while possibly winning a Pulitzer in the process.

"Miss Tate, what you're asking is impossible. The only way I can continue my work is by maintaining strict confidentiality about my clients. I'm not going to jeopardize that by talking to you."

"What if I guarantee to protect your clients' identities?"

"You expect me to put my trust in a reporter? I'm not stupid."

That much is clear. Any other interview subject would have been tracked down days ago. "Look, Max, the way I see it is you have two options. One, you agree to meet with me for a no-holds-barred interview, and I'll draw up a water-tight non-disclosure agreement about whatever elements of the story you need hidden. I'll create aliases for all of your clients and protect their identity fully; yours, too. Or, you can stonewall me, and I when I eventually track you down, and you know damn well I will, nothing will be sacred. I'll lay out the whole mess for everyone to see. Confidentiality be damned."

There's silence on the other end of the line, and I hold my breath in anticipation. I've never been a great card player, because I'm useless at bluffing, but I must admit that sounded damn intimidating, even to me.

The silence goes on for so long, I worry we've been cut off. "Max?" He doesn't reply. "Are you still there?" Still nothing. "Okay, well, guess I'd better go and do some more research then —"

"Stop."

"Oh, so you are still with me."

"I was thinking. I don't like being given ultimatums, especially ones that could affect people other than myself."

I can feel him wavering. "Max, I understand that you'd rather I hadn't found out about you, but I did, and I can't just drop this story. It has the potential to make my career. But that doesn't mean it has to be the end of yours. If you agree to my terms, I'll be careful. I'll protect you."

"And if I don't agree, you'll destroy me?"

"Well, I wouldn't have put it in such Bond-villain terms, but yeah."

He sighs. "I'll think about it, Miss Tate. It's not a decision I take lightly. I need some time."

"Okay. You have forty-eight hours. After that, I can't be held accountable for my actions."

"That sounds pretty Bond-villain to me."

"Yeah, well, you started it. I need your answer by Friday."

"You'll have it. In the meantime, can I trust that you'll halt your investigations?"

"Sure." I don't know if he can tell I'm lying, but he doesn't call me out.

"Fine. Goodnight, Miss Tate."

"Goodnight, Ma–" I say, but he's already hung up.

I take in the door with its creepy mural and high-tech keypad and snap a few pictures for my research file.

I've barely grabbed what I need before my phone buzzes with a message.

<If you don't get off my property within thirty seconds, you'll find out if I was joking about the hounds.>

I laugh, but when I hear dogs barking nearby, my blood runs cold. I get another message.

<Twenty seconds, Miss Tate. They haven't been fed today. I'd start running if I were you.>

I run/walk to the end of the alley and cross the street as quickly as I can. It's only when I step onto the subway car ten minutes later and the door closes behind me, that I stop waiting to be mauled by a hungry pack of dogs.

Four

The Things You Do for Love

I feel him before I see him. A sort of oily, self-satisfied presence at my elbow as I sit at the end of the bar and work my way through a nice, strong gin and tonic.

"Hey, there."

"Not interested."

His shock is palpable. "Excuse me?"

I turn to look at him. Yep. As expected. Expensive suit, sleek hair, not super attractive but handsome enough that he wouldn't experience a lot of rejection. A solid seven.

I give him my most patient smile. "Thanks for whatever it was you were going to say next, but I'm not interested."

Any other day, I'd be tempted to engage in a little sexual therapy, but tonight I'm preoccupied with thoughts of Max and our exchange. Imagining what he looks like based on the sound of his voice, I'm thinking tall and blonde. Probably shirtless.

Despite my indifference, Mr. Seven isn't reading my signals, because he leans on the bar and gives me what I'm sure he believes is his panty-dropper smile.

"Well, I haven't told you what I'm offering yet, so how do you know if you want it?" He smiles again, and even though he's a douche, he has just enough arrogance to have my body interested in finding out more. Specifically, what he looks like without clothes.

What is it about these sleazy assholes I find irresistible? Is it because I've screwed so many of them, whenever they're in my presence, my body expects sex? A horny Pavlovian response? What's more, they seem to home in on me like I have a giant neon sign over my head that flashes, *Strong, independent woman looking for a night of mediocre sex. No strings attached. Orgasms optional. Inquire below.*

I give him a slow and thorough examination, from the shine of his outlet shoes to his carefully cultivated designer stubble.

"Okay," I say. "Let's play a game. I'm going to tell you three things about yourself. If I'm wrong, you can buy me a drink and we'll see what happens. If I'm right, you go elsewhere. Deal?"

He chuckles. "Sounds good. Although I'm not going to lie – I really hope you're wrong."

Part of me is with him. I could certainly use the stress relief, even if I don't need the distraction.

"Okay," I say, "how's this? You go to a different bar every Friday night, and you usually go home with someone, even though you already have three girls on a constant rotation for booty calls when necessary. Your parents are divorced, and part of you blames your mother for not putting in enough effort into keep your dad interested. In high school you had a girlfriend you loved, but she dumped you, and now you avoid anything serious in favor of the classic come and dump." I tilt my head. "How was that?"

He stares, dumbstruck for a second then adjusts his tie. "Uh ... how did you do that? Are you psychic?"

"No, I just know men." Specifically, men like him. "So, thanks for the offer, but as I said, no thanks."

He gives me one more disbelieving look before heading off in the direction of his lookalike friends at the other end of the bar.

As soon as he's gone, Asha slides onto the stool beside me. "Am I imaging things, or did you just brush off a guy?"

"You're not imagining things."

She gestures to Joe the bartender for her usual. He nods and pulls out a tall glass before grabbing some bottles. "Wow. I want to remember this moment forever. It will go down in history as the day my big sister finally learned how to say no."

"Don't be a smartass. I say no all the time."

"Not to guys who look like that. Sleazy finance douches are your Kryptonite. Even more so than unemployed pot-head musicians. Could it be you're finally starting to think with your brain instead of your vagina?"

"Hey, Regina objects to your insinuation that she makes bad decisions."

Asha stifles a laugh. "You know very well Regina Vagina rules your life like the evil queen out of *Alice in Wonderland*. 'Off with their pants!' and all that."

"Yeah, well, if you listened to your honey pot more often, you'd be less uptight."

My sister blushes so fiercely and fast, I have to laugh.

"You said you wouldn't tease me about that name."

"Pfft. That was years ago. I figure the statute of limitations has run out on pet names your high school boyfriend called your pussy."

"You were never supposed to see those texts Jeremy sent me."

"Then you shouldn't have left your phone out where I could find it. Did you expect me to just ignore it when he started sexting you?"

"Yes. That's exactly what I expected."

I shake my head. "Sometimes, Ash, it's like you don't even know me."

Joe delivers Asha's drink, and she takes a sip. I think it's ironic that despite my sister's lackluster sex life, her favorite drink is a vodka cocktail called *One Night Stand.* If she had more of the real deal, she might stop hassling me about my track record.

"So," she says, as she swirls the ice cubes with her swizzle stick. "What's the story with you tonight? You seem to be in a mood."

I sip my drink. "I don't know. I guess I just have stuff on my mind."

"Such as ...?"

I down the rest of my drink and gesture to Joe to bring us another round.

"Well, for a start," I say. "I spoke with Mister Romance earlier."

She almost falls off her stool in shock. "You're kidding. You tracked him down? How? What was he like? Was he gorgeous? What was he wearing? What did he say?"

"Okay, cool it with the questions, Lois Lane. I didn't *see* him. We spoke on the phone."

I went on to explain my P.O. box stakeout, as well as my experience at the warehouse. She listens with rapt fascination.

"Oh, my God. He's so mysterious. Like some hot secret agent." She gets a wistful expression, and I can tell she's imagining him in one of her romance-novel scenarios. I just hope it involves her and not me.

"What if he says no to the interview?" she asks.

"Then I keep investigating."

"But would you really expose him and his clients?"

I give Joe a nod as he places our drinks in front of us. "It would be more beneficial to me if I did. Naming and shaming would be a national scandal. I could really hit it big if I can find out who they are."

Asha sips her drink. "Hmmm. That's true. But the karma wouldn't be good."

As usual with most of my conversations with Asha, I roll my eyes at her idealism. "Ash, you don't get to be a well-respected journalist by being afraid to name names. If I want to create a career-making omelet, I'm going to have to break some eggs."

"Yes, but in this case, the eggs are people's lives. Do you really want that on your conscience?"

"May I remind you that you're the one who told me to pursue this story in the first place?"

She sighs. "As if you ever listen to me." She stands before putting her purse on her seat. "Just be careful, okay? If you decide to light the fuse on this, you'd better be prepared for it to blow up in your face. Now, I gotta go to the bathroom. Try not to sext people on my behalf while I'm gone."

I salute as she leaves, and I don't miss the way the men sitting at the bar turn to stare as she passes. There's no denying my sister is gorgeous. Part of it is her style, sure, but she's also beautiful inside and out. A lot of women who look like her would be egotistical, but not Ash. If anything, I have to keep reminding her how attractive she is.

The only thing more frustrating than my sister's extreme beauty is her failure to capitalize on it. I mean, I get that she doesn't want to waste her time with guys who aren't right, but it's like she needs every box ticked before she even gets to know them, and that's not realistic. At the rate she's going, I'll get married before she does, and I don't even believe in marriage.

When Asha returns, she's wearing an expression that's a mix

between excitement and embarrassment.

"You okay?" I ask.

"Mostly. I just ran into the most gorgeous guy on my way back from the bathroom. Man, he was sexy."

"Ran into him? As in ...?"

"Smashed into his chest as I was exiting the bathroom." Not surprisingly, clumsiness runs in our family. "He smelled so good, I wanted to lick his neck. I don't think I've ever met a man who smelled as good as he did."

"You get his name?"

"Of course not. I mumbled an apology and scampered away. But seriously, Eden, he was *divine*."

"Wait, you're attracted to a guy *before* you give him a thorough interrogation about his life history? He must be something special." When she flips me the bird, I laugh. "Where is he now?"

"Not sure. I think he went out the back to the games room."

"Then why are we still sitting here? Let's go."

She waves me off. "Nah. It's fine. He's probably not even single."

"Well, you'll never find out if you don't talk to him, right?"

She goes to sit down, but I grab her drink and purse before linking my arm through hers. "Come on. At least say hello. He could be your mythical Prince Charming."

Reluctantly, she allows me to drag her to the back of the bar where there are three pool tables set up near a jukebox and small dance floor. Since we moved into our apartment around the corner two years ago, we've spent our fair share of time back here. It's been the setting for more than a few epic pool battles.

As we set up shop at one of the tables to the side, I scan the area for her mystery man. There's a small group of guys on the far side of the room, but none of them strike me as Asha's type.

Way too beardy.

"Do you see him?" I ask.

Ash looks around then points to a large blond guy racking balls on the table nearest us. "He was with that dude, but God knows where he is now." She looks around. "Wait until you see him, Edie. You're going to freak."

He must be amazing to get my sister excited. I can count on one hand the number of times she's gotten giddy like this.

After a couple of minutes, she nudges my foot under the table. "There he is. Be subtle."

I glance over to where a dark-haired hottie is walking out of the back hallway.

The lighting isn't great in this part of the bar, but even in the shadows I recognize the strong jaw and sensuous mouth. And there's no mistaking those delicious arms, either.

As I'm inwardly freaking out, Asha leans over and whispers, "If his looks aren't hot enough for you, be warned. He also has an Irish accent."

"Uh huh." Oh, I know the effect of his accent only too well, and I have no doubt it would do even more intense things to me in this environment, because as delicious as Kieran looked in a tank and shorts at the gym, he's even more delectable in a tight Led Zeppelin T-shirt and well-worn jeans.

Asha turns to see my reaction, and I'm quick to stop staring in slack-jawed awe.

"What do you think?" she asks. "Gorgeous, right?"

I give her an encouraging smile. "I think he's perfect for you. Go say hello." My stomach does a weird tightening thing. It's not pleasant.

She's running a hand over her hair when Kieran turns and sees me. He does a little double-take before smiling and walking over.

"Oh, my God," whispers Asha. "He's coming over to talk to me. What do I do?"

"Just stay calm." As he approaches, I shake my head slightly, trying to tell him not to let on that we know each other. A small frown forms between his brows, and for a second, his smile falters, but by the time he stops in front of us, he seems relaxed and friendly.

"Ladies," he says, as Asha beams at him. "I don't suppose I could interest you in joining our game of pool? A couple of our mates haven't shown up, so we're short."

Asha practically catapults out of her chair. "We'd love to. Right, Eden?"

"Uh, sure."

I get to my feet as Asha gazes up at him and holds out her hand. "I'm Asha by the way."

He takes her hand. "It's a pleasure, Asha. I'm Kieran."

Ash looks like she wants to spread him on toast and eat him for dinner. It's only when I clear my throat that she comes back to reality and gestures to me. "Oh, and this is my sister, Eden."

Kieran takes my hand, and dammit, his effect on me hasn't diminished in the hours since we last saw each other. I half expect him to give away that we've met before, but he doesn't. Instead, he brushes his thumb over the back of my hand and murmurs, "Very nice to meet you, Eden."

I pull my hand away and give him a wan smile. "Hey."

Jesus, my arm feels like it's filled with bath salts. I move around to Asha's other side, so she's between me and Kieran. Let her bear the brunt of his ridiculous sexual magnetism.

Looking even more confused, he leads us over to the pool table where his burly friend is waiting. "Ladies, this is Patrick, but you can call him Pat. Or Paddy."

The larger guy screws up his face. "Please don't call me

Paddy. That's what me ma calls me, and it makes me feel like I'm six-years-old." He sticks out his enormous hand. "Nice to meet you both."

As big as Kieran is, Pat is bigger. His broad shoulders are barely contained in a rugby shirt. He pushes shaggy strawberry-blond hair out of his eyes. Asha and I shake his hand in turn as he whispers, "Thank the Lord you ladies are joining us. It would have been a very boring evening with just me and Kieran playing. I've beaten him so many times, he holds no challenge for me anymore."

Kieran coughs in disbelief. "That's a damn lie. He's just tired of me whupping his ass."

"Sure, sure. Dream on, Flanagan."

God, between the two of them I'm overdosing on the sweet tone of their Irish lilts. Pat's accent is slightly stronger than Kieran's, but Kieran's voice is deeper. Dark and smooth, like good Irish whiskey.

"Now," Kieran says as he turns to me and Ash. "Who wants to join me on the winning team?"

He looks directly at me as he says it, but there's no way I'd take that pleasure away from my sister. After all, she seems far more his type than I am.

"Well, I'd like to be on Pat's team," I say, "if Asha's okay playing with you." My wording makes my sister blush bright crimson. Kieran raises his eyebrows but doesn't protest. Hiding that we know each other feels like an exciting, clandestine secret, and that's not helping me feel less attracted to him. Neither is the way he's holding my gaze. I look away from him and back to my sister. "That okay with you, Ash?"

She nods and tucks some hair behind her ear as she glances at Kieran. "Sure. That works for me."

God, she has it so bad. Could Kieran be the guy who breaks

her cast-iron ban on sleeping with a guy on the first date? Judging from the way she's looking at him, there's a strong chance she's going to throw him onto the pool table and straddle him in front of everyone.

It's bizarre that we're both drawn to the same man. I don't think this has ever happened before. Usually our taste in men is completely different, which works out well, because sisters should never compete for the same guy. But I guess we've finally found that rare creature that bridges the gap between men I want to bang and princes she wants to date. I don't think this is a good thing.

I know I have no reason to be jealous of her crush, considering Kieran and I have only shared one brief conversation, but I can't help feeling disappointed about this turn of events. A low, bitter hum is prickling my blood, and a small childish voice inside me whispers that I saw him first. Asha was clueless to his very existence while he was asking me out.

I shake my head to clear it. How petty can I be? I already made the decision that he's not my type, but even if he was, it wouldn't make a difference now. I'm sure that as soon as he clapped eyes on my sister, he regretted even talking to me. By the time he spends half an hour in her incandescent presence, I'll have well and truly faded into the background.

"Well, alright then," Pat says as he passes pool cues around. "Since Asha is working with a Kieran-shaped handicap, she can break. Not that it will help when Eden and I kick your asses."

Asha flashes Kieran a flirty smile as she walks to the end of the table and waits for Pat to finish racking the balls. When he pulls away the plastic triangle, Asha shrugs and says, "Here goes nothing," before bending over and taking a wild shot.

I roll my eyes. My sister knows her way around a pool table. We both do. And yet whenever we play with guys, she pulls the clueless-girl card. It's kind of ridiculous.

Pat goes next and sinks a solid ball.

"Guess you guys are on stripes," he says to Kieran as he lines up for another shot. "Let the slaughter commence."

Over the next half hour, we take turns trying to sink balls. Well, three of us do. Asha flirts with Kieran and does her best to appear non-threatening by missing most of her shots. At one stage, she even pulls out the old clichéd, "Am I even holding this right?"

If Kieran recognizes her shameless ploy, he doesn't let on. He adjusts her stance and grip as best he can without being all over her, but it still makes me flush with jealousy. I'm slightly placated when he moves away just as she leans back against him.

As for me, I make up for my sister's incompetence by sinking the lion's share of the balls, and even though both Pat and Kieran are good, I dominate the table.

"I'm beginning to think we have a hustler on our hands," Kieran says as I sink another one, and I don't miss how he looks at me when he says it.

"Not at all," I say and give him a smile. "A hustler pretends to suck at first to lull you into a false sense of security. I was happy to let you know how kickass I was from the start."

His stare intensifies, and the heat of it shoots sparks from my head down to my toes. "I guess you were."

It's no surprise to anyone when I sink the winning ball. Pat does a ridiculous victory dance that makes us all laugh. He moves well for a big guy.

"Winners buy drinks?" I say to Kieran and Ash. "What can I get you guys?"

Kieran walks over to me. "I know what Pat wants. I'll give you a hand. Be back in a sec, guys."

He steers me toward the bar, and even though it's starting to get crowded, we find an empty spot down at the end and wait to be noticed.

Kieran stands behind me, gripping the bar with one hand. The heat of his chest seeps into my back, lighting up my skin, and I have to admit Asha was right. He does smell divine.

"So," he says, his mouth close enough to my ear to make me shiver. "What an unexpected surprise to see you here tonight. Don't take this as the corny line it seems to be, but do you come here often?"

I laugh. "Actually, yes. This is our local bar. Ash and I come here a few times a week."

"Oh? So, you live nearby?"

"Just around the corner. What about you? I've never seen you here before."

In my peripheral vision, I see him staring at me. "I've only been in the states for a week. Pat's been here for nearly six months and lives nearby. I'm crashing on his couch, until I can find a place of my own. He's the one who told me about the gym."

"Uh huh."

At this point Joe comes over, and we give him our order. As he's preparing our drinks, Kieran slides in and puts his elbow on the bar as he faces me. He's a head taller than I am, so I have to look up to see his face.

"Do you think it's fate that we saw each other tonight after I asked you out earlier?" he asks.

I focus on his chin, knowing damn well that if I look into his eyes, he'll see exactly how drawn I in am. "More like a coincidence. Either that, or you're stalking me."

He moves closer when someone presses in behind him, and I close my eyes as I experience how good it feels to have his body brush against mine. "I'm not really the stalking type, Eden, but if I were, I'd happily stalk you."

His voice is hypnotizing, and when I submit to looking into his eyes, I'm completely enthralled.

"You look great tonight, by the way," he says, quiet but intense. "And the way you just kicked my ass at pool ... sexy as hell."

The way he's looking at me makes it hard to think. I've had a lot of guys tell me they want me, but very few have done it without using words. Right now, Kieran's eyes are doing all the talking.

He continues staring for a few more moments then says, "Go out with me. Tomorrow night. I promise you'll have a good time."

That takes me by surprise. "Kieran –"

"Don't say no."

"I have to."

"Wrong. A hundred-percent wrong."

"In case you haven't noticed, my sister likes you."

"And?"

"And you should ask her out."

"Why?"

"Because she *likes* you."

His forehead creases. "In case you haven't noticed, I like *you*. I thought I was being clear about that? Was I not?"

"Asha is an amazing person."

"I'm sure she is."

"And she's gorgeous."

"I suppose ..."

"She speaks fluent French and can do the NYT crossword in record time."

"Wow. That's impressive."

"It is. So, why won't you ask her out?"

"Because I'd rather go out with her sister."

I stand there, genuinely lost for words. This has never happened before. Have men moved onto me when they found out Asha wasn't interested? Of course. But it's never been the other way around.

Kieran squints at me. "You can understand me okay, right? Or is the accent throwing you off? You look confused."

"No, I just –"

"Just, what? I like you. I'm attracted to you. I'd like to go out with you. If you're not interested, then please tell me now, because I'm starting to feel like I'm fighting a losing battle here." He stares, waiting for me to reply.

"It's just that ..."

Explaining my logic to him is difficult. Instead, I just get more lost in his remarkable face every second that passes. I'm not even aware I've moved closer, until Joe clears his throat to announce our order is ready.

I blink and step back. I may have only downed a couple of drinks, but my stupidly strong attraction to him makes me feel drunk. I need to be careful if I want to avoid doing something for which my sister will resent me.

I pick up two drinks and let out a breath. "We should get back."

"Wait." His warm hand on my arm stops me. "Just tell me this – if your sister wasn't in the picture, would you go out with me?"

"To be honest ... probably not."

"Because?"

"I don't date."

He raises his eyebrows. "Wait a minute, are you married?"

"No."

"Engaged?"

"No."

"Living with someone?"

"Well, yes, but only my sister."

"And yet, you don't *date*?" He leans closer. "Is it a religious thing? Are you saving yourself for Jesus? Because I can grow a decent beard in just a few days if it would help."

I laugh and shake my head. "Did it occur to you that maybe I just don't like you?"

He takes a step forward, and I'm almost pressing against him. My head is level with his neck, and I stare at the strong muscles there, so I don't have to look up into face.

"Eden?"

I swallow. The moment our eyes meet, I know we both feel the jolt. His smile fades, and I stop myself from curling my fingers into the zeppelin picture stretched across his chest.

"Just to be clear, I have no problem being rejected by women. It happens all the time. But if this is how you react when you don't like someone, I'd be fascinated to see what happens when you do."

It feels like everything is slowing down as the heat from his body seeps into my muscles. "I don't deny that you're attractive."

"Really? Tell me more."

"You're okay to look at."

"Uh huh."

"And I guess your accent doesn't suck."

"I see."

Our heads are getting way too close.

"And you're not really ... boring, or anything."

"So nice of you to say. Not-really-boring is something I've always aspired to be."

"But ..."

He holds up his hand. "You don't have to say the 'but'. Honestly, *buts* are overrated. Except mine. It's fecking glorious."

I laugh at that, and I barely recognize the sound. I'm so horrified by the shrillness, it loosens the magnetic hold he has on my breathing.

I take in some air and let it out. "Even with your glorious butt, and even if my sister wasn't practically drooling over you, I don't have time for dating or relationships. I'm happy to have fun in the bedroom, but that's all I can manage."

He gives me a half-smile. "No offense, but I don't have trouble getting women to sleep with me. That's not what I want from you."

"Then what do you want?"

"I don't know. But it's sure as hell more than a one-night stand."

All sorts of warning bells go off in my brain. It doesn't stop me being drawn to him, but it's enough to make me realize how dangerous this guy is.

"Right now, one night is all I have time for. You should ask my sister out. She's just like me, only nicer. You can wine and dine her to your heart's content."

"And that's your final answer?"

"It is."

He nods and steps back, and it's obvious that we're both breathing faster and deeper than we were a few minutes ago.

"Okay, then," he says, shrugging in defeat. "At least I can say I tried my best." He leans over the bar, grabs a pen, and proceeds to write on a napkin. "However, if you end up changing your mind at any point while I'm still in your lovely country, feel free to call me, alright?"

He holds out the napkin, and I take it. "Absolutely."

With that, we both take a few more deep breaths to collect

ourselves, before he grabs the other two glasses off the bar and steps aside so I can pass. "After you."

When we get back to the table, Pat and Asha are deep in discussion about James Joyce. But as soon as Kieran places a drink in front of Asha and sits next to her, she turns all her attention toward him. I sip my drink with mixed emotions.

I make small talk with Pat as Asha and Kieran chat and laugh, and despite my jealousy, seeing Asha so happy makes me smile. I'd do anything to help my sister find the man of her dreams. If that man is Kieran, I'll do everything I can to stay out of their way.

After finishing my drink in record time, I rub my temple and stand. "Sorry to break up the party, guys, but I'm getting a headache. I'm going to head home."

"Oh," Asha says, putting her drink on the table. "Sure. Let's go. I'll grab you some Advil."

As she stands, I hold out my hand to stop her. "No, you stay. I'll be fine. It's early, and you guys are having a good time." I give Pat a smile. "Nice to meet you. I'm sure I'll see you around." When I look at Kieran, I don't miss the disappointment on his face. "Bye, Kieran."

He pauses then says, "Goodbye, Eden."

I head out of the bar and down the street, and try not to think about what I've just left behind.

Five

Booking It

The next morning, I lie in bed and listen as Asha moves around in the kitchen, preparing her breakfast. The fact that she's humming tells me things with Kieran went well.

I pull my pillow over my eyes and sigh. God, I really don't want to hear all the lurid details. For once, I regret that my sister and I are comfortable enough to share every intimate detail of our lives. Maybe if I hide in here long enough she'll head to work, and I'll be spared for a few hours at least.

That plan takes a major hit when the delicious smell of frying bacon wafts under my door. She's trying to lure me out, and dammit, it's working. If I were a cartoon dog I'd be floating on a stream of bacon fumes, right under the door and out into the kitchen.

"Eden! Get your butt out here! I've cooked you breakfast! Don't you dare let it go cold!" God, she sounds just like Mom when she yells like that.

I sit up and pull my disastrous morning hair back into a ponytail. "No, thanks! I'm good. Not really hungry."

Within three seconds my bedroom door slams open, and my sister gives me a look of concern. "What's going on? Are you sick? You're never not hungry. One of the reasons I resent you is that you eat like a horse but look like you should be strutting the catwalks of Milan. It's unfair and annoying."

"I've told you before, the only reason I'm not three-hundred pounds is because I work my ass off at the gym. My body processes calories the same way yours does."

"Bullshit. My hips and thighs have a vendetta against me and are determined I'll never find jeans that truly fit."

Since we were teenagers, I've coveted her curves, and she's longed for my lack of them. We all want what we don't have, I guess.

"Eden," she says, and I know she's serious, because she puts her dainty hands on her Shakira hips, "unless you're dying, get out here right now and eat. I cooked the bacon in maple syrup, just how you like it. I even made freshly squeezed orange juice. I can't have a glorious Martha Stewart moment unless you come and praise me for my efforts."

I throw up my hands in defeat. "Okay, fine. I guess I should be grateful you're doing the work for once. If this is what I can expect every time you get laid, I hope it happens more often."

She looks at the floor. "Just come eat, please. We need to talk."

After she walks away, I flop back onto the bed and rub my eyes.

Okay, don't be a douche. Get out there and listen to your sister gush about sex with the only guy you've ever thought may be worthy of snuggling after sex. You can do this. She deserves it.

I swing out of bed and pad out into the kitchen. As usual when Asha cooks, she seems to have used every plate and frying pan we own, and they're now piled high in the sink. Still, what she's set out for me looks delicious.

I sit at the breakfast bar and munch on a piece of crispy maple-bacon.

God, yes. Get in me, smoky deliciousness.

"So," I say, before taking a sip of juice. "You seem to be in a good mood. Care to tell me all about the sexy times with your Irish dreamboat?"

She scoops some scrambled egg into her mouth and gives me a closed-mouth smile, then shakes her head.

"What?" I say. "You're not going to tell me? That hurts, Ash. We tell each other everything." Secretly, I'm relieved, but it would be weird if I didn't pretend otherwise.

She swallows and shakes her head again. "No, sorry. I meant, he's not my Irish dreamboat. Nothing happened."

A piece of bacon drops off my fork as I process that. She didn't screw him? I hate how happy that makes me. "Really? You two looked pretty cozy when I left. What was the problem?"

She shrugs. "Nothing. I just wasn't feeling it."

"Asha." I fix her with my serious face. "Are you kidding me? I've never seen you turn your flirt up to eleven like you did with Kieran." I put down my fork and lean forward. "Wait, did he do something to you? Hurt you? Drunkenly grope you? Because if so, I don't care how damn attractive he is, I'll kick his ass all over Brooklyn, and then I'll –"

"Edie, stop." She laughs and grabs some toast. "Kieran was a perfect gentleman. As was Pat. They were nice guys. At the end of the night I just realized Kieran and I didn't have any chemistry. It's not the end of the world. It happens all the time."

"Really? That's it? Did you at least kiss him to come to this conclusion?" I bet he's an amazing kisser. Those lips were made for it.

"Nope, no kissing. The more we spoke, the more I realized he wasn't the guy for me. End of story."

"I see." I look around at the carnage in our kitchen. "Then why the cooking and humming? You're way too happy for a girl who had zero orgasms last night."

"Just because I didn't bring a guy back here, doesn't mean I didn't have fun times by myself."

I laugh then get up and start making a fresh pot of coffee. "Well, good for you, I guess. But I'm sorry things didn't work out. You and Kieran would have made a cute couple." Though it would have been tough watching them together, I wasn't lying.

"So, anyway," Asha says as she adds her empty plate to the Jenga tower of filth in the sink, "we should go out tonight. Just you and me."

"Okay. Where? And also, why?"

"Because I feel like we haven't had any quality time alone recently. You've had a lot on your plate with the whole Mister Romance thing, and I have crappy editorial assignments I'd like to vent about. Let's do Verdi's at eight. We'll eat, get a bottle of wine ... it'll be nice."

"Verdi's is kind of fancy. We can't have quality sister time at a burger bar?"

"No, so don't even think of showing up in jeans and a leather jacket. I've left that cute little blue dress you like on my bed. Wear it, please." I make a noise in protest. "And if that groan is because you think you'll also have to do your hair and makeup, then you're right. A little effort is all I ask. Promise me."

I roll my eyes. "God, you're so demanding. I'm sure we could bond just as easily in our pajamas on the couch with a quart of ice cream, but whatever. We'll do it your way tonight, but next time I get to choose."

"Deal." She kisses me on the cheek. "I'll be coming straight from work, so I'll meet you there. Have a good day."

I gesture to the mess around me. "You're just going to stiff me with all of this?"

"Sure am. Oh, and Nannabeth called earlier. She said if you don't stop blocking her calls, she'll be leaving embarrassing messages for you at work. Byeeeee!"

With that, she grabs her purse and heads out the door, leaving me alone with a stovetop completely caked in maple syrup and bacon grease.

Great. A disaster-zone of a kitchen to clean *and* a Nannabeth call? Thank God it's Friday.

I throw down the rest of my breakfast and get to work cleaning up. Nannabeth will have to wait.

Scrubbing the stove takes longer than expected, and by the time I'm done I'm running late for my meeting with Derek

Lucky for me, he's the patient, forgiving type who won't tear me a new one for being tardy.

Yeah, right.

CR

I'm juggling three coffees and have barely made it through the door, when Derek spots me from where he's giving the advertising department a 'pep' talk.

"Tate! Where the fuck have you been?!"

I hold up the Starbuck's tray and smile. "Stopped on the way here to get your fave, boss, but the line was insane."

He eyes the cups suspiciously then gestures to his office. "Get your ass in there. I'll be done in a minute."

As he goes back to pointing to something on the screen and scaring the bejeezus out of one of our baby-faced interns, I make a quick detour to Toby's desk.

"Mochaccino delivery," I say, plonking the large cup on his

desk. "Consider this partial payment for the illegal activities you've committed on my behalf so far, as well as the ones you're likely to commit today."

He picks up the cup and takes a sip. "God, I'm cheap, but never let it be said that I'm easy. Unless your sister asks. Then you can tell her I'm a complete slut."

"Tate!"

I jump as Derek yells from his office doorway.

I smile at Toby. "Gotta go. If I don't make it out of there, I want to be cremated and stuck into one of those containers that sprouts into a tree."

"No problem. It's totally cool if I plant you in a dog park, right?"

I flip him a sneaky bird behind my back as I hurry into Derek's office and close the door behind me.

"Morning, boss." I give him a sweet smile and place a Grande Latte in front of him. "Six sugars, just how you like it."

He squints at me. "Why are you sucking up to me? Have you fucked up this Mister Romance thing already?"

"Not at all. I just thought you might like some coffee."

"You're not fooling me, Tate. You're not that nice."

"Sure I am. I bought one for Toby, too."

"Toby's your friend. I'm not. So, cut the bullshit and tell me where we're at. Do you have his client list yet?"

"Well, no, but –"

"What about his identity? What's his background?"

"Actually, it's been kind of hard to nail him down as far as –"

"Do you at least have a physical description? He must be quite the stud to have all these women creaming themselves."

"Ahhh, I haven't quite seen him yet, but I think he may be blond."

He slams down his coffee so hard, a glob of foam ejaculates

onto his desk. "Christ, Tate, have you made *any* progress in the four days since I've seen you? What the hell have you been doing?"

I grit my teeth and tell my temper to stand down. "Derek, it's not exactly easy to get to this guy. He's like a ghost. But the good news is, after some long days of surveillance and many dead ends, I managed to have a conversation with him on the phone yesterday."

"To arrange an interview? Thank fuck. I was beginning to think you were completely incompetent. When is it? I'll line up a photographer."

"Well, he hasn't agreed to the interview yet, but I'm confident he will. I just need to talk him into it."

Derek stares at me for a few moments, and his expression tells me he's about three seconds away from forgetting about the whole thing and firing me out of a cannon straight into the Hudson River.

I take evasive maneuvers. "Derek, listen. This entire situation is delicate and needs to be finessed. There are a lot of high-profile clients he's trying to protect. The guy's nervous. If I go in all guns blazing he'll disappear, and we'll never get the story. I just need some time. This isn't something I can deliver overnight."

"Is it something you can deliver at all?"

"Of course."

He opens his desk drawer and pulls out a pack of nicotine gum before shoving some in his mouth and chewing loudly as he studies me. "You have twenty-four hours to secure an interview, or I'm telling payroll you don't work here anymore. Got it?"

"Absolutely. I'll have something by the end of the day and let you know as soon as it's locked down."

"You do that. Now, get the fuck out." He pulls his tablet in front of him and shoos me with his hand.

I leave his office feeling like a death row inmate whose date of execution has been merely delayed.

I pull out my phone and send a text to the number from which Max called me yesterday.

<Have you made a decision yet about allowing me to interview you? Can we meet?>

I sit and watch the screen, half expecting it to light up with a *failure to deliver* status. To my surprise, I quickly get a reply.

<No.>

Okay, so at least I can communicate with him. That's a start.

<Is that your answer about the interview? Or do you mean you haven't decided yet?>

After I press send, the dots at the bottom of the screen blink long enough that I suspect he's writing an essay as to why he can't talk to me, but when his response comes, it's simply *<Yes.>*

I let out a frustrated noise.

<Yes your answer is no? Or yes you've made a decision?>

More blinking dots, then:

<Miss Tate, for a woman who makes her living communicating through the written word, you know how to set up an impressive string of ambiguities.>

I growl in frustration and dial his number. He doesn't pick up. Instead, another text arrives.

<What are you doing?>

<Calling you. We need to talk.>

<No, we don't. I'm busy. Plus, I have another day before I need to give you my decision.>

<Things have changed. Please call me, so I can explain.>

<No.>

I try the number again. Voicemail.

<Please, Max. It won't take long. Just pick up.>

I call again. After three rings, he answers with a distinct edge of annoyance in his voice.

"Miss Tate, I'd like to tell you that it's a pleasure to talk to you again, but that would be a lie. I'm busy. What's with the urgency?"

"My boss is pressuring me for progress on the story. Please, can we just meet and talk? I'd rather get the truth from you than have to start chasing down your clients. I already know about Marla Massey. It's only a question of time before I find the rest."

He's silent for a few beats then says, "So, you think starting our conversation with a threat is going to help your case?"

"It wasn't a threat. It was a fact."

"Yes, a fact in which you threaten to expose me, with or without my cooperation."

"You say potato, I say potahto."

He swears under his breath. "If this is your attitude, why would I help you? I think your claim of wanting the truth is bullshit."

"Why do you say that?"

"Because you're not interested in finding out the real story. You want a scandal, and you'll do everything in your power to get it, whether you talk to me or not."

"That's a little unfair, considering you barely know me."

"I know that you probably sold this story to your boss as a juicy exposé that will cause enough of a stir to win new readers and keep advertisers happy. You no doubt told him you're going to expose me and the seedy underbelly of New York's social elite. Isn't *that* the truth?"

It annoys me that his assessment of the situation is mostly accurate. "That's a pretty dim view of my character, Max. All I want is the full story. I'm a journalist, after all."

"Are you? Journalists have standards. They're supposed to be impartial observers who report the facts and let the public make up their own minds. You're coming into this with strong preconceived ideas of who I am and what I do, and I doubt anything I have to say is going to convince you otherwise."

That gets my hackles up. "Oh, really? Please enlighten me as to what I think of you."

"Put simply, you think I'm a con man. You believe that I'm disgusting and immoral, and even though what I'm doing isn't illegal, you'd like to see me locked up for exploiting rich, lonely women."

"That's not —"

"Please don't insult me by lying, Miss Tate. If you want any chance of convincing me to do this, you at least have to be honest."

I take a breath and resist the urge to tell him to screw himself. "Okay, fine. Yes, I think you're swindling these women out of their money. That you're preying on their insecurities and lining your pockets in the process. And I feel sorry for them being so incredibly gullible that they fall for your ridiculous line of bullshit. How's that for honesty?"

There's a pause, then a low chuckle. "Well, that's a start, I guess. So, you can't comprehend that I might actually have good intentions? That I may even help them?"

"With what? Fake romance? Cheesy role-playing? Please. I think these women live in a fantasy world where they can buy whatever they want, and you're just one more luxury item they can brag about to their friends."

"Hmmm, I'm not sure, but I think you just equated me to a designer handbag."

"Well, aren't you? The difference is, when they spend thousands of dollars on a handbag, they own it forever. You they rent by the hour."

"You make me sound like a prostitute."

"Not at all. That would be an insult to one of the world's oldest professions. When someone pays for a prostitute, at least they *know* they're getting screwed. Your clients have no idea."

I must be finally getting under his skin, because when he speaks again, his voice is hard. "Miss Tate, you don't understand a damn thing about what these women know, or need, or want. You've formed your misguided opinion through shallow assumptions and breathtaking ignorance of the facts."

"Then talk to me and prove me wrong."

There's silence, and I suspect he knows he walked right into that one.

When he speaks again, he's calmer. "If I meet with you and prove you wrong, you'd alter the narrative of your story?"

"Of course."

"Would you give me your word on that?"

"Absolutely." I *almost* have him. I'd swear on a stack of Bibles at this point it that's what it takes. "I want to tell *your* story, Max, whatever that may be. Just tell me what I need to do."

He pauses then says, "Alright, then, Miss Tate, I'll agree to give you the interview, but to make this an even playing field, I'm going to insist on some conditions."

"Like what?"

"I can't talk any further now. I have a date."

"A date? Or an appointment with a client?"

"To me, they're one and the same."

"Well, no, on a real date five-thousand dollars doesn't usually change hands."

"There's that prejudice again. Are you sure you were listening the day your college professors covered impartiality?"

I bite my tongue to stifle another snarky answer. "Please just tell me your conditions, so we can schedule the interview."

"I'll call you later. Have a good afternoon, Miss Tate."

"Wait, Max ..." The line goes dead.

Dammit.

I throw my phone onto my desk and push back my hair. When I turn, I see Derek standing in the doorway of his office, staring at me.

After I smile and give him the thumbs-up signal, he scowls and walks back to his desk.

At least Max has agreed to an interview, even if there's no set time. As long as I can lock him down before tomorrow morning, I have a chance at keeping my job.

Six

Bait and Switch

As I trip over a completely flat piece of floor on my way into Verdi's, I curse my sister for forcing me to wear these impossible shoes with this dress. I'm sure that high heels were invented as an ancient torture device, and women have been brainwashed into believing they're fashion. I've only been wearing these gold, strappy abominations for twenty minutes, and already my feet are screaming in protest.

The restaurant hostess smiles at me as I approach, and I'm not sure if she's being genuinely friendly or taking pleasure in my newborn-foal awkwardness.

"Good evening, and welcome to Verdi's. How can I help you?"

I grip the counter in front of her as one of my ankles decides to freestyle. "Ah, yes. Hi. I have a booking under the name Tate."

She checks her list and smiles again. "Excellent, Miss Tate. I have a table for two all set up. Follow me, please."

She moves through the restaurant with the grace of an elegant swan, and I follow, trying to emulate her technique. Unfortunately, my ankles don't seem to bend the same way hers do, and I end up looking like a Clydesdale trying to scrape gum off its hooves.

"Here we are," she says as we arrive at a secluded table near the back. She pulls out the chair just in time for me to clumsily sink into it. "May I get you a drink to start?"

I blow a stray lock of freshly styled hair out of my eye. "Yes, please. Gin and tonic. Heavy on the gin. Lots of lime."

"Of course. I'll send it right over."

As she leaves, I adjust the low-cut neckline of my dress and look around. Verdi's is a beautiful restaurant, but I don't have any idea why Asha wanted to come here. When she and I get together it usually involves drinking, talking loudly, and laughing. This is a more of a whisper-into-your-lover's-ear kind of place.

I check the time on my phone. 8.12pm. It's weird Asha isn't here yet. She's usually the punctual sister.

I'm about to call to find out if she's okay, when I spot a familiar face at the front of the restaurant.

Oh, come on. What are the chances?

Waiting patiently while the hostess deals with a middle-aged couple in front of him is Kieran, looking like every woman's wet dream come true in a slim-fitting grey suit that hugs him in all the right places.

When he glances in my direction, I snap my head around so he can't see my face.

"Shit, shit, *shit.*" I sneak out of my seat and take cover behind a crystal art piece as I dial Asha's number.

She answers almost immediately. "Hey."

"Hi. Where are you?"

"Oh, well, I don't think I can make it."

"What? I'm here, Ash. Dressed up and everything. I even did my hair and makeup as requested. Why the hell didn't you call earlier, so I could have stayed at home in my PJs and watched

TV?"

"Because you needed to get out for once."

"I get out all the time."

"To somewhere other than the Tar Bar to pick up skanky men."

"So, you made me dress up to have dinner *by myself*? That's not very sociable. And to make matters worse, guess who just showed up?"

"Kieran."

"No, *Kier* –" I stop dead. "Wait, how did you know that?" Before she says anything, the dawning realization of what she's done crawls up my spine like icy spider's legs. "Asha, no ..."

"Edie, don't be mad. He really likes you, and God knows you need to stop sleeping with losers and dropouts and put some effort into a good man for a change."

"I don't put effort into guys. I have *sex* with them. End of story. You're setting me up on a date? What the hell? I don't want or need a boyfriend."

"You just think that, because you've never had one. You should consider this guy for the position. He's lovely, and good-looking, and he smells amaaaaazing."

"Asha!"

"Just one date. For me. If you honestly don't feel anything and decide not to see him again, there's no harm done, right? But if you do like him ... Oh, Edie. It would be nice to see you with someone worthy of you for once."

I can't deny part of me wants to find out what happens with the sexy Irishman, because I have a feeling he would be dynamite in bed, but a bigger part murmurs that he'll be a distraction I neither need nor have time for. I've gone twenty-five years without succumbing to a co-dependent relationship. Despite my attraction to Kieran, I'm not giving that up without a fight. I have zero interest in messy emotional entanglements.

I peek out from behind the artwork and eye him again in his suit. A messy physical entanglement, however, might be all kinds of fun.

I close my eyes and exhale. *No, not a good idea.*

"What happened to *you* liking him?" I hiss at my sister.

"After you left last night, he bombarded me with questions about you. It was pretty clear which Tate sister he was into, and it wasn't me."

"What? How is that possible? You were adorable last night."

"Believe it or not, dear sister, not all men fall at my feet. In fact, it's the guys I like who snub me the most. It's ironic that I'm the one who actually wants a boyfriend and can't find one."

At the front of the restaurant, Kieran steps forward to talk to the hostess. After chatting for a few seconds, she gives him a flirty smile before leading him in my direction. I pull back and make myself as small as possible.

"Dammit, Ash, I can't believe you set me up like this. He's coming over. What should I do?"

"Sit down and have dinner with him. I've already paid for it, so if you leave before eating something, I'll kill you."

"Not if I get to you first. You realize retribution is coming, right?"

"If things work out the way I think they will, you'll be thanking me, not punishing me."

"Unlikely."

"Please hang up now. You have a gorgeous man waiting for you."

"You're evil, and I hate you."

"Neither of those things is even a little bit true."

As I hang up, a deep voice beside me says, "Eden?"

I turn and plaster on my best fake smile. "Heeeey, Kieran.

Hi."

"Hi." He smiles back, and his isn't the least bit fake. In fact, he looks so happy to see me, I almost feel bad about hiding from him. "Thank God you came. When Asha said she could convince you to go out with me, I didn't have much hope, but here you are."

"Yes." I nod and bite my tongue. "Here I am. Asha is a miracle worker."

His smile falters. "Wait ... please tell me you knew I'd be here. That you reconsidered your whole 'no dating' rule because of your overwhelming attraction to me?"

I drop the pretense. "I'm sorry. Asha set this up as a sister date then pulled a bait and switch at the last minute. If I didn't love her so much, I'd be throttling her right about now."

His face drops further. "Oh, I see."

My stomach squirms from the disappointment in his expression. "No, wait," I say, "I don't mean I'm unhappy to see you, because I'm not. It's just the situation ... the setting-up thing, you know? She's such a brat for the deception."

He puts on a brave face, which makes me feel even worse for blurting out hurtful nonsense. "Eden, it's fine. I half expected to show up and find an empty table, so even if we leave now and go our separate ways, I'm still ahead of the game. I'm sorry your sister did this to you, I really am. Let me escort you outside to get a cab."

Before he can turn away, I put my hand on his arm. The contact surprises us both. He takes in a breath as he looks down at my hand, and I'm ashamed to say I blush. How can such a cursory touch flash so much warmth though my whole body?

"We're both here now," I say as I pull back my hand and clutch my purse with tense fingers. "We might as well eat. I'm super hungry. How about you?"

He takes a long look at me. "Starving."

The flush of heat happens again, and it's not helped when he places his hand in the center of my back to guide me to my seat. When he pulls out my chair, I'm struck by the realization I've never had a man do that before. It's a little jarring to register that even moving furniture is sexy when Kieran does it.

After he makes sure I'm seated and comfortable, he unbuttons his jacket and sits opposite me. I fiddle with the edge of the tablecloth as I admire the view. The man sure knows how to wear a suit.

"So," he says, looking a little uncomfortable in the formal surroundings. "Do you come *here* often?"

I laugh. "That's your go-to ice breaker?"

He nods. "When faced with extreme beauty, I lose all cognitive ability, so I stick to small words and short sentences. There's less likelihood of me screwing things up that way." I can't believe someone as attractive as he is could feel nervous around any woman, let alone me. And yet the sincerity of his words makes my stomach flutter. I look down at the table.

Shit. This, right here? This is what it's like to be a girly-girl. To get all giggly and blushy over a man who calls me beautiful without a hint of irony. Goddammit.

I take a breath and try to stifle the euphoria that's bubbling inside of me. It's foreign and unwanted. I don't do bubbly. I'm better than that.

"So," I say, composing myself, "what brings you to America? Are you just here on vacation?"

He nods. "Yeah. I came for eight weeks to spend some time with Pat, but now that I'm here, I'm finding fewer and fewer reasons to go home."

There's that look again. The one that makes me want to forget about all of my reasons for staying single.

As a welcome distraction, a waitress arrives with a G and T for me and some sort of exotic beer for Kieran. We lift our glasses and clink before both drinking deeply. I'm not sure if he's feeling as out-of-control as I am, but alcohol seems to be a comfort to us both right now. I signal our waitress to bring the same again before taking another giant sip.

After draining a good portion of our drinks, we lapse into an awkward silence and assess each other. I squirm a little when Kieran makes no attempt to hide his approval of my appearance.

"Have I mentioned that you look beautiful tonight?"

Flutters again. Many freaking flutters. "Ah ... yes, actually. And thanks. You also look beaut ... uh ... nice."

He raises an eyebrow. "Well, I hope so. I shaved *and* washed my hair for this date. For a guy, that's the equivalent of a full day at the salon."

I laugh and have another sip of alcohol. "I don't mean to say you *just* look nice. I was going to say you looked beautiful too, but it felt weird to say that to a man, so I made an emergency left-turn into *nice*."

He cocks his head. "You think I look ... beautiful?"

"Yes, but in a manly way. Beautifully handsome, okay? I guess I should have just said handsome, but I didn't, and oh well ... too late now. Haha."

Jesus. Could I be any more awkward?

The way his mouth twitches, it's clear he's stifling laughter.

"I appreciate the effort to not openly mock me," I say.

"It's a struggle. You seem uncomfortable giving compliments. Is that not something you usually do?"

"No. Remember that whole conversation about me not dating? This entire situation is something I don't usually do."

His smile fades. "But you've dated before, right? This isn't a new experience for you?"

I swirl the ice cubes around in my glass. "Technically, I've dated. But nothing as romantic as this. It's not really my thing."

"You don't like romance? I thought most girls enjoyed that stuff."

"I'm not most girls."

He takes a sip of beer and licks his lips. "No, you're really not." His eyes sparkle in the low light, and even though I feel like I should look away, I don't. Neither does he. Things are getting tense in the most arousing way possible when my phone buzzes in my purse. We both look at it.

"Do you need to get that?" he asks.

I shake my head and pull my purse into my lap. "Nope. It's probably just Asha checking up on us. She can sweat it out until I get home."

He nods his approval.

When our waitress appears table-side to tell us the specials, I'm grateful for the interruption. My face needs to cool down, and having the menu to shield me from Kieran and his out-of-control hotness helps a little.

After we've both ordered our meals and received fresh drinks, Kieran focuses on me again. "So, tell me, why the ban on dating? Was it a bad experience that turned you off?"

I shrug. "I realized at a young age that I wasn't like other girls who obsessed over romantic fairy tales. I never bought the pipe dream society was selling."

"Which was ...?"

I stir my drink and smile. "Are you sure you want to get into this? Maybe we should stick to safe subjects like religion, or politics, or our favorite serial killers. Once I jump on this soapbox, you might regret asking the question. Or being here. Or meeting me."

"Impossible. It's something you're obviously passionate

about. Hit me."

"Okay." I take a breath. "I believe people have been brainwashed into thinking they deserve perfection. As a woman, it's been drilled into me since I was little that I should be chasing a happy ever after featuring a prince of a husband who'll help me make two genius children, and we'll be so deliriously happy, all our friends and family will gag."

He nods. "Sounds familiar. My ma often asks me when I'm going to settle down. I think that's close to what she has in mind whenever she brings it up."

"Exactly. That's the dream we've all been sold in film, and TV shows, and goddamn romance novels. The shiny, happy ending in which we ride unicorns and always orgasm and have that one guy who just *gets us,* and services us sexually like he was born to do it."

He leans back in his chair, an amused smirk on his face. "You don't think it can happen?"

"Not that it can't, but it's incredibly unlikely. Present company excepted, most men are assholes."

Kieran laughs. "Wow. I'm glad I'm given a free pass, but still. A bit of a generalization, don't you think?"

I look down as my purse vibrates. *God, Ash, give it up.*

I ignore the phone and sip my drink. "I'm sure there are amazing men in the world. I've just never gone out with any of them. In fact, in a city of forty-million people, my unique selling point is that I'm able home in on a douchebag within a five-mile radius."

Kieran laughs and tips his beer at me before taking a sip. "Wow. That's impressive. If you could just find a way to turn that into a quantifiable skill, you'd be set for life."

I smile, and look in fascination at his fingers gripping his glass. "Right? Because if anyone needs a walking asshole-detector, I'm their girl."

We smile at each other, and it quickly turns into another heated moment. I blink as try to ignore the need to touch him. If this is how he makes me feel with only eye contact, God help me if he ever puts his hands or mouth on me.

Without permission, I fantasize about him walking over to my side of the table, sinking to his knees in front of me, and pushing up my dress as he spreads my thighs. Across the table, I don't know if he can tell what I'm thinking, but his expression changes as he stares at me, and the tension between us increases even more.

I'm just getting to the part of my fantasy where he's pressing his mouth against me, when the spell is broken by my phone buzzing again.

Jesus Christ, I'm going to murder my sister. What's the damn emergency?

I put down my drink and grab my purse to dampen the sound. Having it vibrating in my lap while I'm trying to act indifferent to the hunk of a man opposite me is not a great idea, but it's less distracting when it's muffled by my thighs.

"So," Kieran says, before clearing his throat. "Taking into account your douche-detecting skills, how do you explain being attracted to me? Am I an asshole, too?"

I study him with narrowed eyes. "I don't know. Do you have anything you want to tell me? Any deep, dark secrets? Felony convictions? Drug addictions? Jaywalking charges?"

He shakes his head. "I like to keep my owning a few Bieber albums on the down-low during a first date, but that's about it."

"Oh, for sure. That's more of a fourth or even fifth date confession."

"Exactly."

When the phone starts again, my frustration fades into worry.

If Asha is calling this much, there must be something wrong.

I quickly unclip my purse and try to be subtle as I peek at the screen.

Oh, crap! I have three missed calls from Max. It's just my luck that he'd call when I wasn't available.

I look over at Kieran and smile. "Would you excuse me for a minute? I need to visit the ladies' room."

"Of course."

As I stand, he stands, and I wonder how a modern guy even knows to do that. When I glance over my shoulder as I head down the hallway, he's still watching me. It makes me smile.

Ugh. I'm such a girl right now. I like him so much, there's no doubt in my mind there's something wrong with him.

As soon as I'm in the safety of a stall, I pull out my phone and jab Max's number. I hope I haven't missed my opportunity to lock down an interview time.

"Miss Tate. I was beginning to think you were avoiding my calls."

"Not at all. I was just ... busy. Sorry."

"Do you have a moment to talk about my conditions for agreeing to your interview?"

"Absolutely."

"Just to be clear, if you want full disclosure from me, these terms are non-negotiable."

"I'm listening."

"Earlier, you said you thought I was an asshole who's conning my clients out of money, but you swore that if you're proven wrong, you'll change your narrative."

"That's about the size of it."

"Then I'm going to need you to have more of a stake in the truth. If I prove that what I'm doing is helping and not hindering these ladies, you have to promise you'll drop this story and forget you ever heard of me."

That stops me dead in my tracks. "What?" Dropping this story isn't an option. How does he not know that?

"That's my condition. Take it or leave it."

Shit. I need to find a workaround. "Okay, assuming I'm open to this, how do you plan on proving me wrong?"

"Easy. You become one of my clients. If you agree to go on three dates with me with an open mind, I'll offer you as much interview time as you like."

Laughter bubbles out of me. "Oh, wow ... I don't think that's a good idea –"

"Miss Tate, you claim you're able to be impartial. This is how you prove it. Now, from what I know of you, I'm the one who's likely to lose on this deal. You've made your disdain for me and my clients clear, not to mention your contempt for romance in general, and you seem pig-headed enough to stick to your guns no matter what evidence I offer to the contrary. So, what do you have to lose? If you remain unconvinced of my good intentions, you get to print your story as you see fit, names included."

"Seriously? You agree to give me your client list?"

"Yes. If you expose me, there's no way I can continue servicing clients anyway. I'll be ruined. I'll leave it up to your conscience as to how much detail you reveal in your article and hope you're kind enough not to destroy innocent lives."

"Well, the whole innocent issue remains to be seen." God, Derek is going to love this. The entire pie, handed to me on a silver platter, and all I have to do is pretend to date him. Easy. There's no way he'll be able to prove he's some altruistic angel, and if he thinks his tacky playacting will have me swooning and falling over myself, he clearly doesn't know who he's dealing with.

"Okay, Max. You have a deal. I agree to your conditions, and in return you'll give me full disclosure, yes?"

"Within reason. Every answer I give will be truthful, but there may be questions I refrain from answering."

"Sounds doable. Would you like me to draw up a legal document?"

"That depends. Can I trust you?"

"Yes," I say. "But keep in mind if I was going to betray you, I'd say the same thing."

He pauses. "That's true. I guess I'll have trust my gut and take you at your word." I silently punch the air. "Goodbye for now, Miss Tate."

I sit up straight. "Wait! When can we talk?"

"I'll make contact soon. Answer your phone next time."

The line goes dead, and I slump back against the wall in relief. I got him! I actually got him.

The elation is equal to having secured a sit-down with the mythical Sasquatch.

I shoot off a quick text to Derek explaining that I've locked in the interview then head out to wash my hands and check my face. I've been in here for so long Kieran must think I have some sort of bowel impaction. Great. Just what every girl wants her hot Irish date to think.

I sway a little as I fix my hair. I shouldn't have slammed back those drinks so fast, especially on an empty stomach. Of course, the stupid heels don't help.

When I pull open the door and attempt to strut down the hallway, I squeal when I run straight into Kieran.

"Shit!"

After smashing into his chest, my ankles buckle, and I'm on my way to a spectacular fall when he wraps his arms around me and pulls me tight against him.

As he pulls me up and braces against the wall, we both

freeze. Adrenaline blasts through me, partly from the collision, but mostly because we're pressed together in ways that make the epic sexual tension I felt across the table seem weak and pale in comparison.

He looks down at me, and his arms are so tight I can barely breathe. "When you didn't come back, I got worried you may be sick, so I came to see if you were okay." He searches my face, mouth soft and eyes dark. "Are you? Okay?"

"Yes ... fine." My heart is thrumming in my chest, and I can see the pulse in his neck is racing just as fast. "Sorry. I seem to keep throwing myself at the floor whenever you're around. I did warn you that my clumsiness was extra sexy in heels." My voice is breathy, and he's looking at me like he has no intention of letting me go.

"You did," he whispers as he gazes down at me. "But if holding you like this is the result, then please throw yourself at the floor at every opportunity."

For a moment, I feel like laughing, because there's no way in the world Max will be able to even come close to Kieran's levels of hotness. His heat, and smell, and rumbling whispers make me do something I never thought I would. I swoon. I wasn't sure I even knew the meaning of the word until now, but I'm certain that what I'm doing right now is definitely swooning.

"Your voice is amazing," I say. "So is your accent."

"Thank you. Your lips are incredible."

"Would you do something for me?"

"Anything."

"Say 'top of the mornin' for me."

He chuckles, low and rumbly in his chest. "You know that Irish people don't say that anymore, right?"

"I don't care. Say it." I press against him and smile when he clenches his jaw in response.

"Top 'o the mornin' to ye, Eden."

I close my eyes and moan. "God. So sexy."

Before thinking too much about it, I put my hand on his chest and feel the hard planes of his muscles beneath his shirt.

"You know," I say. "We could forget about dinner and go back to my apartment. My sister is working late. We'd have the place to ourselves."

He drops his head back. "I'm not sure that's a good idea."

"Why not?"

He brushes some hair away from my face. "Because I told you last night I'm trying to date you, not get into your pants."

"Can't you do both?"

"Not unless I break several personal and professional rules."

I lean into him. "Break them. I'll make it worth your while."

Unexpectedly, he sets me back on my feet and puts distance between us. "Eden, we can't."

"We can. Honestly, I'm really good at it."

When I go to touch him again, he grabs my hands and spins me around so my back is against the wall. "Miss Tate, please stop. Perhaps now is the appropriate time to explain the dos and don'ts of our upcoming interactions."

For a full five seconds, I blink in confusion. Kieran's sexy accent has suddenly vanished, and his voice is now deeper and more resonant, if that's goddamn possible. "Wait, what?"

He lets me go then runs his fingers through his hair to push it back into place. "I'm sorry for the deception, but I had to get to know you, so I could be prepared for what I'd be dealing with." He straightens his tie. "We have a lot to talk about. Shall we go back to the table? And please, call me Max."

Seven

Maximum Max

There have been few times in my life I've been angrier than I am now.

The artist formerly known as Kieran sits across from me, looking the same as he did five minutes ago, but sounding and acting completely different. I can't believe he duped me so completely.

Pig.

"So," I say. "I guess my asshole detection ability is still running at a hundred-percent accuracy, then. Good to know."

He sips his beer and smiles. "Why so angry, Miss Tate? Because I lied to you? Or because you enjoyed it so much?"

"For the record, I don't enjoy being lied to. No woman does."

"No, but you enjoyed Kieran. A lot. In fact, if I didn't have strict rules about physical interactions on dates, I have no doubt you would have enjoyed him all night long. Am I right?"

He knows damn well he's right. Even though we haven't eaten yet, Kieran was most definitely on my menu for dessert. Now, facing the serene asshole opposite me, I have no idea what I was thinking.

"I'm glad you're amused by this," I say. "Perhaps I was wrong.

It's not money that motivates you after all. It's your pathological need to manipulate people and laugh at their reactions." I white-knuckle my glass. "So, Kieran was just a ploy to make me feel like an idiot?"

"Not at all. He was a way of getting to know you without your guard being up. I needed to be convinced I could trust you."

"So, you betrayed my trust to prove I was trustworthy. Wow. Your reasoning is astounding. How long had you planned 'running into me' at the gym?"

"Technically, you ran into me. But to answer your question, I'd been tailing you since I received your questionnaire."

"Tailing? You mean stalking."

"You tell me, Miss Tate. You were the one perched outside my P.O. Box with the telephoto lens. Is it only acceptable when you're the predator and not the prey?"

God, I need another drink. I down what's left in my glass and glare at Max. He looks as cool as a cucumber. Of course he does. He's not the one who just made a complete fool of himself.

"So, big Irish Pat the pool player," I say. "Not your best friend, I take it."

"He's a friend, and an actor. I have a stable of people I use from time to time."

"What about the phone calls you made to me during dinner? Did you have a person for that as well?"

He pulls his phone out of his pants. "Pocket dial. Not very sophisticated, but it got the job done."

I shake my head and let out a bitter laugh. "I should have listened to my instincts. I knew there was something off when you claimed to be interested in me and not my sister."

That makes something flash behind his eyes. "For the record, Kieran was very taken with you. He had zero interest in your sister."

"*You* are Kieran."

"Not really. He's a version of me, and to be honest, I preferred the way you looked at him. There was far less glaring."

God, I want to smack him. And the most infuriating thing is, I'm certain he knows it and is getting a kick out of it. How dare he be so smooth in the face of my fury?

I ramp up my death-stare. "Give me one good reason why I shouldn't walk out of here right now and write the most damaging story I can about you and your little harem."

He runs his fingers through the condensation on the outside of his beer glass. "I'll give you three good reasons. First, despite your tendency to be prematurely judgmental, I believe you are a true journalist, and walking out just because you're pissed and want payback isn't your style. Two, you're genuinely intrigued by me and want to learn my story, even if you have to fight the urge to hit me. And three, you know you're onto a scoop here, and you'd like nothing better than to prove to your boss that your talent is being wasted on mind-numbing click bait." He leans back in his chair. "How'd I do?"

I hate how spot-on he is. I don't like smug people at the best of times, but he takes it to a whole new level.

"You do realize there's a fine line between being confident and flat-out obnoxious, right?"

He shrugs. "Obnoxious only applies if confidence is misplaced. Mine rarely is."

"Confidence in your ability to annoy me? You're right. Not misplaced at all."

He gives me a slow smile. "You didn't seem too annoyed ten minutes ago when you practically begged me for sex. I'm *confident* I could have taken you in that hallway if I was so inclined. Is that an obnoxious statement? Or the cold, hard truth?"

I close my eyes and breathe deeply. I'm so turned around right now, I can't find my equilibrium. I liked Kieran, a lot. And yes, I was attracted to him in profound ways and would have very much liked to have fucked him. But *Kieran* doesn't exist, and now Max is sitting there with his face and body like a goddamn evil twin, and my hormones are having a hard time knowing the difference.

I don't think of myself as someone who's ruled by her emotions, but tonight's events have me hot, bothered, and confused. I have a suspicion that's exactly what Max intended. His entire shtick revolves around getting certain reactions out of women, but I'll be damned if I'm going to be a good little sheep and play along. I'm more than happy to fight his romantic bullshit every step of the way.

I take a few more breaths and try to let go of my tension. When I open my eyes, I find him sitting patiently, staring at me. It's clear he's enjoying my struggle.

"Feeling better?" he asks.

"Much. Thank you." I pull out my phone and bring up the voice memo app. "I assume you're okay with me recording this conversation for the sake of accuracy?"

"Sure."

"Good." I hit record. "Interview with Mister Romance. 8:57 p.m. Friday May fifth."

"I'd rather you call me Max. Or Mr. Riley, if you want to be formal."

I place the phone between us on the table and give him a pointed look. "So, *Mister Romance* ..." I pause. "Wait, Max Riley? As in M.R.?" I think back to the note he gave me and the emails about Mason Richards stables. "I thought M.R. stood for Mister Romance."

"No. My clients came up with that title. I've never referred to myself that way. I'd ask you not to, as well."

"Very well. So, Mr. Riley, how did you get into the business of screwing women for cash?" He opens his mouth to object, but I hold up my hand. "Sorry, let me rephrase – screwing *with* women for cash."

I give him a blithe smile. He gives one back. "I didn't go into this with a business plan, if that's what you think. It happened slowly, over time. I realized I had an ability to help women feel good about themselves, and –"

"Decided to bleed them dry?"

Unexpectedly, Max leans forward and turns off the recording. "Okay, we're done here."

As he gestures to our waitress for what I'm assuming is the check, I start to panic.

He's leaving? Dammit, Eden, you had to push him. You and your stupid wounded pride.

"Max, wait ..."

He holds up his hand to shush me as our waitress arrives, and then pulls out a billfold and peels off four hundreds before handing them to her.

"I'm sorry, but something's come up and we have to go. Could you please box up our meals and take them over to the homeless shelter on West 41st Street?"

He's vetoing our food, too? Goddammit! I'm starving.

"Max, come on. I'm –"

Once again he holds up his hand as the waitress leans down and whispers, "Sir, I can't take your money. Your meal has already been paid for by Miss Tate's sister."

He pushes the cash into her hand. "Then this money is for your cab fare to the shelter and back, as well as your time and the inconvenience to your employer. Please make sure those folks get the food while it's hot. Thanks."

As the girl takes the money with a bewildered expression and walks away, Max pushes back his chair and comes over to my side of the table.

"Up, Miss Tate."

"Max, please sit down. We haven't finished the interview."

"And we're not going to." He pulls back my chair and urges me to stand. "Not here anyway. Let's go."

"Where?"

"Somewhere we can relax. I know a place."

He puts his hand in the center of my back to steer me away from the table, but I stand my ground. "What if I don't want to go somewhere else with you?"

He turns to me, and even though there's tension in his face, his voice is quiet. "Listen, Miss Tate, I'm sorry I deceived you, and I'm also sorry I then baited you. I shouldn't have been a dick. It was petty and unnecessary, and it put you in a bad mood that you're having trouble shaking. This was never my intention. I'd like to wipe the slate clean and start over."

"We can't do that here?"

"Neither of us is comfortable in this environment. Let me take you to a place where you can kick off those shoes, and we can just be ourselves and talk." When I continue to hesitate, he moves closer. "Please. You need this interview, and I need to convince you I'm not the asshole you believe me to be."

He stares at me expectantly as I consider his proposal. It's true I'd get down on my knees and fellate Satan if I thought he could take away the pain in my feet, and I'm not proud of how I've behaved tonight. I never thought I'd be guilty of letting my emotions get in the way of my professional duty, but here we are. Perhaps a change of scenery will help me put my feelings aside and treat this more like a job and less like a ruined date.

"Does this place you're talking about have food?"

He puts his arm around me again, and this time I let him guide me toward the exit. "Yes. Amazing food. And unlike here, we won't have to auction off body parts to be able to afford it."

CR

I doubted Max when he said he was taking us to a place where I could remove my shoes. After all, bare feet in a restaurant isn't usually a thing. However, as a short Greek man leads us down a long hallway of plush carpet lined on both sides by pale, chiffon curtains, I'm indeed carrying my shoes. So is Max. I snort when I notice the tiny pattern on his black socks is a whole bunch of multi-colored jelly beans. It doesn't gel with his suave, sexy image.

In the middle of the hallway, our guide stops and pulls back the curtains to reveal a spacious area featuring a square wooden table, close to the ground, surrounded by brightly colored cushions. It reminds me of something out of a movie, and even though I can hear the faint murmur of other diners over the gentle background music, the space still feels isolated and private.

And here I thought Verdi's was romantic. This place makes it look like a tacky shopping mall food court.

"Here you are, Mr. Riley," the man says with a flourish as we enter. "I hope this is to your liking."

"Thank you, Georgios." Max shakes the man's hand, and I hear the faint crinkle of money between their palms. "I appreciate you fitting us in on such late notice. Would you please organize a serving of all the entrees as soon as possible, followed by the lamb platter? Also, a bottle of the Breakwater Merlot. Thanks."

After Georgios bows deeply and exits, Max takes my shoes from me and places them in the corner next to his, then gestures for me to sit on one of the cushions. "Make yourself at home."

I'm grateful the dress Asha chose has a floaty skirt, and I manage to sit cross-legged without flashing my underwear.

"Comfortable?" Max asks, looking down at me as he pulls off his tie and shoves it into his jacket pocket.

"Yes."

He slips off his jacket and places it on his shoes. Then he pops the top button of his shirt, followed by the second.

I raise an eyebrow. "Did we need to be this secluded so you could perform a full striptease, or ...?"

He gives me a slow smile. "Not at all, but it's interesting that's where your mind went. Would you like me to strip for you?" He unclips his cuffs and starts to roll up his sleeves.

The truth is, just watching him reveal his delicious forearms is enough to make me feel warm in interesting places. With the amount of alcohol that's still effervescing in my system, I may lunge at him if he reveals any more flesh.

"I doubt I could afford your stripper services," I say with a shrug as I pour myself some ice water from the carafe on the table. "I'm still not sure if I'm going to get a bill from you for the whole Kieran thing."

I sip my water and try not to stare at his arms.

"No money is going to pass between us, Miss Tate," he says. "But even if it did, I assure you, my rates for stripping are very reasonable. Lap dances, however –"

I almost spit out my water, partly because I didn't expect him to admit something like that so freely, and partly because I have a mental image of women throwing cash at him to get a good, hard look at his good, hard body. I saw parts of it at the gym. I know damn well it would be worth the money.

When he sees my expression, he chuckles as he finishes rolling up his sleeves. "I'm kidding. I never strip for clients. And

I'm sorry if removing my jacket got you excited, but I'm simply getting comfortable. Suits aren't my usual thing, and I always feel like an imposter when I wear one."

"But then again, don't you make your living out of being an imposter?" He flashes me a look, but I hold up my hands in defense. "I'm not being a bitch. That's a legitimate question."

I pull out my phone and start recording again.

Max eyes the device as he walks back to the table. "How much do you know about what I do?"

I'm surprised when he sits adjacent to me instead of on the opposite side. Is he torturing me on purpose with his stupid pheromones?

As much as I hate to admit it, having him this close is distracting, so I adjust my position to put a little more space between us.

"Well," I say. "I've heard you act out romance novel scenarios. Play different characters and whatnot."

He presses his lips together. "I guess if you break it down into basic terms, that's accurate, but it's not as simple as throwing on a dime-store costume and saying lines. A lot of planning and research goes into every encounter."

"Is that why prospective clients have to fill out a questionnaire thicker than some books?"

He nods. "That's a big part of it. Learning about a client's life history and what she's passionate about helps me predict her behavior. And sometimes figuring out what it is she's *not* telling me is most important."

"So, they don't just stipulate that they want you to be a sexy cowboy, or biker boy, or whatever?"

"They can, but that doesn't mean that's what they'll get. Their favorite books and movies tell me a lot about what they crave from their escapism."

"Uh huh. So, what did my list say about me?"

He chuckles. "A lot. In fact, it's what tipped me off that you weren't who you said you were. Not a big believer in happy endings, are you, Miss Tate?"

"No, because I'm a grownup, and I know damn well the only real happy endings are those that occur in certain massage parlors."

"I'm not disagreeing, but most of us like to escape the dark reality of our existence through entertainment. But not you. In fact, I don't think I've ever seen so many books that deal with a bleak, dystopian future on one list before. It makes me wonder what you do for fun."

"You don't think I have fun?" He gives a non-committal shrug, which immediately puts me on the defensive. "Oh, I have fun, Mr. Riley. Believe me. You'd be surprised by the amount of fun I have."

"When was the last time you had some?"

I start to say the other night when we were playing pool, but it will be Turtleneck Tuesday at Hooters before I admit that I enjoyed being with him.

I ignore his question and move on. "Tell me about your fee. It's kind of outrageous, don't you think?"

He takes a sip of water. "We all need money to survive. I'm not deceiving anyone about the price of my services."

"So you think you're worth *five-thousand dollars* per date?"

Something flashes in his eyes, and it looks a lot like shame.

He gazes down at the table. "I'd like to tell you money isn't important to me, but it is. I'm not going to apologize for that."

Max goes quiet and stays that way as Georgios and four waiters bring in a selection of platters and plates, as well as our wine.

After everyone's gone, Max pushes a plate overflowing with

chargrilled meat and vegetables toward me. "Go ahead. I can feel how hungry you are."

He's not wrong. I'm salivating so hard right now, I have to swallow several times before I open my mouth to reply. "Do you want to pause the interview while we eat?"

He shrugs. "Doesn't matter to me. I don't think you're going to end up publishing this article, so I'm easy either way. It usually only takes one date for a woman to fall for me. I stipulated three for you, because I've discovered you're completely closed to the concept of romance enriching your life. Three gives me a little more time to crack you." With that, he pops a chunk of bread into his mouth.

"Wait," I say, gobsmacked. "You think I'm going to *fall in love* with you?"

He chuckles. "No." He takes a sip of wine and smiles. "I know it."

I'm rendered speechless by his ridiculousness, and that just makes him smile even more.

"If you think I'll be easily swayed by your charms," I say as I spoon food onto my plate, "you're going to be disappointed."

He closes his hand over mine, and I take in a tight breath as he gently strokes my skin. "Are you forgetting your reaction to Kieran? If you think you're immune to my charms, you're fooling yourself."

I pull my hand away and ignore how fiercely it tingles as I place it in my lap. "So, you don't think any woman can resist you?"

"I'm sure plenty of women could. But you? No. You're so starved of romance in your life, you're like an emotional skeleton. I intend to put some meat back on your bones. Make you believe in something other than a bleak apocalypse."

I'm filled with a sudden and fiery determination to prove him wrong. God, how dare he? Does he think he's the first man to push my buttons? He has no clue how many inflated egos I've smacked down in my life. His will just be one more.

"Well, I guess we'll see soon enough," I say.

"I guess we will."

We eat in silence for a while, and even though I'm still fuming over his outrageous assumptions, I can't deny he did well with the choice of restaurant. The food is delicious, and I manage to demolish a full plate in less than three minutes.

When I look up, I find Max staring at me.

"What?" I ask, my mouth half full.

"You don't care what people think of you, do you?"

Embarrassed, I take stock of myself hunched over my plate like a barbarian, shoving food into my mouth as quickly as I can to stave off my hunger pangs. I sit up and daintily dab at my mouth with my napkin, but I'm pretty sure the damage to my ladylike image has already been done.

"Sorry. I was hungry."

"Don't be embarrassed. It was a compliment, not a criticism." He scoops more food onto his plate then adds some to mine. "Plus, that little moan of pleasure you make in the back of your throat every now and then is ... stimulating. Feel free to do that as often as you like."

The way he says it sends a flash of goosebumps over my skin, but I keep my face impassive. "If that's an example of the cheesy lines you'll be hitting me with on our 'dates', I'll go ahead right now and say you don't have a chance in hell of winning me over."

He stops what he's doing. "Miss Tate, you'll soon discover I don't have any 'lines'. Generally, I say what I think, whether I'm in character or not. I rarely lie."

"You'll forgive me if I maintain my cynicism about that."

"Sure. I get the feeling your cynicism is your security blanket in most situations, so go for it."

That statement takes me by surprise, and even though it raises my hackles enough to want to find out what he means, part of me doesn't want to know.

I wipe my hands on my napkin and grab my wine glass. "So, tell me, how do these dates work?"

Max swallows his food and takes a sip of wine. "Well, with a new client, after I get a handle on their personality and work up several scenarios, I choose the one I think will be most effective and arrange to 'accidentally' run into them somewhere."

"Are they all like what you did with me at the gym?"

He gives me a half-smile. "I knew you wouldn't respond to traditional romance tropes, so with Kieran I took a more ... realistic approach. Most of my dates involve a fantasy element. Larger-than-life characters."

I grab a bowl of rice and spoon some onto my plate before offering it to Max. "So, like, costumes?"

He takes the bowl and helps himself. "Yes, as well as more extreme situations than they'd usually find themselves in."

"Will you do that for my dates?"

He puts the bowl on the other side of the table and shrugs. "Perhaps. I haven't planned your dates yet. Why? Are you eager to get started?"

"Not really," I say, determined to not let on that I'm intrigued about what he'd choose for me. "Just trying to understand what to expect. I should probably warn you that if you come at me with some crazy, unrealistic scenario, I'll probably laugh my ass off."

He gives me a knowing look. "Miss Tate, the only time you'll laugh while I'm romancing you is if I tell a joke."

I lean toward him. "You really don't know who you're

messing with, Mr. Riley. I'm not that easy to pleaser."

He passes me some bread. "That sounds a lot like a challenge."

"Take it however you like."

He distributes more food between us, and I find myself watching as he eats. The way the muscles in his jaw move is fascinating.

"So," I say, to distract myself from staring. "How far do things go on these dates?"

He wipes his mouth with his napkin and picks up his wine glass. "Talking, light touching, nothing too explicit. If the date goes well, a natural progression will lead to kissing and light intimate contact."

"What do you define as 'light intimate contact?'"

I'm shocked when he reaches over and cups my face, before grazing a thumb across my cheek and down to my mouth.

"Something like this," he says quietly. I stop breathing as he continues to stroke my skin. The sensation is intoxicating.

As he continues to stare, he seems to glaze over for a few seconds before he blinks and clears his throat. "It depends on the situation." He pulls back and looks away.

I try to act like I'm unaffected, but I have no control over how fiercely I blush. "Are ... uh ... women allowed to touch you back?"

"Yes, within reason." He adjusts his position. "Areas not covered by underwear are fine."

"And if they go for the underwear areas?"

He looks at me and a muscle in his jaw jumps. "The date is immediately terminated, and the client is blacklisted."

"Wow. Harsh."

He pours us both more wine. "I'm not a whore, Miss Tate. It's important to make that clear."

"So you've never had sex with a client?"

"Never."

"Have you ever wanted to?"

He pauses for a moment then says, "Next question."

I file that piece of information away for further investigation.

"So," I say, "*Light intimate contact* is all you offer? Or can ladies bribe you for more?"

"Just so there's no confusion ..." He picks up my phone and holds it up to his mouth. "*I do not have sex for money.*" He puts the phone back down. "However, if ladies would like something more intense, they can pay extra for a more immersive experience."

"Oh, so you take them scuba diving?" He stares at me, unimpressed. I drop my smile and move some food around with my fork. "Please, continue."

"Tier two involves the client also taking on a different character. It's popular with ladies who want to escape their everyday lives."

"Will you do that with me?"

"I'd like to, yes. I think you'd gain a lot from stepping outside of yourself for a while."

It grates that he's so self-assured about what I need. "You barely know me, and yet you think you know what's good for me?"

He runs his forefinger over the table cloth next to my hand. "We all have issues we're trying to overcome, Miss Tate. Everyone wants to feel special, whether we admit it or not. And loving without limits and allowing ourselves to be loved in return is what life's all about. Or at least, what it should be about. Everything else just gets in the way."

I want to refute him, but I've never been in love, so I have no idea if he speaks the truth. What I do know is that I have disdain for women who fall apart over men. Surely they're not stupid. They've heard the songs and seen the movies. If you buy a ticket on the Love Express, it comes with compulsory stops at Painville, The Isle of Co-Dependence, and Betrayal Central, so why get onboard in the first place?

I think Max is waiting for me to contradict him, and when I don't, he gives me another of those goddamn enigmatic smiles.

It's off-putting how confident he is. I mean, I'm used to men who are as attractive as he is being egotistical dicks, but this is something else. He possesses a self-assuredness that has nothing to do with what he looks like and everything to do with who he is. Or at least, who he believes himself to be. He has a Zen-like calm that's somehow wildly exciting.

As if he senses my thoughts, the corners of his lips curl. I have a horrifying image of me attempting to find out if those lips taste as good as they look, but I quickly push it away.

As I try to get back on topic, I form what I hope is an expression of barely suppressed boredom and clear my throat. "Okay, so the big question is, why no sex on dates?"

"Sex is for the body. Romance is for the soul."

"Nice catchphrase. You should sell T-shirts. What does it mean?"

"Sex complicates things that should be kept simple," he says. "I can make my clients feel more special if mutual attraction doesn't escalate into the bedroom."

"And how do you do that?"

He gives me a knowing smile. "Never underestimate the power of a good kiss."

I try to disguise my intense skepticism. "A kiss? You're kidding, right?"

"Not at all. Haven't you ever had a truly life-altering kiss?"

"Not one that could compete with a good hard fuck, no."

He leans forward and studies me, and I struggle to maintain

my composure under his intense scrutiny.

"A lot of men think the way you do," he says quietly. "And that's why so many of them take their women for granted. Guys see kissing as the first rung on the ladder to sex." He draws an arc in the air. *"Kiss ... grope ... strip ... penetrate.* It's a straight line for them. But kissing is most powerful when it's a circle. A long, meandering journey of sensation."

God, his voice. His stupidly resonant, sexy-as-hell voice. Even without the Irish accent, it's devastating.

He leans forward, and he's too close for me to ignore how his body sets mine on high alert. I lean back to compensate, but his expression tells me he knows exactly what I'm doing.

"Miss Tate, you might think that a kiss is nothing special, but kissing a woman with no intention of it leading to something else? That's how you discover the meaning of sensuality. I can find an ocean of pleasure in every inhale and moan; every soft, slow sweep of her tongue. The taste of her lips. The shape of her face beneath my hands. The way her body curves into mine as she stops thinking and finally gives herself over to how she feels." His voice is barely above a whisper, but every word vibrates through my skin and into my bones.

He gazes at my mouth with open fascination for several long seconds before coming back to my eyes. "You can live and die within the lifetime of a decent kiss. Trust me on that."

He seems to wait for my reaction, but I'm so mesmerized, all I can manage is, "Uh huh."

"You have to understand that most of the ladies who engage my services haven't been kissed properly in years. Their partners do it to initiate sex, and they've forgotten how to make their women feel loved instead of merely wanted."

I squirm under his intensity, hot and viciously aroused. "I don't see the difference."

He goes back to staring at my mouth, and every single trace of his smile has vanished. "Maybe one night I'll kiss you properly to help you understand."

I struggle to keep my breathing even as he continues to stare. There's no way I'm letting him know how stupidly attracted to him I am right now.

"I didn't agree to be kissed as part of our deal."

"You agreed to the dates. Kissing is part of the package."

"Then I'd like to order the non-kissing version. The dates I can pass off as research, but I'd never live it down if my editor found out I was macking on the subject of my exposé."

I think I see a flash of disappointment in his expression, but that's more likely a projection of my own regret.

"Are you sure that's how you want to play this?" he asks.

"I am."

He gives a small shrug. "Okay, I'll hold back from kissing you. But for the record, if you kiss me, all bets are off."

"That's never going to happen."

He smiles and goes back to his meal. "If you say so, Miss Tate."

C&R

After polishing off enough food to satisfy a handful of NFL teams, Max and I watch in sated silence as Georgios leads a brigade of waiters in clearing the table. When he places the check between us in a fancy leather wallet, I'm quick to grab it before Max can.

He isn't amused. "Hand it over, Miss Tate."

"No," I say. "You paid at Verdi's. I'm paying here. This isn't a date. It's a business meeting."

He removes his hand and shrugs. "As you wish."

I grab some cash from my purse and slide it into the wallet. "Besides, that thousand dollars you refunded was company money, so really my boss is paying for this, not me."

"From what I've learned of your boss, he's not the easiest man to work for."

I close my purse. "*Not easy to work for* is probably the nicest thing anybody's ever said about Derek. For someone who doesn't seem to be packing much in his pants, he's certainly the biggest dick I've ever known. It doesn't help that he hates me."

Max stands and holds out his hand to help me up. "Then go somewhere else."

I take it, and he pulls me to my feet. "I intend to, but I can't until I have some frequent headline miles under my belt. This story will help me achieve that."

Before I can move away, he brings his hand over mine and says, "Miss Tate, until you write your final piece on me, I'd ask you not to give Derek too many details about what we discuss. In fact, the fewer people who know about me, the better, at least until the article is published. Can I trust your discretion?"

"I can try to keep everything on the down-low as much as possible, but if Derek pushes me, it'll be hard to deny him. I'll do my best, though."

We're quiet as we slip back into our shoes and head out into the street. Max loops his jacket over his arm and shoves his hands in his pockets as we amble in the direction of the west river. It's a cool night, but right now walking off the metric ton of food in my swollen belly seems like a good idea.

Seemingly at random, Max passes behind me, so he's nearest the curb before continuing on.

"Superstitious?" I ask, amused.

He points to the water lining the road. "Trying to protect you from a dry-cleaning bill if someone drives too close."

"Do you get your moves from an eighteenth-century edition of *A Gentlemen's Guide to Chivalry* or something?"

He glances at me, his expression darkening. "If you knew how ungentlemanly I've been in my life, you wouldn't say that."

"Sounds like something I should investigate further. Care to explain?"

"Not tonight, no." His tone suggests we're done discussing it.

As we continue, walking beside him feels bizarre. Going to dinner with a man to whom I'm attracted, followed by heading to a destination that isn't a bedroom isn't usually my thing. The strangeness of it makes me shiver.

"Are you cold?"

I shake my head, but already Max is unfurling his jacket and draping it over my shoulders. "You don't have to," I say. "I'm fine."

"It's no trouble." He stands in front of me and pulls at the lapels until it's securely wrapped around me. "Besides, you look better in it that I do."

He gives me a look that's almost affectionate, then seems to realize he's not with one of his fawning fans and clears his throat before going back to his place beside me.

When I look at my phone, I'm surprised to note it's nearly one a.m. The past few hours have flown by. I should be thinking about heading home, but I still have so many questions running through my mind, I don't want to lose the opportunity to ask them, just in case Max rethinks his decision to talk to me and disappears.

"So," I say, "I know this is probably a silly question, but do you have a girlfriend?"

Max looks down and chuckles. "Yes. Several. Isn't that why we're here?"

"Excluding clients."

"Well, in that case, no."

"Have you ever? Since you've been doing this?"

He puts his hand on my lower back as we cross the street. "Once. Didn't last long. It seems sharing a man with other women can be a relationship killer."

"Did you love her?"

"Honestly? No. She was more an experiment than anything else."

"In?"

"My ability to practice what I preach."

"And it didn't work?" I catch my heel on an uneven bit of pavement and stumble. Max grabs me and keeps me upright. When I regain my footing, I expect him to let me go, but he doesn't.

"Sometimes we confuse hormones with happiness," he says. "I was guilty of that. Beyond some basic chemistry, we had nothing in common."

His arms are strong around me, and looking up into his face makes me think I'm going to stumble again.

"Did she love you?"

He pauses. "You'd have to ask her that."

"Okay. Can I have her name and number?"

He laughs and makes sure I'm steady before letting go. "You're tenacious, Miss Tate. I'll give you that."

"Yes, I am, and I think it should be rewarded. How about some info on your upbringing? School, parents, friends–" He walks away from me, and I scramble to catch up. "No? Not even a tidbit?"

"You've exhausted my supply of tidbits."

"You know you're going to have to give me something about your identity eventually, right?"

"Maybe. But not tonight."

When we get to the river, we walk south. I tilt my head to look up at the sky. As spectacular as the river view is, it's hard to make out the stars in the city. Too much light. Whenever I'd give Asha shit about her quest for Mr. Right, she'd tell me that her prince is like the constellation of Orion – just because she can't see him, doesn't mean he isn't there. Only my sister could make her girl-boner for true love sound like a creepy religion.

Max follows my gaze. "What are you thinking about?"

"Oh, you know. The Cult of Love."

"Cult?"

"Yeah. People who are in it won't shut up about how wonderful and fulfilling it is, but after a while they realize it's all borderline-crazy, and forever-happiness is a giant con. Getting through life is hard enough without the burden of carrying someone else with you."

Max gives a soft laugh and shakes his head. "Every time I think you can't get more cynical, you prove me wrong. I take it you don't believe in marriage, then?"

"No."

"Care to explain?"

"Do I even have to? Look at the world. Love fades. Couples break up. It's part of growing and developing as people. It's ridiculous to think that you should be attracted to the same person for decades, so what's the point of standing up in front of your friends and family and swearing to love and cherish *forever*? Why not swear to stay together for a few years, and then, when the boredom and bitterness sets in, go your separate ways? That's more realistic."

He stops in front of me. "What about keeping a family together?"

"What about it? Some families are healthier apart."

He looks out at the water. "I can't argue with that."

He seems to get lost in his own thoughts for a moment, but when an approaching cyclist rings his bell, he pulls me toward him, making sure we're both out of the way. With his hand still on my arm, he looks down at me, and I see something in his expression. Something needful I'd seen earlier when he was pretending to be Kieran. It makes my stomach curl and my heart speed up, and I'm reminded that I've spent my whole life avoiding this kind of connection for good reason.

I step back, pretending to yawn. "Wow, it's getting late, huh?"

He nods. "Yes. Far too late. I'll get you a cab."

I have more questions, but I guess they'll have to wait for another time. I peel his jacket off as he steps into the street and hails a taxi. When it pulls over, he takes his jacket from me before opening the door and holding out his hand.

I shake it firmly. "Well, goodnight, Mr. Riley. Thank you for your time."

He gives me a perplexed smile and tenses his arm to stop me from pumping his hand. "I want to hold your hand to help you into the car, Miss Tate. Still, now that I have it ..." He brings it up to his mouth and presses his lips against my skin. I restrain myself from full-on trembling from the rush of sensation that races up my arm. "Goodnight. I'll see you soon."

"When?"

"For our next interview? Or our first date?"

"Either. Both." Jesus, do I sound as hyper as I feel? "I'm talking way too fast, aren't I?"

He chuckles and helps me into the car, then leans through the door. "I'll call you. And make no mistake, Miss Tate, by the time I'm done, you'll have shed your cynical husk and be a romance junkie like the rest of us. Have a good weekend."

Just as I'm about to tell him how wrong he is, he closes the door. I sigh in frustration and give the driver my address, and when we pull into traffic and head east, I lean my head back and think about tonight's events.

On the one hand, I know without a doubt this story is going to be as hot as Hades when I get more details. On the other, my resolve about Max's charms not working on me isn't quite as rock solid as I thought. There's no doubt he's gorgeous, and he can certainly flirt when the mood takes him, but is that him being himself? Or him being the Max he wants me to believe is real?

Whatever the answer, I know I'm going to have to develop a tolerance for how he makes me feel, or I'll end up as just one more giddy client on his roster. To that end, I conjure up negative thoughts about him all the way home.

Eight

Look Before You Buy

The next day, Asha and I are wandering through the bustle and noise of the Brooklyn Flea market while I regale her with the revelation that Mister Romance and Irish Kieran are the same man.

"Holy snapping duckshit, Edie, are you serious?"

"Unfortunately, yes."

She stops dead and whips off her Jackie O sunglasses in dramatic fashion. "So, that whole Kieran ploy was just to *scope you out*?"

"Seems that way."

"And you went on your whole anti-love, fuck-relationships rant, and he *still*s said he's going to win you over? Was he drunk?"

"He actually said he's going to make me *fall in love* with him. Like this is some big game, and my affection is the prize."

She gives me an incredulous look. "I hope he realizes he's going to lose. Of all the women in the world to bet on going gooey for him, you're the least likely. I invested two-hundred dollars into that date, thinking it was a down payment on a potential boyfriend for you. It turns out I was buying a delusional fool. God!" She stomps off while sucking angrily on her organic wheatgrass smoothie.

"To be fair," I say. "You did get great value for money. I mean, that's still forty-eight-hundred dollars less than his regular going rate."

"And he's not even Irish?"

"Nope."

"Oh, man! I got all hot-and-bothered over his accent for nothing. What a dick." She stops in front of one of the stalls and sniffs some homemade soap. "I was so sure he was into you, too. The way he spoke about you ... Edie, what I wouldn't give for some guy to get that same wistful expression when he talks about me. Of course, I'd like it to be a real man with real emotions and not some faking faker who fakes, but still ..." She moves down the line of displays, smelling samples as she goes. "I'll say one thing for Max – the dude is a committed actor. I was totally picking up what he was laying down." She holds the soap out to me. "Ooh, smell this."

I lean forward and breathe in, and I'm surprised that the familiar aroma gives me goosebumps.

"Lemongrass," Asha says. "That's exactly what Kieran ... shit, I mean *Max* smells like." She pulls a couple of dollars out of her purse and hands them to the vendor.

"Why are you buying it if it reminds you of Max?" I ask.

She pops the soap into her tote. "He may be a dick, but he still smelled delicious."

We head down the aisle of tents and browse the crazy collection of wares. It's still early, so some people haven't finished setting up, but if you ever doubted that Brooklyn has become the hipster capital of the world, you only need come to these markets to get proof. Everything is artisanal, free-range, and organic, even the furniture. There's some dude selling cat-fur scarves. He doesn't skin cats, mind you; that would be wrong on so many levels. No, he just spins the excess fur from his five Persians into wool and then lovingly knits it into neck warmers, no doubt while listening to sixties bands on vinyl and sipping his free-range, organic, recycled tea.

The mere thought makes me shudder.

Cat-man catches me staring and gives me a smile. Or, at least I think it's a smile. His beard is so epic, it's hard to tell.

"Pussy warmer?" he asks, gesturing to his collection.

I have a suspicion he started this whole thing for the express purpose of asking women that when they pass.

"No, thanks," I say, trying not to act as skeeved-out as I feel. "I'm all good in the pussy wool department."

Beside me, Asha snorts. "You can say that again." As we walk away, she whispers, "This is your gentle sisterly reminder to get yourself a Brazilian. It's been a while."

"How the hell do you know my waxing schedule?"

"You walk funny the day after you get it done. That hasn't happened in over a month."

Dammit, she's right. I make a mental note to schedule an appointment with Francesca as soon as possible.

We're just about to reach the end of the aisle, when both of our phones ding. We stop and check our screens.

<No rush, but if U gurls cud cum b4 Xmas, that'd B gr8!!!!>

Asha and I turn to each other and say simultaneously, "Nannabeth," and then pick up the pace.

"Why does she always have to text like a thirteen-year-old?" Asha asks.

"You know she dresses like a teenager. It's only natural she should text like one."

When we turn the corner, we head toward a large yellow tent, under which we can see Nannabeth bustling around, getting her wares organized for the morning rush. Today she's wearing one of her tamer ensembles—a bright pink midriff top, floral overalls, and red Chucks. From this distance, when her back is turned, she even looks like a teenage girl. It's only when you get closer and notice the wrinkly skin around her waist and the streaks of grey in her mess of curly red hair, that you realize she's an old woman in disguise.

"Hey, Nannabeth!"

She turns, and when she sees us, her face lights up behind her trendy purple glasses.

"My girls! My beautiful but sleepy-headed girls. Thought you'd never get here. It's almost lunchtime."

She pulls us both into a hug, and as usual, we grunt in pain. The woman may be five-foot-three and would blow away in a strong breeze, but she's still as strong as an ox.

"Nan," I say, my voice straining beneath her vice-like grip, "It's 7.30 in the morning, which is barely breakfast time. And to be fair, we were both up before six this morning, even though it's Saturday."

She pulls back and puts her hands on her hips. "Well, I'm up at 4am every day. I've told you girls before that life's too short to spend it sleeping. Still, I'm grateful you could come and help today. I couldn't cope without you."

Nan usually has a couple of neighbors helping each Saturday, but occasionally they're unavailable, and she gets Ash and me to step in. We don't mind. Working with Nan is never dull.

"Okay, darlings," she says as she grabs a nearby trestle table and unfolds its legs. "Help me get these up. I'm running behind. Moby was sick this morning, so I couldn't get out of the house until he was all tucked into bed. Poor thing looked so small and pale when I left, I might have to duck home at lunchtime to make sure he's okay."

Asha and I exchange a smile as we set up the tables.

Nan saying she has to 'duck home' to check on Moby is hilarious, mainly because Moby is a duck. Think about that. She named him *Moby Duck*.

At first, Asha gave her props for her shout-out to Herman Melville, but Nan insisted she named him after the music artist. I thought she was kidding, until I discovered she does indeed have all of his albums. It still makes me laugh.

Another fun fact is that Moby is a girl. The duck, not the musician. When Nan first brought her tiny duckling home, she just assumed it was a boy, and by the time 'he' got around to laying his first egg, Nan was set in her ways and couldn't face the inconvenience of a sex change. So, yeah. Moby has been Nan's faux-transgender best friend and roommate since Grandad died, and Nan wouldn't have it any other way.

I pull a tray of duck eggs out of a basket and place them carefully on the table. "Whoa. Moby's been busy this week."

Nan nods proudly. "He's been binge-watching *Game of Thrones*. The stress of all the character deaths sometimes makes him pop twice a day. It's fantastic for his laying but not so good for his blood pressure."

It's also hilarious that even though Nan has barely had a single sick day in all of her seventy-five years, Moby seems to be suffering from three or four chronic illnesses at any one time.

"So, Eden," Nan says, as she stacks some crates to display her fruit and veggies. "How's your love life? Found a nice boy yet?"

I sigh. "Nan, how come you always ask me that question and never Ash?"

"Because I know your sister is at least looking. You're not."

"So? *You've* managed to live a full and happy life without a man for over a decade."

"It's not the same. You don't even have a duck."

"I'll go and get a duck today if it will stop you from hassling me about men."

"Actually, Nan," Ash says, shooting me a look. "Eden had a date last night."

Nan stops dead and stares at me. "Eden Marigold Tate – why didn't you tell me? I want to know everything."

Asha pushes her sunglasses up onto her head before setting up Nanna's cashbox. "Oh, Nan, this guy was *hot*. Like, seriously, *stupidly* hot." She grabs her bag and fishes out her bar of recently purchased soap. "And the best thing was, he smelled like *this*."

Nan takes a whiff then lets out a low whistle. "Wowee. Sounds like a dreamboat." She turns to me and raises her eyebrows. "When's the wedding? I need to buy a new pantsuit."

I throw the cloth I was using to dust the table at Asha, who bats it away and giggles.

"Ash is exaggerating, Nan. He wasn't all that. And he turned out to be a total douche, so I won't be seeing him again."

"Except you will be," Ash says. "For at least three dates."

"Different guy," I clarify to Nan.

"Did he smell just as good as the first guy?" she asks.

Asha grins. "Yes. Maybe even better."

"Then what's the problem?"

"She *liked* the first guy. She's not that keen on the second guy."

"Actually," I say. "The second guy is just a business contact. I have no interest in him beyond a professional relationship."

"But this business guy is still hot?" Nan asks.

"So hot!" Ash says.

Nan looks at her in confusion. "Then why isn't she dating him?"

God, this conversation is going nowhere, fast.

"Nan, let me make this as simple as possible. I'm not dating anyone. I don't *wish* to date anyone. I'm single and happy, and I'm not changing that any time soon. Don't listen to a word Asha says. She's just being a brat."

Nan throws up her hands. "You girls go and get my hopes up just to shatter them like glass. You know I'm not going to be around forever, right? I'd like to hold at least one chubby grandchild before I die. Stop baby blocking me, and put those nice, young uteruses to good use!"

As frustrating as Nan's obsession with my dating schedule is, I laugh as she continues to mumble about my aging baby-maker while we finish setting up.

Twenty minutes later, we've just gotten everything into place when customers start arriving, and the three of us go to work.

For years, Nannabeth's stall has been one of the most popular at the market. Apart from her amazing range of fresh fruit, veggies, and herbs, she also has her own brand of honey. Believe it or not, she raises bees, right in the heart of Brooklyn. Amazing what you can achieve when you've lived in the same apartment building for sixty years and have claimed the entire giant rooftop as your own private hobby farm.

Down at the other end of the tent are several boxes of old records, as well as a collection of furniture pieces and bric-a-brac dating from the sixties to the eighties. All of the secondhand wares sell incredibly well, even the ugly stuff. Nothing is ever out of fashion in Brooklyn.

As the morning rush hits us, the first few hours fly by, but by mid-morning things have calmed down. We've just hit our first big lull when a familiar platinum blonde in head-to-toe Chanel approaches Asha. In the midst of the reclaimed, recycled, and pre-loved nirvana of the markets, she's kind of out of place.

"Joanna!" Asha says, and I recognize that thing she does

when she's sort of pleased to see someone and sort of not. "Hey. I didn't expect to see you here." I wander over, and Asha grabs me by the arm. "You remember my sister, Eden. You guys met at last year's Christmas party, remember?"

I wave and smile as Joanna almost squeals, "Of course! Hiiiiii, Eden!"

I remember Joanna well. When we first met, she'd gone into disturbing detail about how her ex-boyfriend had given her gonorrhea and that until she finished the medication, she had to keep extra underwear in her drawer at work 'just in case'. Never having had gonorrhea myself, I had no idea what she was talking about. Then she drilled me for a solid ten minutes about my sex life, including a full assessment of how many STDs I'd had. It wasn't fun. She's one of those people who over-shares at every opportunity and expects you to do the same. She's also constantly smiling and yet never seems happy.

"What are you doing here?" Asha asks. "I thought Midtown was about as far as you like to roam from the Upper East Side. Isn't Brooklyn a little out of your comfort zone?"

Joanna nods and looks around as if she's assessing an alien planet. "Yes, but you told me about how cute your Nan's stall was, so I thought I'd come check it out." She looks over to where Nan is dealing with a young couple looking at furniture. "Oh, my God. Are things so tight that she has to sell her furniture? That's so sad."

Asha laughs. "No. She just has a lot of elderly friends, and when they pass, she helps out their families by selling their possessions for top dollar." Asha points at a small, scuffed mahogany plant stand. "She just sold that for two-hundred dollars.

Joanna scrunches up her nose. "Wow. But it's, like, way old."

"Yes," I say. "Some would even say *antique*."

"You know who has cool antiques?" Joanna asks, her face lighting up. "Pottery Barn. They look old, but they smell new. Your gran should totally check it out."

"Yeah, Ash," I say, nudging her with my elbow. "You should tell Nan about Pottery Barn. You know how much she loves it when people replace rather than recycle."

Joanna spies the bottles of honey and grabs two. "Ooh! Honey facial, here I come."

"Take your time browsing," I say to Joanna as I tug on Asha's arm. "We'll be right over here if you need us."

I pull my sister over to the produce section and keep an eye on Joanna as I whisper, "So, you guys are outside-of-work friends now? That's a new twist."

My sister gets the same expression she always does when she knows she's done something wrong but doesn't want to admit it.

"Ahhh, I might have invited her down here so she'd think we were friends."

"And why would you do that?"

"Because, she has tickets to see Kingdom of Stone tomorrow night and I was angling to be her date."

"What the heck is Kingdom of Stone."

"A band. A really good one."

Joanna glances over and waves at us. When Asha and I smile and wave back, she heads down to look at Nannabeth's collection of homemade Fimo jewelry from the eighties. "So gnarly!" she squeals. "It's like ugly-chic."

I turn to Asha. "So, you prostituted yourself to see some band?"

"Not *some* band, Edie. *The* band. They're the biggest thing to come out of the east village in years, and I happen to love their music."

"And ...?" Knowing Asha, I'm sure there's more to it than a

few catchy tunes.

Asha slumps. "And I think I'm in love with their bass player. He's gorgeous, and from reading articles about them, I think he has the soul of a poet. He writes a lot of their songs."

"So you're lusting after him? Okay. I can get on board with that. Does he have a girlfriend?"

She crosses her arms. "I'm not looking to be his girlfriend. I'm not one of those delusional women who thinks he's going to bring me up onstage and fall in love with me. It's a harmless rock star fantasy. Everybody has one. I remember when you used to have Justin Timberlake posters all over your room."

"That's different. JT could dance. There's nothing sexier than a man who can dance."

A short distance away, Joanna holds up an ugly flower necklace. "Girls! Don't you just love it?"

"So much love," I say, giving her a thumbs up.

"She's not that bad," Asha whispers. "Plus, she was the one who told us about Mister Romance, so I figure we kind of owe her one."

Joanna walks over with her collection of items and drops them in front of us. "How much for all of this?"

Ash goes through her pile and adds everything up. "Thirty-five."

Joanna reaches into her purse and pulls out some cash. "I think I'm going wear the flowery thing tomorrow night. Do you think?"

"Totally," says Ash. "You should wear it with that cute red dress you rocked at work the other day."

"Yes! So cute, right?" Joanna turns to me. "Did Ash tell you we're seeing the Stoners tomorrow night?" When I hesitate, she says, "That's what the fans call the Kingdom of Stone guys. I'm pretty sure they're not real stoners. Or maybe they are. Who am

I to judge, right? Anyway, I'm good friends with their manager, so if you want me to get a ticket for you, too, I totally could."

"Uh ... thanks, but I don't really know their stuff."

She waves off my concern. "Who cares? They're hot guys playing rock music. What's not to like, right?"

I smile as I wrap up her purchases, and when I give them to her, she grabs my hand and leans forward in a conspiratorial way. "So, Eden, did Asha tell you about the whole ..." She looks around. "... *Mister Romance* legend?"

I take a quick glance at Asha, who nods. "Uh ... yes," I say. "Thanks for the tip about him. I think it would make a great story."

"No problem. And just so you know, if you need to, like, do some research or whatever, my cousin and her friends are having a big fundraiser thing next week, and I can totally get you an invite."

Now my gratitude is real. I know I told Max I'd stop investigating the identity of his clients, but if I happened to be at a party and some of them were there, and I just happened to run into them ... well, that's just a good old-fashioned coincidence, isn't it?

"Wow, Joanna, that's a great offer. Can I get back to you?"

"Sure. I'll RSVP that I'm bringing another guest just in case, and if you decide not to go, Asha can come instead. There'll be some rich single dudes there. Maybe even royalty. You never know what could happen."

She lets go of my arm and shoves her purchases into her giant tote, and I realize Asha's right – she's not that bad. In fact, she might be useful in finding out some facts Max is hesitant to tell me.

"Hey, Joanna," I say. "Why don't you come over to our place tomorrow night and get ready there? Ash can do your hair, and we can have cocktails before you guys go to the concert."

For a second, she looks shocked, but then her face breaks into a giant smile; a real one this time. "Are you serious? That would be ah-maaaaayzing! I'd love to! We'll have such a good time!"

"Great. We'll see you around six?"

"Yes! Perfect! See you then."

She's just about vibrating with excitement as she waves goodbye and walks away.

When she's gone, Ash nudges me with her shoulder. "Aw, that was a nice thing to do. Are you getting soft in your old age?"

I glare at her. "You shut your filthy mouth, Asha Rose. You'll ruin my reputation."

ơ

I'm weaving through the waning afternoon crowd with fresh coffee for me, Nan, and Asha when I get a text from Nannabeth.

<Found a man 4 U. GORGEOUS! Lawyer!!! Single!!! Hurry bck b4 he leaves!!!!!>

I groan and drop my head back. I wonder how much time I could waste if I went all the way around the other side of the markets to get back. The only trouble is, the coffee would be cold by then, and I'd have to make another run. Still, if it helped me avoid Little Nanna Matchmaker...

I compromise by dawdling all the way back, and when I arrive, I'm relieved to see Nan is alone at the stall.

"Awww," I say. "I missed him? Total bummer."

I hand Nan a coffee, and she pats my forearm. "I'm immune to your sarcasm by now, dear, you should know that. Besides, he'll be back. I'm going to sell some furniture for him next weekend, and he's just gone away for a few minutes to organize someone to deliver it."

I look around. "Where's Ash?"

"Bathroom break, but she's been gone longer than you. No doubt she's found a clothing stall somewhere and is trawling it for vintage Valentino."

"Oh, well. Her loss." I put Asha's coffee on the table and sip mine. *Ahhhh, sweet caffeine.* Normally, I'd have had four or five by now, but this is only number two. My brain sighs in relief.

When I look up, I see Nan's smiling at me.

"What?"

She blinks, and I notice how her eyes are a touch misty. "Nothing. Just always surprises me how much you look like your mother when she was your age. Asha looks more like your dad, but you ... you're a dead ringer for Liz." She touches my face. "I wish she'd lived to see you girls grow into such beautiful young women."

I pat Nan's hand and smile back as best as I can. Thinking about Mom always makes my throat tight. "Yeah. Me, too."

Mom was too young to die, and Ash and I were too young to lose her. Everything should have been different. She shouldn't have had to kill herself working two jobs to keep our heads above water, and Dad shouldn't have been a Houdini husband who disappeared whenever it suited him.

Ash blames it on them getting married too young, but I blame the swinging dick who broke Mom's heart a little more each time he left.

"You finished your coffee?" Nan asks.

I take one final sip and nod.

"Good. Then go take off your smartass pants and put on some lip gloss. I want you to look your best for when Sean gets back."

"Sure, Mah," I say in my best redneck accent. "Ah'll go pretty mahself up, so the hawt cowboy you wanna sell me to can check mah teef befow he rahds me!" I'm in the middle of a gross yokel guffaw when Nan's eyes go wide as she focuses on a point over my shoulder.

I stand up straight and drop the act. "He's right behind me, isn't he?"

Nan winces and nods.

A deep voice says, "So, I'm the cowboy in this scenario? Do I have to wear chaps and a hat? Because as luck would have it, I own both."

The familiar resonance sends a shiver up my spine, and sure enough, when I turn I see Max standing there, an amused smirk on his face.

What the hell is he doing here? Did he really go to all of the trouble of tracking down my grandmother, so he can recruit her in his quest to make me see the error of my anti-romance ways?

A flush of anger fills me. Involving my Nan like this feels like a violation. He's had the balls to lecture me several times about professional behavior, and then he does something like this? Not cool.

"Oh, Sean," Nan says as she sidles up to him. "There's that sense of humor again. Women love witty men. By the way, this is my lovely granddaughter, Eden." Nan smiles and through gritted teeth says, "Say hello, Eden." Then she leans over and whispers, "Isn't he handsome?"

Max holds out his hand and acts innocent. "Very nice to meet you, Miss ... uh ... Eden." It ridiculous how awkward he sounds calling me by my first name.

I ignore his hand and go for a level-ten glare instead. "Oh, please ... *Sean*, is it? Feel free to call me Miss Tate."

"Or call her anytime!" Nan says with a giggle. "She's single." When neither Max nor I laugh, she glances between us. "Wait, do you two know each other?"

"No," I say. "I've never met *Sean* before. Wow, you're a lawyer, huh? Impressive. Perhaps you can enlighten me – what can I do if a guy is stalking me?"

"Well, first," he says in his calmest voice, "you'd have to establish that his presence is nefarious and not just a coincidence."

"That's unlikely."

"Not really. If two people live in the same area, it's conceivable they'd run into each other from time to time."

"After not running into each other for years before that? Seems strange."

"Perhaps he's recently moved to the area."

"And perhaps he's full of horseshit."

He tilts his head. "Not bullshit?"

"I thought horseshit would be more appropriate, considering the whole cowboy thing."

Nan continues watching us like a tennis match, until a couple of girls wearing flowers in their hair pick up some herbs and wave at her.

"Well, if you'll both excuse me," she says, giving one more glance between us. "I have customers to attend to. Eden, don't forget to get a contact number for Sean before he leaves. See you next weekend! We're going to make you some money."

When she's out of earshot, Max goes to say something, but I cut him off. "How dare you use my grandmother to get to me!"

"Miss Tate –"

"I mean, seriously. She's an old woman whose only wish is to see me married off and churning out tiny, red-headed babies. She doesn't need *Sean the lawyer* coming in here and being all tall and single."

"I didn't –"

"I know you're probably nervous about convincing me that your whole romance shtick isn't a con, but clearly we need to set some professional boundaries about how and when we contact each other, because I find this *totally* unacceptable. Call me on the phone. Don't just show up and charm my Nan into liking you."

"That wasn't my –"

"I can't believe you'd just ..." I'm shocked into silence when Max takes a step well inside my buffer zone and whispers, "Miss Tate, if you don't stop and listen for five seconds, I'm going to kiss the hell out of you in front of your gran then drop to one knee and propose. If you think she's obsessed with marrying you off now, imagine what she'd be like after that."

He's so close it takes me a second to get used to the heat of his proximity. "You wouldn't."

"Keep talking and find out."

"You agreed you wouldn't kiss me."

"On a date. Since we're not on a date right now ..."

"Seems like you're just looking for an excuse to kiss me, Mr. Riley."

"I'm not, but if that's what it takes to get a word in, I'm willing to take the hit."

Looking up at him like this is uncomfortable on my neck, but I'll be damned if I'm the first one to step back.

"Wow, you sweet talker. I can see what all the ladies see in you. I'm swooning so hard right now."

"I assume your failure to stop means you'd like to find out how my mouth tastes? Maybe it's you who's looking for an excuse."

I tell myself that threatening to shut someone up with a kiss should not be sexy. Unfortunately, my body doesn't listen. He stares, waiting to find out what I'll do, and I deliberately press my lips together to show him I'm done. I'm still not moving back, though. He can be the one to retreat.

I hold my breath for the full three seconds he takes to register my compliance, and then exhale as he finally steps back.

"Now," he says, "if you care to know the truth, I came down here today because a friend recommended Nannabeth as someone who could sell secondhand furniture fast and for a decent price. I had no idea she was your grandmother, until I returned from my phone call to find you doing your best Jerry Lewis impersonation."

"It was Lucille Ball mixed with Holly Hunter, actually, but whatever."

"I know this may be hard to believe, Miss Tate, but my world doesn't revolve around finding excuses to spend time with you. I have a life outside of my work and separate from your story, so if you've finished yelling at me, I have better things to do than stand here and argue."

He's about to leave when I say, "Why are you selling your furniture?"

He looks back at me and hesitates before saying, "For personal reasons."

"It just seems strange to me that someone who earns as much as you would need to sell furniture on the side."

"I inherited some pieces. I'd rather sell them through Nannabeth than worry about registering with a dealer or auction house."

"Because then you don't have to give your real name?"

"That's part of it, yes." He takes a step back. "Oh, and just so you're clear on when and how I'm going to be contacting you in the near future, you'll receive an email from me tomorrow about the etiquette of our upcoming dates. Please read the guidelines carefully and commit them to memory. I'll call you tomorrow night to discuss them and answer any questions you might have."

I don't know why I bristle from his assumption that I won't

have anything better to do on a Sunday night than talk to him, but I do, and without thinking too much about it I say, "I'm not available tomorrow night. I'm going to a concert."

He pushes his hands into his pockets. "Let me guess – Kingdom of Stone."

"How did you know?"

He looks over at the line of clouds forming on the horizon. "I think half the women in Manhattan are going. I'd considered taking a client, but if you're going to be there …"

"You don't think I could maintain a professional distance?"

"I think it would be a challenge for you."

"Would you prefer it if I didn't go?"

He gives a one-shoulder shrug. "I won't presume to tell you what to do, Miss Tate. I'll make other arrangements."

"Don't," I say. Getting a chance to see him in action is too good to pass up. "I don't care about the band, so don't change your plans because of me. I have plenty of work I can do at home."

A look of relief settles on his face. "Okay. That'd be great. Thank you."

"You're welcome."

"Will you be available to talk Monday morning?"

"Sure."

He walks over to the back of the tent and picks up a paper carry bag overflowing with fresh flowers. "Nannabeth stashed these for me earlier."

"They're gorgeous," I say. "Are they for a date?"

He gives me a serene smile. "Goodbye, Miss Tate. Enjoy the rest of your weekend."

He walks down the aisle, and I'm ashamed to say I watch his back until he disappears.

I'm still staring off into space when Asha gets back.

"What did I miss?" she asks, carrying two bags filled with clothes. Guess Nan was right about where she's been.

"Could you call Joanna?" I say. "I'm going to need a ticket to that concert tomorrow night after all."

Nine

Rock Shop

"Eden, do you want another drink?" Asha ducks her head around my bedroom door and frowns when she sees me working on my laptop. "Hey, come on. It's Sunday night. Time to kick back and let your hair down."

I gesture to the funky hairstyle she and Joanna inflicted upon me half-an-hour ago. My regular frizz has been flat-ironed into smooth, sexy curls. "It's down, even though I would have rather put it in a ponytail and been done with it."

"Don't be grumpy. We're going to a club. You need to look club-hot."

"Is that different from normal-hot?"

"Of course. How do you not know this?"

"Because I don't go to clubs."

"Okay, then just take my word for it. Do you want another cocktail? We have time for one more before we have to leave."

I look back at my computer screen and shake my head. "No, I'm good."

"K. Be ready to go in twenty."

"Will do."

When she leaves, I continue sifting through some of the

information Toby sent me regarding the warehouse we found in Greenpoint. There's so much stuff here, I don't even know where to start. There are deeds to the building, leases, past tenants – but trying to find a thread that will lead me to Max's real identity is like finding a needle in a haystack. He must have some connection to Reggie Baker, or else why was his name registered to the mailbox?

I'm searching for more info on Reggie when an email alert pops up. I click it open.

From: Maxwell Riley <mr@email.com>
To: Eden Tate <etate@email.com>
Subject: Behavioral Guidelines
Date: Sunday May 7
Dear Miss Tate,

Further to our conversation yesterday, following is a list of guidelines to be used in our upcoming dates. Please do your best to strictly adhere to them.

1. When you encounter me in the coming days, I may look/ sound/act differently than you expect. Please respect the integrity of my characterization and do not block or dispute the information I give you. For any role-play to be successful, the participants need to suspend their disbelief. I know you're a natural skeptic, so accepting me as a different character may be difficult, but I'd ask that you do your best to immerse yourself in the experience.

2. Whatever character I choose for our date will be attracted to you. Please put your mistrust of me aside and accept the truth of that scenario. The only way for you to write a balanced article about me and my popularity is to fully understand my clients and their thinking, and that means opening your mind to a world of uplifting and life-affirming romance. Pretending and deception are two totally different beasts, and for you to understand why I believe my work isn't immoral, it's important you learn the difference.

3. Trying to break my concentration or pulling me out of my chosen character will not succeed. I advise you to mentally catalogue burning questions you have regarding my methods, and I will answer them in a separate interview session after the date. Addressing me as Max or breaking the illusion for any reason will result in the termination of the date, and our arrangement.

4. Until we reach the end of this experiment, describing my methods to outsiders is strictly forbidden. I understand that your sister is privy to sensitive information regarding me and my identity, and that's partly due to my choice to involve her in the Kieran scenario, but please, no one but her must know. By all means, keep notes of what you discover for the purposes of research, but make sure that research remains confidential.

5. Our dates may involve physical contact. I want to reassure you that I will not force you to do anything you're not comfortable with. I do not engage in, nor do I condone, sexual assault. I may have threatened to kiss you yesterday without your consent, but I had no intention of going through with it. To that end, if at any time you feel I am overstepping my bounds regarding intimate physical contact, simply use the word, 'veto', and I will stop. These experiences are designed to empower you, not make you feel threatened or frightened. If you are in extreme distress, saying veto three times in a row will immediately end the role play. Because you've made it clear that you do not wish to be kissed during our interactions, I will require a verbal directive from you to overturn this decision.

6. As I've previously mentioned, clients are free to touch most of my body. This includes, but is not limited to, my face, hair, arms, chest, and back. You may not touch me below the waist without express verbal permission. Any violations of this guideline will result in the immediate termination of our date. I will also limit my physical interaction with you to the aforementioned areas. I will naturally refrain from touching your chest unless expressly invited to do so. Overt sexual contact is not part of my service. You may ask me to touch you in more intimate ways, but it will be at my sole discretion as to whether or not I comply. My decision on these matters is final. Prolonged or continued coercion on your part will result in the immediate termination of our date.

If you have specific problems or objections to anything contained in this correspondence, please let me know by return email immediately. Lack of response will be interpreted as a tacit verbal agreement to abide by this document.

I look forward to seeing you soon.

Regards,

Max.

As I finish reading, I shake my head. How the hell do women find this process romantic? There are so many rules about how to behave and what to think, it must suck all the joy out of being spontaneous. I know I should keep an open mind to get the story, but I'm still skeptical that going on these dates will achieve anything except reinforce my idea that what Max does is tacky and unscrupulous. I don't care how attractive he is. There's no way he can create a real, meaningful connection with someone while being constrained by all of this nonsense. I'd be willing to admit that women fall in lust with him, but not love.

I look up as Joanna knocks on my door. "Hey! You might

want to get dressed. We're heading out soon."

I look down at my skinny jeans and gray V-neck T-shirt. "I am dressed."

Joanna raises her eyebrows and gives me one of those smiles that has a definite edge of, *Oh, God, really?*

She smiles at me, and I smile back, until she finally says, "Okay, then. Let's go get our party on!"

Asha calls out that our car will arrive in ten as I pack away my computer and pull on my boots.

Conscious that Ash and Joanna look like they just stepped off the set of *Young, Hot, and Hip in Manhattan,* I slap on some smoky eye makeup and clear gloss before the girls drag me downstairs and out into the street to meet our car.

Half-an-hour later, we pull up in front of The Rock Shop, one of NYC's trendier live music venues. Even though we're an hour early to see the headline act, the building is already teeming with people.

"God, I'm soooo excited," Joanna says as she bypasses the huge line waiting to get in and leads us straight up to the two enormous bouncers. "This night is going to rock!"

The bouncers barely glance at Joanna before lifting the velvet rope and ushering us inside. Asha and I exchange a glance.

"How?" I whisper.

Ash shrugs. "I have no idea, but the more time I spend with her, the more I realize she knows *everyone.* Maybe all those tall stories she's famous for are true after all."

We push through the heavy door and are immediately hit with a wall of sound. Within five minutes of stepping into the packed space, I remember why I rarely see live bands. If the ear-splitting noise, sticky floor, and huge crowds weren't enough to turn me off, then the faceless ass-grabbing as we push toward the bar is.

"Let's line up for shots!" Joanna yells over the music. "I'm buying!"

We've all downed two cocktails already, but I'm still feeling stone-cold sober. I smile when Joanna gets the bartender to line up shots of Patron.

I lean into her. "Now we're talking!" I figure that if all else fails, switch to tequila to let the good times roll.

We all slam back a shot, and I shudder as it burns in all the right ways.

"Wow, these guys are really good!" Asha says into my ear as she points to the guys rocking it out onstage. "They're just one of the opening acts, but they've really got the crowd pumping!"

I look out over the sea of bodies in front of the stage. They certainly seem to be having a good time.

After I down my second shot, I start feeling no pain. Then Joanna suggests we get closer to the stage, so we all hold hands and push our way through the gyrating throng.

I must admit, this music is growing on me. With some alcohol in my system, I can understand how the energy of this kind of event could turn people on. The lights, the sound, the seething mass of passionate people. It's all working for me.

I have a brief look around for Max, but I can't see him anywhere. In fact, there are few guys here tonight, and those that are seem to have taken up permanent residence at the bar. There are several women nearby who look high-end enough to be among Max's clientele. I edge close to one who seems to be wearing way too much diamond jewelry to be here just for the music.

"This is great!" I say to her, and she smiles and nods. "Are you here with someone?"

She gives me a sympathetic smile. "Oh, sweetie, you're very cute, but I'm waiting for my boyfriend. He'll be here in ten."

I sigh in mock-disappointment. "Oh, well. Bummer for me. Enjoy your night."

Okay, so she's a potential.

I move away but make sure I still have a clear view of her, just in case.

Asha pokes me. "What are you doing?"

"Nothing."

"Then stop hassling strangers and dance with us."

I continue scoping the room as I dance with the girls, but I still try to have good time. When we've pushed to the front of the stage, we join everyone in throwing our arms above our heads in time with the music. I don't think I've ever done this before, and right now I can't figure out why it's taken me so long. Max may have had a point about me not having enough fun in my life.

I scream and clap along with everyone else as the band finishes their set. The M.C. comes onstage to chat to the crowd and cover the next setup, and we silently agree to have a well-deserved rest.

"Do you guys want water?" Asha asks.

Joanna and I nod vigorously.

"I'll come with you," Joanna says.

They look back at me to see if I want to follow, but I'd rather scope the room for Mr. Riley.

"I'm good," I say. "I'll wait here." I keep my eye on my mark, who's now talking to a couple of other luxe ladies. Perhaps they're all a part of the exclusive M.R. fan club.

While they chat, I push my fingers through my hair and move to lean against the giant stack of speakers, so I can catch my breath. There's a flurry of movement onstage as they swap over equipment for the next act.

After a few minutes, the M.C. comes back on to address us.

"And now, we have one of our most popular singer/songwriters here to take us up to show time. Please give a huge Rock Show welcome to Caleb Sykes!"

The women around me scream their heads off, and it makes me wish I'd brought earplugs like I'd planned.

I head over to the stage just as a driving rock beats starts up, followed by a voice so appealing, it immediately has all of my attention. When I move out to get a better view of the stage, a rush of shock and disbelief hits me. The tall, muscled singer with the dreamy voice, chaotic hair, and two-day scruff is ... Max.

"Holy goddamn Mother of Shit."

CR

My mind is reeling. What the hell is happening right now? Maybe this is just someone who looks like Max, and I've been so obsessed with him and this story, I'm making myself see things that aren't there.

I study the guy in front of me. Dark, low-ride jeans with thick belt, snug black T that shows an impressive range of tattoos. Muscled arms strum a Gibson guitar as sensual lips brush against the microphone. There's no denying it anymore. It's Max. Just a totally different Max than the version I know.

I look around, desperate for Asha to confirm what I'm seeing, but I can't spot her anywhere. It doesn't help that the women around me have taken it upon themselves to swarm the stage, and even as I try to move toward the bar to find my sister, I'm swept forward until I'm standing just a few yards away from Max's crotch.

I stand there gaping as the first song ends and the next one starts. So, this is the date he had planned for his client? A classic rock star fantasy? Man, Asha was right. Everybody does have one. And judging from how my body is reacting to this whole situation, that includes me.

The luxe women are still in a group, gazing at him with fierce adoration. Max seems completely oblivious to anything but the music. That pleases me, because I have a strong suspicion that if he looks down and spots me, I won't get a positive reaction. I flat out told him I wasn't coming so he could work unobserved, and he doesn't seem to be the kind of man who'd appreciate bald-faced lies.

For good measure, I try to hide behind the girl in front of me. She's shorter than I am, so it's not a great fit, but I do what I can. Trying to remain as inconspicuous as possible, I turn to the blonde girl next to me, who's staring at Max like he's a sexy rocker messiah.

"Do you know this guy?" I ask.

She nods. "I've seen him play here a few times. So gorgeous, right? And his voice ..."

"Yeah, he's great. Have you seen him play anywhere else? Does he have an album?" I want to find out exactly how meta this setup is.

The woman nods. "He sells CDs after the show. He'll sign them and everything. In my opinion, it's worth the twenty bucks just to talk to him for a few minutes." So, he sells furniture and now CDs? How many revenue streams does this guy have?

The woman looks over my shoulder. "Don't tell my boyfriend, but I've bought his album three times in the past few months." She winks at me, and it doesn't do a single thing to convince me I haven't fallen through some sort of weird wormhole into an alternate universe.

I look back at rock-god Max. He seems so comfortable up

there, singing and playing like he was born to do it. Nothing about it looks even remotely fake. I thought his speaking voice was sexy, but I have no words to describe his singing voice. It's rough and smooth at the same time. Black velvet wrapped around sandpaper.

I have no idea if the songs he's singing are his own, but he sure as hell sells them. He's one of those people who looks like every word is coming from deep inside. He's not singing words, he's expressing emotions.

I continue to marvel over the scope of this illusion, as well as his talent, as he and his band mates play another four songs. By the end, I don't even care if this whole thing is pretend. I'm a fan of Caleb Sykes and his sultry, heartfelt music.

After they finish up their fifth song, Max pushes his hair out of his eyes and smiles. The women around me scream and clap.

"We've only got time for one more. Any requests?"

Without any hesitation, at least a dozen voices yell out, "Deep!"

Max raises his eyebrows. "You want 'Deep?'" They all scream that they do. "Really?" They scream again. "Are you sure? I mean, we always do 'Deep'. Don't you want something different tonight?" They yell that they don't, and Max shrugs in defeat. "Well, okay then, but you know what that means, right?" They all scream again. God, I'm seriously on the verge of going completely deaf. "It means I need to bring a lovely lady up on stage to be serenaded." More screaming, louder now as they all throw up their hands and jump, trying to get noticed.

Ooooohkay. Now I'm going to find out who his date is. I grab my phone in preparation. If I can take a quick picture, I might be able to figure out her identity. I doubt someone high profile would allow themselves to be involved in such a public display, but you never know. Some of these society women have influential connections. She may be famous by association.

Max scans the crowd, pretending to consider all of his options. *Yeah, nice acting, buddy.*

I keep an eye on the rich chicks. Like every other woman, they're all holding up their hands and jumping in the air, desperate to be chosen.

Just when the crowd has reached the climax of their frenzy, Max looks me dead in the eyes and points. "You, pretty redhead. Come on up here."

My jaw hits the floor. "Ah ... I ... uh..."

"Now please, sweetheart. Don't make me wait." The crowd whoops and hollers their approval, and I feel hands pushing me forward as voices yell how lucky I am and how jealous they are.

God. This isn't how I saw this night going at all.

Max walks to the front of the stage and holds out his hand. "Don't be nervous." He gives me lusty smile. "I'll take good care of you."

Goddamn shit bastard crap. So, *I'm* his client? Oh, for the love of...

Did he pull all that stuff in the market just to reverse psychology me? Tell me I shouldn't come to make sure I would?

Man, I feel so freaking stupid. And now an entire club of people is cheering as I put my hand in Max's and walk up the stairs to the stage.

This is insane.

I hover on the verge of hysterical laughter as Max brings me behind the mic stand. Being the center of attention isn't something I've ever enjoyed.

"So, what's your name?" he asks and tilts the mic toward me. I flash him a glare but he doesn't react.

"Uh, hi ... I'm ... uh ... Eden." Everyone screams. Goddamn, *none* of these women are going to have voices tomorrow.

"Nice to meet you, Eden," Max says with this slow-lidded blink that makes me feel like he's imagining me naked, but not in a disgusting way. More of an *I'd like to see if you taste as good as you look* way.

To reinforce my suspicions, he licks his lips before saying, "So, do you play guitar, Eden?" When I swallow and shake my head, he gives me a mischievous smile. "You do now."

He pulls me in front of him and loops his guitar over my shoulder. "Let's get you set up here." I shiver as he sweeps my hair out from under the thick leather strap. He's close behind me, and the heat of the stage lights is nothing compared to the heat coming from him. I tense up when he puts a pick in my right hand and guides it over the strings.

"Just like this," he murmurs as he envelopes my hand in his and makes me strum in an even rhythm. "Very good. You're a natural." His head is nearly on my shoulder, and the ladies in the audience whistle in response. I shut my eyes and breathe evenly.

Okay, this is the part where I have to remind myself it's all pretend. I know Max told me to suspend my disbelief, but that was before I fully understood what the hell I was in for. I thought Kieran was one of the sexiest men I'd ever met, but this Caleb guy makes Kieran seem like a virgin choirboy. He even smells different. Kieran smelled like lemongrass. Caleb smells like pine. Fresh, sexy, phallic pine.

"That's perfect," Max whispers as I continue to strum after he takes his hand away. "If you keep stroking like that, I'll be a very happy man."

Sweet Horny Jesus.

He takes my left hand and places it on his left wrist. "Now, hold on tight, Eden. We're going to have some fun together."

He curls his fingers around the neck of the guitar and changes chords as I continue to strum, and then the drums and bass kick in with a slow, seductive riff. I've barely had time to register the thrill of making music before Max's front presses flush against my back, and he leans forward into the microphone.

"I can feel you on the inside. I lose my fingers in your hair. Your body's my religion. Your name's my favorite prayer."

God, the sensation of his chest and throat vibrating against me, not to mention the timbre of his voice. His freaking dark, sensual voice.

The ladies in the audience are no longer screaming. Now, they're all watching in rapt fascination, mesmerized by 'Caleb' and his insane sex appeal. The lyrics and music vibrate through me so powerfully, my whole body feels it.

Deep is how I want you.
Deep is where you live.
Wrap me in your legs now
Drown me in your kiss.
Keep me safe inside you.
Let me see your soul
I'm half a monster without you.
When I'm deep, you make me whole."

The song continues to build, and by the time it climaxes and ends, I've never felt the need for a cigarette more in my life. As the final chord dies away, there's silence for a full three seconds before the audience erupts. My hands shake from the adrenaline firing in my system. I've never felt anything like this before. Is this why musicians are so passionate? Because performing makes them feel like they've taken a whole crate of high-quality drugs?

Max is still close, mouth near my ear, when he says, "You were amazing, Eden. Thank you." Then he lifts his guitar off me and steps away, but I can still feel the echo of his body on my skin.

"Give Eden a hand. Wasn't she great?"

They all scream again, and I look around in a daze. As Max escorts me back down into the audience, I feel lightheaded and groggy, like I've woken up from an intense dream.

What the actual hell did I just experience?

I push through the crowd toward the bar as the M.C. says, "Give another hand for Caleb Sykes! If you want Caleb's album, he'll be signing them in the foyer in just a few minutes. We're going to take a short break while we reset for the main event tonight, Kingdom of Stooooone! So, refill your drinks, and we'll see you back here in thirty minutes."

The lights come up as pre-recorded music filters through the room, and people murmur and laugh as they wander off the dance floor.

I look up and down the length of the bar, but there's still no sign of Asha and Joanna. On unsteady legs, I signal to the barman to bring me a beer.

"What kind?"

"Anything. I don't care."

He places a bottle of craft beer in front of me, and I drink half of it without stopping. It does nothing to help bring me back to reality.

☙

Fifteen minutes later, I'm coming down from whatever screaming cloud of bizarre my rock star experience put me on, and am feeling mostly like myself again. A few ladies come up and gush about how jealous they are of me getting so close to Caleb, and I try to be polite, even though I'm starting to panic that I still can't find Joanna and Asha. I've texted Ash three times in the past five minutes and haven't received a response, which is worrying considering I know for damn sure she rarely has her phone out of her hand, even when she sleeps. Her not texting me back is a definite red flag.

Leaving the bar behind, I push through to the lobby and search every corner of it. Still no Asha.

"Shit."

I'm about to head outside when I see 'Caleb' standing among a throng of women, signing CDs and Rock Shop T-shirts. I have to hand it to Max. This setup is pretty extensive. He certainly goes the extra mile to make his scenarios believable.

He glances over at me. "Eden, hey. Thanks for waiting for me, sweetheart."

A very loud *WTF* is on the tip of my tongue as he hands a CD to a busty brunette. She gazes up at him the same way Asha gazes at Sprinkles cupcakes; which is to say with deep and abiding lust. All the ladies make a groaning noise as he extricates himself from them and heads over to me.

"Sorry, ladies, I'd love to stay and chat, but I promised my beautiful girlfriend we'd go to dinner after the show."

So, it would seem that the onstage cameo wasn't the full date. I guess that makes sense. Not to diminish the smoking-hot experience of having Max wrapped around me while he crooned about being deep, but as a client I'd be pissed if I paid five grand for four minutes.

"Oh, she's your girlfriend?" the brunette says, not even bothering to conceal her envy. "I thought you two looked too cozy on stage to be strangers."

"What can I say?" Max says as he puts his arm around my waist. "I just can't hide my feelings when she's near, no matter how hard I try." He bends and grazes his lips over my cheek. It sends a rush of tingles through me that are so powerful, I suppress a full-body shiver.

The brunette's friend lets out a snort. "Oh, I bet it's hard when she's around." They all gaze at his crotch then giggle again.

See? This is exactly what I'm trying to avoid becoming. I'm sure all these ladies are strong, accomplished, and clever in their own ways. And yet, right now, they're like a gaggle of school girls.

My face must show my inner thoughts, because Max whispers, "Just smile and nod. And don't show any fear. They can smell it." Then he turns back to his admirers. "Well, gotta go, ladies. Nice to see you all. Have a great night."

There's a general murmur of disappointment as he takes my hand and leads me past two burly security guards monitoring the door to the backstage area.

"Thanks for the cover," he says as we walk down a long corridor. "Getting away from them can be tough."

His hand is warm around mine.

"Where are you taking me?" I ask.

He stops, confusion coloring his expression. "Back to my dressing room to fuck, of course. I'm sorry, have you not read the groupie handbook? It's one of the first things they teach you."

I pull my hand back. "What?!"

He holds his serious expression for half a second before breaking into a smile. "Jesus, I'm kidding. I was going to take you into the green room for a drink. Don't worry. Fucking is strictly prohibited in there."

He goes to take my hand again, but I pull back. "I can't. I'm sorry. I have to find Asha."

"And Asha is ...?"

Oh, right. Even though Max knows Ash, Caleb doesn't. I have to get used to this new reality. "She's my little sister. I came with her and a friend, and they've disappeared."

"What does she look like? Maybe I can help find her."

"Five foot six. Red hair. Red lips. Gorgeous."

"You've just described yourself. Is she a twin?"

I roll my eyes. He's quick on the draw with those corny compliments. As I finish the thought, he hits me with a self-deprecating smile, and for some reason, 'corny' is instantly transformed into 'charming'. How weird.

"Wait," he says and snaps his fingers. "Was your sister with a blonde girl wearing an ugly eighties necklace?"

I nod. "You've seen them?"

He gestures for me to go with him. "I take it your sister is a fan of the Stoners?"

"Yes. She's crushing on the bass player."

"Yeah, I already guessed that part."

He leads me into a big room filled with couches and lined with tables of food and drink. He points to the far corner where Asha is sucking face with a guy I've never seen before.

"That her?"

"Holy crap. Yes."

My first response is total surprise that she's acting like a regular horny twenty-three-year-old for a change, followed closely by the urge to chew her out for not letting me know where the hell she was. However, before I can open my mouth to yell at her, Max puts his hand on my arm.

"I don't know your sister, but she seems to be enjoying herself. Maybe now's not the best time to pull the big-sister card."

"So that's the bass player?"

"Bingo." He points to the other corner, where I can see the back of Joanna's head as she sits next to another band member on a giant couch. "And that's the drummer." He goes to the impressive table of alcohol and grabs some beers. "They'll be going on for their set soon, so it won't be long before your sister and friend are out of their clutches, but until then ... why don't you come to my dressing room for a drink?"

I look over at the girls. "Are you sure there's no weird stuff in here?"

"Positive. The security guys have cameras all over this place, and I've seen them swoop on a guy for adjusting himself too often. The girls will be safe."

"And your dressing room? Is that safe?"

He shrugs one shoulder. "There are no cameras in there, but also no fucking. Just drinking. Maybe a little unrestrained adjusting if the mood hits me."

His eyes actually sparkle as he says this, and against my better judgment, I smile. I suppose 'Caleb' is a required part of my research, and I could think of worse ways of spending my time than having a beer with him. "Sure. Why not?"

Max nods and leads me out of the green room to a nearby dressing room. Then he pushes open the door and holds it so I can step past him.

"Nice," I say, taking in the surprisingly clean and stylish decor. "Forgive me for saying it, but this doesn't seem very rock and roll."

He uncaps the beers before handing one to me. "Really? Why not?"

I take a sip from the cold bottle and wander around the room. "Where's the harem of groupies? The mountains of cocaine? Hell, there's not even any broken furniture."

He puts down his beer and packs the guitar lying across the

couch into its case. "Well, the furniture in here is sturdier than it looks, so smashing it is more trouble than it's worth; I've been off cocaine for four years now, so that's out; and as for the whole groupie thing ..." He snaps the guitar case shut and stands. "It's never been high on my list of life goals. I find it hard to keep any artistic integrity if I devolve into a horny teenager the minute I get some female attention."

"So, wait ... you're telling me you're actually doing this for the *music*? What sort of maniac are you?"

He chuckles and packs the remainder of his belongings into a large duffle bag. "My band mates wonder the same thing. That's why we don't share a dressing room. I like my own space, and all of their cocaine, broken furniture, and groupies cramp my style."

I laugh and sit on the white leather couch while Max finishes packing up. It's amazing to me that he can be so different as Caleb. I don't have any experience with role-playing, but I didn't think it would be this believable. To be honest, I really like Caleb. He's rough around the edges, has a great sense of humor, and the scruff coloring his jaw is hot as hell. Also, he's more open than White-Bread Max, which isn't a bad thing.

When everything's packed away, Rocker Max joins me on the couch. Having him this close, I can get a better look at the ink on his arms. I have no idea how he suddenly has tatts everywhere, but it's damn convincing.

I trace a dragon that snakes from his wrist to his bicep. "This looks amazing. What is it?"

I look up to see Max staring at me, his expression intense. "I was born in the year of the dragon, so ..."

"No," I say, unable to look away from his eyes. "The ... uh ... ink. How did you get all of this onto your skin?" He had to have gotten them sometime between yesterday morning and tonight.

"A hulk named Brian strapped me into a chair and attacked me with a needle gun for hours on end." Oh, yeah. His guidelines said if I ask him things out of character, he won't take the bait. Very good.

"Did it hurt?" I raise knowing eyebrows, expecting another dig might provoke a flicker of irritation, but again, nothing.

He keeps looking me dead in the eye. "I don't mind suffering every now and then. Pain reminds us we're alive."

"Is life something you forget about?"

He looks down at his beer and fiddles with the edge of the label. "I think that when we're kids, we start out feeling everything. The whole world is amazing and magical. But as we grow up, we're trained to believe everything is ordinary, and magic only exists in fairytales. That's total bullshit, of course, but that's how it goes."

I lean back and study him. "You believe in magic?"

He nods. "Sure. Not Harry Potter magic, but magic nonetheless. I mean, look at this ..." He extends his finger then gently and slowly trails it from my elbow to my wrist. His touch is so light, it's barely there, and yet I can feel the thrum of his energy in every part of my body. All of my hair stands on end, and I notice there are goosebumps forming on his skin, too.

"I'm barely touching you, and yet, we're making electricity. It's firing in every inch of skin." He drags his fingers back down, watching it the whole way. "Edison and Tesla worked for years to harness something this powerful, and we just created it out of thin air." His voice gets softer, and he looks at me with a hint of awe. "If that's not magic, I don't know what is."

He pulls back, but he's still too close. If he was any other man right now, sitting that close and looking at me with seventeen shades of sex-eyes, I'd be crawling into his lap and tearing off his shirt. But he's not another man. He's the one guy I need to keep my distance from, for personal and professional reasons.

He keeps eye contact as he takes a sip of beer then glances down my body. "Sorry. I kind of hijacked the conversation there. We were talking about tattoos. How about you? Got any ink you'd like to show me?"

I lean back and say, "Can you see any?"

"No, but you strike me as the kind of woman who might have something hidden." His voice gets quiet. "You wouldn't feel the need to show it off. It would be just for you."

He's not wrong, and for a few seconds I sit there and consider what to do.

"You don't have to show me," he says. "I mean, we've just met, and I'm basically asking you to take off your clothes, but ... I'd love to see it."

He's looking at me so earnestly, it's disarming. I've never shown someone my tattoo before. People have seen it, of course; after all, I've been naked with my fair share of men. But none of them knew me.

Is that why I'm hesitating? Because on some level, I think this man, who's sitting there pretending to be another man, sees through the person I'm pretending to be?

Throwing caution to the wind, I put my beer on the table and kneel on the couch next to Max. Then I take a breath and pull up my shirt.

Max leans forward to study the two lines of cursive letters that stretch up the right side of my ribcage from my hip to the band of my bra.

He looks up at me. "May I?"

When I give him a tight nod, he grazes his fingers over the elegant lettering. Stupid move, letting him touch me. My physical reactions are insane. There's no way a man should affect me like this. Any man. But especially not a man about whom I'm trying to remain objective.

He trails over the letters again, and I close my eyes and clench my teeth.

" *'Screw you and all the ways you didn't love me.'* " When I open my eyes, I find him looking up at me. "Bad relationship?"

"You could say that." I can't stand the contact anymore, so I drop my shirt, sit down, and take a large swig of beer to try and calm my runaway heart.

"Did he hurt you?" There's an edge to his tone, and when I glance over, I'm surprised he's wearing a hard expression.

I blink as old memories roll and stir, threatening to wake. "It was a long time ago."

He tightens his hold on his beer bottle. "Do you still think about him?"

"I do my best not to." The less I think about him, the easier it is to ignore how angry I am all of the time.

When the thudding bass of live music starts up, Max drains his beer and sighs. "Sounds like the Stoners have finally made it to the stage."

Almost at the same time, my phone buzzes with a message.

<Edie, where are you?! The band is on. We're waiting at the door.>

I stand and push my phone into my back pocket. "Well, thanks for the beer."

Max stands, too. "Where are you going?"

"My sister's waiting."

When I grab the door handle, he covers my hand with his, and for the second time tonight my back tingles where his chest presses against it.

"Don't go," he says quietly. "Come with me instead."

I look down at where he's lazily stroking my fingers with his. "Where to?"

"My place."

"I thought you didn't do the groupie thing."

"I don't. You think all musicians just want women for free, easy sex?"

"Seems to be a perk of the job."

"Do you think that's what I want from you?"

"I don't know what you want from me."

He looks down at our hands. "Neither do I. That's why you should come with me. I'd really like to find out."

He reaches behind me and slides my phone out of my pocket. "Text your sister. She'll survive without you for one night."

I take the phone from him, and I'm surprised how tight my breathing is as he watches me type out a message.

<You and Joanna go have a good time. I've run into a friend. I'll see you at home.>

I press send.

No doubt Asha will interpret my words to mean I've hooked up and won't be home until morning. Let her believe that.

I'm more comfortable with her assuming I'm sleeping with a stranger than staying fully clothed with Max, and I have no idea why.

Max steps back and grabs his duffle and guitar case. "Come on, pretty Eden. Let's get out of here."

Ten

Interlude

Forty minutes in the back seat of a cab with Max feels like an eternity, and I'm relieved when we climb out into the cool night air in front of an impressive industrial building.

"The old Brooklyn Pencil Factory?" I say, looking up at the iconic facade.

"You know it?"

"Yeah. my grandmother lives a few blocks away, so I've seen it heaps of times. Just never been inside."

"Well, then, now's your chance." He holds the door open for me. "After you."

We climb up to the top floor, where Max slides open a huge metal door to reveal his apartment. Well, *an* apartment. God knows who it belongs to, but it's everything and nothing like what I'd expect from a musician. It's a large industrial space, but even with the concrete floors and exposed brick, the way it's been decorated makes it seem warm and elegant. There are several different areas defined by furniture, a large kitchen, and at the back is what seems to be an enclosed bedroom and bathroom.

"You live here by yourself?"

He nods as he dumps his bags and opens the fridge. "Used to belong to a friend of mine. When he moved out to L.A., he passed it along to me."

In the corner of the room is an impressive studio setup, complete with an array of instruments including a violin, saxophone, clarinet, trumpet, full drum kit, tuba, and a well-worn baby grand piano.

"Do you play all of those?" I ask, pointing at the musical collection.

He nods. "Not well, but yeah. That's what comes from having musical A.D.D as a kid. I could never figure out which instrument I liked the best, so I gave them all a try."

"Is there much call for a rock-n-roll tuba these days?"

He laughs. "Not as much as I'd like. Nothing better than getting down with some phat brass."

"Word."

He moves over to an impressive bar set up on one side of the room, and I follow. I'm not sure if I should have another drink. For the entire cab ride over here, I've felt ... off. Dizzy and feverish. It's not my usual reaction to alcohol, which tends to mellow me out. Maybe I'm getting sick.

Even now as I watch Max slide behind the bar, I find myself staring and not blinking. I'm wired but it feels too intense.

"What can I get you?" he asks.

I look over the bottles lined up on the scuffed wood. Screw it. I'll have one more drink. Maybe it will help with the tension in my muscles. I feel like I have so much pent-up energy, I could run a marathon. "Can you do a G and T?"

He raises an eyebrow. "I even have ice." As he goes about mixing our drinks, he glances over at me. "So, you didn't seem too heartbroken about missing the Stoners tonight."

"My sister was the fan. I was just tagging along. Live gigs

really aren't my thing."

He brings my drink around and stands closer than I expect. He leans on the bar, and I don't miss how extraordinary his arms are. Again, my attention is drawn to his tatts. I didn't think I had a thing for ink on men, but he may very well change my mind. Also, his chest is spectacular in that T-shirt. And although I've never had a strong opinion on belts, the one he's wearing, which is drawing my line of sight to his crotch like a magnet, is disturbingly hot.

See? This is another symptom of my current wrongness: noticing everything about him; wanting to touch everything. I'm craving to run my fingers over his skin; crumple the fabric of his T-Shirt in my fist; press my forehead against the cool metal of his belt buckle.

"Well," he says, either ignoring how hard I'm staring or not noticing. "I'm glad you tagged along. And I'm glad I picked you." He takes a step forward, and it makes the air between us way too thick. "And above all, I'm *very* glad you're here now."

I grip the edge of the bar to keep my hand from acting out. "I have the impression you wouldn't be starved for company even if I wasn't."

"Maybe not, but out of all of the lottery tickets in the world, there are very few jackpots."

"You think I'm a jackpot?"

"I think you're *all* the jackpots."

Warmth runs through me, and okay, I'll admit it. I get why he's so popular. I doubted him being able to take a contrived situation like a rock star romancing a fan and make it convincing, but his commitment is extraordinary. He has me believing every word he's saying, and I really don't want to. I can only imagine how he affects women who are into all of this romantic crap. I guess I can understand that it's nice to feel less insignificant for a while.

"What's it like to have all those women lusting after you?" I ask, studying his face. I'm talking about his clients, but it works in Caleb's context as well. "Does it ever get old? Having them project their fantasies onto you."

He keeps his eyes on me, but there's tension in his jaw. "We all need fantasies now and then. Sometimes believing our lives can be different is the only thing that keeps us going."

"And what fantasies keep you going?"

For a second he just stares at me, and for the first time since I met Max, I see his rock-solid composure slip.

"Discussing my fantasies right now isn't a good idea. I'm trying hard to be a gentleman tonight, and telling you everything I'm thinking would ruin that." He sips his beer. "How about you? Care to confess your current fantasies?"

He expects me to come up with a coherent answer when I can barely focus on anything that's not him? I search for something vaguely intelligent. "I fantasize about ... being a successful journalist."

"No, you don't."

"Excuse me?"

He moves closer. "You'd *like* to be a successful journalist, sure, but that's not what you fantasize about. Fantasies are what we desire, whether we like it or not." He puts down his drink and places his hand over my eyes. I tense as my whole body flushes. "Now, tell me what you see."

I take in a sharp breath as I'm bombarded by images.

Him, peeling off my shirt and kissing a line from my jaw to my chest. Him wrapping me in thick, painted arms, groaning in need as he tears off my underwear.

"Tell me," he whispers.

Him, sweeping the bottles off the bar, so he can lie me down

and mount me and have me screaming in pleasure as I come,
and come, and come –

I pull his hand away and walk to the other side of the room. This attraction is getting out of control. Apart from Justin Timberlake, I've never fantasized about a man in my life, sexually or otherwise. And these fantasies were so powerful, I can feel an echo of his hands on parts of me he's never touched. What the hell is wrong with me?

"You okay?"

I nod and press my cold glass against my cheek. "Just feeling a little dizzy from the alcohol. I'll be fine."

"Come sit on the couch 'til it passes."

"No, thanks. I'm good." The last time I sat on a couch with him, I lifted my shirt and showed him my bra. In my current state, I can only imagine what would happen.

He walks into the kitchen and opens the fridge before coming over and replacing the alcohol in my hand with a cold bottle of water. "You may be dehydrated. Sip this until your head clears."

Ugh. Again with the sweetness. Doesn't he understand that until he stops with that, my head is never going to clear?

I take a sip of water then put some distance between us by wandering over to look at the piano. I'm still shaky, but it's easier to cope when he's not near me.

"It's a beauty."

"Take a seat," he says. "She does more than just look good."

I put my water on the floor and wipe my hands on my jeans before grazing my fingers over the keys. "I've always loved the piano. I'm jealous you can play."

"Wow," he says, deadpan. "I've never met a woman before who has pianist envy."

When I groan, he smiles.

"Okay, fine," I say. "I do envy you. I wanted to learn piano when I was a kid, but there always seemed to be more important things to do."

Max comes over and sits beside me on the wide stool, and his thigh presses against mine. "More important than music? There's no such thing."

He plays a few jazz licks, and I realize why I'm having such a hard time with this date; well, apart from being so goddamned turned on, I can barely see straight. My issue is this: there's nothing in Max's manner or speech that seems even a little bit insincere. He sings and plays the guitar like a pro. Right now, he's playing the piano like he's done it his whole life. And I have zero doubt that if I asked him to break out some hot violin or rock-and-roll tuba, he could do that, too. Surely he hasn't learned all of this just for his business. It seems too natural. In fact, if someone told me that Caleb is his real personality and Max is the fake one, I'd believe them. His acting is impeccable.

Why the hell he's wasting his time being an escort in New York instead of getting on the first flight to L.A. and landing a movie deal, I'll never know.

He stops playing and looks at me. "Okay, your expression is hard to read. Do you just hate jazz or ...?"

"The jazz was great. I'm just thinking that with all your talents, you should be on a Hollywood billboard somewhere."

"Yeah, well, I'm not going to deny that getting a record deal is my dream. Maybe it will happen one day." Once again, I'm not sure if this is Caleb or Max talking. I make a mental note to ask him about his real-life musical aspirations in our post-date interview.

"Will you play something for me?"

He smiles. "I have a better idea. You play something."

"I doubt your ego could withstand my epic rendition of Chopsticks. It's twelve minutes long, and I perform part of it with my nose. You'd be shamed beyond belief and never play again."

He chuckles. "Maybe you should play something less impressive."

"Sorry. Impressive isn't a choice for me. I was born this way."

"That's becoming more evident each moment I spend with you." He stares for a few moments then clears his throat. "Still ... maybe I can help with your pianist aspirations. Stand up."

When I stand, he slides over to the center of the bench and pulls me to sit on his lap. When I hesitate, he whispers, "Trust me. I promise I won't violate you. Well, not unless you ask me to."

Gritting my teeth against the flood of lust I feel, I perch on his thighs, and he moves his arms forward and places his fingers on the keys. "Put your hands on top of mine."

I do as he asks and line my fingers up with his. The spark of his skin against mine makes my heart race and my breath quicken, and a gust of warm breath skates over my neck as he leans forward.

"You okay?" he asks.

"Yeah, fine. I'm just not used to this."

"What? The piano?"

"No, sitting on a man while fully clothed."

There's a beat before he chuckles. "Well, I'd invite you take off your clothes if it would make you more comfortable, but that would annihilate my concentration, so ..." He moves his fingers over the keys, and my fingers follow. "What do you want to play? Old-time rock and roll?" He plays some Jerry Lee Lewis. "Or some pop." I laugh when I recognize Britney Spears. "Or perhaps you're more of a classical girl. Mozart?" He launches into something complicated and pretty, and I'm amazed how proficient he is.

The Mozart morphs into some slow, contemporary chords. "So, what's your choice?"

"Did you write the music you performed tonight?"

"Yes. Some of the songs were collaborations, but they're mostly mine. Why?"

Note to self: Also, ask him about his songwriting abilities tomorrow. "How do you even do that? Create something out of nothing?"

"It always starts from something. An emotion. An image. Something you've seen painted on someone's skin." He plays a couple of more chords then softly sings:

"Screw you, and all the reasons you wouldn't love me.
Screw you, and all the ways you didn't care.
You're the one who killed my heart in stages ...
every time I found that you weren't there."

His lyrics send goosebumps up my spine. How can he just do that? Pull out phrases that are the exact shape of my pain?

He keeps playing as he whispers, "Now, it's your turn."

"I can't." I don't have his talent for lyrics or emotional awareness.

"Just try. It doesn't have to be perfect. It just has to be how you feel." He plays the chord progression again as I close my eyes and think. There are so many memories I usually suppress. It feels strange to let them come to the surface.

I can't even open my mouth. The only place I ever sing is in the shower, and even then, not loud enough for my neighbors to hear.

"I don't care what you sound like," Max says. "Just take the plunge. It will feel good, I promise."

I take a breath and try to follow his melody in my mediocre, quavering voice.

"You taught me love was like a weapon.
You made me see-through from the start.
Now all I have is faded pictures,
and this hard, bomb-shelter heart. "

Max sings the chorus again, and I join him, my voice stronger when melded with his. He finishes the song with a slow run up the notes, and when he's done, we both don't move. For three breaths we stay silent, and then he opens his fingers to allow mine to slide between them.

"I don't know about you, but I thought that left Chopsticks for dead."

I close my eyes as I try to shut the floodgates on my emotions. "How many women have you done this with?"

"One. You."

"Don't lie to me."

"I'm not. The thing onstage? Yes, I've done that with others. This? Never before. Only you."

His words and his convictions do something strange to me. I feel ... special. And then a lump forms in my throat, and I push down an urgent and disturbing need to cry.

I know he's just playing a part, but it still feels good to hear that. Way too good.

I stand, and he pushes back the stool as he follows. Before I can move away, he places his hands either side of me on the piano.

"Wait, what's wrong?" he asks.

"Nothing."

"Was it me? The song?"

"No, I loved the song." And that's true. It's like that song pierced some of the anger I've carried around for most of my life and softened it, but I don't think that's a good thing. "The song was amazing."

"Then, what?"

I shake my head and try to regain my equilibrium. "I'm sorry. This isn't like me."

"It's fine. Don't worry." He pulls me into his arms, and stupidly, I let him. "There's no judgment here."

I press my cheek into his chest as he tightens his arms around me. Why does this feel so good? Why do I feel so safe with him?

When he strokes my back, the sensation makes me moan. This is unnatural. I want to tear his shirt in half, so I can press my cheek to his bare chest. I want to bury my nose in his neck and overdose on his scent. I want to straddle him, and ravage him, and have him ravage me in return, and I want it all right the hell now.

I dig my fingers into his back as my common sense fights my animal instincts. None of what I want to do to him is appropriate, and yet part of me thinks it's the best idea I've ever had. I'm dizzy, and blurry, and...

Oh, my God.

Realization hits me like a lightning bolt from a clear blue sky.

I've only felt like this once before, and it was anything but natural. Asha once dragged me to the after-party for an off-Broadway play, and we unknowingly downed test tubes filled with shots of Molly, otherwise known as liquid ecstasy. I'd felt like this then. Too full of sensation but desperate for more. It turned me on so much, I hooked up with a geeky guy in glasses who was on the stage crew. I nearly destroyed him. That night I was insatiable, and that's exactly how I feel with Max. Like I could go ten rounds with him in the Sexcathalon and still be left wanting more.

I pull back and look up at him. "Jesus, did you ...?"

He pulls his body back, and I swear I see a flicker of fear in his eyes. "Did I what?"

Disorientation floods me as I stare up at him. How the ever-loving fuck does he become more attractive with each passing second?

"What was in that drink you gave me?"

"Gin, tonic, lime. Why?"

God, he plays innocent so well, but I know that what I'm feeling isn't right, and whatever he spiked my drink with is powerful. Too powerful to fight. Is this his secret weapon? He was supremely confident he could make me fall for him. Could it be a little chemical helper has his back?

Now that I think of it, this all started back in the club. He must have dropped something into the beer I had in his dressing room. Sly bastard.

"Hey, you okay?"

It has to be drugs. Nothing else makes sense. At least this way my hair-trigger emotions and arousal overload have a viable explanation.

"Oh, you're good," I say as I put my hands on his chest and push away. I'm still dizzy from his proximity as I look around for my purse. Then I realize I didn't bring a purse. "Just not quite good enough to fool me."

"Eden?" I head toward the door, but within three strides, he's in front of me. "Hey, wait up. Where are you going? "

"Home."

"Why?"

"You know why. Do you think I'm stupid? That I wouldn't figure it out?" I watch as his face morphs from confusion to realization, and finally lands on shame.

"It wasn't intentional." I step around him, but he catches my wrist. "Eden, let me explain –"

I look down at his hand then back up to his face. "I'm vetoing this date and you. Now, let me go."

With reluctance, he releases me then pulls the door open, and I give him one final glare before escaping.

Eleven

Manic Monday

"Goddamn asshole!"

I slap at the printer as I try to wrench my crumpled document from its stupid, electronic clutches. "Let ... the fuck ... go! Bastard!"

Large hands close around my shoulders. "The poor, innocent printer was beaten so viciously by its human master, it never recovered, and it never forgave. And thus, the war with the machines began."

I slump in frustration. "Tobes ..."

"It's fine, Eden. Just step away from the equipment, okay? You're in no state to handle this." He gently moves me back then bends down to get a better look at the paper jam. "So, is this regular Monday-morning rage? Or is there something else going on?"

"I don't know what you're talking about. I'm fine."

"Sure. That's why you look like you slept here and have yelled at nearly everything that's crossed your path, including your phone, the vending machine, and now the printer."

"I have not yelled!"

When he turns to me and raises his eyebrows, I let out a breath and say much more quietly, "Okay. Maybe I yelled a little."

"Do I need to go grab some therapy brownies? Or does this have something to do with your story?"

He gives a final tug, and the mangled remnants of my document pull free. He looks them over. "Wait, this isn't what you've been working on. It's the story on the street artist you were telling me about. The one who penises potholes."

I take it from him and ball it up before tossing it into the recycling bin. "Yeah. I thought I might be able to prove my worth to Derek with something other than the Mister Romance story."

"And you want to do that because ...?"

I shrug and reload fresh paper into the machine. "He's ... well, he's an impossible man to deal with."

"Uh huh. Impossible in what way?"

"All the ways." I don't tell him that I suspect he drugged me last night, or about my trip this morning to my friend who works in a lab, so he could test my blood. Saying it out loud would make it all too real, and don't want it to be. I think some part of me was rooting for Max to change my mind about him, but this morning I've all but given up hope. I've rolled the events of last night around in my memory time and again, wondering if it's possible my extreme reaction was all in my head, but I don't think it was. Feeling that much for someone I hardly know can't possibly be natural. I don't think Max is a rapist or even sexually assaulting anyone, because God knows, he's got more physical boundaries than a child care worker. But even if he's just slipping his ladies something to relax them and make them feel good, it's still wrong. And illegal.

All of a sudden, the loyalty his clients display is understandable. They're all drinking the Kool-Aid. Literally.

I shove the paper tray back into the machine as my phone

vibrates in my pocket. I pull it out to see the fourth text Max has sent me this morning.

<We need to talk. Meet me for lunch.>

"Nope," I say and shove the phone back into my pocket.

"Wow," Toby says. "Who's on your shit list?"

"No one. Don't worry about it."

"If you say so." He leans over my laptop and prints the document again. "But if I were that guy and valued my balls, I'd steer clear of you for a while."

He walks back to his cubicle as I slump into my chair and watch the printer spit out my pages. He wasn't wrong about me looking like I slept here. I hadn't felt like facing Ash last night, so I came here and worked off my excess energy by writing.

Fueled by my experience with Max, I pumped out six-hundred words on the Brooklyn parking fine con, and a thousand words on the pothole penises. I figured if I could use them to convince Derek of my value as a journalist and drop Max and his whole romance routine, I'd never have to see him again. Depending on the results of the blood test, I also have to decide whether to go to the police. All of his messages this morning tell me he knows he's busted, but I don't want to confront him until I have all the facts. Besides, I'm feeling too raw right now to even see him.

When the printer finishes, I staple my articles together and march into Derek's office.

He doesn't even look up as he mutters, "Get out."

"Derek, I have something I want to –"

"No."

"But I –"

Now he looks up, and his expression isn't happy. He points to the papers I'm holding "Is that your completed feature on Mister Romance?"

"No, but –"

"Then get the fuck out. I'm not interested."

I clench my jaw to stop the bitch goddess inside of me from picking up the pretty chrome chair and smacking him in the face with it. Instead, I slap the articles on his desk so forcefully, he jumps.

"I wrote these last night," I say. "Read them. They're good."

He scowls before picking them up and scanning through the pages. "If you finish them and don't think I deserve a chair on the features desk, then –"

He throws them back across his desk to me. "They're shit. Not only have they already been reported by at least three major news outlets, but they've been covered better and expressed more eloquently. What the fuck are you playing at, Tate? Where's the Mister Romance piece?"

"It's proving more challenging than I thought."

"So, what? You're giving up? How can you call yourself a journalist?"

"Derek, you don't understand."

He slaps his hand on the desk. "No, I fucking don't! You begged me for this story. You guaranteed me you could get it and that it would be an exclusive scandal-bomb that would blow the underwear off my advertisers. Then you tucked a thousand bucks into your bra for fucking 'expenses', and what? Completely failed to deliver? Not on my watch, Tate. Your bullshit doesn't play with me. Either you walk out of here to finish that story, or your keep walking to the unemployment line. Which will it be?"

God, I'm so tempted to just tell him to shove his job up his miserable ass and start afresh, but I don't have enough money to cope with being out of work, even for a week. So I swallow my pride, and my fears about Max, and accept my fate. Still, I promise myself that someday, somehow, I'm going to pay Derek back for being such an almighty asshole.

"I'll get the story," I mutter and take back my articles.

"I should fucking think so." Derek picks up his tablet and jabs at it. "This company is in enough goddamn trouble without you screwing up our most promising scoop in years. And don't you dare think you're not going to give me names. I mean you're not stupid enough to cut a deal promising him you'll protect his clients, right?"

Oh, shit.

"He's reluctant to name them, unless I can protect their identity."

"Then you do the same as I do when I deal with my ex-wife you – tell them whatever's necessary to get your way then do whatever you want."

He's divorced? What a shocker.

"And if I'm not comfortable doing that?"

"Then you don't have a story. Or a job."

"Derek, what happened to journalistic integrity? The right to protect our sources?"

He throws his tablet onto his desk and leans back in his chair. "For Christ's sake, Tate, we live in a society where ethical journalism is going the way of the dinosaurs. These days, any asshole with an internet connection and an opinion can become a 'journalist'. People don't give a shit about integrity. Every major news corp. in the country is struggling, because people only want to read stuff that either doesn't challenge their current belief system or makes them feel superior to others. Do you think we're going to gain any readers by tiptoeing around the precious celebrities involved in this scam? Fuck, no. And even if you play Mother Teresa and keep the whole thing anonymous, some asshole at a competing agency will dig up the truth anyway, and then *they'll* get the scoop. So, if you're going to do this, it's all or nothing. Am I making myself clear?"

I grit my teeth and nod. "Yes. Crystal clear."

"Good. Then tell me something that will make me think I didn't make a mistake in trusting you. Do you have anything new to tell me at all?"

I'm really not in the mood for this conversation, but what choice do I have?

"I went on a date with him last night," I say, gripping the back of the chair in front of me. "A fake date, of course. Rock star fantasy."

He sits forward. "And?"

"And ..." I swallow. "I suspect he may be drugging his clients."

Derek goes totally still. "Are you screwing with me right now?" When I shake my head, he says, "He rapes them?"

"I don't think so. It's more about relaxing them. Making them feel ... uh ... good." I clear my throat. "Aroused."

He chews the inside of his cheek. "Still a crime if he's doing it without permission. Do you have proof?"

"No. I'll get the results of my blood test this evening."

Derek stares at me, and I can feel his excitement growing.

"You'd better hope that test comes back positive, because this is what's known as a *bombshell*, Tate. It could blow this whole thing wide open. Lover boy is not only a petty conman, but also a criminal? Nothing would make me happier."

Sometimes, I really hate the vampiric nature of mass media. "Can I go?"

He nods. "Yeah, yeah. Sure. Let me know when you hear from the lab."

Deep breathing helps me remove myself from his office without shoving the paper I'm holding down his throat. When I get back to my desk I crumple up my articles, toss them into the trash, and slump into my chair where I rest my head in my hands.

Well played, Monday. Well goddamn played.

I grab my phone and text Asha.

<I hope you're not tired from bass-player shenanigans, because we're going out tonight. No excuses.>

After everything that's happened, I need to refresh and reboot, and that means finding myself a male-shaped palette cleanser to remove the taste of conman from my body and mind. By tomorrow morning, I want to have had enough sex with anyone who's not Max Riley, I can't walk straight.

CR

The music blares from the jukebox as I dance my ass off and work what God gave me. There are several candidates here tonight auditioning for the role of 'man I'll be riding later', but I'm leaning toward the Wall Street douche in the pin-striped suit who's already asked me about the color of my underwear. Sure, he's blonder than any man should be, and clearly plucks his eyebrows, but the main reason I like him is because if Max was on one side of the hotness see-saw, this guy would be his perfect opposite. Not too attractive. Not too bright. Not too sexy. In other words, perfectly mediocre. Exactly how I usually like my men.

Asha says most of the guys I sleep with are like *Fast and the Furious* movies – they're fun for a couple of hours, but hard to remember the next day.

My soon-to-be inside-trader is named Brick, and it's kind of perfect considering how thick he is.

"You dance so good," he says as he flails to the music like he has some sort of palsy. "You're like ... hot. So fucking hot.

Are you a real redhead? Does the carpet match the drapes?" He waggles his eyebrows at me, and I bite back a groan.

Ugh, shut up, dude. There's fun-dumb, and then there's just plain dumb-dumb. He's quickly veering into the latter.

"It's hard to hear you over the music," I say, pointing at my ear. "Probably best not to talk."

He nods enthusiastically and moves closer, dancing in that weird way so many men think is sexy where they lead with their crotch. It must be some throwback to ancient mating rituals or something, but I doubt females ever found it appealing. It's right up there with unsolicited dick picks as the top way to turn women off. Having known the delightful Brick for less than half an hour, I would bet money on him having a whole folder of dick pics on his phone, all photoshopped larger than life and ready for some poor, unsuspecting girl's eyeballs. I pray it won't be mine.

We dance for a bit longer, and just when I'd given up hope that Asha's going to join me tonight, she shows up on the edge of the dance floor looking like the cat that caught the canary. When I'd called her earlier, she was just about to go into a late meeting and didn't think she could make it. I'm so glad she was wrong.

She mimes the drinkies gesture and points to the bar, and I nod. I don't really feel like talking about the whole thing with Max, but just being with her always makes me feel better.

I lean into Brick and put a hand on his chest. "Let's take a break. I need to talk to my sister."

"Cool," he says. "Gotta spend some time hanging with my homies, anyway." Ugh. He calls his bro-dudes *homies*? He's getting less attractive by the second.

Before I can escape, he leans in so close I can smell the delicate aroma of Budweiser on his breath. "I'll be down the end of the bar when you need me, hot stuff."

I smile, but as soon as he turns away, I drop the pretense and head over to the bar.

God, why am I being so intolerant tonight? Brick isn't any more heinous than most of the men I've hooked up with, and yet my eye-rolling has gotten so severe, I can feel a headache coming on. I rub my temples as I make my way over to where Asha is waving to Joe and ordering our usual drinks.

"What's up?" I say, giving her a quick hug. "The meeting wrapped up quickly."

"Actually, I'm just on dinner break, but I needed to come here first and tell you my *amazing* news in person."

I gasp in mock surprise. "O.M.G.! You and bass boy from the Stoners are getting married, and you want me to be chief bridesmaid for your wedding? Oh, Ash! Yes, yes, a thousand times, *yes!*"

She rolls her eyes. "As if. He was hot, but it turns out he's as dumb as a post. After the concert, I started talking to him about his songwriting process, because, you know, his lyrics are half the reason my panties melted in the first place. Well, it turns out he pays some *other guy* to write the lyrics, and then *he* takes credit for it."

"What?" Joe delivers our drinks, and I take a sip. "Why would he admit that?"

"Because," she says, stirring her cocktail, "he was drunk, and dumb, and more than a little high. Apparently, I should have been rubbing myself all over some guy named Caleb Sykes."

I cough on my drink, and Ash pats me on the back. "You okay?"

"I'm fine." I take a breath. "Really? Caleb, huh? Wow." I grab some napkins and dab at the mess on my chin.

"Wasn't he playing at the Rock Shop last night? I heard his

name announced, but I was too busy lusting after an imposter to catch his set."

Seems like lusting after imposters is something we have in common at the moment.

"For all I know," Ash says, "he looks like one of the less attractive cousins out of *Deliverance*. I mean, you just know that anyone named *Caleb* is a total hillbilly, right?"

I cough again and nod. "Oh, yeah. Definitely. He's probably ... you know ... totally gross." My whole body lights up just thinking about how not-gross Max was as Caleb.

Dammit! For a while there, I was doing so well. I know I should level with her about Caleb's real identity, but I honestly just want to put last night behind me, and if I tell Ash about how Max made me feel and that it was possibly chemically induced, we're not getting off the topic any time this year.

"So," Ash says, swiveling around to face me. "How about you? Hook up with anyone I know?"

I shake my head. "Nope. Just some random musician. It was pretty forgettable." At least, that's what I'm telling myself.

"Anyway," Ash says, "my amazing news has nothing to do with boys and everything to do with my job. Guess which junior editor has been chosen to go with the head of publishing and the foreign rights director to the *European Book Fair* next week in *Paris*?"

My mouth drops open in shock. "No way!"

"*Yes, way!* I leave on Friday. We have a whole bunch of meetings lined up in London the week before the fair, so I'll be gone for just over two weeks!"

"Oh, my God, Ash! That's amazing!"

"I know, right?!"

I pull her into a hug, and after she almost squeezes me to death, I hold up my glass in a toast.

"To my baby sister. May she have a wonderful trip and find a hot Frenchman to romance the bejesus out of her."

"Oh, hell, yes!"

We clink glasses, and after Ash sips her drink, she puts her hand on my leg. "Will you be okay dealing with Nannabeth by yourself for a while?"

"Don't worry about it. As long as Nan stays out of my love life, we'll be fine."

Ash laughs. "Yeah, like that's going to happen."

For a few minutes, we chat about everything she wants to do in Paris, and I've almost put everything with Max out of my mind when she looks off into space and says, "So, what's going on with the whole Mister Romance thing? When are you going on those dates with Max?"

Again, I'm tempted to tell her about the whole rock star debacle, but I just don't have the energy right now. I've finally gotten my blood pressure down to healthy levels. No need to spike it again.

"I don't know, Ash. Derek's breathing down my neck about the whole thing, but I'm not sure I even want to go through with it, anymore."

"Well, I think Max wants you to go through with it."

"Why do you say that?"

She points over my shoulder. "Because he's heading straight toward you."

I swivel around, and sure enough I spot Max, looking very much like Caleb in jeans and a snug Clash t-shirt, striding over to me. I immediately tense up, and every step he takes winds me a little tighter. By the time he's standing in front of me, I'm lightheaded and full of conflicting emotions.

He shoves his hands in his pockets and looks at my sister. "Asha, nice to see you again."

"Uh, hi." Asha's expression tells me she's contemplating the fastest way to extricate herself from this awkward threesome. "How are you, Max?"

"I'm great, thanks." He gives my sister the briefest nod before turning to me. "May I speak with you, Miss Tate?"

I hate the way he can make a formal greeting feel intensely intimate.

"I don't think that's necessary, Mr. Riley."

"I do." He turns to my sister. "Asha, would you please excuse us for a minute?"

Taking the opportunity to bail, Asha swallows the rest of her drink and grabs her purse off the bar. "Sure. In fact, I have to get back to work. No rest for the wicked. I'll be late, Edie, so I'll see you in the morning." She smiles at Max as she books it toward the exit, and I silently curse her for looking so gleeful about leaving me alone with him.

I take a sip of my drink and try not to look at him. "What do you want, Max?"

"We need to talk about last night."

"Why? So you can try to excuse it? I trusted you."

"I know, and I'm sorry. That's not how I usually like to operate."

I let out a short laugh. "Oh, really? That was just for me? I'm honored."

"It wasn't intentional, I assure you. I jus–"

"Not intentional?" I put my glass down on the bar. "How on earth do you spike someone's drink by mistake? Are you saying it's not a normal part of your routine? Please. It's easy to make women fall for you with a designer love potion helping you along, right? Guaranteed success."

He stops dead and stares at me. "What are you talking about? You think I *spiked* your *drink*?"

Now that I'm on a roll, it's easy to let my anger drive me. "Of course you did. I just can't figure out when. It had to be at the Rock Shop with that first beer you gave me."

He's now looking at me like I'm speaking another language. "And what, *exactly*, do you think I put into that sealed bottle of beer which I opened in front of you?"

"I'm not sure. Some sort of GHB or Molly. Strong stuff, too. It had me rolling for hours. If I wasn't so goddamn angry, I'd ask you to give me the name of your dealer."

His stare intensifies. I try to maintain eye contact, but he's making that difficult. "Why on *earth* do you think I drugged you?"

I waver under his scrutiny. "Because I've had that stuff before, so I know what it feels like." I check points off on my fingers. "Overstimulation. Heightened senses. Dizziness. Sensitive skin. I had it all."

"So did I. Are you saying I spiked my own drink as well?"

That stops me in my tracks. "Uh ... you did?"

"Yes, I did." Now, he looks beyond furious about what I'm accusing him of.

"So you're saying you didn't –?"

"Commit a goddamn *felony*? Of course not!" His eyes flash with anger, and the serene, Zen-Max I'm used to is nowhere to be seen.

"But ..." I say, feeling the need to backpedal. "When I left last night, I mentioned it and you looked guilty. And you just apologized about how you –"

"I was talking about something else. Jesus *Christ* ..." He steps forward and lowers his voice. "Do you honestly think I'm the kind of man who would use a *date rape* drug on you, Miss Tate?"

"Well ... to be honest, I don't know you that well."

"Yes, you do." The certainty in his tone takes me by surprise. "You know me better than you'd like. And that's what this is about, isn't it? You're looking for a reason to *dislike* me. To continue believing I have immoral methods, because whenever you're with me, you're terrified of how I make you feel. I could see it every time I touched you last night, and I can see it now."

"No ... you're ..."

He steps closer, so we're almost touching. In an instant, every hair on my body stands on end, and he looks at the goosebumps on my arm before leaning down to whisper in my ear.

"*This* is what you were feeling last night, isn't it? The rush of hormones. The lightheadedness. The craving for my hands and mouth on every inch of skin. The way your blood rushes so hard and fast, you think you might pass out." I can see the pulse in his neck thrumming double time. "I hate to break it to you, Miss Tate, but the so-called *drug* you're so strung out on is *me*."

He leans back just enough to look into my eyes. "Go ahead. Tell me I'm wrong."

My head is spinning, and I blink too fast as I try to resist pushing him away so I can think. "You're ..."

When I don't continue, he says, "Finish your sentence. I'm ... what?"

Infuriating. Arousing. Not the type of male pushover I'm used to or comfortable with.

"You're wrong."

He keeps staring. "Am I?"

Now, I have no choice but to put my hand on his chest and push. I'm certain the frantic rush of blood I'm experiencing isn't healthy, and it's not going to calm down with him so close. He steps back but continues staring at me.

I try to match him. "Do you know that your constant eye contact is uncomfortable to endure?"

His expression softens, but he continues focusing on my eyes. "In my opinion, people don't look at each other enough. Eyes speak truths mouths refuse to, and liars always find a reason to glance away." He looks from one of my eyes to the other. "So, tell me – why does it distress you so much to be this attracted to me?"

Before I can come up with anything resembling an acceptable response, I become aware of another presence at my side.

"Is this guy bothering you, sweetheart?" I turn to see Brick there, puffed up like a lizard in a suit, glaring at Max. "Just say the word, and I'll save you."

I bristle at his noxious sexism, but I can't think too badly of him. He did save me from having to answer Max's minefield of a question.

When I turn back to Max, I see him give Brick an openly disdainful head-to-toe assessment, but he doesn't say anything.

"Uh ... Brick, hey. This is my ... uh ..." I take a breath. "This is Max. Max, Brick."

To my surprise, Max holds out his hand. He doesn't go so far as to smile, but he acts friendly enough. "Hi. Nice to meet you."

Brick isn't quite as evolved and grab's Max's hand way too hard to be considered anything but a dick move. "Yeah. Cool shirt, bro." He's heavy on the sarcasm, and I bristle on Max's behalf. That shirt is hella cool.

For several long moments, Max and Brick just stare each other down, and I have no doubt they're doing that stupid macho thing where they squeeze each other's hands and see who bails first. I'm not surprised to see it's Brick. One thing I know for sure is that Max didn't get biceps the size of grapefruits from stroking kittens.

Brick subtly massages his hand as he turns back to me with a questioning look. "So, babe, are we going to dance or what?"

I grind my teeth. One of my least favorite things in the world is to be called *babe* by a guy I hardly know. "Uh ... actually, Brick, Max and I were just talking, so–"

Max draws up to his full height, which is about six inches taller than Brick. "No, we're done, Miss Tate, so by all means don't let me keep you from dancing with ... Brick."

"Uh ... well, I..."

Brick holds out his hands. "Hey, Clash-boy says we're cool, so let's go."

I flash Max a dirty look as Brick leads me out to the dance floor. I don't feel like dancing anymore, but what am I going to do? Admit to Max I'd rather keep talking to him? Just the idea of that makes me break out in a cold sweat.

I shake off the heaviness in my limbs and try to dance. Elvis is blaring from the jukebox, and Brick must be a fan, because he knows all the moves.

As we continue dancing, I can see Max watching us from the bar. His expression is unreadable, which means I'm passionately compelled to figure out what he's thinking. God, why are even his facial expressions fascinating?

I'm hoping that when I get more information on his background, I'll find him way less attractive. I'm aware that part of his appeal right now is his air of mystery. If I can find a way to pull back the curtain, I have no doubt I'll discover that the Mighty and Powerful Oz is just an ordinary man after all.

In all honestly, that day can't come soon enough.

I'm one of those people who hates going to see illusionists, because I can't stand the feeling of ignorant wonder. Max may believe in magic, but I don't. I believe in clever people using smoke and mirrors to fool the masses, and Max may be clever, but he's still just a fraud wrapped in misdirection, and one day soon I'm going to prove it.

CR

By the time 'Viva Las Vegas' ends, I'm almost danced out. Brick is sweating profusely but still insists on hugging me, and in the process his hands get way more acquainted with my ass than I'd like. That's when I feel the hair stand up on the back of my neck. After we pull apart, I find Max right beside us.

"Miss Tate? A word."

Brick doesn't look happy about it, but I think his hand is still suffering from earlier, so he knows better than to push his luck.

"Go for it, babe," he says to me. "I need to refuel the old tequila tank, anyway. Be right back."

As Brick leaves the dance floor, Max steps toward me. The heat of his gaze is scorching, and when the next song is slow and sexy, he looks at me for a few seconds before saying, "I'd like to walk you home. I have something I need to say."

"Dancing isn't your thing?" I ask as the other couples on the dance floor get close and grind to the sensuous beat. Not that I'm angling for him to press that rock-hard bod of his against mine or anything. It's just that the music is there. It's kind of rude not to take advantage of it.

His posture is stiff, like he's a soldier standing at attention. "Not tonight."

I dislike how disappointed I am by his response.

"You know," I say. "If we were on one of your romance-novel dates, you would have laid out Brick for daring to touch my ass."

He shoves his hand in his pockets. "I considered it. Would you have liked that?"

"I don't know. I guess there's something sexy about an alpha willing to fight off the attentions of the other males."

"Uh huh. There's also something unhinged about a man who resorts to violence with minimal provocation. Besides, Brick is a lightweight. Me fighting him would be like swatting a fly with a bazooka."

My phone buzzes, and I check the screen.

It's from my friend at the lab. My blood test came back negative.

Shit.

It's official; there are no drugs in my system except my insane attraction to Max.

I drop my head and sigh. That knowledge should make me feel better, but it does the opposite. There's a chill in the air without my cozy, convenient denial to protect me.

When I look up, Max is staring, and it seems he caught a glimpse of the text, because he crosses his arms over his chest and looks at me expectantly.

"So," I say with a weak laugh. "Good news. You didn't drug me last night."

He continues to stare, unimpressed. "I already knew that. Do you have something you'd like to say to me?"

Apologizing isn't something with which I have a lot of experience, but I can't deny I was in the wrong. Sucking up my embarrassment, I shove my phone back into my pocket and mumble, "I'm sorry I accused you of something you didn't do."

He holds his hand up to his ear. "What was that? It's pretty loud in here. You'll have to speak up."

I take a breath and talk louder. "I said, I was wrong about you. I'm sorry."

There's still a look of disappointment on his face, but at least he's not glaring anymore. "You're forgiven. For now." He nods toward the exit. "I still have my own apology to make, but not here. Let's go somewhere quieter."

I cross my arms. My purpose in coming here tonight was to try and get him out of my system, and judging by the way I'm still fighting tooth and nail to keep my hands off him, my objective has yet to be achieved.

"I'm not ready to go home. And I'm definitely not ready to go home alone."

"You wouldn't be. I'd be with you."

"Yes, but unless you intend on giving me orgasms, you're not the kind of company I was thinking of." I raise my eyebrows. "Were you planning on giving me orgasms, Max?"

Please let him say no. If he doesn't, I'm well and truly screwed, and not in a good way.

He tenses his jaw. "They aren't one of my regular services, no." He looks over his shoulder at where Brick and his buddies are doing shots like it's a competitive sport. "Are you honestly going to let that swamp dweller touch you? If his brain were dynamite, it wouldn't blow a part in his hair."

The mental image makes me smile. "I'm not looking for a life-partner, Max. Just sex." *With a man who doesn't dominate my thoughts and hijack all my fantasies.*

He jabs his finger in Brick's direction. "I would bet you a million dollars *that* man has never made a woman come in his life. But if you're determined to confirm he's a lousy lay firsthand, be my guest. I'll be at the bar when you're done with him."

He goes back to perch on a stool as Brick rejoins me, smelling like he's been on a week-long bender in Tijuana.

"Ready to show everyone else how it's done, sweetheart?"

I fake a smile as I admit to myself that if Max weren't here, I would have left this loser in my wake an hour ago. But something small and vicious in me gets satisfaction in making Max believe I'd still consider taking Brick home.

Despite my souring mood, Brick keeps me occupied for a few more songs, and when Hound Dog comes on, he forces me into the world's most awkward jive. He dances like a drunk guy trying to appear sober, and his terrible technique makes me laugh when he spins me out before pulling me back. It's a wonder I stay upright, considering how tipsy I am.

"Jump," he says to me, as he grips my waist.

"Oh, no, don't think that's —"

"Come on, babe! The song's almost over. Jump!"

He hoists me off the floor, and I don't have much choice but to place my legs on either side of his hips as he dips me down then pushes me up into the air. I feel something go in my back and make a noise.

"Shit." I grip his shoulders as I start my descent. "Brick, don't —"

"I got you, babe. Chill!" The words are barely out of his mouth when he overbalances, and before I know it, the dance floor is rushing up to meet me.

"Miss Tate!"

I'm vaguely aware of Max's concerned voice as I land heavily on my back, and a sharp pain makes me say several words that would make my Nan blush.

"Oh, shit, babe. You okay?" I wince and roll onto my side as Brick hovers over me, the stench of tequila on him making it hard for me to breathe.

"Move, asshole!" Brick is hauled backwards as Max appears. Strong hands that just shoved Brick halfway across the room are gentle as they touch my shoulder. "Where does it hurt?"

"My back. Not from the fall. I think I pulled a muscle when he dipped me."

"Can you move everything?"

"Yes."

"I should call an ambulance."

"No, really, I'm fine." I let out a breath and glance up at him. *Whoa.*

Never in my life have I seen a man look at me like that. As if the pain I'm feeling is being felt twice over by him.

"Miss Tate, you shouldn't move."

I wave him off and sit up. "I'm not paralyzed, Max. I just have an owie. I need some aspirin and an ice pack."

He helps me to my feet before wrapping his arm around my waist to support me as we move off the dance floor.

"I'll take you home."

"Whoa, whoa, whoa." Brick steps in front of us. "That's my job, pal. I haven't been hanging around this smoking-hot ginger all night just to lose her at the last minute. If anyone's taking her home, it's going to be me.

Max's body tightens like razor wire, and even though he doesn't raise his voice, the intensity he radiates through his glare makes Brick take a step back. "She's not a toy you get to buy with your time, *pal.* Have some fucking respect. You injured her, and if you don't get the fuck out of my way this second, I'm going to injure you. Understand?"

I don't know if I've heard Max use the "F" word before, but even with my back pain, my body reacts positively.

By now, Brick has had enough booze to forget how Max crushed his hand earlier, and when he belligerently grabs my arm, Max gives him a look that's truly terrifying before grabbing his wrist and squeezing. Brick sinks to the floor with a strangled cry.

"Brick, I know you're not an intelligent man, so I'm going to use small words. If I ever see you lay your hands on Miss Tate, or any woman, ever again without permission, I'm going to shatter your arm in three places."

Having been on the receiving end of Max's brutal sincerity, I know Brick believes every word. That would explain why he looks like he's about to pee himself as Max towers over him. When Max releases him, he skulks back to his frat-boy brat-pack, red faced and not willing to even look back at me.

Max doesn't spare him another glance. He just scoops me into his arms and heads toward the exit.

"What was thing you said earlier about resorting to violence at the slightest provocation?" I say, struggling to deal with both the pain in my back and the vicious arousal that comes from being in his arms.

His face still looks like thunder. "That wasn't violence. It was restraint. And there was definite provocation. Brick was an asshole who needed to be taught that women aren't vending machines that trade attention for sex. I hope the little shit bruises easily."

I notice how everyone stares and smiles as he carries me down the street toward my apartment. "I feel like you should be wearing a white Navy uniform right now."

"I have one of those. If you play your cards right, I'll bust it out someday." He shoots me a look, but I see the corner of his mouth twitch as he begins to hum, *Up Where We Belong.*

Twelve

Shirtless Houseboy

Twenty minutes and two muscle relaxants later, and I'm feeling nooooo pain. Max has set me up on my couch with an ice pack nestled on my lower back, and now he's in my kitchen making tea. I told him I don't drink tea, but he didn't listen. He's opening and closing cupboards as he searches for stuff, and I'm pretending that he's my sexy houseboy. I've always wanted one of those. It would be so useful to have one around in case I needed to ... well ... you know, get stuff off high shelves. Or ... I don't know ... open jars. His only real job would be to walk around without a shirt and occasionally flex. Oh, and provide orgasms on request.

"Max?"

"Yeah?"

"Do you ever just take off your shirt and flex in front of a mirror? You know, to perv on your own hotness?"

"No. Do you ever take off your shirt and caress your breasts, just for the hell of it?"

I shrug. "Sometimes. When I get stressed, I cup my boobs and give them a reassuring squeeze."

"Good information. Next time you're stressing I'll have to

try that."

I flop back into the cushions. My boobs are now tingling. Great.

More doors open and close, and I hear him mutter. "Jesus."

"Everything okay?"

"There's zero logic to your cupboard contents. I've now found tea in three separate places."

"Yeah, if only I had a decent *shirtless houseboy* to take care of me and rearrange everything."

He walks over and stands above me, all tall and broad-shouldered, with those long legs and a butt I'd like to sink my teeth into. "Are you suggesting I should take off my shirt?"

I blink up at him. "I don't know. Maybe. It's pretty warm in here. You can if you want. Okay, fine, stop hassling me. I won't stop you."

He stares me down as he grabs the bottom of his T-shirt. "You want this?"

He pulls up his shirt to reveal a crazy-impressive six-pack, but as I try to sit up to get a better look, my wince of pain makes him drop to his knees in concern.

"Relax," he says, pushing me back down and readjusting my ice pack. "If you behave yourself and stay still, I'll take off my shirt later."

"Really?"

"No. But stay still anyway. How are you feeling?"

"Awesome. The drugs have kicked in, and I'm fiiiiine." I touch his face, because ... well, why not? It's there, and it's pretty, and wow ... his mouth is *so* pretty. And so annoying. It's annoying how symmetrical he is. And how piercing his eyes are. And don't even get me started on the eyebrows, eyelashes, and cheek bones, not to mention the mouth. "You're handsome."

His lips quirk. "And you're stoned. Is your back still

spasming?"

"Nope, it's loosey-goosey, salmon-moosey." I giggle as I graze my hand down his neck and onto his chest, because he's so fracking attractive, it's hilarious.

Max doesn't giggle, however. He presses his lips together as I investigate the muscles of his chest. He shouldn't look perturbed. After all, I'm an *investigative* journalist. This is a natural extension of my craft.

He must not appreciate my technique, because everywhere I touch, tenses.

"What are you doing?" His voice is doing that dark, sexy thing.

"Research."

"Miss Tate —"

"Stop calling me that. My name's Eden."

"I call you Miss Tate because it helps me try to keep things more formal between us."

"Uh huh." His eyelids flutter as I graze his nipple through his T-shirt. "How's that working out for you?"

He puts his hand over mine to stop my exploration. "Well, it's freaking pointless when you touch me like that. Do you realize you're a handsy drunk?"

"Yes. Is that a problem?"

He stands and mutters, "Only when I'm trying to ignore how goddamn attracted I am to you." He stalks back into the kitchen, and I flop back into the couch and stare at the ceiling.

Honestly, having him in my apartment is weird. He's not a friend. He's not a lover. He's a walking, breathing erogenous zone who fascinates me and infuriates me in equal measure. He's like a wild beast that can rip out my internal organs with no effort at all, and now that he's invading my inner sanctum, I'm horrified to find I enjoy having him here. It's bizarre and unsettling.

"May I ask you something?" I ask while blinking to try and focus my fuzzy vision.

"If you must."

"If Brick hadn't taken his hand off me tonight, would you really have broken his arm?"

Something clatters in the sink. "You don't have to hit someone to do it damage."

"Sounds like you speak from experience."

He doesn't answer me. I wish I had a notebook nearby, because while I can usually catalogue this stuff in my head, my brain is too fuzzy, and I want to come back to this subject when I'm sober.

"Have you ever gotten into a fight over a woman?" I ask.

"Several times."

"And? Did you always win?"

Again, silence. Then he says, "No. But that doesn't mean I wouldn't do it again ... and do it better." When the electric kettle beeps, I hear all manner of pouring and stirring.

A couple of minutes later, he places a steaming cup on the coffee table in front of me and pulls the table closer, so I can reach it. Holding his own cup, he sits in the armchair next to me.

I sip the tea, surprised that I like it. "Thanks."

"You're welcome. And for the record, I didn't spike it. Just in case you were wondering."

He watches me as I drink, and I don't know if I'll ever get used to how he looks at me. It's like he's trying to show me his true self through clairvoyance, while hiding everything else about him.

"I'm sorry I got angry with you earlier," he says quietly. "When I came to the bar tonight, I wasn't expecting to be accused of criminal activity. It took me by surprise."

"Why did you come?"

He holds his cup with both hands and looks down into it, as if he's searching for answers. "I wanted to apologize. I thought you ran out on me because of what happened when I hugged you."

"Which was?"

He looks up at me, surprised. "You don't know?"

I shake my head. "I was too busy being paranoid about being dosed and high. Did you steal my Starbucks loyalty card from my purse when I wasn't looking or something? Because that would piss me off. I'm one star off getting a freebie."

He puts his cup on the table and rests his elbows on his knees. "Miss Tate, I usually manage to keep a certain veneer of professionalism between myself and my clients, but last night with you, I ... failed."

"Failed, how?"

He takes in a breath and exhales. "Do you really need me to say it?"

"Max, I'm highly medicated right now, and my brain isn't firing on all cylinders, so, yeah. Please say it, so I can stop feeling dumb."

Embarrassment flits across his features. "When you were upset after the song and I hugged you, I was ... aroused. I didn't mean to be, but having you on my lap, and then hugging you, I ..." He looks at the floor and shakes his head. "I thought you felt it when I pressed against you. Or heard it when I moaned. That's why I was ashamed of myself when you ran out."

To be honest, I barely hear anything after 'aroused'. That word uttered in his white-hot voice has set fire to my face and body. For the first time in a long time, I'm at a loss for words.

I do my best space cadet impersonation as I struggle to find something witty to say.

He looks over at me. "Miss Tate? Did you hear me?"

"Yes, I just ... uh .... apology accepted, I guess. Don't beat yourself up." When I realize my pun, I squeeze my eyes shut in embarrassment. "Sorry. Total accident. Plus, I have no idea if you beat yourself after I left. If you did, great. Go, you."

A heavy silence falls between us, but my brain is still fixated on what he just told me.

"So," I say, trying to connect the dots, "*you* were attracted to me? Or was is *Caleb?*"

He pauses for so long, I wonder if he's going to answer. Then he says, "Both, and that's something that I haven't experienced before." I stare at him, and he shifts in his seat. "Why do you seem so surprised?"

"I just didn't think I'd be your type."

He makes a scoffing noise in his throat. "You're everyone's type."

My hackles rise. "Are you judging me for having a healthy sex life? Because it might not have filtered into your eighteenth-century gentleman's brain, but these days women are free to sleep with whomever they choose, as often as they like, and in whatever position floats their boat. And I don't think it's fair for you to –"

"Miss Tate ..." He gives me a patient look. "I wasn't making a moral judgement. I was trying to say that you're an amazing woman, and you'd be hard-pressed to find a man who wasn't attracted to you."

Goddammit. That's even worse. "You don't have to say that. We're not on a date right now."

"I'm aware of that."

I drop my gaze and look at his chest. "Men say those things all the time without meaning them."

"I'm saying them because they're true."

He stares, unflinching in his conviction. I stare back, more affected by him and his smooth words than I should be. Despite the commotion that starts in my body every time we're together, I don't crave this feeling, and I don't crave *him*. He may be different from any man I've met, but that doesn't make him a good man. There must be something wrong with someone who gets his jollies by turning women into piles of aroused goo.

"Why aren't you out tonight with some client?"

"I'm not seeing clients right now."

"Because?"

He sips his tea. "I'm seeing you."

"You can't do both?"

"I'd rather not." He looks down at his hands. "Out of all the ladies I know, I find you the most ... interesting."

"I'm not interesting at all. I'm a simple creature with simple needs."

"I disagree. You're one of the most complicated women I've ever met." He leans forward and brushes my hair away from my face, and I blame the drugs for making me feel so entirely mesmerized by him.

"Miss Tate, may I ask you a personal question?"

"Hmmm?"

"Have you ever had sex with someone you loved?"

For a second, I think he's making another criticism about my sex life, but when I check his expression, I see only open sincerity.

"No," I say, unsure whether I should be admitting that. "Have you?"

"Off the record?"

"Yeah."

He shakes his head. "The one thing I've learned while doing this work is that as much as I enjoy playing out romantic fantasies, it's still just pretend, and more and more I'm craving something real."

For a few seconds he studies my face, seemingly lost in his own thoughts. Then he comes and sits next to me on the couch and coaxes me up until my back is facing him. "Lift your shirt. I want to assess the damage." I help him ease up my shirt, so he can see my lower back. "Still painful?"

"A little."

He places his hand over the area and presses gently. The heat of his skin is a nice change after the ice. He lowers the shirt then runs his fingers slowly up and down my spine over the top of the fabric. It makes me shiver with goosebumps and at the same time drains the tension from my muscles. When I drop my head forward to give him better access, he gently scrapes his nails from my tailbone up into the hair at the base of my neck. The sensation is so incredible, I moan.

"Feel good?"

"God ... yessss." He keeps going, and I can't remember a time when a man has touched me in such a selfless way. Why is he doing this? Hanging around. Making sure I'm okay. I mean, he gets bonus points for just escorting me home. Why the rest of this charade?

"Max, do you usually pamper clients in your spare time?"

He pauses his movements. "No. In fact, I make a point of not interacting with them outside of a business setting. Otherwise, the situation can get complicated."

"I figured. So why are you here? Taking care of me?"

"Because you needed someone to make sure you were okay."

"Not really. I would have coped by myself."

"Is that your goal in life? To just cope? Alone?"

"No, I just ... if you're trying to suck up so I'll give you a good write up, or whatever, well ..." He starts with his fingernails again, and I let out a low moan. "Oh, maaaaan. Good job."

He chuckles, and I close my eyes and sigh. I'm going to have to amend my opinion on magic to exclude Max's hands. drop my head forward and hover in a bizarre zone of part relaxation, part arousal.

"Max, have your clients ever complained about your whole sex ban on dates? I mean, you're an attractive guy. How can they be satisfied with only kissing you?"

He takes his hands away, and when I turn to look at him, I can see amusement on his face.

"Tell me," he says. "What's the point of sex?"

"Do you think that because I'm a woman I'll say 'intimacy', or 'the physical expression of love'?"

"No. Give me your honest answer. Why do you have sex?"

I tilt my chin up. "Orgasms."

"But you can have them by yourself."

Okay. Good point. "It feels better when someone else does it."

"Why?"

"I ... don't know."

He maneuvers me so my back is against the arm of the couch before shoving some pillows behind me for support.

"Okay, then I'll tell you. Sex is a *ritual*. It's more than just physical reactions." He pulls my legs up into his lap then takes my hand and lays it, palm up, in his. As he talks, he draws a spiral on the sensitive skin over and over again. "If you think of sex as a generator, fueled by the relentless build-up of tension, then the release happens when the tension snaps, providing waves of pleasure. Yes?"

Jesus, that single finger moving over my palm is drawing me tighter each second. With the amount of sex I've had over the years, how the hell is this the most erotic experience that's ever happened to me?

"Miss Tate?"

"What? I mean, uh ... yes."

"We don't need to be naked to simulate a similar concept."

He places my hand back in my lap and focuses on my mouth. "When you kiss someone for the first time, adrenaline courses through your veins." He inches forward, just enough for me to become fixated on his mouth. "See how our muscles tighten? And the closer we get, the stronger the sensations become." His eyelids become heavy as he gazes at me. "This intense sexual tension is pleasurable in itself, right? It makes your heart race. Your lungs seize."

At this point I realize how shallow my breaths are. How ragged and fast. The tension he's speaking of is turning in on itself and creating a ball that's filling my chest.

When he cups my cheek, the brush of his skin against mine makes the ball expand.

"And as my lips move closer and closer," he says, his voice soft, "... the tension is almost unbearable. Want turns into *need*, which turns into *compulsion*."

He's so close now, we're breathing the same air, and I can almost feel the crackle of electricity surrounding us.

"And when our lips finally touch," he whispers, closer still. "all the breath will rush from our lungs, because it's like a tightrope has snapped beneath our feet, and all we can do is close our eyes and revel in how it feels to fall."

He stays there, keeping me at the pinnacle of sensation, dizzy and breathless and trembling with more need than I knew my body could feel.

His deep, rough voice adds another layer to my reaction.

"Do you want me to kiss you, Miss Tate?"

God, yes.

And God, no.

There's no easy answer to this question. Kissing him would be wonderful and terrible. It would be like claiming a lion as a pet and counting down the days until it mauled me.

"It's not a hard question," he says. "Either you want it to or you don't."

"Is this your way of seducing me into dropping my story?"

His nose brushes mine, and I shiver as I grip the front of his shirt.

"That's one explanation. A cynical one, of course, but I've come to expect that from you. Maybe I want to kiss you. Find out how your lips taste."

"Then why don't you just do it?"

"Because I promised I wouldn't without your permission, and honestly, you're too out of it right now to give informed consent."

I lean my head against his, so desperate, the ache inside me borders on painful. "Then why are you still torturing me?"

He angles my head the other way, keeping his mouth tantalizingly out of reach.

"Because I wanted you to understand that what you're feeling right now ... this *euphoria* ... *this* is where the essence of romance lives. Have you ever felt this way with any of your sexual partners?"

"Hell, no." I've never felt this with anyone. It's like every single nerve ending is being magnetically drawn to him, so desperate for contact it's painful to deny.

He makes a needful sound in his throat. "Then maybe you should move onto a better class of man. One who doesn't treat you like a vending machine. One you're genuinely attracted to instead of one who's just convenient."

I'm so blurred by hormones and pain killers, it takes me a

moment to notice he's moved off the couch and is now staring down at me. I feel foolish when I realize I'm still pursing my lips, expecting contact.

I clear my throat and compose myself. My heart is hammering so hard, I'm sure he can hear it.

I look up at him. From the expression on his face, I don't think I'm the only one feeling tortured right now. Then my focus lowers down to his crotch, and dear *God* ... the long hardness I can spy straining the denim of his jeans is not helping anything right now.

He follows my gaze. "In case you're wondering, it's exactly as painful as it looks."

"You sure I can't help you out?"

"I'm positive you could, but that would violate even more rules from my personal code of conduct, and considering I've already set a record for unprofessional behavior tonight, I'm going to leave." He looks around the apartment. "Is there anything else you need before I go?"

I want to say his hand down my pants, but I don't think that's the type of thing he means.

"Maybe you could take off your shirt and do some cleaning."

He comes over and scoops me off the couch. "Or how about I put you into bed and stay with you until you fall asleep?"

He places me on the bed, and I wince as I turn on my side to get comfortable.

"I liked my idea better," I say with a pout, as he pulls the covers over me. "Honestly, Max, you're the worst shirtless-houseboy I've ever owned." I yawn. "We're going to have words at your next employee review."

He chuckles as I close my eyes and start to fade. "Sorry to disappoint you, Miss Tate. I hope to please you more next time we meet."

Unconsciousness begins to wrap me in soft grayness as I mumble, "You do that. More pleasing, less shirts. Your mistress demands it."

I sink fast, but I'm still conscious enough to feel warm fingers brush my hair away from my face. "Goodnight, Eden. Sweet dreams."

As soon as I hear the door to the apartment open and then close with a quiet click, I'm out.

CR

"Sooooo," Asha says the next morning as she spoons some scrambled eggs onto my plate. "I ran into a certain hot-bodied escort as I was coming home last night. Care to spill about what happened with him?"

"There's nothing to spill. I hurt my back at the bar. He brought me home. End of story."

"Oh, what crap, Eden. I saw his face when he arrived at the bar last night, and I saw it when he left our apartment. That man has it bad, so don't tell me he didn't get happy in his pants over you, because that's a damn lie."

I finish off my breakfast as quickly as possible. "Ash, come on. It's too early for this." *Plus, I can't tell you about Max, because that would make what I'm feeling for him way too real, and I'd rather just ignore it.*

"Look, sis, I don't want to make a big deal about this, but just between us ... how big a deal are we talking about?" She holds her hands five inches apart. "I'm just going to keep widening this gap, and you tell me when I've reached his Max-imum length, okay?"

I laugh as she keeps widening the gap. When she reaches

what looks to be about nine inches, I raise my eyebrows, and she slaps the counter with both hands. "No way! Seriously?"

I walk around to wash up my plate. "Ash, I'm writing a story on him, and he's sucking up to make sure I don't crucify him. That's it. We aren't a thing. Please stop trying to make us one."

"It *is* a thing if that man is carrying around a gargantuan boner for you. Don't tell me you aren't desperate to ride that fine piece of maleness."

I kiss her on the cheek. "I have to go. I'll see you tonight."

"Eden! Have mercy! I've been waiting years for you to meet someone like him, and now you're freezing me out? No fair!"

I can still hear her calling out to me when I close the door and head down the stairs. I'm halfway to the subway station when my phone buzzes with a message.

<How's the back?>

I feel myself smiling and immediately force myself to stop. I also put a kibosh on the urge to text him right back. And that giant swarm of butterflies that just took flight in my stomach can bite me, too. Feeling this way over a guy is not on my to-do list today; or ever, for that matter.

Maybe he didn't drug me, but he certainly isn't playing fair. He knows how attractive I find him and is systematically wearing me down so he can claim victory on our bet. Well, he'll soon come to learn that conning a woman who slaps down dozens of romantic fantasies before breakfast is going to be harder than he thinks.

I hit my favorite caffeine supplier near the subway station and get myself a big, fat triple-shotter. I need coffee like air this morning. Even with the muscle relaxants and alcohol, I didn't sleep well. I kept having dreams that Max was in bed with me, all hard and warm and smelling like a spring orchard, touching me like I was precious and making me feel like I could do anything as long as he was by my side. It was the closest thing to a nightmare I've had in years.

The only good to come out of it is that it kept me tossing and turning enough to make sure my back didn't seize up, and even though I get twinges of pain if I bend the wrong way, on the whole I'm feeling much better this morning.

By the time I get to work the coffee has hit my system hard, and I practically bound through the doors to see Toby.

"Good morning, friend!" I hug his back as he continues typing on his keyboard.

"Good morning, friend-who-never-hugs-me-unless-she-wants-something. What can I do for you this fine day?"

I give him my best shocked face. "Toby! I resent the implication that our friendship is based entirely on favors."

He spins around and leans back in his chair as he crosses his arms over his chest. "Oh. Okay. Then you don't want something?"

I scoff. "No, I don't. Only the pleasure of your sunny disposition and the sight of your handsome face." I flash my most dazzling smile.

He raises his eyebrows and waits.

I look around at the hive of activity around me and say "Soooo ... I'll just be ... you know, going to my cubicle now." I roll back onto my heels. "Yep. Nothing more I want to talk to you about."

I take a step away from him, and he cocks his head expectantly, maintaining his stony silence.

"Soooo, yeah." I take another step. "Talk to you later, Tobes." He watches as I reach the edge of his cubicle and play with an errant thumbtack. "Byeeee."

I let out a sigh as I head into my office space and collapse into my chair. Within seconds, his head appears above our shared wall. "You're not fooling anyone, you know. What do you want?"

I lean forward onto my desk. "You're the best, Tobes. I don't know who else I can ask about this stuff."

He rolls his eyes and gives me the 'get on with it' gesture.

"So," I say, "I need to find out more about Max, AKA Mister Romance, but the dude isn't exactly forthcoming. I have to get inside that warehouse we found in Greenpoint, but it's locked up tighter than my sister's thighs." I pull out my phone and bring up the picture of the digital keypad I snapped when I was there. "This is guarding the one accessible door, and it's right below a camera that feeds to Max's phone the second anyone activates it. Is there a way to disable it? Or work out the passcode?"

Toby takes my phone and studies the photo. "This looks like a pretty standard six-digit system." He hands the phone back to me. "Hang on a second. I may have something."

He disappears for a few seconds then pops up again and shows me a high-tech-looking stainless-steel rectangle that has a small digital display on one side. He looks around to make sure no one is listening before holding out the device like it's the Holy Grail. "Take this. When you get it close enough to the keypad, press the black button. It will emit a high-density electronic pulse that should be powerful enough to knock out the lock and the camera in one fell swoop."

I widen my eyes and reach for the device. "Holy shit, Tobes. Really?"

He slaps my hands away and laughs. "No, not really. Jesus Christ, Tate, I'm not James fucking Bond. What the hell do I know about covert warehouse infiltration?"

I point to the thing he's holding. "Then what's that?"

"It's my portable phone charger." He tosses it back onto his desk and laughs when he sees my crestfallen face. "Aw, don't pout. You look ridiculous. Forgive me for not being a superhero security expert."

I flop into my chair. "But you know so much about really obscure crap, I thought you might have had a clue."

"Nope. Zero clues about these sorts of things. Hacking I can do. Anything else you see in spy movies, not so much. Couldn't you just *ask* Max what's inside the warehouse?"

"Sure, but then he'll just tell me what he wants me to know, and I'm after the stuff he wants to keep hidden. If he has that much security, there must be valuable info inside, right? I just need to find a way to get to it."

"Oh, you know I have your back as much as I can. If you can give me any solid facts about this guy, I can go to town tracking his real identity, but I need a place to start."

"I know, Tobes. Thanks. I'll see what I can find."

Toby goes back to his computer, and I pull my hair back into a rough bun as I think about where to go from here. I need biographical info on Max, as well as testimonials from his clients. Then I'll be able to start painting a balanced portrait that can serve as the jumping-off point for my story.

My computer beeps as an inter-office message pops up on my screen.

I want your first 800 words on Mister Romance on my desk by next week.
Derek.

Oh, goody. Right now, that will be eight-hundred words of filler and bullshit, and I don't think Derek would be pleased with that.

I type my reply.

Sure thing, bossman! I'm on it!

203

I sign it with three happy faces, just to piss him off.

I'm still wracking my brain for a solution ten minutes later when my phone lights up with Max's name.

I answer with, "Unless you start being more forthcoming, I'm going to give you a very unfavorable review on Yelp, Mister Romance."

There's an amused chuckle before he says, "Well, good morning to you, too. Would you like some cheese to go with that whine?"

"I'm serious, Max. I agreed to your conditions, and you promised me full disclosure, but so far all I've gotten is a lot of talk and a night with a non-existent musician. I need more."

"Such as?"

"Your history. A list of your clients. Testimonials. Interviews. You know, the usual stuff a journalist needs for a story. I have so many questions about why these ladies are so dedicated to you and how they feel about the whole situation. You telling me how they feel and me hearing it from their own mouths are two totally different things."

"I've told you before, my clients won't divulge anything to a journalist. Apart from the non-disclosure agreements they all signed, talking to you will jeopardize their identities."

"Then you'd better come up with something that will help me, because I'm on a deadline, and I need to start showing results. If I get kicked from this story, I have no doubt Derek will put someone else on it, and you'll lose whatever leverage you've gained with the whole being nice and taking care of me routine."

"You honestly can't comprehend I did that because I care, can you?"

"Pure intentions from a man who manipulates women for a living? Sure. That makes perfect sense. Now, about my story ..."

He pauses then says, "I have an idea that might work, and

coincidentally, it meshes with the plans I had for our second date."

"I'm listening."

"I want to do an immersive date with you, which means you'll also play a character."

"Oh, Max, I don't know. I'm not much of an actress. The only theatrical experience I've had is playing second turnip from the left in my third-grade nativity scene, and even then I was so nervous, I almost peed."

"There's nothing to be nervous about. None of my clients are actresses. You'll be fine. Although, if you still have that turnip costume somewhere, let me know. I can always find a way to work it in."

I laugh, and it's a real, pure, girly laugh. I throw my head back and everything. Oh, Lord. What's become of me?

"Be available Friday night," he says. "I'll send through details shortly."

"Will I need to wear pants and a bra?" I ask. "Because that's a whole other level of commitment right there, and I don't know if I'm ready to be that intimate with you yet."

"Then by all means, consider pants and bras optional. God knows, I won't be wearing a bra." He pauses, and it sounds like he's covering the phone to talk to someone in the background. When he comes back, he says, "I'm sorry, Miss Tate, but I have to go. I'll be in contact soon."

"Okay."

"Take care of your back, and have a great week."

"You, too. I mean, the great week part. Your back's fine." *Jesus, stop with the babble.* "Okay, bye."

I hang up, a grin splitting my face. I put down my good mood to being excited about finally moving forward with my story.

Yeah, of course. That's the reason.

When I spin my chair around to go and get a fresh cup of coffee, Derek is standing two feet away from me, arms folded across his chest.

"Jesus!" I say, pressing my hand over my skipping heart. "Sneak up much, Derek? Isn't that against company policy or something?"

"No, but do you know what is against company policy? Chatting to your boyfriend on the phone and making heart-eyes so big, I can see them from my office."

"There's a wall that blocks me from your view."

"And yet, here I am to remind you that I don't pay you to make personal calls."

"I wasn't –"

"Of course you weren't. You just look like a giddy school girl because you were speaking to your accountant. I understand. Now, get the fuck back to work."

Before I can say anything else, he stalks off toward Accounts.

I swear to God, that man gets more unpleasant every time I see him. If and when this story hits big, I'll find incredible satisfaction in moving on to a new job where I never have to look at his bastard face again.

Heart-eyes. Pfft. I don't even know what the hell that is, let alone how to make them.

Thirteen

Bon Voyage

"Do you have your passport?"

"Yes."

"A photocopy of your passport? And your credit cards?"

"Yes, and yes."

"What about antibiotics? Take them with you, just in case you catch a UTI from having crazy euro-sex with a dude named Jacques who has a monster baguette-dick."

"Eden, chill."

Asha grabs my shoulders to stop me from repacking her suitcase. Staying still isn't fun for me right now. I need to keep busy.

"What's going on? You've been on edge all week."

"Nothing. I'm just nervous about my baby sister traveling thousands of miles in a flying tin can, that's all."

"You know I have more chance of being kicked to death by a donkey than dying in a plane crash, right?"

I look at her in horror. "Holy shit. What? Is there some sort of evil donkey cartel going around killing people? Where did this information come from? Do they have *Mafioso* donkeys in France?"

"Eden!" She laughs and squeezes my shoulders. "I'm going to be fine, both on the plane and around random donkeys. Stop panicking."

I sit on the bed and drop my head into my hands. Honestly, I'm also on edge about Max. We haven't spoken since Tuesday. It's now Friday morning and still no contact. We supposedly have a date tonight, but I know nothing about it. Where, what time, how I'm supposed to dress. I mean, sure, I have that whole 'pants and bra are optional' directive, but that's it.

I grab my phone and dial the movie information line again, just to make sure there's no reason he can't get through.

Nope. Everything's working.

Then why hasn't he called?

If I weren't so badass, and he wasn't completely off the grid, I'd be stalking every piece of his social media right about now to find out what the hell's going on.

Asha clips shut the Ziploc bag containing her toiletries and gives me the side-eye. "You know, I can't help noticing you haven't seen Max this week. What's up with that?"

"Don't know. Don't care."

"Uh huh. Because to someone who knows you, it seems as though you might actually miss him."

I roll my eyes multiple times before checking the time. "Wow. Would you look at that? Your car will be here soon. Better get that case shut."

She gives me a knowing look before pressing her last few items into the overflowing suitcase and gesturing for me to push it down, so she can zip it. "Have it your way, but I hope you realize that denial isn't healthy. He likes you, and you like him. Story or not, you two have issues to sort out."

Her phone buzzes with an alert at almost the same time mine does. She checks her screen. "Ten minutes."

I check mine and get a vicious flutter in my belly when I see it's a text from Max.

<You have mail.>

I tap into my email app so fast I almost drop the phone, and sure enough, there it is. A fresh, shiny email.

I click it open.

From: Maxwell Riley <mr@email.com>
To: Eden Tate <etate@email.com>
Subject: Behavioral Guidelines
Date: Friday May 12
Dear Miss Tate,

I apologize for not contacting you sooner. Something came up unexpectedly, and I've been indisposed for most of the week. I hope your back has recovered and that you're feeling well.

Regarding tonight's date, please read the following guidelines and let me know by reply email if you have any questions.

First, I'm confirming that this is an immersive date, in which you will step out of your own personality and into someone else's. Your character description, along with mine, is detailed below. Read it carefully. Understand it. Live it. For this to be a success, you will genuinely have to try to be someone else for the night. I have faith that you can do it.

Character: Eden Crane, a top-notch New York journalist with a thirst for the truth. (Very much like yourself.)

Personality: Open-minded. Unguarded. Craves intimacy and intense connections. (Totally unlike yourself. These traits are your Everest, Miss Tate. Embrace them.)

Setting: Black-tie charity event

Background: You've been invited to the event by Maxwell

Roberts, a wealthy philanthropist who also runs a successful escort business for high-profile clients. (Don't think too much about the logic of this. It's a fantasy, after all.) You met Maxwell earlier in the day when you were interviewing him for a feature story for the online news source, Pulse. *(Sound familiar?) When you met, you both felt an instant attraction, and he's invited you to the charity gala to get to know you better. You've accepted his invitation, because you need more information for your story, and also because, despite your best efforts to remain impassive, you feel a powerful and passionate attraction to him. (Use your imagination if you must.)*

Please note: You may ask me real-world questions about my business in this scenario, and I will try to provide answers. I won't consider this breaking the reality of the scenario. The people you encounter will give you real information. By the end of the night, you should have increased your research file substantially.

Existing guidelines regarding physical contact apply, as do the procedures for canceling the date should you become uncomfortable. I will continue my promise to not kiss you unless invited to do so.

I would advise you to call in sick to work today. I need you well rested and prepared for tonight, and you will need to be home in the afternoon for reasons that will become clear. So, Miss Tate, try to relax. Take off your pants and bra, if you wish. Watch a movie. Eat some ice cream. I look forward to seeing you later this evening. Or rather, I'll enjoy spending time with your alter ego.

Have a wonderful day.

Warmest regards,

Max.

As I finish reading, I hear a shutter go off and turn to see Asha pointing her phone at me.

"What are you doing?"

"Nothing. Capturing a moment." She puts her phone away. "Walk me down?"

I take the suitcase as she grabs her computer bag and giant purse, and within a few minutes we're waiting on the sidewalk.

"Edie?" When I turn to look at her, she smiles. "I hope you know I only want the best for you."

I take her hands, already feeling a painful lump forming in my throat. "Of course I know that. I feel the same way about you."

"Good, because I want to make sure you know how much I love you before I do this." She slaps the top of my head.

"Ow! Ash!"

"Don't look a gift horse in the mouth. Opportunity is not a lengthy visitor. Fortune favors the brave. Big risks lead to big rewards."

"Do you want to inform me why you suddenly turned into a talking fortune cookie?"

She sighs. "I know that preaching gets nowhere with you. Just know that if I were you, I wouldn't let my stupid pride and self-preservation mess up something that could be amazing."

I open my mouth to reply, but she holds up her hand. "No. Don't tell me I'm wrong or make excuses. Just think about it."

Her car pulls up to the curb, and we hug as the driver loads her gear into the trunk.

"I'm going to miss you, Edie."

"Not as much as I'll miss you." I swallow and blink to push back the tears. Crying isn't something I do. I learned a long time ago that it hurts less to keep it in than let it out. Also, Asha cries less if I'm strong, and I'd do pretty much anything to prevent

Asha from crying.

"Take care of Nannabeth while I'm gone. See you in a couple of weeks."

"I'll be here."

She climbs into the back seat of the slick SUV, and I stand at the curb and wave until she disappears into the rush-hour traffic.

When I get back upstairs, I slump into the sofa, already feeling her absence. It's so quiet without her, I jump when my phone buzzes with a text. It's from her, and there's a picture attached.

I open it and find the photo she took when I was reading Max's email.

<*Just for the record, I've NEVER seen this expression on your face before. EVER. Look at yourself, Edie. You look HAPPY. Just thought you should know. I love you and miss you already.*>

She's right. I look so happy, I barely recognize myself. What the hell is happening to me?

I breathe through another urge to cry. God, I'm such a baby right now. I think I'll take Max's advice and call in sick to work.

At the mere thought of his name, I feel myself smile. I don't think I've ever done that over a man before and take great pains to make my face stand down.

As much as Asha loves me and thinks she know what's best for me, there's a simple truth she didn't articulate: those who don't jump off cliffs are a hundred percent less likely to wind up road kill than those who do.

Fourteen

Everyone Loves a Makeover

I stand in the middle of my living room surrounded by flowers, gift boxes, and people I don't know, as I genuinely wonder if I'd fallen asleep and conjured up this elaborate dream.

"Miss Crane? How do you feel?"

I stare at myself in the full-length mirror a girl named Teresa is holding, and I honestly can't express what I'm feeling. The surrealism began at lunchtime, when a delivery man knocked on my door armed with the most stunning long-stemmed roses I've ever seen. The card read:

> *Dear Miss Crane,*
> *I can't wait to see you tonight. Please save a dance for me.*
> *Maxwell Roberts.*

This was my first hint that I had no idea the extent to which Max would go to take this date to the next level.

After that, I received several other gifts: perfume, shoes, and even expensive lingerie. I've never thought of myself as sexually prudish, but the thought of Max picking out that underwear made me blush.

Then, at four this afternoon, I opened the door to find a woman holding a Marchesa garment bag, along with Venus the beauty therapist and a hairdresser named Peter. For the past few hours, I've been pampered beyond my wildest expectations and am now thoroughly polished, waxed, and slickly styled. My body is wrapped in the most stunning gown I've ever seen. It's midnight blue, strapless, and dreamy, and I've never worn something that's made me feel so thoroughly feminine before. The layers of silk chiffon wrap around my body like it was made for me, and the prettiness is given an edge by the way the skirt breaks into a high split on one side that reveals my freshly waxed leg and one of the glittery, strappy heels I'm wearing.

The real kicker about this entire transformation is that, even though I've never felt the need to have impeccable makeup, hair, and designer clothes to enhance my worth, I can't deny that right now, looking like a sky-dipped goddess, I feel amazing.

"Miss Crane?"

I stop gawking at myself and turn to Teresa. "I'm sorry, what?"

She gives me a patient smile. "How do you feel?"

I run my hands over the luxe fabric. "Teresa, how much is this dress worth?"

Her smile falters. "Uh ... I'm not really authorized to tell you that."

"Come on," I urge. "I won't tell him you told me."

She looks at Venus and Peter, then back to me. "Let's just say, for the money it would take to buy that dress, you could have a car."

"A really nice car," Peter says.

I swallow and stop stroking the fabric. Damn. I'd better not spill anything on this. I have no doubt Max will have to return it to whichever high-end boutique he borrowed it from.

There's a knock at my door, and I groan, because I don't think I can handle any more surprises. Venus runs over to open it, and a smartly dressed man is waiting.

"I'm Daryl. Miss Crane's limo is ready."

A limo? Dear God. The most glamorous mode of transport I've ever experienced up until now is a Toyota Prius.

Teresa hands me a bejeweled clutch bag. "Have a great time, Miss Crane."

In a daze, I follow Daryl out of my apartment as Teresa, Peter, and Venus wish me well.

And as I make my way down to the car, all I have echoing in my brain is a silent scream as I prepare to jump off a cliff.

෬

The incredible building at 583 Park Avenue is one of those venues I've heard about over the years but have never been rich or well-connected enough to visit. Even though I've heard tales of the extravagant galas in the glamorous ballroom, being here is on a whole other level of, *Oh my God.*

The entire double-height room is swathed in gauzy white fabric, and the giant crystal chandelier that hovers fifty feet above the action casts infinite tiny rainbows around the room. The crowd is a sea of men in crisp dinner suits and glamorous ladies of all ages, and I've never felt more like a fish out of water in my entire life.

I take a deep breath and squeeze my fancy clutch purse like a stress-relief toy as I look around the room.

So, this is how the other half lives, huh? Good to know.

The ballroom is enormous, and even though I estimate there are about five-hundred people milling around, they're dwarfed by the massive space. On the screen is a slide announcing that this is the *Valentine Foundation Annual Fundraising Gala.* I've hear of this foundation. It works to help low income and underprivileged women gain training and employment. From what I've heard, it's a fantastic cause, and it's lovely that it seems to be patronized by the largest group of attractive people I've ever seen.

I self-consciously run my hand over my hair, grateful I've been professionally styled. I might not feel like I belong with this blue-blooded crowd, but at least I look the part.

A slick team of waiters moves between groups of people distributing fancy, microscopic canapés and sparkling glasses of champagne.

When a waiter passes near me, I snag myself some bubbly. God knows I'm going to need to calm my nerves if I have any chance of pulling off this charade. I down the champagne in three swallows and deposit my glass on a nearby table.

"Miss Crane?" I look around to see an older lady approaching me, beyond glamorous in a silver sheath that matches her silver hair. "I'm so glad you could make it. I'm Vivian Roberts, one of the patrons of the Valentine Foundation. I'm very pleased to meet you."

She gives me a warm smile and holds out her hand, and though it feels wrong to tarnish it with my peasant flesh, I do it anyway, if only to be polite.

"You're so beautiful," I say then realize I sound ridiculous. "I mean, it's lovely to meet you, too."

She lets go of my hand to snag some more champagne from a nearby waiter and passes me one. "I've heard a lot about you. I don't think Maxwell has ever gushed about a woman before, but he can't seem to stop talking about you."

"Well, that's so kind of you to say. I notice you and Maxwell share a last name. Are you related?"

She shakes her head. "Not technically, but he feels like my son. I understand you're doing a story on him."

"Yes. He's certainly a fascinating subject."

She gets a wistful expression on her face. "He is. And one of the best men I know."

Okay, lady, don't oversell it.

I vaguely wonder if that was planned or if she's going off-script.

"Is Maxwell here, yet?" I ask, as I search the crowd. I'm not eager to see him or anything. Just curious. After all, I should thank him for all the presents.

The tiniest raise of Vivian's eyebrow tells me she thinks I like him. Well, I suppose I don't dislike him, so she's half right.

"He's speaking with some of our committee members right now, but he should be finished shortly. He asked me to take you up to the gallery to wait."

"Oh, okay."

"Follow me."

She leads me to the side of the room where a wide staircase leads to the horseshoe-shaped balcony. I'm grateful that not only are there fewer people up here, but it also gives a fantastic view of the event below. She leads me over to the balustrade near a group of women who are standing and chatting.

"Would you mind waiting here for just a few minutes?" Vivian asks. "I'll let Maxwell know you've arrived."

"Great. Thank you."

I take a brief glance at the women beside me. My God, they all look like entrants in the Mrs. America pageant. Gorgeous dresses, beautiful hair. Faces that are so smooth and wrinkle free, I'm betting they've had some sort of cosmetic enhancement.

A perfect primp of princesses.

I'm about to turn away, when one of the blonde ladies catches my eye.

Holy shit!

It's Marla Massey. *The* Marla Massey who inspired this whole investigation. I study the ladies with her. Could some of them also be Max's clients?

I'm concentrating so hard on trying to identify them, I jump when a perky voice behind me says, "Oh, my God, Eden! Hiiiii!" I turn to see Joanna there, beaming at me. She's wearing a blush-pink gown with a plunging neckline. Nice if you have the boobs, I suppose.

"It's so great to see you!" she says as she takes in my full appearance. Her jaw drops in disbelief. "Holy crap, woman, you look amaaaaaaaazing. What happened? Did Asha help you?"

I'm slightly insulted that she doesn't think I could have put this ensemble together by myself. I mean, we've only hung out couple of times. How dare she already know about my complete lack of style?

Joanna reads my face and laughs. "Sorry, I just meant that I'm not used to you looking this attractive. If it weren't for the color of your hair, I never would have recognized you."

I smile. "You're wonderful for a girl's ego, Joanna. Has anyone ever told you that?"

"Actually, no."

"Huh. This is my surprised face."

She laughs and pushes my arm. "You're funny." After giving me another onceover, she says, "What are you doing here, anyway? I didn't think this was your kind of event."

"I was invited by a friend." Not sure how true that statement is, but I'm going with it. "What about you? This isn't really the kind of place I'd expect to find an assistant from a publishing company."

Joanna gestures to the group beside me. "The brunette in the red gown is my cousin, Alice."

I squint, trying to place her. "Have I met your cousin? She looks familiar."

"Oh, you've probably seen her in the news. She got married a few months ago to that oil magnate's son. Cristos whatshisname."

The penny drops. "Cristos *Callas*? Holy crap, Joanna, your cousin is Alice Kennedy?"

She shrugs. "Yeah."

No wonder she's so well connected. Not only is Alice a congressmen's daughter, but her brother is a best-selling author. And yes, they're related to *those* Kennedys.

I gesture for Joanna to lean closer, then whisper, "Joanna, you know how I'm looking into the whole Mister Romance thing?"

"Yes! So cool!"

"Do you know if any of those ladies use his services?"

She nods. "All of them, except Alice. It's not really her thing, but she still likes to hear about it."

Holy crap. I've just hit the client mother lode.

I grab my phone out of my purse and pull Joanna into my side. "Hey, let's take some selfies!" I've never taken a selfie in my life, but I quickly figure out it's not too difficult to also frame in the ladies behind us.

When I'm done, I bring up the notes app. "Could you write down your cousin's friends for me?"

Joanna looks at the phone with a dubious expression. "Are you going to write bad things about them? Because Alice would kill me if that happened."

"I'm going to try to keep their identities a secret. I just need to know who they are for my research."

"Okay. I guess." She types into the phone, and when I scan down the list, their names jog my memory in ways their faces don't. One is the daughter of a prominent Supreme Court judge. Another is an actress who's had some success on Broadway. There's even a well-known magazine editor whose publication specializes in stories like, *15 WAYS TO TELL IF A MAN IS CHEATING ON YOU*. I'm not sure if all of them are married or in relationship, but wow. That's a whole lot of platinum-plated scandal right there. If Derek found out, he'd have a major revenue boner.

I'm sure these ladies don't represent all of Max's clients, but it's enough to give me an idea of the types of women who use his services. I suddenly feel inferior in comparison. They're so glamorous and accomplished, and I'm ... well ... I look down at myself ... a Brooklyn girl masquerading as a Park Avenue princess.

"Eden?" I look up to see Joanna staring at me. "You okay?"

"Just thinking." I give her a smile. "Do me a favor? Introduce me to your cousin and her friends."

Joanna leans in and drops her voice to a whisper. "Oh, my God. What are you going to do?"

"Try and infiltrate them. Find out more info about Mister Romance. Let's just hope all those hours I spent playing a turnip pay off." I hit record on my voice memo and put the phone back into my purse.

Joanna beams. "This is so exciting! I've never been a part of a secret mission before. Let's go!"

I exhale slowly as we move toward the group. Marla Massey is talking, and the ladies around her listen with eager interest.

"The other day my son asked me how his father and I make up after our many arguments, and I said it was simple – we reach a compromise. I end up lying and tell Walter I was wrong, and then he agrees with me." The women all laugh. Their reaction is so synchronized, it's like they share a hive mind.

Joanna moves us into position beside her cousin. "Good

evening, ladies. Alice, I want you to meet my friend, Eden."

I hold out my hand. "Eden Crane. Nice to meet you."

As Alice shakes my hand, I can feel the other ladies assessing me, taking note of my dress and accessories; weighing up whether or not I'm the same species. I must pass the test, because Marla Massey is the first to smile.

"Crane, you say? Are you related to Samuel, by any chance?"

God, I wish. Samuel Crane is the heir apparent to one of the biggest media empires in the country. If I was related to him I wouldn't have to go through all of this crap to get a decent job.

I hit Marla with my most sincere smile. "Yes, actually. Sam is my second cousin. With his family's fortune, I don't have any idea why he chooses to work for a living, but then, he was always a strange child."

The ladies laugh, and I try to hide how disgusted I am with myself right now. *Anything for the story,* I tell myself. I hold my clutch a little higher, so it's sure to get a decent sound level on the conversation.

"Actually, I'm glad I met you tonight, Mrs. Massey," I say.

"Oh, please. Call me Marla."

I act like it's an honor. "Thank you. I believe we have a mutual friend."

Marla raises her eyebrows. "Oh?"

"Yes, a certain gorgeous stallion I recently met at the Mason Richards stables."

For a brief moment the women freeze, and I worry I've made a terrible mistake.

But then Marla gives the group a knowing smile and says, "From the moment I saw you, I knew you had good taste."

There's a smattering of laughter, and I let out a relieved breath. Okay, now let's see what we can find out about a certain stallion from his stable of fillies.

Fifteen

Inside Information

"I think for me, it's like getting vitamin B injections," says Candice, a well-preserved forty-year-old whose family owns a chain of luxury hotels. "Seeing Max regularly keeps me healthy, happy, and youthful. It's like after a date with him, I've purged a whole lot of negative energy and feel totally refreshed."

"Is it the same for all of you?" I ask.

The ladies nod in agreement as a waiter refills our glasses.

Candice cocks her head and studies me. "Is it not like that for you?"

I tense up as everyone waits for my answer. "Uh ... well, not exactly." Now they all seem concerned.

"Talk to us, Eden," Marla says. "We'll help you if we can. The Sisterhood of the Romancing Pants is here for you."

I take a sip of champagne. *Great. Now, I have no choice but to share.*

"Well, I've never really been a romantic person, so I have issues with the tender sentiments, and ... I don't know. I guess I just find it hard to trust a guy who gets paid to make women feel good. Like, how can I take any of his compliments seriously?"

There's a murmur of understanding. "You've been hurt,"

Marla says. "Not wanting to trust is a symptom of that. But Max doesn't say things he doesn't mean. If he tells you you're beautiful, it's because he thinks you are. Then again, he's the kind of man who finds beauty in most places."

"And you don't think that's strange?"

Candice touches my arm. "I used to be like you. But the only way to get the full benefits from a date is to surrender to the fantasy. We've all been hurt. We're all broken in places. But romance gives us a way to forget about that for a while and believe that fairytales can come true." The other ladies nod in agreement. "We live in a world of flawed men. There's no shame in letting ourselves believe in a perfect one for a while."

"Do any of your husbands or partners know about Max?"

Several of them nod, including Marla. "I told my husband about him. God knows, I've put up with his enough of his 'secretaries' for all these years. The least he can do is support my emotional therapy."

"And have any of you developed real feelings for Max?" I ask. "I mean, it must be hard to let go of the emotions he brings out in your dates, right?" Despite my knowledge he's playing me, I can't deny he knows how to press all of my buttons. "Does the euphoria from the romance become an addiction?"

Some of them laugh, then Candice says, "Sure, it's an amazing feeling to be the center of the universe of a man like Max, and there's no doubt he's incredible at knowing just how far to push, but none of us is fooling ourselves that it's real. For those of us who've had money our whole lives, we're used to men pretending they love us to get their golden ticket. It happens all the time. Max gives us the adrenaline rush of that kind of attention without any of the strings."

"Or alimony payments," Marla says with a laugh.

I'm about to ask another question when Vivian appears

beside Marla and smiles at me. "Ladies, I'm sorry to interrupt the stallion appreciation society, but I'm afraid I have to steal Miss Crane."

Several highly arched eyebrows are raised, including Marla's. "Do you happen to have a date tonight, Eden?" In a strange twist, she seems excited for me.

"Uh, yes, actually."

"I was wondering who he'd bring to this event. He helped organize it, you know."

Actually, I didn't know.

She leans over to me. "Enjoy yourself. Try not to think too much. You're a queen. Let Max treat you like one for a change. Goodness knows, we've all had our fill of being treated like part of the furniture."

That statement stays with me as I smile at her and bid the ladies goodnight. I must admit to myself that I underestimated them. I figured they'd all be rich and bitchy, but they seem determined to support each other, and Max is the glue that binds them all together.

As I leave, I tell Joanna I'll talk to her later before following Vivian toward the stairs.

"Did you get what you needed, Miss Crane?"

I reach into my purse to turn off my voice recorder. "You knew those ladies were there when you stood me next to them, didn't you?" She smiles but doesn't answer. "And from your stallion comment, I'm assuming you know all about Max and his extracurricular activities."

She stops and turns to me. "Who do you think set him up with his client base in the first place?"

I do a mental jaw drop. "You ... manage him?" I never even considered that Max would have a pimp. Or, more accurately, a madam.

She laughs. "Hardly. Max is capable of managing himself. I merely suggested there was a definite market for his talents and introduced him to some of my friends. He did the rest."

"And how did you learn about his talents in the first place?"

She looks down at my purse. "Do you want this on record?"

"Is that okay?"

"I wouldn't have suggested it if it wasn't."

After I turn the recorder back on she says, "A few years ago, I was at my lowest point. I won't go into all the details, but the short story is that my husband of thirty years informed me he'd never loved me and then left me for a woman half my age."

"Oh, God. I'm sorry."

"Don't be. It was the best thing that ever happened to me; but at the time I couldn't see that. Everything I'd taken for granted about my life was destroyed. Then one night I was drowning my sorrows in a bar downtown where Max was bartending. I don't know how he could tell I was struggling, but he could. He spent the rest of the night trying to make me feel better."

"Did he succeed?"

She laughs softly. "Remarkably, yes. I've never considered myself vulnerable to the charms of beautiful young men, but he wasn't just handsome. He was also wickedly intelligent and one of the most caring souls I'd ever met. That night, within the space of a few hours, he made me realize that my husband was a moron for letting me go, and I was better off without him."

"How did he do that?"

She narrows her eyes a little. "I still don't know. But he did. Over the following weeks, whenever I'd feel down, I'd go the bar and see Max. He was my human booster shot of self-esteem. On those nights, I tipped him well. He'd resist, of course, but I insisted. From there, I started recommending that bar to my friends who were struggling. Max became very popular, very quickly."

"So how did he transform from Max the friendly bartender into Mister Romance?"

She hesitates then says, "When we became friends, he admitted to having some issues of his own. He wasn't in a good place emotionally or financially, and I realized he'd have to make a change in order to get ahead. The concept for Mister Romance seemed a good way to capitalize on his skills. Thankfully, he agreed."

"What sort of problems was he having?" This is the first time I've heard any hint that Max isn't the perfectly put-together cover model he always seems to be. I'm intrigued to hear he may have a jaded past.

"That's not my story to tell. And besides, I've been gabbing long enough. If we don't wrap this up, he'll come looking for you, and the character he's playing tonight doesn't take kindly to being kept waiting." She points toward the stairs. "Head on down. He's at the bottom. And he'll probably kill me for telling you this, but he's been anxious to see you all week."

I click off the recorder and close my purse. "Why are you helping me? If I end up publishing this story, it would ruin everything you've helped him build."

She touches my arm. "I don't know you, Eden, but from what I can tell, you're a decent person. I trust that after you have all of the information about Max, you'll make the right decision."

With that, she pats my arm and heads off to the other side of the balcony.

☙

I take a breath as I absorb everything I've learned tonight. Max wasn't kidding when he said he'd give me access. I've gone from an information famine to a feast, and it's going to take a while for me to digest it all.

I smooth my dress and head down the stairs. As I turn onto the landing, my breath catches when I spy Max. He's a few yards away from the bottom of the stairs, talking to a beautiful woman in black. I stop short and grab the railing when the full force of his appearance hits me.

Dear God. I'm in trouble.

There's no denying that Max is an attractive man no matter what he wears, but tonight in that laser-sharp dinner suit, with his hair slick and neat, pure, undiluted sex rolls off him in waves. I don't have the words to describe how entirely screwed I am.

I take a couple of calming breaths. Predictably, they don't work. It doesn't help that whenever I'm hit with a bout of dizzying attraction to Max, it's accompanied by an equally strong amount of panic. Perhaps the ladies upstairs were right; I need to surrender to this feeling rather than fight it. But will that make being around him less debilitating? Is it possible for me to embrace the attraction without involving my locked-down emotions?

I decide to embrace the acting exercise and try to channel what Eden Crane would do.

I continue my breathing technique while I watch Max interact with his lady friend. She really is stunning. I dislike the sensation I get when she laughs and puts her hand on his chest. I dislike it even more when she stretches up to whisper in his ear. And when Max smiles as he cups her elbow, I get a pain in my jaw from clenching my teeth too hard.

No doubt she's a client, but seeing him being so affectionate with another woman is ... irritating.

After the whispered exchange, she kisses him on the cheek,

and I try to shake off my tension as I continue down the steps toward him.

When I'm almost to the bottom, he turns and sees me, and ... oh, dear Lord ... the expression on his face. It's like the whole universe is expanding in his chest. His gaze sweeps all over me as I walk, and even though I try to play it cool, feeling my heart slamming against my ribcage makes that difficult.

When I stop in front of him, he shakes his head the tiniest amount before swallowing with effort. After a few seconds of staring, he says in a low voice, "Miss Crane, you're ... stunning."

Okay, so, yes. He's playing a character, and so am I. I'm going to be someone else. Someone open to how he's looking at me. Maybe even someone who's able to be gracious.

I try to smile. "You're too kind, Mr. Roberts."

"Actually, I'm not." He takes my hand and brings it up to his mouth where he presses a warm, lingering kiss to my skin. I feel those lips everywhere at once, as if the back of my hand it a conductor for every other cell in my body.

When he lowers my hand, he doesn't let it go. "If I had a better vocabulary to describe how amazing you look, I'd use it. Unfortunately, 'stunning' is all I can come up with."

I look away. Taking on his compliments is more difficult than I thought, especially when I'm trying to minimize my sarcasm.

"Is this what usually happens when you invite a woman out?" I ask, laughing off my tension. "You dress her up like a goddess then melt her panties with your sex voice?"

"Yes, that's the general idea. At least, I hope the thing about melting your panties is true." He glances at my body. "Are you wearing the underwear I bought you?" I give a tight nod. "Good. Then the mental image I have right now is accurate."

I glance up at him and realize instantly it's not a great idea. I've had men undress me with their eyes before, but that's not what Max is doing. From what I can tell, he's mentally tearing my clothes off with his teeth.

I squirm under his scrutiny. This is feeling way too intimate, and I'm not the slightest bit equipped to deal with him on this level. I shift my weight, becoming more and more uncomfortable every second.

"What are you doing?" he asks as I look anywhere but at him.

"I don't know. This is too strange for me."

"No, it's not. Stop fidgeting and relax." There's an edge to his voice I haven't heard before. Rough and bossy. Believably raw.

"Relaxing isn't in my nature." I close my eyes and roll my . neck. Then I exhale and open my eyes to see him staring at me in concern. "I'm sorry. I'm trying."

"I can see that."

"You know, I ran into some interesting women upstairs. They gave me valuable advice."

He looks wary. "Which was?"

"Stop fighting and surrender. I'm just not sure I'm the sort of person who can do that."

"Then let me help you." He steps closer and takes hold of my chin. "Tonight, you'll do as you're told. You'll answer my questions truthfully, accept every compliment I give you, and not flinch away from me or how I make you feel. Am I clear?"

"I –"

"Don't argue with me, Eden. Am ... I ... clear?" He looks like the god of thunder, ready to strike me down if I defy him.

"Yes. Clear."

His eyelids get heavy as he continues to stare at me. "Good." He steps back and glances at my neck. "Before we go any further, there's one more gift I forgot to send." He pulls a black velvet bag out of his pocket and turns it upside down into his palm. Inside is a stunning necklace, sparkling in the low light.

I assume the stones are crystals, because if they were diamonds he'd need to hire a bodyguard to follow me around all night to make sure I didn't lose it.

He puts the bag on a nearby table. "When you wear it, think of me."

He holds it up to unclasp it, and even if it is costume jewelry, it's still the most extravagant present I've ever received.

"Max, I can't accept that. It's –"

"... not up for discussion. Turn around, please."

When I do, he reaches in front of me and leans close as he secures the clasp. I draw in a breath when he grazes his fingers along the edge of my shoulder. "Of all the women I know, Eden, you're the one who deserves to be dripping in diamonds."

I turn to him. "These are diamonds?"

"Do you think I'd give you glass?"

I touch the stones around my neck. "No, I just ..." I have no idea what's going on right now. Is this a normal part of the scenario? Are they really diamonds, or are we just playing pretend?

"Eden?" When I look at him, I see his expression has softened. "Don't fight it."

I take a step back. I'm too hot and way too vulnerable. "I need a drink."

He steps forward and cups my face. "No. No more drinking tonight." He looks into my eyes. "You're going to be stone-cold sober when you ask me to kiss you later, because there's no way I'm letting you blame what's going to happen between us on alcohol."

I can't stop staring at him. "I'm not here to kiss you. I'm here for the story."

"Actually, you're here to understand my methods and my clients. Kissing plays into both of those." He glances at my lips. "And I'm going to enjoy every second while I thoroughly explain myself to you."

The tension between us is reaching uncomfortable levels when I hear buzzing. With an apologetic look, he reaches into his pocket and pulls out his phone. When he glances at the screen, his face looks like the sky before a tornado.

"Excuse, Miss Crane. I have to take this."

He stalks off to the side of the room and disappears into an open hallway. I look around, feeling conspicuously alone. I know he walked away to have privacy, but I'm curious about who on earth could make him look so murderous.

I casually make my way over to the hallway and peek around the corner. He's nowhere to be seen.

There are several open doorways farther along, and when I get enough away from the ballroom to make out anything but the sound of the band, I can hear Max. He's not yelling, but his voice is definitely raised in anger.

"I don't care where you go or what you do, but stay the hell away from me. You and I are done." There's a pause, then a bitter laugh. "Do you think you scare me? You don't. You're a pathetic excuse for a man, and if I'm ever in a room with you again, you'd better bring bodyguards, because you're not getting out of there in one piece, asshole."

For a second there's silence, then I hear a frustrated, "Fuck!" before a huge crashing sound.

I walk over and peek into the room. It's set up with several large tables covered in white cloths. One of the tables is on its side, surrounded by toppled chairs. Max is standing with his phone in one hand, his shoulders slumped and head down. His other hand is clenched into a tight fist. I can almost feel his rage from where I'm standing.

I used to think Max had solid-gold composure, but after the

thing with Brick earlier in the week, and now this? My already-eager curiosity has switched into overdrive.

Who the hell was he talking to? And why did they push him over the edge?

Knowing he has this kind of rage inside him is troubling. Is that why he always seems so studiously calm? To keep this part of him under control? And after his statement about violence at the bar the other night, it's ironic to hear him threaten someone so vehemently.

I have the strongest urge to go to him and ask what's wrong ... to try to help somehow. But how do I do that?

After a few seconds, I make the decision that maybe it's best to leave him alone to gather himself. I don't know if I've ever been as angry as he is, but I can imagine it's not something you want other people around to witness.

As quietly as I can I step away from the door, but I must not be stealthy enough, because before I get two steps, he bellows, "Miss Crane!"

I freeze, thinking that maybe he's like a T-rex and won't see me if I stay still. That doesn't seem to be the case, because he says, "I know you're there. Come in here."

Like a kid who's been caught sneaking in the morning after prom night, I walk into the room.

His glare nearly pins me to the wall. "Shut the door."

I slowly turn and close the door behind me, and there's way too much going on in my body right now to make sense of it. This Maxwell character is like regular-Max turned up to eleven, and that's eleven points too much for me to handle.

"Do you often eavesdrop on private conversations?" he asks, his voice is quiet but intense.

"No."

"But you thought it was acceptable to listen to mine?"

I want to play the submissive role, but there are so many questions swirling in my head right now, it's difficult to stop them from spilling from my mouth.

"You looked upset. I wanted to find out why."

He comes over to me, cups my face, and then runs his thumb over my lips. "It's not worth discussing. I'm sorry we were interrupted. All I wanted to do tonight was have a nice time with you."

The warmth that's spreading from his hand to my face increases, and I struggle to not close my eyes.

The stroke of his thumb on my lips has grown softer, and even though some of the anger has drained from his posture, it's still bright behind his eyes.

"You started out thinking I was a conman, Miss Crane. Is that still your opinion?"

"Your clients don't think you are."

"My clients hardly know me."

"Are you saying that you're a bad person?"

He leans his forehead against mine. "I'm saying that everyone is someone's monster, and I'm no exception."

Again, a slew of questions flare up in my brain, but before I can articulate any of them, he goes over to pick up the table he assaulted.

"Go back to the party, Miss Crane. I'll join you shortly."

I want to stay with him, but I understand he needs some space in order to calm down. His broad shoulders are back to looking like he's carrying the weight of the world on them, so I close the door and head back down the hallway to the ballroom.

It's clear that as much as I think I know Max, he's still a total stranger to me. For the sake of the truth, I'm going to have to fill in those blank spaces about his private life in the near future, by whatever means necessary.

CR

"Do you think we're strange creatures?"

I turn to see Vivian standing beside me as I watch the interactions in the room. "Excuse me?"

"The expression on your face is one of incredulity. Is it the decorations? The music? The people?"

I shake my head and smile. "I'm sorry. I didn't realize what my face was doing. It's just so bizarre for me to be among the rich and the beautiful. When I was a little girl, I trained myself out of having princess fantasies."

She waves at a couple passing by. "And rightly so. We should encourage girls to drop the fairy tales. They create unrealistic expectations that make us think men can complete our lives, when very often, they destroy them."

"Wow. It's nice to meet a likeminded soul. There aren't too many of us around."

"Miss Crane, when you've lived as long as I have, you know how the world works. Now, don't get me wrong. I generally love men, and my current boyfriend is one of the best I've ever met, but you only have to look around this room to see a symptom of what's wrong with the world." She points to Marla Massey, who's standing in a group with her husband.

"Congressman Massey there portrays himself as a man who believes in good, Christian values. He's an ex-preacher and a government representative, and yet he treats his wife like an object he owns rather than a partner in life. And don't even get me started on the number of affairs he's had over the years."

She points to the group of ladies I was talking to earlier, who are now gathered near a group of men, presumably their husbands. "In this world, Miss Crane, people don't necessarily marry for love. A large number of these women are treated like possessions. Their partners give them sex, but what they truly crave is for someone to *see* them. Value them. *Love* them. That's what Maxwell does."

I think about that for a moment. I never thought it possible to have sympathy for women who pay more for a pair of shoes than I do in rent, but after getting to know them tonight, I've discovered it is. I wonder if I could live like that – rich, but miserable.

Vivian turns to me. "Exposing the seedy underbelly of the social elite would make a wonderful addition to your story, wouldn't it?"

I feel small beneath her scrutiny. "Of course. It's newsworthy."

"Yes, because scandal is the most popular type of news there is these days. We just love to see the high and mighty fall. It makes us all feel better about our own pathetic lives. But as much as I'd like to see Walter Massey taken down, because he's an insufferable, sexist pig, Marla would be taken down with him. And that woman has enough to deal with. All of Max's clients do. I don't know a single one of them who deserves to be publicly humiliated." She gestures to the crowd. "All of these women are here tonight to support a charity that empowers other women. Skills-training programs, safe havens from domestic abuse, philanthropic grants, and special housing for homeless women and children. Maybe you could highlight their *work* rather than what they do in their spare time."

From her words I feel like I'm receiving a lecture, but her tone and face still remain kind. "My editor wants me to name names."

"Of course he does. But I think you're clever enough to write the story you want and still make it newsworthy."

I watch as Marla and her husband take to the dance floor.

With the knowledge I have, I can now see how Marla's blithe smile seems hollow.

"Did Max tell you we have a bet?" I ask. "If I develop feelings for him, I have to drop the story altogether."

"And how's that working out for you?"

"Right now? I have no idea."

"You like him."

"I guess."

"That wasn't a question. And he likes you."

I laugh. "Let's be honest; he likes a lot of women."

"I'm not going to argue that point, but he's never, and I mean *ever*, looked at any woman the way he looks at you." She directs her attention over my shoulder and smiles before coming back to me. "Now, if you'll excuse me, I have to attend to other guests."

As she walks away, Max appears next to me.

"Should I be nervous that you were talking with Vivian?"

"You tell me."

He doesn't look at me. Instead, he glances at the stage. He's trying to appear calm, but I can still feel his anger. It's in the hunch of his shoulders and the clench of his fists.

"I'm sorry about before," he says. "I wasn't expecting that call tonight, and it put me on edge."

"To put it mildly," I say, trying to lighten the mood.

He glances down, not meeting my eyes, like he's just exposed a part of himself he'd rather have kept hidden. "I didn't mean to leave you alone."

"Are you okay now?"

He nods but still looks as if he'd like to pick up another table and throw it across the room.

"Can I do anything for you?" I ask, moving closer. "Get you a drink? A Valium? Maybe a backrub?"

The corners of his mouth lift, but it doesn't quite become

a full-blown smile. With his eyes still downcast, he takes my hand. "I might take you up on the backrub later, but for now, just dance with me."

I squeeze his hand in silent agreement, and he leads me to the dance floor. The band is playing smooth big-band music from the forties, and even though there are a dozen or so other couples around us, when he pulls me into his arms, the whole room fades away, until all I'm aware of is him.

As we come together, something shifts in the air between us. The music gets softer. The edges of my vision blur. There's a tunnel of energy straight from me to him, and it's the most exciting and terrifying experience I've ever encountered.

When he presses his cheek against my temple, his skin is hot. He takes some deep breaths, and as I stroke the hair at the base of his neck, he lets out a noise that's a mix between a groan and a sigh.

"That feels good."

Comforting him feels oddly affectionate, but then, that's a perfect summation of my feelings toward Max.

"It's ironic," he says as we sway to the music. "So many women hold me up as the paragon of a perfect man, and they couldn't be more wrong. If they only knew the truth."

His statement surprises me. I mean, I know he's too good to be true, I just don't know why. But to hear him admit it confirms something I've thought all along.

"What truth are you talking about?"

He pulls me closer. "Can we just dance? I'd like a little more time before you look at me like I'm a piece of shit."

I don't know what to say to that, so I hold him closer and keep moving.

By the time the song ends, his muscles are less bunched, but he doesn't step away from me. He just stands there, pressing against me and breathing deep.

"Have you ever felt true joy, Eden?"

I think about it for a few seconds. I've spent so long dulling my pain, joy kind of got lost in the mix. "I don't think so. Or at least if I have, I don't remember."

"Me, neither. I've found a lot ways to simulate it over the years, but that's like renting a fancy car for the day and pretending you're a millionaire. It's self-delusion, and that's the saddest, most pathetic delusion of all." He runs his hand up my spine, until his palm is pressed against the skin between my shoulder blades. "But standing here, holding you ... this feels like the real deal."

The next song starts, and we sway once more. I wish I could turn my brain off around him, but I can't. Distrusting smooth men is second nature to me by now, and I have no idea how to train myself out of it.

"Did you like my gifts today?" he asks softly.

"To be honest, I don't usually go in for the whole hearts and flowers deal," I say. "But I must admit, you doing all of that ... going to so much trouble ..." I take a breath. "It made me feel like I'm not ordinary for once. I felt ... special."

He pulls back and looks at me as if I've just said the most obvious statement in the history of language. "That's because you are special. But sometimes it's nice to have someone remind you."

I look up at him. "And that's what you do, isn't it? Remind these women of their worth?"

He smiles. "My God, she's finally got it."

I pull a face and dig my fingers into his shoulder. "Yes, I catch on fast. Doesn't mean I don't still have a ton of questions."

"I'd expect nothing less of you, Miss Crane." A furrow forms between his eyebrows. "You know what? Let's kill the role-playing. I just want to dance with you. No characters. Just us. Okay?"

I try to drop my thorny demeanor and find out if I'm able to unlock my joy. "Okay."

For a few minutes, I let my guard down and enjoy being a regular girl who's dancing with a handsome man, but I'm brought unceremoniously out of the moment by my stomach growling so loudly, Max looks down at it and laughs.

"Jesus. Are you keeping wildlife in there?"

I put my hand on my abdomen. "Wow. So, that's what it sounds like when I forget to eat. It's never happened before."

Max puts his hand over mine. "Do you want to get out of here? I know where we can get New York's best pizza."

"God, yes. Please."

He takes my hand and leads me toward the exit. "Great. And since I sprang for the diamonds, you're buying."

Sixteen

Pizza and Epiphanies

I laugh as Max stands as far away from me as he can in the elevator, both of us carrying a pizza box.

"Max, come on."

"No. Keep your disgusting fruit pizza away from me. It's an abomination that will frighten my pure-blooded pepperoni."

"It's a little bit of pineapple, for God's sake. Not the Pizzapocalypse."

He glares as if I just insulted his mother. "Fruit on pizzas is unnatural, and those who eat it are monsters." He looks up at the lit numbers as we climb floors. "God, I was really starting to believe we could have something, Miss Tate. A real connection. But, now that you've revealed your true nature, I can barely look at you."

"Max –"

He holds up his hand. "No. Don't talk to me. I don't even know who you are anymore."

I suppress a smile as he grimaces in disgust. This is the most relaxed we've ever been with each other, and I have to admit, I like it. His mood from earlier has completely gone, and I wonder if ending the official part of the 'date' had something to do with it. Now that he's not playing a role, he's a mixture between Kieran, Caleb, and Maxwell, and I wonder if that's his secret to being so believable – all his roles are just different shades of himself.

"Max, can I –?"

"Stop talking. In fact, don't even look at me." He gestures with his head. "Turn around and face the wall. Go on."

I roll my eyes and humor him, and I hear the smile in his voice when he says, "Good girl. Now, take some time to think about what you've done."

I laugh, surprised that when he lets his guard down, he's actually a regular guy. I decide that for tonight, I'm going to try to ban all thoughts of mistrusting him. I still need to get answers to my questions, but maybe I can do it while enjoying hanging out and eating pizza.

I peek over my shoulder to find him staring at me. More specifically, at my ass.

I clear my throat, and he looks away.

"So," I say, feeling smug. "We're going to Maxwell's penthouse?"

He nods. "Each character has a different apartment. Maxwell's is kind of ... impressive."

"Do you own all of these?"

He snorts. "If I owned that much real estate, I could retire a wealthy man. Most of them I book through Air BnB."

Now it's my turn to snort. "Yeah, right."

He shrugs. "Don't really care if you don't believe me. You're a disgusting lover of fruit pizzas. You're barely human."

I'm still snickering when the elevator doors open to reveal the most incredible apartment I've ever seen.

"Oh ... my ... God." I walk into the huge penthouse, mouth gaping. It's plush and luxurious and has an entire wall of glass that showcases the breathtaking view, including the Empire State Building, front and center.

"What sort of freakazoid puts this up on Air BnB?"

"Someone who's not here a lot and wants to share the view." I barely notice when he takes my pizza box and walks into the kitchen. "Now, get your butt in here and eat. I can hear your stomach still growling, and it's getting louder."

I gawk at the view for another thirty seconds before turning to see him moving around in the gleaming white kitchen. He places a plate and napkin next to my pizza box then takes up position at the opposite end of the huge granite island.

"You stay down there with your monstrosity," he says as he opens his lid. "And if you tell me you need utensils to eat pizza, then we're done. Get the hell out of my presence with that nonsense." He shoves a giant slice of pizza in his mouth as I walk over and open my box.

God, it smells amazing, but there's no way I can eat pizza in the most beautiful dress on the planet. I'd ruin it within seconds.

I look at Max, who's inhaling his slice with impressive speed. "I don't suppose you have a robe or something. There's no way I could live with myself if I got pizza-grease on this gown.

He puts down his slice and wipes his hands on a napkin. "No robe, but I might have something that could work. Come with me."

I follow him across the living room and into the bedroom. The leather duffle bag he used as Caleb is there sitting on the bed, and a few articles of clothing are poking out the top. After throwing his phone and keycard onto the nightstand, he rifles through the bag and pulls out black sweatpants and a gray Led Zeppelin T-shirt and hands them to me. "These should do the trick. They're clean, in case you're wondering."

The shirt is the same one he wore as Kieran when we 'ran

into each other' at the bar. It seems I've come a long way since then, because I no longer have the urge to smack him for that deception.

"Thanks," I say as I put the clothes on the bed and pull my hair over my shoulder. "Could you unzip me?"

"Uh ... sure." He steps behind me, and I freeze as he slowly lowers my zipper. When it's all the way down, I hear him exhale but don't turn around. I assume he's just gotten a full view of the expensive underwear he sent me, and if I want to have any chance of resisting my attraction to him, I need to avoid seeing his face right now.

"Thank you. I'll be out in a minute."

I feel tension in the air for a few seconds, and then the warmth behind me disappears before the door closes with a quiet click. I blow out a breath as I take off the dress and lay it carefully on the bed. Then I remove my shoes and pull on the soft T-shirt.

Oh, Lord. It smells like him. Well, like Kieran, anyway. Lemongrass. My sense memory makes parts of me pulse uncomfortably. The shirt's so big it reaches the top of my thighs, and my body registers that Max's size definitely isn't a turn-off.

I pull on the pants, but the legs are so long, they cover my feet. Not to mention they fall straight down over my non-existent hips.

I pick them up and fold them neatly on the bed then take a deep breath.

Okay. I'm just going to eat pizza with him. Press him for information about his past. Get the story. Easy.

I pad back out into the kitchen to find Max has already polished off half of his pizza. When he looks over at me, he freezes mid-chew, his eyes wide and his jaw slack.

I go to my end of the bench and attack the largest piece in the box. He wasn't wrong about this being the best pie in New

York. Even with my heathen fruit tainting the flavor, it's freaking delicious.

"Oh, God. So good." I moan as try to fill the black hole inside me. Of course, only part of that hunger has to do with food.

When I finally look up from stuffing my face, Max is still frozen, watching me. After he catches me looking at him, he chews and swallows what's in his mouth, his eyes flashing with something that looks a hell of a lot like irritation.

"Where are the pants?"

"What?" My speech is muffled by the huge bite of pizza stuffed in my mouth.

"The pants I put out. You decided to not wear them?"

I shrug. "They were too big. I figured the shirt covered the important parts."

"Okay," he says. "No problem." He swipes the napkin across his mouth before placing it onto the counter. Then he slips off his jacket, throws it onto a nearby stool, and unclips his silver cufflinks before placing them next to the pizza box. While keeping his eyes locked onto me, he removes his tie and slowly begins popping open the black-enamel buttons on his dress shirt.

The temperature in the apartment suddenly skyrockets.

It takes effort to swallow as I watch him. "Uh ... what's happening?"

"I'm taking off my shirt."

"Why?"

"Because we've apparently reached the portion of the evening where we get semi-naked to torture the other person."

He pulls off his shirt and throws it onto the stool with his jacket, and I'll admit it, I gape. He looks at me coolly as he goes back to eating, as if he can't tell I'm being engulfed in the most scorching bout of lust to ever be felt by a human female.

Sweet Hot-Bodied Moses.

I've seen glimpses of his naked torso before now, but never the whole thing. And here he is, standing there wearing only his slim-cut dinner suit pants and a pissed-off expression, and I can't remember a single reason why I haven't licked him yet. I'm so turned on, my entire head could be on fire right now, and I wouldn't even notice.

His body is divine. Lean, hard pecs, beautiful arms, abs for days, and those amazing little muscles on the sides of his ribs that you just know would look like tiny waterfalls when he takes a shower.

I can feel my mouth hanging open, but I don't have the focus to do anything about it.

Jesus.

Who knew eating pizza would require so many muscles to bulge and flex? It's mesmerizing.

He notes my expression and smiles while chewing. "Are you done eating, Miss Tate? Or are you just hungry for something else now?" I don't understand how his face can do absolutely nothing and yet say so much.

Through sheer unwillingness to let my attraction dictate my actions, I pull my gaze away from him and go back to my pizza, which doesn't help banish the urge to eat the rest of my pie straight off his abs.

We chow down in silence for a while, both of us stealing glances when we think the other isn't looking, and even though the penthouse is the most spacious apartment I've ever been in, the tension in the air makes it feel tiny.

How had it come to this? I've never wanted to sleep with a man as much as I want to sleep with Max. I want it so much, I feel ill. My stomach is twisting around itself, my skin is hot, my heart is racing like I've just sprinted a few miles, and my brain is fuzzy with a dizzying rush of hormones. The worst part is

245

that, despite my earlier protestations, I'm seriously considering asking him to kiss me ... and not just on my mouth.

I think about how he'd taste as I stare at the thick muscles of his neck. Would he be gentle? Rough? Maybe a bit of both? I shift my attention to the delectable roundness of his shoulders; the plump curve of his biceps; the gentle slopes of his forearms. How long could I kiss him before my body screamed at me for more? A few minutes? Judging by my current state, it would take seconds, maybe less. I stare at his broad chest and taut stomach then become entranced by the angled grooves above his hipbones, the ones right where his pants are sitting. That leads me to notice that the front of his pants is bulging. Could it be he's just as aroused as I am? And if he is, how can this possibly be anything but disastrous for both of us and our so-called professionalism?

"Hey." He bends over until his face is in my line of sight. "Eyes up here, missy." When he straightens, I finish my last piece of pizza and wipe my face and hands.

"Got any alcohol?" I ask. I desperately need something to take the edge off my emotions. Staying down at this end of the island is getting more and more difficult.

"Nope. But I do have some soda." He goes to the fridge and gets out two bottles of Coke. "Why are you so determined to self-medicate around me? Or is it just the way you deal with life?" When he reaches into an overhead cabinet to get glasses, I marvel how his back flexes and the firm roundness of his butt in those snug pants. "You chug caffeine to stimulate you during the day and binge on alcohol at night. Does it help to numb you from the burning need to connect with someone on more than just a physical level?"

I laugh as he grabs ice from the freezer and fills the glasses. "And here I was thinking it was just my nan and sister who enjoyed browbeating me about my love life."

After pouring the soda, he walks over and hands me a glass. "You realize that people only browbeat you because they care, right?"

I look down at the bubbles as they rise to the surface and pop. "I don't know why it's such a big deal that I don't want a relationship. It's insane how society views people who are conscientiously single. If I'd gotten married to some loser and divorced him by now, no one would say a word. But a never-attached twenty-five-year-old is like a mythical harbinger of doom."

He leans against the island and crosses his arms over his chest. "So, you're telling me that you're happy, and determined to go through life alone?"

"I've done pretty well so far. I don't need another person to make me complete."

"Not needing someone and not *letting* yourself need someone are two different things. I'm not sure you know the difference."

"Then why don't you educate me? I know you want to."

He leans forward. "One is called independence. The other is denial. Humans need love and affection. We're pack animals. We're not designed to be alone."

"I like being alone. There's a certain peace in solitude."

"I agree. But are you sure you're not confusing solitude for loneliness? All animals need physical contact to feel love. Is that why you have sex with strangers? So you can pretend your need for affection is being fulfilled?"

I stare him down and try to think. I'm not used to being challenged in this way. Explaining my innermost thoughts and opinions isn't my idea of a good time. I like how things are with my life. Or at least how they were before I met him.

"Do you realize how often you Dr. Phil me?"

"Do realize how often you avoid my questions when I do?"

"I don't know why you keep turning this interview around to be about me."

He shrugs. "I just find you fascinating, that's all. It's like you think solitude is a logical defense against love, but it isn't. If cupid were real and needed to literally shoot you with an arrow to make you fall in love, then sure, your idea of locking yourself in a tower with no doors might work. But love is like a dormant disease." He puts down his glass and steps forward, and when he presses his cool hand over my heart, I pull in a tight breath. "It's already inside you, Eden. Just waiting for the right person to activate it."

I force myself to take even breaths and avoid the urge to look away. I hold my head high and wear my best poker face. "Maybe I'm just naturally immune."

His expression shows glimmers of sympathy, like he's a doctor giving a fatal prognosis. "No one's immune. But I do believe you're stubborn enough to ignore the symptoms for as long as you can, and one day you'll find out denying it damages you far more than giving someone your heart ever could."

Just when I've reached my last scrap of restraint in either having to kiss him or step away, he makes the decision for me. He takes his glass and strides into the living room, where he proceeds to flick through the impressive range of vinyl albums lining one of the bookcases.

Without looking at me he says, "But, hey ... what do I know, right? I'm just a college dropout who romances women for a living."

I take a cleansing breath and go and sit on the plush leather couch as he pulls out albums to examine them before placing them back.

"You dropped out of college?" I ask. "This is new information.

Care to elaborate?"

He studies the front of an album then flips it over to read the back. "Not really. I was in college when my life went to hell, and I dropped out to deal with it. End of story." He puts his drink down, so he can slide the record out of its sleeve.

"*End* of story? That seems like the beginning to me. At least tell me what you were studying."

He opens the record player and places the disc on the spindle, and even though he doesn't look at me as he sets the stylus, I can sense the tension in his face. "Music."

Sultry jazz filters through the high-end speakers as he comes to sit next to me, and he slides down until his head is leaning against the back of the couch. Then he man-spreads until his thigh is touching mine. "I really enjoyed it, too. Maybe I'll go back one day."

"So, that's why Caleb is such a convincing character? He's a lot like the real you?"

"I guess. I enjoy playing him the most."

"Where did you attend music school?"

He sighs. "If I tell you that, you'll try to track down my information, so ... no."

"Max, come on." I put my glass on the coffee table and kneel on the couch, so I can face him. "Full disclosure. That's what you told me. Do you not know the meaning of those words?"

He turns his head to look at me, and for the first time since I met him, he looks tired. As if the burden of being so many people other than himself sits heavy on his shoulders.

"Would you stop trying to make every moment with me about the damn story? Please, just sit here and relax." When I sit back down, he puts his arm around me and pulls me until I'm curled into his side, my head resting on his shoulder. "Just let's ... *be*, tonight. I'll worry about exposing my dark secrets to you another time. I promise."

I brace against him by placing my hand on his chest, and dear God ... part of me really wants to relish the casual intimacy of this position, but I don't know how.

"Just listen to the music," he says, his tone heavy with fatigue. "Breathe. Relax. Stop talking yourself out of experiences you should be talking yourself into."

I try to let go. I really do. I close my eyes and lean into him, and he slouches down so we're both more comfortable. The strong thud of his heart beneath my ear is strangely hypnotic.

"See?" he says, his voice quiet. "Would it be so bad to have something like this in your life? Someone like me?"

I take steady breaths, ignoring the thrumming currents racing from his body into mine.

"Can you feel that?" he whispers.

I squeeze my eyes tighter. "No."

He chuckles. "You're the worst liar I've ever met."

The music swirls around us, smooth and elegant. Max lightly runs his fingers down to my elbow, then back up to my shoulder, and the sensation is beyond incredible. I curl my hand into his chest and take his lead by using my fingertips to glide up to his clavicle, then down to the waistband of his pants. His skin contracts with goosebumps, and he makes a growly noise in his chest as he presses his head back into the couch.

"God, yes. That feels too good."

I love the feel of his skin, and he's basically given me permission to keep going, so I do. I run my hand over his shoulder and down to his bicep, where I press lightly before making my way to his forearm and feel thick muscles under smooth skin.

"If you're trying to drive me insane, Miss Tate, you're succeeding."

I look down to see that his crotch is swelling in response.

"Are you being unprofessional around me again, Mr. Riley? Because this is becoming a habit for you."

He lets out a humorless chuckle. "When we're together, I have no control over my body. I've given up trying."

"My offer stands to help take care of your urges."

"Don't tempt me. I'm trying to be Zen about what I want to do to you, but you don't make it easy."

The need in his voice pushes me over the edge, and moving slowly, I draw myself up and crawl into his lap. His eyes snap open as my knees settle on either side of his hips.

"What are you doing?"

"Getting comfortable. That's the idea, right? Relaxing with each other?" Following my body's directive and not much else, I lower down until the insistent throbbing in my groin is pressed against the hardest part of him, and we both moan the second I make contact.

"Fuck ... Eden." He closes his eyes again. "This is a bad idea."

"Then tell me you don't want it." I slide up while pressing against him. Then I close my eyes and moan as I slide down again, sharp pleasure piercing through me.

He pushes a breath out through his teeth as he closes his hands around my hips. "Oh, I want it, and if we were different people, I'd have already given into the hundreds of urges I have regarding you. But I suspect you're doing this for all the wrong reasons."

"When something feels this good," I say, as I press down, "how can it be wrong?"

I grip his bare shoulders as I circle my pelvis, and every time I hit the spot that makes him groan, I try to make him do it again. God. *This.*

It's exactly what I need from him; the antidote to the relentless pressure he builds within me. The grinding and moaning and pleasureable gasps. Not the other stuff that can't be cured by his hand, or dick, or well-trained tongue.

This is my solution, and if I can get it without taking my clothes off or getting my heart involved, great. Right now, I'll take whatever relief I can get.

I rise up and slide down, over and over again, riding the long ridge of him through his pants as I curl my hands into his hair and pretend he's just like all the other men I've had beneath me.

"Eden ... Jesus."

I tug at his hair, trying to block out anything that distracts me from lighting this powder keg. I'm kindling, and his body is flint, and if I do this right, it will be a cleansing fire that will reset my ridiculous body and its gravitational pull to him.

He groans beneath me and tightens his hands on my hips, and just as I open my eyes to see his tortured expression, he grunts in frustration and stands, making me squeal as he takes me with him. We're both panting when he sets me onto my feet and steps back.

"Eden, this isn't what I'm about. It's not what *we* should be about." He exhales and rubs the back of his neck. "I know what you're trying to do, and ... no. You can't make something that's beautiful but complicated into something simple and ugly out of sheer force of will."

"Max, I –"

"No, just listen for a minute. There's a difference between making love and having sex. And there's also a difference between having sex and fucking." He walks to the window, as if he doesn't trust himself if he remains close to me. "Sex is just body parts creating friction to get a physical release. *Fucking* is more intense. It's desperation. It's not that you'd *like* to have sex, it's that you *need* it. And you need it with that particular person, right the fuck now."

He paces, not looking at me. "And then there's making love. That's when you need to be a part of that person, and whether or not you come is irrelevant. You get so much pleasure from just being inside them, everything else is unimportant."

"I understand, but –"

He stops moving and faces me. "No, you don't, because you're goddamn terrified that out of those three options, sex is what you want the *least* from me."

I throw up my hands. "My vagina would disagree."

"That's because you're used to listening to it above all else while stifling your heart." He squares his shoulders, challenging me. "Just stop fighting the goddman obvious for five seconds and admit you have feelings for me."

I laugh. "Oh, that would make your night, wouldn't it? To prove your domination over me. The great Mister Romance and his unfailing ability to tie women into emotional pretzels."

"This isn't about our bet."

"Of course it is. Everything you do to me is about protecting yourself."

We glare at each other, but I'm not backing down. I'll be damned if he wins this easily. It's bad enough that he can read me like a book and play my body like he was born to do it. There's no goddamn way I'm going to admit to all the ways he owns me.

"If you want me to admit to something," I say, "… then here it is: I don't want to ride off into some mythical sunset with you, Max. That's not who I am. I want to fuck you and get my story, preferably in that order, and that's it."

He clenches his jaw before raking his hand through his hair in frustration. "For God's sake, Eden!"

"So, Miss Tate is finally out the window?"

He scowls. "You think I can even *pretend* to remain

professional with you anymore? You're so strong in so many ways, but right now, you look like a scared little girl. Why is it so difficult to cope with the thought that you *like* me?"

"My *God,* your ego —"

I stop short when he strides over to me, eyes flashing with fire. "Then deny it. Go ahead. But you better look into my goddamn eyes when you do it."

He's leaning down so his head is level to mine, and every smart-ass comment I had lined up to hurl at him dies in an instant. "Max ... I ..." I can't deal with the way he's looking at me, like he's itching to pounce on any half-truths.

"Okay, yes," I admit. "I'm attracted to you, but that doesn't mean I have feelings beyond desire."

"No? Okay then, if you're so sure that all you feel for me is physical ... let's go." He starts unbuckling his belt.

"What?"

"Take off your underwear and get over here." He walks over to the kitchen and slaps the marble bench. "We could start here then move the couch. Maybe up against the windows. That would be hot. You taking in the view while I fuck you from behind. We could give the tourists on the observation deck a real show."

"Max —"

He notices that I haven't moved. "Come on, Eden. If sex is the answer, then tell me what you want, in what position, how many orgasms you'd like ... I'll do it all. Free of charge."

"So all that crap about you not sleeping with your clients —"

"Is *a hundred percent* true. You're not my client. You never have been. And even if you were, I'd break every fucking rule I've ever held sacred just to be inside you right now. I've *never* wanted a woman as much as I want you, so if you want to fool yourself that this is just about hormones ... *fine*. I'll help you work me out of your system one thrust at a time. But then, that's it. After we've had our way with each other, we're done."

He's so worked up, he's panting, and my breathing isn't much better. The mere thought of not seeing him again makes me feel sick.

"Come on, Max," I say, attempting a smile. "This is crazy." I try to laugh it off, but he's being serious enough right now for the both of us.

He walks to where I am, the intensity of his eyes drilling into me. "You just looked me in the eyes and told me sex is all you want from me, Eden, so let's do it. Fuck me until all those inconvenient urges go away, and then I'm out of your life forever. I'll never inflict myself upon you again."

"I ... I still need to see you for the story."

"You can email me questions. I'll email back. Strictly business. Is that how you want it between us?"

He's standing close now, and because I can't look into his eyes anymore, I watch his fists clenching and releasing instead.

"Max, I don't ... I don't know what I want."

He exhales, and when he speaks again, it's softer. "Yes, you do. You're just too damn stubborn to say it. You want me, but not for one night. You want me in your life. You want me in ways you've never desired any other man, and that has you fucking *terrified*. You want me *exactly* the same way I want you."

"No."

"Yes." When I look up at him, I see such raw disappointment in his expression that my stomach squirms with guilt. "But if you're not ready to accept that, then there's nothing I can do. I can't force you to take a chance on me." He swallows and shakes his head. "Go get dressed. I'll take you home."

I look at him for a moment, feeling more lost and confused and ... *small* than I ever though possible. He's asking me to open a door that's been closed my whole adult life, but not only do I not have the key, I have absolutely no idea where to even look for it.

I turn and head toward the bedroom. Just before I reach it, he says, "Do you know why you avoid real connections, Eden?"

I look back at him. He has his hands in his pockets, and he's staring in my direction but not looking directly at me.

"Why?"

"Because it's easier for you to think being alone is a choice rather than admitting you might be unlovable." He looks me in the eyes. "Let me tell you, you're not. Not even a little. The man who made you think that – whoever the hell he was – couldn't have been more wrong."

I hold his gaze while trying to lock down a storm of emotions that are filling me up in unfamiliar and painful ways. And when he gives up waiting for me to change my mind

and looks away, I head into the bedroom and gently close the door.

CR

Getting back into my dress by myself is difficult. Honestly, I'd rather just curl into a ball on the massive bed and sleep for a week, if only to forget about everything that just happened. Instead, I awkwardly zip myself up as best as I can and bite my tongue every time I even think about calling out for Max to help.

I've just finished pulling on my shoes when I hear a buzzing noise. I turn to see his phone on the nightstand, screen bright in the dim room as it skitters and vibrates.

Unable to resist, I walk over and check the screen. A text message is there from someone called Dyson:

<Hey, buddy. Me & Rosco will be at the warehouse at 7am tomorrow to grab furniture. Should make it to markets by 8. See you then.>

The warehouse? God, I'd almost forgotten he'd arranged for Nannabeth to sell his furniture at her stall tomorrow. And they're picking it up at the warehouse? Intriguing.

I glance at the door, but it's still safely closed. I shouldn't be thinking about showing up and seeing what I can find, right? I should wait until he's ready to level with me about what he's hiding. But judging by how tonight has gone, the day he trusts me with his secrets may never come.

I grab my purse and exhale before pulling open the door and walking out. When I get out to the living room, Max is seated, fully dressed at the desk, staring at his computer screen. When he sees me, he closes the lid and stands, his face unreadable. "Ready?"

"You don't have to take me home."

"Yes, I do. This was a date night. The least I can do is escort you to your door."

After the world's most awkward elevator ride, we head out into the street and he flags a taxi. We're both silent as we ride through Manhattan and across the Brooklyn Bridge, and it feels wrong to be on one side of the cab while he's on the other.

I glance at his hand splayed on the seat next to his thigh as he gazes out the window. I have the strongest feeling that if I just reached over and slid my fingers between his, this revolting tension would melt away, but maybe things cooling down between us is for the best. One of the first things I learned as a journalism student was to beware of getting too close to my sources, and now I know why. I've gotten so close to Max I've lost every ounce of my objectivity, and that's unacceptable. I'm supposed to report the story, not become part of it.

I shake my head at how miserably I've screwed everything up and go back to staring out the window. There's no danger of me being too close to Max anymore. Right now it feels like the distance between us is growing wider every minute.

The whole journey passes without either of us saying a word, and it's not until we're standing outside the door to my apartment that we even make eye contact.

Max gives me a tight smile before lifting my hand to his mouth and kissing it. "Thank you for your company tonight, Miss Tate. It was a pleasure."

It bothers me that he's gone back to calling me Miss Tate. It feels wrong now. Cold.

I take my keys from my purse and try to look happy. "Thank you, Mr. Riley. Despite everything, I ... I had a really great time."

He smiles, but I can't help feeling he's being someone else right now. Someone who I haven't disappointed and hurt.

He takes my keys and leans over to unlock the door, but before he does, he stops.

"Eden ... the man who hurt you. Was it your father?"

He doesn't look at me, which is good. Maybe I can try to be honest if we don't make eye contact. "Why do you think that?"

"I went back and looked at your questionnaire. When you were asked for a paragraph about your parents, you said a lot about your mother but didn't mention your father once. If it was him, it would explain why you distrust men so much."

He unlocks the door and hands me back the keys. "Plenty of women are hurt by men, but the deepest wounds are left by our parents." He says it gently, like he's afraid of how I might react.

He doesn't understand how many times I've practiced being unaffected by my father's actions.

He clears his throat. "What did he do to you?"

I don't know if he's expecting some shocking tale of sexual

abuse, but that's not what happened. There are dozens of hideous ways to ruin a child. My dad used the simplest one.

"He ignored me. Saw through me like I wasn't there."

I've never admitted that to another person. Telling Max doesn't feel good, but it does feel right.

"I always thought fathers had to love their kids," I say, staring at the buttons on Max's shirt. "Like it was a requirement or something. But whenever I tried to hug Dad or get him to play with me, he treated me like an inconvenience. Like my existence annoyed him." Even now, with all the time that's passed, those memories have surprising power to hurt me. "Mom would say 'Daddy's just tired', or 'Daddy doesn't like to play', but I knew. Kids always know."

I hear a noise, and when I glance at Max's face, he looks just as furious as he did earlier on the phone.

"Tell me everything," he says, his voice gentler than his expression.

I shrug. "When Asha came along, he was a completely different person. She was his angel, and I was just ... the other one."

"Do you have any idea why he was like that?"

I look at the window down the end of the hallway. "Once, when Mom and Dad were fighting, I heard my name. Mom was saying that he couldn't treat me like nothing and Asha like everything ... that it wasn't fair. He countered by saying I was the chain Mom used to keep him with her, so how could she expect him to love me?"

"Your mom was pregnant before they got married?"

I nod. "Once I found out, it explained a lot. I wasn't his daughter. I was the weight around his legs, drowning him in his own life."

He steps closer and wraps his fingers around mine. "Eden ...

I'm sorry."

I give him a faltering smile. "Don't be. It wasn't your fault."

"I'm still sorry it happened to you."

I look down at my purse and fiddle with the line of pearls around the edge. "Even after he left us all high and dry, Mom never stopped believing he just needed time to 'find himself' or whatever. Sometimes when he needed money, he'd come back for a few days. He'd bring flowers and chocolates and tell Mom he loved her, and she'd take him back every time."

I look at Max with a bitter smile. "He was a lying sack of shit. Why the hell would she do that?"

He nods like he understands only too well. "Sometimes, people stick with what they know, even if all they've known is misery."

"The thing I'll never understand is, even while Mom worked herself to the bone supporting two kids by herself, she never allowed us to say a bad word against him." I shake my head. "I vowed I'd never be like her. In so many ways she was a strong woman, but when it came to my father, she was weak. He *made* her weak. That's not going to happen to me."

I see understanding in his eyes, and his posture falls, as if he's discovered the hill he thought he'd been climbing with me is actually a mountain.

"Maybe that's why you scare me," I say. "In a lot of ways, you remind me of him. He was handsome like you. He had green eyes like you. He had a way of melting women with a glance like you."

He cups my face and urges me to look into his eyes. "There's one important difference between him and me."

"Which is?"

"I have no idea how he treated you like you were invisible. When I'm with you, you're all I see."

He stares at me for a second before stepping forward and pressing his lips to my forehead. "You should get some rest. I'll call you tomorrow."

He gets one step away before I grab his hand to stop him. When he turns back with a perplexed expression, I step forward and stand on my toes to press my lips against his. For the longest second in human history, we freeze, lips conducting enough shared energy to detonate a supernova. I move first, releasing his lips and then moving in again. I press against his warmth, tasting his top lip and then the bottom. He doesn't move and is still standing rigid when I pull back to see his face.

"Max?"

He stares at me, his jaw tight. "I promised you I wouldn't."

I grab his shirtfront and pull him forward. "For the love of God, Max ... I give you permission to kiss me."

With those words, it's like I've released a lion from its cage. He grabs my face with both hands and presses me back into the wall as he takes my lips. I groan and open my mouth to him, and I've never felt the kind of hunger that consumes me as his taste filters through all my senses. When his tongue slides softly against mine, it unleashes more sensation than I know how to handle. I drop my purse and grasp at him, all the areas I can reach; his arms and shoulders, the curve of his butt, his chest, the back of his neck. Every part of him feels incredible, and it all makes me ache for more.

When I slide my fingers into his hair and pull, he makes an animalistic sound before reaching around to grab my butt with both hands and pressing me tightly against him.

"God, Max ..." He's rock hard, and knowing it's me who's done that to him only makes me kiss him more passionately.

He moans against my tongue, his hands angling me exactly where he wants me as the unbelievable taste of him drives me insane. I grunt against the tidal wave of need that hits me. As crazy as my attraction to Max has been, nothing could prepare me for this feeling of pure insatiability. No matter how hard I try, there's no way for me to get close enough, or kiss him deep enough, and the more I try, the dizzier I get.

I've never felt like this with any other man ... nothing even remotely close to this. I'm not equipped to deal with it. The desperation is raw and relentless. He seems to feel it too because he grunts as he presses me against walls then pulls me away, only to push me to the opposite side, shoving me noisily against the dated wallpaper.

I knew kissing him would be something I could never come back from, and right now even my fear isn't strong enough to ruin it. For the first time in my life, I feel like I'm wide awake and dreaming at the same time.

For long, hazy minutes we kiss each other like we're afraid to stop. Like the world could come crashing down in a fiery apocalypse around us, and neither of us would notice.

In fact, neither of us does notice when Mrs. Levine from the apartment next door comes to see what all the commotion is about. It's only when she clears her throat loudly that we pull back, both surprised by our elderly spectator.

"Eden," Mrs. Levine says with a tight nod. She gives Max a long look up and down as he tidies himself up and runs his hand through his hair. "Man attached to Eden."

I lean against the wall and try to calm the hell down as Max steps forward, who despite his best efforts, still looks the victim of an animal attack. His tie is half off, his shirt is untucked, and his hair is everywhere.

Still, he smiles at Mrs. Levine as if nothing has happened and holds out his hand. "Maxwell Riley, ma'am. Pleased to meet you."

Mrs. Levine glares at him for two seconds before breaking into a toothless grin. Oh, man, I hate it when she doesn't wear her dentures.

She puts her hand in his, and he gives it a gentle squeeze. Mrs. Levine bends sideways to look at me around his body. "Oh, Eden, he's lovely."

I smooth down my dress and give her an unsteady smile. He is lovely, but in the emotionally stunted world of Eden Tate, that doesn't make all my trust issues pack up and leave. If anything, it makes them worse.

"Sorry to disturb you, Mrs. Levine," I say with a wave. "It won't happen again. Have a good night."

She gives Max one more head-to-toe assessment before giggling under her breath and going back into her apartment.

Max turns back to me, looking as shell-shocked as I feel. Tonight, we've gone from romance, to arguing, to making out like demons in a public hallway, and those things combined with the fact I laid bare my pathetic childhood makes things become awkward again real fast.

After I open my apartment door and turn back to him, he steps forward, hesitantly. "Eden ... I –"

"I should go in. Goodnight, Max." I can't deal with any more emotional upheaval tonight, even if the concept of not kissing him again is physically painful.

For a moment, it looks as though he's going to say something, but then he shoves his hands in his pockets and nods. "Goodnight, Eden."

I close the door and then lean my head against the cool wood until his footsteps disappear down the hallway.

What the hell am I doing?

Perfect good looks, perfect body, perfect mouth, and perfect, caring heart. I didn't think someone as perfect as Max could possibly exist in the world, and that's why my stomach is sitting in my shoes. Because if I know one truth above all others in this world, it's this: if something seems too good to be true, it usually is.

Even if I could contemplate letting him into my life, for all I know, the passionate man with the mysterious past I spent the evening with is just one more character in his romantic arsenal. Until I find out more about who he was before he became New York's favorite escort, the jury is out, and there's no way in hell I can allow myself to get in any deeper. Especially considering the volatile temper I saw on him tonight.

I swallow down the paranoid scenarios playing in my mind as I strip off the trappings of the glamorous woman I've been for the past few hours and get ready for bed. And when I set my alarm for six a.m., I tell myself I'm not doing it so I can get up early enough to scope out the warehouse that could contain all of Max's secrets.

Seventeen

Family Secrets

I poke my head out from behind the dumpster to see if there's a truck outside the warehouse yet. There isn't. It seems that whoever this Dyson person is, his idea of 7am is vague and inaccurate. It's now 7:18, and there's still no sign of him.

I'm torn about this mission to snoop on Max, especially considering everything that happened between us last night, but I can no longer let my emotions sideline my objectivity. No matter how charming and magnetic he might be, I still have a job to do, and with Derek breathing down my neck to see a partial draft of my story on Monday, I don't have time for Max to keep stalling about his past. If he has skeletons in his closet, that's fine, but I'd rather know about it now than be blindsided later.

"Any truck action?" Toby asks from behind me.

"Not yet."

He sighs, loudly. "You wake me up at the asscrack of dawn, get me all excited about being spies, and now we're just sitting around, waiting."

I turn to him. He's leaning again the wall behind the dumpster, sipping his soy milk latte and munching on a seven-dollar granola bar he picked up on the way. When I called him at 6:30

to see if he could help me out, he jumped at the chance, but I didn't count on him dressing up in his best paramilitary gear. Of course, for Toby that means khaki skinny jeans, a grungy black T-shirt, a black beanie, and a camouflage-print cardigan. Yes, I said a *camo* cardigan.

"Have I mentioned what you're wearing yet?" I ask. "Because seriously ... I have so many thoughts."

He looks down at himself then back to me. "What? You said we'd be doing crime, so I wore my most crimey outfit."

"Toby, first of all, you don't 'do' crime; you commit crime, and the only person committing anything this morning will be me. You're just my distraction. And second, never in the history of the world has any criminal thought to themselves, 'Hmmm, you know what this felony calls for? A nice camo cardigan.' Where on earth did you even find that thing?"

"I've had it for years. It's both kickass and comfortable, so you can stop giving me shit about it."

"You look like you belong in a retirement home for hipster bird watchers."

He waves his giant leather-cuff wrist watch in front of his face. "*Sching! Sching!* Just deflected all of your negative energy."

"How many cardigans do you own, anyway?"

He shrugs and has another sip of coffee. "The usual amount. Thirty. Forty."

I roll my eyes and go back to staking out the warehouse. When I see a truck making its way down the alley, I elbow Toby. "Showtime, Soy Rambo."

He comes over and looks out, his head sitting above mine. The truck backs up to the roller door right next to the mural stairs, and two guys get out. I recognize one of them as my former pool partner, 'Pat', the giant Irishman. I'm guessing he's Dyson.

Huh. Actor and furniture mover. Multi-talented.

"You know," Toby says, "if you wanted someone to distract those burly dudes, you should have brought your sister. I know she's in France, but as attractive as I am, I'm not sure they'll take much notice of me."

"Sure they will. You know that stupid character of yours you do around the office?"

"Hertzog, the Particularly Dense German Tourist? Oh, *ja.*"

I hand him a map of Manhattan I snagged at a news stand on the way. "Feel free to make him extra dense today."

"*Ja, ja, ja!*" He takes the map. "*Wunderbar!*"

After his buddy opens the back of the truck, Dyson goes straight to the keypad and punches in a number. Clearly, he's in Max's inner circle. The door buzzes as it unlocks, and he yanks it open before heading inside. Within a minute, the roller door opens, and he ushers the other dude, who I'm assuming is Rosco, to follow him. They emerge a short time later carrying a large and expensive-looking dining table.

"And today on *Removalist Wars*," Toby whispers in a British accent, "Danny and Brett are going for the gold with an oak eight-seater. They've loaded it onto the truck, now let's see what they do ... Oh, yes, I think they're going back for the chairs. Well, this is good form from the New York boys. If they keep it up, we could see them in the final."

I stifle my laughter as I nudge Toby. If I get arrested for trespassing, at least I'll be smiling in my mug shot.

"You ready?" I say.

"I was born ready, fräulein. You want me to hang around until you get out?"

"Nah. As soon as I'm done I have to go and help Nannabeth at the markets. Thanks, Tobe. You're a life saver."

"Yeah, well, what can I say? I'm a giver. Still, if you wanna pay me back by taking a few pics of yourself in a Leia slave outfit, I'd be down with that. See you next week."

I pat him on the arm as he passes.

When he gets to the dock, the guys have their arms full with padded chairs. He waves the map at them and loudly says, "Excuse me! You can help me? Zis subvay system is most confusing, *ja*? Vere am I finding ze Times Square? It is near here?"

The guys put their chairs down and laugh. "Pal, you've taken about a dozen wrong turns. You're not even in Manhattan any more. You have to get back on the subway."

"You will show me vere to go?"

For a few minutes they try verbal instructions, but when Hertzog can't understand them, they jump down off the dock to point to the map. Hertzog walks them away from the truck as he struggles with their directions, and as soon as they're at a safe distance, I make my move. Running as quietly as I can, I dash to the dock, climb up, and duck inside the roller door. The urge to commando roll hits me, but I have no time for that right now.

As soon as I step inside the warehouse, I'm hit by the sheer size of it. For the most part, it's a massive empty space that would make a fantastic mega skating rink. Then I notice that to my left are some overhead lights illuminating a stack of furniture and boxes, and the end of the area is blocked off with wire fencing like a security cage. I can see a collection of old office furniture in there, including bookcases that are being used for storage.

I quickly run down to the end, and when I discover the door on the cage is unlocked, I scoot inside and hide behind what looks like a tall clothing rack, covered in a dust cloth. Toby must have taken off, because I can hear Dyson and Rosco's voices clearer now as they come to grab more furniture.

"We'd better hustle," Dyson says. "Max will shit if we keep

the old lady waiting for this stuff." Not a hint of Irish today. He sounds like he's from Queens.

"Where's he been, anyway?" Rosco asks. "He's missed poker night two weeks in a row."

"He's freaking out about some reporter who's been sniffing around. I guess he's trying to get rid of her or whatever."

I take in a sharp breath.

Those words cut through the parts of me that had begun to trust Max. The parts that wanted to believe what he felt for me was more than just a con. Of course, the bitter side of me that's been trying to avoid falling for him this whole time feels vindicated my mistrust was founded.

"Come on," Rosco says. "Grab the end tables first, and we'll come back for the credenza."

"What the hell is a credenza?"

"That big thing with the drawers."

"Then just say 'that big thing with the drawers'. What are you? The King of England?"

I sit cross-legged on the floor as they finish loading the truck and try to tell myself that knowing Max has been playing me doesn't hurt.

See? This is exactly why I don't put myself out there. Men lie. They flatter and flirt and kiss you stupid whenever it suits them and fucking *lie* to make you feel things. And then they break you, the same way my father broke my mother. I shouldn't be surprised that Max is no different from the rest of them, but I am. Surprised and more disappointed than I've ever been in my life.

I close my eyes and push down the hurt. It only fuels my determination to find out what the hell he's so intent on hiding.

At last the guys finish up, and the warehouse is plunged into darkness as they turn out the lights and close the door. When the rumbling of the truck fades away, I grab my phone and turn on the flashlight.

"Okay, Max. Let's see what all this stuff is."

The first thing I do is find the light switch and turn the lights back on, so I can take a quick inventory of what's underneath the dust cloths. Even after the Dyson and Rosco removed a truck full of furniture, there's still some left, and from what I can tell, Max has a pretty swanky collection. It leads me to wonder why he'd want to sell it for cash with my Nan, when he could probably get more money through a dealer. He said he inherited it, but from whom?

Alongside the furniture are some cardboard boxes. I open the closest one and look through the contents. There are several trophies with the name Max Roberts on them—baseball, football, and even one for music. So, I guess the guy I spent the evening with yesterday was the real Max after all. I'm not sure how I feel about that, considering I've never felt so intensely intimate with someone before. Beneath the trophies is a certificate for achievement in music made out to Max Riley Roberts.

So, Riley is his middle name.

At the bottom of the box I find a few crumpled photographs of Max in high school. It's strange, but the boy in the pictures looks quite different from the Max I know. Grown-up Max might be a little too smug for my liking, but young Max looks flat-out arrogant. And more than a little aggressive. In most pictures, he seems to be scowling, not smiling.

I go to another box. It contains files and some printouts of news reports about something called Fulcrum Financial. As I rifle through the faded articles, one of the headlines jumps out at me. *Carl Roberts Faces Fraud Charges Over Fulcrum Financial Collapse.*

I scan through the article. From the picture of the handsome middle-aged man below the article, I assume Carl was Max's dad. None of the other articles tell me what happened to him, so I do a quick search on my phone.

"Oh, shit."

Seems like Daddy Dearest got hit up on a class-B felony for embezzlement and insider trading and was sentenced to eight years. The date indicates it was three years ago, and I'm guessing that was around the same time Max dropped out of college.

I spread the articles on the floor and photograph them. They may come in handy for background info.

Checking the time on my phone, I realize I need to speed this up or risk Nannabeth's wrath, not to mention getting caught. I quickly put the boxes back where I found them and move into the fenced-off area. When I lift up the dust cloths draped over the clothing rack, I discover it's filled with dozens of costumes. Max wasn't joking when he said he had a cowboy hat and chaps. And yes, he also has a white navy uniform, similar to the one Richard Gere filled out so nicely in *An Officer and a Gentlemen*. I can see that would be a popular fantasy.

He also has costumes for a firefighter, biker, and army dude, among others. I wonder if he's used all of them. Then I get powerful flash of jealousy at the thought of him playacting with other women.

Goddammit.

Why couldn't I just resist feeling anything for him? Liking someone I'll never have isn't a feeling I've ever wanted to experience.

At the side of the room, there's a small set of mahogany drawers sitting on a table. When I open the top drawer, I gasp. It's shallow and lined with black velvet, and inside is a collection of stunning jewelry. By the looks of it, the stones are real.

"Whoa."

This must be where he got the necklace he gave me last night.

All of a sudden, a horrible possibility occurs to me. Could Max be using his position of trust with these rich women to relieve them of their finery? A little involuntary tip for his services. Is that his big secret?

God, no. He wouldn't.

The thought makes me queasy. I know I'm just speculating, but I can't discount it as a possibility. His father was a thief and a criminal. Maybe Max is following in his footsteps.

I'm so focused on scanning my memories for further proof of corruption, I jump when I hear, "They were my mother's."

I whip around to see Max there, standing a few feet away with his hands shoved deep into the pockets of his leather jacket. His expression is one of supreme disappointment. He looks like I feel, which is sick to the stomach.

"I'm not a thief, Eden."

There's so much raw emotion in his voice, I'm taken aback. "I didn't think you –"

"Yes, you did. I know how your mind works by now."

I feel my face flush in embarrassment. "There are a lot of beautiful pieces here. Your mom had good taste. Expensive, too."

"My father bought them for her."

I nod. "Ah, so he was Mister Romance senior?"

His face twists, and he laughs, short and bitter. "No. Not at all." His shoulders bunch. "What are you doing here?"

I close the drawer and slide my phone into my pocket. "I'm just trying to find out the truth, Max."

"I had every intention of telling you the truth."

"When?" He stares at me, unblinking. "I know I shouldn't be here, but you're the king of stonewalling. For all the time we've spent together, I still know virtually nothing about you

– the *real* you. Is it any wonder I'm having trouble trusting your motivations? Yes, we've been getting close, but you're a fantastic actor. And let's not forget, you gloated you could make me feel something for you as a way of killing the story. So the fun time at Maxwell's apartment and then the kiss ... For all I know, this is all part of your grand plan to protect yourself."

"My grand plan went out the window the moment I realized I was the one developing feelings."

"That's what you say, but according to the steroid twins who moved your furniture today, you're freaking out about a reporter who's been sniffing around and working your ass off to get rid of me."

A muscle in his jaw ticks as he stares at me. "And you found it all too easy to believe, didn't you?"

"I honestly don't know what to believe anymore. My brain hurts, and for the first time since I was eleven years old, my heart hurts. And neither of those things feels good." I rub my face, feeling tired and thoroughly confused. "All I wanted out of this arrangement was a story. That's it. Not whatever the hell is happening between us."

"Do you think I had any intention of feeling like this? Because in case you don't already know it, you're a pain in the ass. You complicate my life in the most intoxicating ways, and everything I used to want has been thrown into chaos because of my intense goddamn *need* for you."

Every time he says something like that, he carves another chink in my armor. But if I accept him at his word, I have everything to lose, and he has everything to gain. Admitting I want him means he's won, and the moment I kill my story, he'll have a free pass to say, "Oh, oops. Never mind. All those pesky feelings have conveniently vanished. See ya!"

He waits for me to say something, and when I don't, he walks over to the desk beside me and pulls a framed picture from the top drawer. "Okay, fine. It looks like we're doing this." He hands me the picture. "This is my fucked-up family." I study the faces looking back at me. "At least it *was*. I don't have a family anymore."

The picture was taken in a garden, with what must be his mom and dad laughing as they hug their two tall sons. I recognize Max but not the other good-looking boy.

"That's my older brother, Spencer. He died of a drug overdose when I was seventeen." He points to his father. "That piece of shit is my dad, and he's currently lazing around in a cushy white-collar prison for screwing hundreds of people out of their life savings. And that ..." He swallows as he brushes his finger over the pretty woman's face. "That's ... my mom." He stares at her with a haunted expression. "She killed herself three weeks after Dad was arrested, which was six months after Spencer died."

He opens the back of the frame and pulls out the picture. "Here," he says. "You'll need to scan this for the story. Spencer overdosed on heroin, in case your editor asks. And mom took sleeping pills. Dad's due for parole in a few months, but I really hope he doesn't get it. He doesn't deserve to be free after everything he's done. He's dead to me." Max thrusts the photo into my hand. "Take it. You're right, I've been holding out on you. I promised you full exposure, so here it is."

"Max ..."

He walks over to a filing cabinet and yanks open the drawer. "I have more pictures of Spence in here somewhere. Even a couple taken at a party where he looks like he's out of his mind on drugs, which he probably was. And there's a nice one of Mom that was from a charity event a few weeks before she died." He rifles through a box of photos in the bottom of the drawer. "There are even a few of me at my high school prom.

I'm sure you'll get a laugh out of them."

When I walk over and put my hand in the middle of his back, he freezes.

"I'm sorry," I say. "I shouldn't have come here. I should have waited until you were ready, and I –"

That's as far as I get before he spins around and pushes me up against the filing cabinet as he kisses me. The unexpectedness of it shocks me into stillness for a second, but as soon as I register the warmth of his lips against mine, I moan and open my mouth to him.

Jesus, the taste of him. The white-hot hunger that flares when he kisses me as deep as he can. He groans in relief as I kiss him back, and then things go from hot to downright incendiary when he picks me up, and I wrap my legs around his waist. He shoves my back flush against the filing cabinet as he grinds against me. The metal clangs loudly when he plants his hand on top of it to get more leverage. The rock-solid feel of him, even through his jeans and mine, launches my body into a level of arousal it's never felt before. I squirm and pull him closer, trying to get some relief from the incessant pulsing between my legs.

"God ... Max."

I anchor my hands in his hair as he kisses my neck, nipping and sucking, his breath hot and ragged. I want to get naked with him. Tear off the clothes separating us and press my fevered flesh to his hard, warm skin. He talked last night about the difference between sex and fucking, and right now, there is zero doubt in my mind I need Max Riley to fuck me, furiously and with zero restraint.

With rough, desperate hands, I shove his jacket off his shoulders, and he puts me back onto my feet so he can help. My jacket is next, flying onto the desk as I press Max against the wire fencing and palm his erection.

He throws his head back and closes his eyes. "Fuck, Eden."

"I need this," I say, savoring the hard line of him. "Please."

I fall to my knees and start on his belt, but before I can get it unbuckled, strong hands close over mine. "Wait."

I look up at him in confusion. "You can't tell me you don't want this."

"I'm not. I'd like nothing more right now than to fuck you until we both can't see straight ... but I can't."

"Sure, you can," I say as I stroke him through the thick denim. His eyelids flutter, and his fingers curl around the chain link fence. "You take off your clothes, I take off mine. We do what we want to each other and get relief from the hell our bodies are in. This doesn't have to be complicated."

He gently pulls me to my feet. "Whether we like it or not, it *is* complicated. And with what I still have to tell you, it's about to get worse." He retrieves my jacket and hands it to me. "When we have sex, Eden, I intend it to be the start of something special. Not some desperate quickie in a dusty warehouse. And once you hear my full story, you might decide even that's more than you want from me."

He pulls out the chair from behind the desk and gestures to it. "Please, sit."

He grabs another chair from near the wall and sits at the end of the desk, facing me. The positioning makes me feel like I'm conducting a job interview. In a way, I guess I am. With most men, the only thing I'm interested in is their body. Once the flush of arousal fades, so does my desire to have them anywhere near me. With Max, I want him near me all the time, whether he's touching me or not, which is why I'm vaguely hoping that what he's about to tell me will be so unforgivable, I'll never want to see him again.

Max leans forward, forearms on his thighs, hands clasped

together. His expression is so grave, I become genuinely concerned.

"I didn't bring up my family before now, because I was ... ashamed. I wasn't ready for you to know the person I used to be. But ... nothing I'm about to say changes how I feel about you. I need you to know that."

"Jesus, Max, you're really starting to freak me out. Did you kill someone or something?"

I expect him to laugh at that, because I was going for ridiculous to lighten the mood, but he doesn't.

"What would you say if I did?"

I look for any sign that he's joking and swallow nervously when I don't find one. When he sees the horror dawning on my face, he looks away. "The first thing you need to know is that as far back as I can remember, my dad tortured my mom."

That makes my skin crawl. "He was violent?"

"Not with his fists, but he pummeled the hell out of her with his words every damn day. Taunted her. Belittled her. Committed psychological warfare every chance he got. I've since discovered that he's a malignant narcissist, so that should tell you something about how bad he was. And the most shameful admission I can possibly make to the woman I have feelings for is that ..." He takes a breath. "... there was a time when I wanted to be just like him."

I'm shell-shocked. This man – the one who's chivalrous and polite, who holds chairs and doors with such deference and care – he looked up to his abusive father?

"Max, I find that hard to believe."

His expression turns steely. "Believe it. Before everything went to hell, people thought we were a great family. Rich, loving, successful. It was all a lie." He gazes at a spot on the wall behind me, and it's clear admitting this stuff is easier when he's not looking at me.

"Dad treated Mom like she was a second-class citizen, while making Spence and me think we were gods. We were indoctrinated to believe that men ruled the world and women did what they were told, so we didn't even question the way he treated Mom. It was natural. When we were old enough to realize that not all women were treated like that, it was too late."

He shakes his head, angry at himself. "In our minds, Mom's job was to keep us fed and the house organized, as well as look pretty and play nice for Dad's rich, society friends. Her whole world was made to revolve around us, and that was the way we liked it. Especially Dad. Toxic masculinity at its finest."

He looks over at the jewelry box, shame etched into his features. "There's no doubt in my mind that we were the reason she killed herself. Her blood is on our hands. Especially mine." He's squeezing his hands together so hard, his knuckles crack.

I don't know how he'd react to me touching him right now, so instead I try to make my voice as soothing as possible. "Max ... I can't talk about the reasons your mom did what she did, but you can't take responsibility for –"

"She asked for my help." He clenches his jaw. "She tried talking to me about how she was feeling, and I ... I brushed her off. I didn't have the time. I had more important things to do." He goes quiet. "She tried to tell me she was struggling with depression, and I ignored it."

I don't know what to say. How can I possibly console him over that? It's something he'll have to live with for the rest of his life.

"I'm sorry."

He stares at a spot on the floor. "I look back at how I treated my girlfriends in high school, even the few I dated in college, and I'm horrified. I'm disgusted that I allowed myself to be molded into my father's image." He looks over at me, a world of regret in his eyes. "I know you don't trust me ... that you may never trust me ... but I'm genuinely trying to tip the karmic scales back to make up for what I did. I give my clients the man they need, whoever the hell that may be. I couldn't do it for my mom, but I can sure as hell do it for them."

It's hard for me to think of Max treating women like possessions, but perhaps the anger I saw in him last night, the hard, dominating side of Maxwell, was a glimpse into how that might look.

"The phone call last night—"

"Was from my dad. He kept talking about all the things he wants us to do together when he gets out. I just want to beat him senseless for what he did to Mom. But as satisfying as I'd find that, it wouldn't bring her back. And it wouldn't change him. No matter how many people he destroys, he'll always think he's the sun, and the rest of the solar system should revolve around him." He shakes his head. "I don't care anymore. I have no father."

Well, there's something we both have in common. "Maybe your dad and my dad should get together and go bowling. Form a vortex of douche." He tries to smile but doesn't quite succeed.

"Vivian said you had to become Mister Romance because of financial problems."

He nods. "Dad gambled. Compulsively. By the time he was caught with his hand in the company till, our house was mortgaged to the hilt, the business was dying, and he'd sold off most of our assets. Then the trial costs piled on top of that, and I dropped out of college, because I couldn't afford the fees."

He gestures around him. "Mom left me this warehouse in her brother's name, but no one wanted to buy it. After I sold our family home and the house in the Hamptons, there was still a mountain of debt. Most of what I make these days goes to paying it off. A portion goes to the Valentine Foundation to help women like my mother, and every few months I sell off what's left of our possessions and live off the cash. I haven't started selling the jewelry yet out of respect to Mom, but I'll have to one day."

"The necklace you gave me ..."

"That was her favorite. At least, I think it was. I never asked. She wore it the most."

I lean forward and put my hand on his. "God, Max, I'm so sorry."

He plays with my fingers. "Last night, when you were talking about how your dad made you feel, it hit home. I wondered how many times my dad looked through Mom like she wasn't there. I sure as hell know that Spence and I did it all the time. We damaged her the same way your dad damaged you, so ... yeah. I guess you're right to be scared of me."

He gets up and goes back to pulling out photos and putting them on the desk. "So, there's a juicy backstory for you. Tortured son tries to make amends by helping women like his mother feel loved. Your editor will piss himself in delight from the possible headlines."

"Max, I don't have to write this. You've definitely changed my mind about your motivation, and according to our agreement –"

"Screw the agreement. Write the story, Eden. I'll brace for the backlash." His expression becomes hard. "I've run from all of this long enough. Time to face the music and move on. We all have moments in our lives when we have to decide if we're going to stay comfortable in our bubble of ignorance or strive to be more than we were. I'm determined to be more. A better man than I was brought up to be. Only time will tell if I succeed."

I want to hug him and tell him that sometimes, good people

do bad things, because it's so clear he's already succeeded. But after so much truth he's closed down, and when I go to touch him, he steps away from me.

"I have to go," he says. "Don't want to get on the wrong side of Nannabeth by being late to my own furniture sale." He puts the box of photos on the desk and looks at them for a few moments. "Stay here as long as you like. Take whatever you need. Call me if you have any follow-up questions." The look he gives me is of a defeated man. "Just promise me you won't pull any punches. The one thing I don't deserve is mercy."

Then he walks away, and when the door closes behind him, I feel about as empty as the space around me.

CR

After what just happened, I don't really feel like collating the research, but I get the impression it's important to Max that I write his story, so I promise myself to do it as sensitively as possible. After I shove the photos and documents into my bag, I turn out the lights and leave.

Knowing what he used to be like, my feelings for him are even more conflicted. He admits that he used to be exactly the type of man who inflicted so many scars on me. And yet, it hasn't made it any easier to ignore the clawing, desperate need I have to be with him. Perhaps I'm more like my mother than I'd care to admit. Or, maybe, he's less like my father than he'd ever believe.

I'm coming up the stairs from the subway station and heading toward the markets, when my phone buzzes. I smile at the screen before answering.

"I'm on my way, Nannabeth. Sorry I'm running late."

"Darling granddaughter, it's fine. The day you show up on time is the day I keel over and die of shock." She laughs, which makes me smile. Nannabeth's laugh is wicked and infectious, and it can make the most tragic of situations bearable. "I just wanted you to know that Sean the Lawyer has just arrived, and he's looking even more attractive and single than usual."

"Nan –"

"Wait, just hear me out before you dismiss this as meddling. It's not. It's lifestyle advice. Do you think someone like him comes along every day? Because I'm here to tell you, they don't. He's clean, has great taste in clothes, smells fantastic, is polite to old women – just stop me when I've convinced you – has a great body, his eyes are amazing, he has a killer sense of humor, he's –"

"An imposter." God, I hate throwing cold water on Nan, but here goes. "He's not Sean, Nan, he's Max, and he's New York's highest paid male escort."

There's silence for a few beats, then she sighs. "Oh, Eden. You and your bizarre sense of humor."

"Nan, I'm serious. I'm doing a story on him. I've been researching him for weeks, and he's just told me his father was a malignant narcissist who brought him up to be a sexist pig. He says he's changed and is trying to make up for all the harm he's caused, so ..."

"But he seems so ... lovely. You're telling me he used to be an ass and now has sex for money?"

"No. It's a long story. Anyway, I have to reevaluate how I feel after receiving this new information."

"Has he ever mistreated you? Your radar for assholes is pretty good, honey. Goodness knows you've slept with enough of them. What does your gut say?"

I look both ways before crossing the busy street. "I don't

know, Nan. I think he's worked really hard to become a good guy, but part of me still doesn't trust him."

"Could that possibly be the part of you who's a pathological commitment-phobe?"

I roll my eyes as I get in line at a coffee place near the subway station. "I suppose that's possible."

"I'm not telling you what to do, sweetie, but you seem to have a genuine connection with him. Maybe you should give him a chance to prove what kind of man he is."

"That sounds an awful lot like telling me what to do."

She pauses. "Edie, I just want to make sure you don't screw things up with him, because you're too pig-headed. I never want you to make the same mistakes I have."

"Men mistakes?"

"Yes, men mistakes. Haven't you ever wondered why I never remarried?"

"I ... well, I – "

"Let me guess. You think I loved your grandpa so much, I couldn't face replacing him? Oh, Edie." I hear a quiet sigh. "Your grandpa was a good man, and I did love him in my own way, but his death didn't break me. I just never felt the need to replace him. Hearts are funny things. If they spend too much time being one size, they end up stuck that way."

I finally reach the front of the line and signal to the barista for a large latte. Nan will be hankering for caffeine right about now, and this place is her favorite. "So, you've dated over the years?"

"More than you could possibly know. But I'd told myself so many times I didn't need anyone, I started to believe it. Sound like anyone you know?"

"Nan ..." I hand over some cash before moving to the side to wait for my order. I'm feeling way too raw to have this discussion this morning, especially after what just happened.

"Sweetie, let me just say this one thing, and then I'll shut up. Being alone for too long isn't healthy. Loneliness is like a big, empty room inside you that echoes with the sounds of the life you're not living. So you fill it with stuff – work, friends, pets – and over the years it becomes bearable, then comfortable. And after many years it's so safe and warm, it becomes the new normal. And the worst part is, it's so full of fake comforts, there's no room for anyone else. But you deserve more than that. You deserve the world, and this Max ..."

I lean against the wall and close my eyes. "Nan, please don't tell me he can give me the world. My feminist heart couldn't take it."

"I was going to say he could *be* your world, and you could be his. If you let him."

Is that all I have to do? Let him be my world? She might as well ask me to catch the moon and slingshot around the stars.

"I'll think about it, Nan, okay?" The barista calls my name, and I grab the coffee and head out into the street.

"That's all I ask, muffin. I want to see you happy. When I was your age, I was –" She stops abruptly and makes a noise I've never heard her make before.

"Nan? Are you okay?"

"Yes," she says, but her voice wavers. "I'm just ... a little dizzy. Haven't had much to eat yet. Or my coffee."

"I'm bringing it now. If you're really lucky, I'll also stop to grab one of those double-choc brownies you love so much, but only if you promise to drop all topics related to men."

"Sounds ... good. I –"

She goes quiet, and then I hear a crunching sound and cries of alarm.

"Nan?" My heart leaps into my throat. "Nan? Are you there?"

I hear running footsteps and scuffling, and then Max's voice cuts through the rest of the noise. His tone is wrong. Too hard and way too panicked.

"Nannabeth! Nannabeth, wake up. Hey, come on. Just wake up for me." There's a pause. "Shit. She's bleeding. Someone call an ambulance! Now!"

There's a scraping sound before he comes on the line. "Eden?"

"Max, what the hell is going on?"

"Nannabeth collapsed. I think she cracked her head on the pavement."

"Is she okay?" The half a second he pauses is a lifetime too long. "Max!"

"I don't know. I have a pulse, but it's weak. The ambulance is on its way."

Without hearing anything else, I drop the coffee and break into a run.

Eighteen

Weathering the Storm

By the time I got to her booth, Nannabeth had already been taken away, so I grabbed the first cab I could to the local hospital. When I race into the emergency room I'm so full of fear and concern I can barely breathe. I'm sure the receptionist is used to people showing up out of their minds with worry and demanding answers, and yet she sees something in my face that makes her hold up her hands before I've even opened my mouth.

"Ma'am, just calm –"

"Elizabeth Shannon. Where is she?"

"She's with the doctors, so if you'll just take a –"

"What happened? What's her condition? Is she conscious? Is she...?" The word won't even get past my throat. I can't comprehend a world in which Nannabeth doesn't exist. I just can't. She has to be okay.

"Are you a relative?"

I nod, my heart pounding so hard it hurts. "I'm her granddaughter." When I say that, I realize I need to call Asha to let her know what's going on. She'll probably want to come back.

Wait, no. She'll cry, and if she cries then I'll cry, and I can do that right now. I need to be strong.

"Miss?"

I glance up to see the receptionist holding out a clipboard. "If you could fill in these forms and give us Elizabeth's details, I'll get you some news as soon as I can."

"Nannabeth," I say, my tone clipped.

"I'm sorry?"

"She doesn't like being called Elizabeth. Said that's the name of a queen, and she's barely a lady. Her name is Nannabeth."

Her expression softens. "Of course. Just take a seat, and I'll try to find out Nannabeth's condition."

I wander over to the plastic chairs and sit, my breathing ragged as I write in answers. I don't know her insurance details or even if she has insurance. As far as I know, she's never been in a hospital before today. For my whole life, she's been the healthiest person I've ever met.

I pause when I get to the question about next of kin. It's such a weird phrase. It should have a subheading that reads, *Who should we call if your loved one dies?*

My hands get clammy, and I wipe them on my jeans before attempting to write my name. My hand is shaking so hard, it's barely legible. When I finish, I go and put the clipboard back on the receptionist's desk. There's a different lady now, and she takes it without looking at me.

I sit back down in the uncomfortable plastic and close my eyes. The room is spinning, and the last thing I need right now is to pass out, so I take deep breaths and lean down to get my head below my heart.

I keep telling myself she'll be fine and that she's one of the strongest people I know. At Mom's funeral she was the only one who wasn't blubbering. Asha was nine at the time, and I was eleven. I'd held Asha's hand, and we both cried our eyes out as Nannabeth said a few words to the small crowd, which not surprisingly didn't include my father.

A few weeks later when I asked Nan about controlling her tears, she said, "Sweetheart, I'm a person who cries at everything, so I've learned to cry at nothing." I'd begged her to teach me, but she said no, because hardening your heart isn't something kids should do.

I did it anyway. I never wanted to feel anything as deeply as I felt that day. So every time I'd feel too scared, or angry, or sad, to keep it inside I did this thing where I'd visualize I was on the deck of a ship being hammered by a vicious storm. I'd see myself diving into the ocean and swimming deep underwater. Even though I could see the mayhem above, everything was muffled and quiet down there, and as long as I could hold my breath, I could watch the boat get destroyed from a safe distance, without ever being in danger.

Right now I'm trying to see that boat, but I can't. All I see is the storm.

"Eden?"

I look up and see Max standing there, wearing blue scrubs and a white jacket. He even has a stethoscope around his neck. My confusion must show on my face, because he shrugs like it's not a big deal. "They wouldn't let me go in, because I wasn't family, so I improvised. I've played a doctor a few times. I know how to fake it."

For some reason, that makes me laugh, but it's too shrill and high-pitched, and Max looks at me in concern. Then I feel bad, because Nan could be in there dying, and I'm out here laughing with my ... well ... whatever Max is to me.

"They won't tell me anything," I say. "What's going on?"

He squats in front of me and takes my hands, but I pull back. He can't touch me right now. No one can.

He frowns then says, "They think she passed out because of low blood sugar. When she fell ... I couldn't get to her in time." He looks at me like what he's about to say will push me over the edge. "Her head smashed into the pavement. Her brain is so swollen that ..." Guilt etches into his expression. "Eden, she's in a coma. When I left they were taking her for a CT and an MRI."

She's in a coma.

I try to process that and can't. My Nan is a dynamo. A seventy-five-year-old force of nature. She can't be in a coma. It's not possible.

"She fainted because of low blood sugar?"

"They think so, yes."

She hadn't had her morning coffee with three sugars. I didn't bring her breakfast. If it weren't for me snooping around in Max's warehouse instead of being there for her, none of this would have happened. We'd be in her booth, selling second-hand stuff to hipsters for stupidly inflated prices.

The guilt twists through me, adding another layer to my increasing anxiety.

"Eden?"

When I open my eyes, Max looks at me like he's afraid I'll crumble into an emotional heap. He doesn't understand how long and hard I've fought to train myself for these kinds of situations. Father who didn't love me. Mother who died. Nan who ...

I close my eyes and make myself see the boat in the storm. I become the girl on the deck and sigh in relief as I dive into the dark, muffled waters.

When I open my eyes, I can breathe again. "When can I see her?"

Max seems taken aback by my sudden calm. "I don't know. I'm sorry. Do you need anything? A coffee? Something to eat?" I shake my head. "Have you called Asha? Would you like me to?"

I shake my head again. "So, you've called her?"

His constant questions are irritating me. "It will ruin her trip."

"You know your sister better than I do, but if I were her ..."

His voice is quiet, but I hear the judgement in it, loud and clear.

I don't want him here hovering and judging and making me weak. I'd rather deal with this alone. It's what I'm used to.

"Everything's fine, Max. Thanks for coming." I try to be warm and dismissive at the same time, but I think I just end up being the second thing. Still, it has the desired effect because he steps back.

"Yeah, of course," he says. "I'll get out of your hair. Sorry I couldn't be more helpful."

He pushes through the doors leading into the emergency area, and a ball of lead falls into my stomach as I watch him go.

I don't need him, I repeat to myself, over and over again. There's only room beneath this boat for one person, and that's me.

I don't need him.

CR

It's three hours later when I'm shown into a room in the ICU to see Nan for the first time. I clench my jaw against the sight of her in a huge bed, tubes poking out of her mouth, nose, and arms, surrounded by machines. She's always been my superwoman role model. If I did nothing else in my life but grow up to be like her, I could die a happy woman. But seeing her now, so pale, and small, and ... broken, my only wish is to be in that bed instead of her.

"She's stable for now," the doctor says in hushed tones, "and we've relieved the pressure on her brain, so now we just have to be patient."

"How long will she remain in a coma?"

"I don't know. Everyone heals at their own pace. Even if she wakes up, there may be some issues related to possible brain damage. Impaired speech, memory loss, partial paralysis. We just don't know for sure yet."

"*When* she wakes."

"Excuse me?"

"You said *if* she wakes. But you meant *when*, right?"

He gives me a reassuring smile. "Of course. From what you've told me, she's a strong woman. If anyone can get through this, she can." Then he gives my arm a squeeze and leaves me there, staring at Nan and feeling more and more useless by the second.

A nurse is taking readings from machines and writing stuff down. She looks over at me and gestures for me to come closer.

"You can sit with her," she says, indicating the chair near the window. "It helps if you talk to her."

I sleepwalk to the chair and sink into it. "What do I talk about?"

"Anything. Tell her about your day. The doctors believe that talking to coma patients helps them wake up."

She finishes up what she's doing and gives me a smile before she leaves. Then it's just me and Nan, and the scraping and beeping of the machines around us.

Okay. I'll just talk like she's not lying there half-dead.

"Hey, Nan." My voice is tight. I try to swallow, but I have zero saliva, so my tongue feels three sizes too big for my mouth. "How's it going?"

I didn't think I'd ever miss Nan's incessant chatter, but right now I'd give anything to hear her say just one word.

I try again, while attempting to keep my tone light. "You

know, I've never really thought of you as a tubes and machines kind of girl, but I have to say, you pull it off. I take issue with the dowdy gown, but otherwise, you're really rocking the hospital chic."

In my mind she agrees with me, and that makes me smile. But it's one of those smiles that you know is fragile, like a mask, and it's just one half-breath away from splintering in two.

"So, listen ... I don't think I've said it enough, but ... I love you." I stroke her hand over and over again. "You make the world a better place, so just ... stay ... okay? Stay with me."

My throat tightens, but I refuse to cry. "The nurse said it would be helpful for me to talk to you, so I will. I'll talk until I lose my voice. Here goes." I take a deep breath. "I found this website the other day for beekeepers called 'To Bee or not to Bee', which is all kinds of adorable, but I didn't get around to telling you about it." I grab my phone and bring it up in the browser. "But we have plenty of time now, so just lie back and relax, and I'll tell you what they have to say." I clear my throat. "To bee, or not to bee, that is the question ..."

℘

When I open my eyes, I see a large red-headed male nurse taking Nan's vitals. I blink and cough to get the dryness out of my throat. "Morning."

He smiles. "Hey."

I look down at myself, bent out of shape in the uncomfortable visitor's chair. I'm wrapped in a blanket, which is weird, because I didn't go to sleep with one.

The nurse checks the saline drip then mutters, "Be right back," before leaving the room.

"Morning, Nan," I say, as I stretch up and wince when my back cracks. "Did you see how hard that nurse was flirting with me? Shameless. Then again, he is pretty cute. Maybe I'll throw over that Max guy for him. I mean, he won't earn as much, but with his red hair and my fiery locks? We could make the ultimate ginger child. Can you imagine? The kid would be unstoppable. Sure, he'd survive by feeding on the souls of his enemies and burst into flames in full sunlight, but still. Super Ginger!"

The nurse comes back in and hands me a leather duffle bag. Max's duffle bag. I look at it in confusion.

"Your brother left this for you."

"My ... *brother*. Right."

He goes to Nan's drip and swaps out the saline bag. "He's hot. And sweet. I practically swooned when he came in with a blanket and tucked you in. Not enough men like him around. Is he single?"

Well, there goes my super-baby idea.

Then the gears in my brain start to grind, and I shake my head to understand what he just said. "Wait, Max gave me this blanket?"

"Yeah. Sat and talked with your gran while you were asleep, too." He finishes up with the drip and scribbles something on Nan's chart. "What I wouldn't give for my brother to be more like him."

I lean down and open the bag. On the top of a pile of my clothes is a handwritten note.

Hey, Eden.

I hope you're doing okay.

I thought you might like a change of clothes and some toiletries, considering you'll want to stay with your Nan. I hope you don't mind that I conned the super of you building into letting into your apartment. In case he says anything, the FBI agent apologized for thinking you owned bomb-making equipment and were a threat to national security. If he gives you any trouble, let me know. Agent Richards can always make a return visit to set him straight.

I hope Nannabeth is doing better today.

Please let me know if you need anything. I'm just a phone call away.

Max x

"You okay?"

I look up to see the nurse staring at me.

"Uh ... yeah, I'm fine."

He gives me a sympathetic look. "Miss your brother, huh?"

I nod and pack the note away. "Yeah. Unfortunately."

❦

For three days I live at the hospital. I get used to washing up in the public bathroom, grabbing takeout food from the cafeteria, and sleeping in the cot they set up for me. I talk to Nan all day long about anything and everything that comes to mind. I make up stories about amazing men I'm going to date and have children with, because really, if anything's going to call her back from the great beyond, it will be the prospect of me finally ending my filthy single-lady ways and settling down.

Toby has been running interference for me at work, but even so, I knew I couldn't avoid Derek forever. When my phone lights up with his number on the afternoon of the third day, I sigh and answer it.

"Hey, Derek."

"Eden. Hi." His voice is strange. Soft. Not pissed off. And he used my first name.

Oh, God, is he firing me?

"Look," I say, sitting up straighter. "I know my partial draft was due yesterday, but I have a lot going on right now, so if you could –"

"Eden, it's fine. I'm not calling to harass you."

"You're not?" Now I'm more confused than worried.

"Toby used every excuse in the book to explain where you've been for the past few days, but he finally spilled the beans about your grandmother. I just wanted to call and send you some good thought. I lost my gran two years ago, so I sympathize with what you're going through. I really hope she pulls through."

That was the last thing I expected from him. I slump back into my chair. "Thanks, Derek. That means a lot."

"This doesn't mean I'm giving you a free pass on the story, mind you. But it does mean you can have some extra time. Where are you with your research?"

"I have everything I need. I just have to write it. And to be honest, right now, I can't think about much except being with my Nan."

I hear rustling papers in the background. "I get it. I'm heading off to Europe tomorrow to meet some possible investors for *Pulse*, so you can have until I get back to finish up."

"How long will you be gone?"

"Two weeks. Can you get it done?"

"I think so."

"Good." There's a pause, and then he clears his throat. "Okay, so it's weird speaking to you for this long without yelling, so I'm gonna go."

I laugh. "Thanks for calling, Derek. I really appreciate it."

"Yeah, sure. Take care of yourself. And as soon as you can

face it, get writing."

"I will."

We sign off, and I sigh. I never thought I'd see the day Derek would act like a regular person with human feelings, but I guess in times of crisis, people can surprise you.

I look over at Nan and take her hand. "See, Nan? Everyone's on your side, even my asshole boss. That's got to count for something, right?"

I stroke her skin and yawn as the sun kisses the tops of the buildings outside the window. I'm trying to stay positive, but it's hard. Telling myself she's going to be okay is one thing. Believing it is another.

"Ash called today. She was so excited, I didn't have the heart to tell her about you. I know you'd approve, because you'd hate it if she gave up this opportunity and got on the first plane home. Besides, what can she do? The position of chief hand holder and chatterbox is filled. She'd have no purpose."

I stroke her paper-thin skin and trace my fingertip over her tiny blue veins. "But of course if you wake up, I can call her and say you've had an accident but that you're fine, which would work out well for everyone. So, just ... wake up, okay?" I look over at her and will her to move. "You don't have to do anything major. Just open your eyes. Or squeeze my hand. You could squeeze my hand. That would be fine."

I stop talking, because I get that pain in my throat that tells me I'm about to lose control. So instead, I press my forehead against her wrist. In this position I can feel her pulse, and I have to believe that as long as her heart's beating, there's a chance she'll make it through.

When I hear footsteps come into the room, I figure it's just one of the battalion of nurses that checks on Nan every half hour. I flinch when a warm hand cups my shoulder.

"Eden, come on. You need to rest. Let me take you home."

I shouldn't be surprised he's here. All week, my 'brother' has been leaving care packages for me. He's very popular with the nurses. Of course he is. All the ladies fall for Mister Romance, whether they want to or not.

When I raise my head, he strokes my back. "Hey, there."

"Hey." I'm so tired, my voice breaks.

"Wow," he says, pushing hair away from my face. "I didn't think it was possible, but ... you look like crap. Very beautiful crap, but still ..."

I let out a hoarse laugh. "Awww. You really are the sweetest man I know."

Without waiting for my permission, he grabs my phone and purse and pulls me to my feet. "Come on. You're exhausted."

"Max, I can't leave."

"You can and you will. The nurses have told me they'll call the second Nan's condition changes. But tonight, you're going to eat, shower, and sleep in a nice, warm bed, and I'm not taking no for an answer."

"But she needs someone to talk to her."

He stops and faces me then says, "I have that covered. Our wonderful *cousin* Dyson is going to stay here tonight and read to her."

Dyson, AKA Pat, walks in carrying a collection of books. "Hey, Cousin Eden." He squeezes my arm. "I'm so sorry about Nan. But don't worry, I took a course in audiobook narration. I got this. Tonight, we're going to crack open *Pride and Prejudice*. I do a killer Mr. Darcy. "

Max waits for my reaction. I sigh and nod. "Okay. But I'm coming back first thing in the morning."

Max leads me down the hallway and toward the exit, his arm around my waist. It's so comforting, I feel like I'm already asleep and wrapped in a warm, tall, good-looking dream.

When we get in the elevator, I turn to him. "Can you take me to Nan's instead of my place?"

"Sure. Why?"

"There are a few things I have to do."

Nineteen

Fragile Strength

Max wanders around Nan's apartment, seeming contemporary and out of place among her vintage chintz and clutter.

"You were a cute kid," he says as he picks up an old family photo.

I grab some of Nan's stuff and put it in an overnight bag. "Well, yeah. Tell me something I don't know." I take the engagement photo of her and grandad, the clock she's kept by her bed for fifty years, and the throw pillow she embroidered with a noble portrait of Moby Duck.

Speaking of Moby, the neighbors have been feeding him since the accident, but I think the poor thing is missing Nan, because from the moment I set foot inside the door, he's followed my every step. When I grab some of Nan's favorite lavender moisturizer from the bathroom cabinet, he perches on the closed toilet seat and quacks at me.

"It's okay, Moby. She'll be home soon." He quacks again, and when I look at him, I realize I've never seen a duck look sad until this moment. "Aw, buddy. Come on. It's okay." I smear some of the fragrant cream on my arms and pick him up. He snuggles into me and the familiar scent, and I stroke his feathers.

"She's going to be okay, Moby. I promise."

I hear a noise in the hallway and turn to see Max watching us, looking way too large for the small space. "Everything okay?"

"I think he's fretting. He's not used to being without her for so long."

He walks over and gently pats the duck. "I can come and ... uh ... duck sit ... while you're at the hospital, if that will help. I mean, I'm pretty good with dogs and cats. How different can it be for a duck, right?"

The emotional lump in my throat from earlier doubles in size, and I'm not even a little equipped to deal with him and his caring ways right now.

"I'm going to take him up to the roof." I squeeze past Max and head for the door. "His pond is up there, and he likes swimming."

"Mind if I tag along?"

"If you want. But you're too big for the pond. Plus, Moby doesn't like to share."

I hug Moby to my chest as I lead Max up the back stairs to the roof. Moby quacks as soon as he sees his pond, which is really just a kiddy pool Nan fancied up with fiberglass boulders and potted palms to seem more organic. As soon as I put Moby in the water, he flaps his wings and splashes around. When he's settled and happy, I grab the hose Nan has jerry-rigged to the rainwater tank up here and water her vegetables and herbs.

Max doesn't say anything, but I can tell he's impressed with Nan's setup. He bends over one of the garden beds and pulls out some tiny weeds.

"Your Nan's quite amazing, isn't she?"

I nod and walk the hose over to the pool to raise the water level. "Yeah. She is."

"It's clear you take after her." He walks over and stands

beside me, and we both watch Moby as he swims in circles. "How are you feeling?"

"I'm fine."

"You don't have to be, you know. Most people in your situation would be struggling. There's no shame in that."

"I'm not ashamed."

"Okay, then just humor me for a second."

He takes the hose from me and puts it into the pool, then with gentle grace he pulls me into his arms and presses his head into my neck.

It feels incredible, but I instinctively tense up. Doing anything else right now will lead to me crumbling like ash and flying away in the wind. "What are you doing?"

"Helping you." Warm breath on my skin makes me shiver. "Prolonged hugging relieves stress and lowers cortisol levels. Just relax into it, Eden. Let go. You'll feel better, I promise."

I want to tell him that having him pressed tight against me feels better than anything I've felt in my life up until now, but the words get stuck behind the ever-growing knot in my throat. All of the good stuff stays inside of me, stuck to my fear like it's flypaper. The only words I'm capable of right now are thorny.

"Max, I can't do this."

"Really? Because, so far, you're doing pretty well." He tightens his arms. "Being more enthusiastic about hugging me back would help, but still ... it's a solid seven out of ten."

I pull out of his arms and go over to the side of the roof. The sun is setting, and everything is bathed in golden light. In moments like this, it's easy to forget how devastatingly crappy life can be.

"I meant, I can't do this. You and me."

My back is to him, but I hear him walk over and stand behind me. "I'm not asking for anything, Eden."

"Yes, you are. You want to be there for me. To support me. Take care of me."

"And that's a bad thing?"

I turn to him. "I've been taking care of myself for years. I don't need you to hold my hand."

"I know that. I just don't think you should be alone right now."

"I'm not alone. I have Moby. In fact, I think I'll stay here for a while and make sure he's okay."

He moves closer and puts his hands on my shoulders. "And who's going to make sure you're okay?"

I feel so small standing close to him. It would be so easy to get lost in his size, and warmth, and smell, which is exactly why I can't.

I look down at his chest. "Max, you have to stop treating me like I'm a bomb that's about to detonate. I'm fine."

"You're not. Do you think I can't see through this tough-girl act?"

"That's rich, coming from the Great Pretender."

That gets to him. "Yes, I'm a pretender, but the difference is I know I'm doing it. You don't. You're so used to being strong you can't see that sometimes, admitting you need someone is the brave option."

When I don't say anything, he gives me an understanding nod before looking over at Moby. "Okay, so ... If you get lonely and need a friend, I'll be at the Pencil Factory loft."

He turns and heads toward the stairwell, and just as the door closes behind him, the last sliver of sunlight fades over the horizon.

Twenty

A Soft Place to Land

I'm more exhausted than I've ever been – both physically and emotionally – but as I wander around Nan's apartment, I can't relax. I end up eating beans out of a can for dinner, and then when Moby crawls onto his side of Nan's bed and puts his head under his wing for the night, I clean. I scrub her bathroom until the smell of bleach makes me dizzy. I dust every surface in the living room. I even wash the floors. And still, I'm filled with a type of anxious restlessness I've never felt before.

Maybe staying here is a bad idea. Every time I turn around, I see a ghost of Nan as her beautiful, vibrant self, but that's quickly followed by the memory of her in the hospital, frail and unconscious, dwarfed by the litany of machines around her.

I have to get out.

I make sure Moby's food and water bowls are full, and then I lock up the apartment and just walk. The fresh night air helps a little, and the bustling streets of Brooklyn seem to quell my rising need for human connection. However, the longer I walk, the more I notice that everyone seems to have a place to go except for me. And someone to be with. I pass couples holding hands, couples sitting on park benches, couples looking lovingly at each other across tables in restaurants and cafés. I don't think I've ever noticed before how the whole damn world seems to be paired off, and the more I notice it, the more agitated I become.

No wonder single people become bitter. It's like the universe is conspiring to make us feel defective. Every happy couple that passes is a slap in the face, as the world yells, "See? Look at the joy you're missing out on. You think you're content, but you're not. Those two over there sucking face near the subway station – *they're* the content ones. They have each other. You're just alone and lonely, and trying to convince yourself you like it that way."

I turn a corner and see a bar. "Oh, yes."

Nothing like some hard liquor to dull stupid urges. I walk in and order a triple whiskey, no ice. The bartender gives me a look but complies. As soon as he hands it to me, I down the entire thing in three painful mouthfuls, which is an achievement considering I despise whiskey. "Thanks," I say through a burning throat.

It tasted awful, but at least it has the desired effect of distracting me from deeper thoughts. I throw down some cash and go on my way.

As I turn east, I tell myself I'm wandering aimlessly, but I'm not. I try to be content in my aloneness, but I'm not. I contemplate calling Asha and sharing the burden of Nannabeth and how I'm feeling, but I don't.

Instead, I see the familiar building in the distance and walk faster. By the time I climb the steps and stand outside the huge metal door, I'm puffing.

Emotions churning, I take a few deep breaths then knock. I can hear classical music coming from inside, as well the aroma of something cooking that smells delicious.

I hear footsteps, and then the door pulls back to reveal Max, devastatingly shirtless and barefoot in his jeans. For a moment, he seems surprised to see me, then relieved. "Hey."

"Hey."

He waits for me to speak, and when I don't he says, "Come in."

I nod, and he steps aside, so I can enter. After he closes the door, he walks around to stand in front of me. The distance between us chafes. So does the silence.

"Eden?"

I look at my feet. It's easier than looking at his face. "Maybe you were right. Maybe I do get lonely."

He's silent, but I can feel him staring at me. I see his bare feet poking out of the bottom of his jeans. They're handsome, just like him. Large and attractive. When they move closer, I feel the heat of his whole body just inches away.

"Admitting it is the first step," he says, his voice soft. "And?"

"And ... I guess tonight, I don't feel like being alone. I want to be with someone."

He's so close now, his cheek grazes my temple, but still he doesn't touch me. Warm breath against my ear makes me shiver when he talks. "Don't do that. Don't seek me out and pretend it's just because you need someone. The world is full of someones. You came here because you needed *me*."

He puts a hand on my waist, and I let him. "Say it, Eden. I promise, it doesn't make you weak."

"Yes, it does. Every time I'm with you, I'm weak, and getting weaker every second."

He takes my hands and presses them flat into his chest. "There's no shame in needing me. I need you, too."

I shake my head. "I don't know how to do this."

"Neither do I, but we'll figure it out together. Just let me help you."

There comes a point where holding everything in is too hard. The pain of containing all of the things you don't want to feel becomes too overwhelming, and as much as I despise crying, and as much as I try to stop the tears, they bully their way out of my eyes and onto my cheeks. I think tensing my jaw will stop them, but it doesn't. I think digging my fingers into Max's chest will help, but it doesn't. My fear is too big for my body, and it squeezes out of me into the fresh air where it thrives and multiplies into giant, heaving sobs.

"I could l-lose her, Max."

"You won't. She's strong."

"She's old. I'll lose her and then ... the only person left on the planet who l-loves me, is Asha ... and she'll be gone one day, too. Married and happy ... and I'll be truly alone."

"Never going to happen. Not while I'm around. Come here."

He pulls me into his arms, and I let myself feel comforted, and I let myself be weak and vulnerable. It's so alien to me, I don't recognize the tortured sounds I'm making. I haven't cried like this since Mom's funeral, and it's just as painful now as it was then.

I hate it, I hate it, I hate it.

This is what loving gets you. This expanding world of pain. Because no one stays forever. They all leave in the end.

"I can't picture a world ... without N-Nan. I don't kn-know who I am ... without her."

Max holds me closer and strokes my back, and when he encourages me to let it all out, I do. I cling to him like he's my life preserver. He whispers to me, tells me it's going to be okay. Tells me I'm amazing and beautiful. For some reason, that makes me cry harder. I know I'm making his chest wet with my tears, but he doesn't seem to care, so neither do I.

I don't know how long we stand there, but it's long enough that when I'm done, I'm so drained I practically fall asleep in his arms.

Without a word, he scoops me up and strides into the bedroom where he lays me down on the crisp, white duvet and pulls a blanket over me. Then he lies beside me and strokes the tears from my face, until I close my eyes and drift off.

CR

The next morning, I wake to find myself wrapped around a half-naked and unconscious man. His arm is beneath my neck, and I'm snuggled into his side, my head on his chest, my hand resting on his stomach. I look down to see my bare leg draped over his. I vaguely remember struggling out of my jeans during the night to get more comfortable, and it seems Max did the same, because he's only wearing a pair of black boxer briefs.

I close my eyes and suck in some deep breaths.

It takes me a moment to understand how I got to his loft and why I'm in his bed, but then it comes back in excruciating detail. Oh, yeah. I inflicted my mental and emotional breakdown on him. As I was blubbering all over his chest, he must have patted himself on the back for being attracted to a crazy woman.

I slowly move out of his arms and retreat to the other side of the bed. As mortifying as my ugly crying was, I can't deny that I feel better today. The simmering anxiety that's been with me since Nan's accident has faded to a dull buzz rather than a deafening roar. Of course, I now have a different brand of anxiety brewing – the type that comes from my ever-expanding feelings for Max. Even watching him sleep inspires an uncomfortable level of affection.

I study his face, so relaxed as he dreams. He really is beautiful, and that has nothing to do with his chiseled jaw or perfect face. It's because he has one of the biggest hearts I've ever known.

He thinks he used to be a terrible person, and maybe he was, but I don't see that in him now. Everything he's done for me since Nan's accident proves it. I've never had a man want to take care of me like this before. And even though I'd like to believe I don't need him, maybe I do. And maybe I can learn to be okay with that.

Goddammit. Why did he have to complicate everything by being so amazing?

I squeeze my eyes shut and lie flat on my back as an epiphany hits me, making the room spin.

Sometimes when self-awareness comes, it's in shadows and stealth, like a cat; winding around your body until it settles in your chest, comforting and warm. And at other times, it crashes down like a sky-diving elephant looking for a soft place to land.

Right now, the elephant is sitting squarely on my heart, and its name is *I'm in Love with This Man.*

I drape my arm over my face and sigh.

Shit.

I wasn't lying last night when I told Max I didn't know how to do this. A real, grownup relationship is something I have zero experience with, and I'm sure that if there are a hundred different ways to fuck it up, I'll find each and every one, plus a few no one's ever thought of. Furthermore, *avoiding* fucking this up is something I have no time for while Nan's sick, so if Max thinks I'm going to drop everything to become some perfect little girlfriend, he can just ...

I jump in surprise when a warm hand takes mine, and I open my eyes to see Max lying on his side, watching me as my heart skips several dozen beats.

"Sorry," he says with an amused expression. "Didn't mean to startle you."

"Maybe not, but your grin tells me you're enjoying it, right?"

He gives a non-committal shrug. "The noise you made was cute. Like a gerbil having shock therapy."

He looks down at our hands as he links his fingers through mine. "How are you feeling this morning?"

I run my other hand over his and allow myself to enjoy the soft brush of skin on skin. I've never thought twice about putting my hand in a man's pants, but stroking Max's fingers? It's such an everyday gesture for most people, but for me it's a whole new world of intimate contact.

"I feel a bit better,' I say. "Thanks to you. I'm sorry for falling apart. I don't usually do that."

"There's no need to be embarrassed."

"Really?" I tuck some hair behind my ear. "I went full-on emotional disaster area. Can't think of anything more embarrassing than that."

"I can." He props his head up with his hand, and against my will, I stare at his bicep.

"Would you like to share?"

"Well, you did wake up once and look at me like I was an axe murderer waiting to kill you. Then recognition sank in, and you ... uh, well ... then you made yourself comfortable by putting your hand on my crotch."

"Really?"

"Yep. At first, I thought you were making a semi-conscious pass at me, but no. You just put your hand there and went back to sleep."

"Did you move my hand away?"

"No. Cupping that general area seemed to soothe you, which is the only reason I didn't do anything to stop it."

"Wow. Selfless."

He shrugs. "Eh. I do what I can."

"I don't remember that at all."

He glances down at my bare legs then back up to my face. "That's okay. I remember it vividly enough for both of us."

I know he's thinking about touching me, because there's no disguising his current arousal in those boxer briefs, but even though I want him more than is probably healthy, how on earth can I contemplate taking something for myself when Nan's in the condition she is?

"I should go."

"No, you should rest. You still look exhausted."

"I wanted to be back at the hospital by now."

"Dyson's already there. Honestly, Eden, the best way to help your Nan is to take some time for yourself. We can call to see how she is, but then you need to take a day off."

He's just picked up his phone from the nightstand when it buzzes with a message. He checks the screen then holds it out so I can see. It's from Dyson.

<No change in Nan's condition, despite some of my best work as Darcy. Never fear, this morning I'm starting on Dickens. My Nicholas Nickleby is sure to do the trick. Tell Eden to relax and get some rest. I got this.>

I smile. I barely know Dyson, and yet he's giving up his time to help me.

"Are you paying him?" I ask.

Max shakes his head and puts his phone back on the nightstand. "Nope. When he heard, he wanted to help. I think he could tell how worried I was about you. And how important your Nan is to you." He turns back to me. "So, there you have it. Stay in bed today. I'll provide whatever you want. Food, drink, emotional support ..." He looks into my eyes. "Physical release ... just tell me what you need."

We both go quiet as the air fills with tension. A big part of it is sexual, but there's also a sense of awkwardness that comes from not knowing where we go from here. I can no longer deny I need him. Last night proved that. But a few hours of emotional intimacy doesn't make any of the issues I have go away. It just puts pressure on me to try to be different, and I don't know how.

"So," he says then clears his throat. "You ... uh ... never mentioned the stuff we talked about at the warehouse. About my family."

I take his hand again. "Do we need to?"

"Well, I hit you with the confession that I was raised to be a chauvinistic misogynist, and you have yet to comment. I'm not stupid enough to think you don't have an opinion on it. In fact, I have no doubt your opinions have opinions."

I push up on my elbow and stare down at him. "Max ..." I struggle to find the right words. I begin slowly, so I don't say the wrong thing. "I don't know who you used to be, but I like who you are now, and that's enough for me." I'm so unused to being this emotionally expressive, my voice is shaking. "And I know you've been told this by a lot of women, but I ..." I look into his face. "I've never said anything like this to a man before, so for me, this is a big deal. You're ... *amazing*. And what you do is amazing. If you see your work as some kind of penance, then I think you've more than made up for your past."

He lets out a noisy breath though his nose, like he's been holding it in since he confessed his most shameful sins. Honestly, with what I now know about his family, I'm surprised he didn't devolve into a class-A asshole and declare war on the world, but I guess those sorts of major life events define you. There's a choice whether to give in to the darkness or struggle toward the light, and Max ended up being full of light.

He stares up at me. "So ... I'm glad you didn't take out a restraining order, but ... where do we go from here?"

I suck up my fear and start with trying to be honest. "I've

never had a healthy emotional relationship with a man. Or, *any* relationship with a man, really." I say it fast, thinking it might sound less pathetic that way. It doesn't. "I don't even know where to start in trying to be with you."

He moves closer, so we're almost nose to nose. "I've had a lot of perfect relationships, but none of them have been real. This whole thing will be one big learning curve for me, too."

Swallowing my rising panic, I graze my fingers from his temple to his chin. Being so affectionate with him is all new to me, and I'm nervous I'm not doing it right. "I have trust issues. I'm impatient and judgmental. And I've never admitted this before, but I never refill ice cube trays when they're empty. I leave them for Asha, every single time."

He slides his hand from my shoulder, down over my butt, to the back of my knee, and he pulls my leg up to his hip, so he can slide his thigh between my legs. He keeps looking me in the eyes as he rocks a little, pressing his erection against where I'm aching the most.

"I hate myself on so many levels," he says, his voice becoming breathy, "I should probably be in therapy. And when I used to share a bathroom with my brother, I'd leave a single square of toilet paper, so he'd have to change the roll."

I circle my hips and press down on his thigh while gripping his back to give myself better leverage.

"So," I say, "we both agree we're terrible people and that falling for each other is probably a bad idea."

"Absolutely." He climbs on top of me, so he's fully between my legs, and I spread my thighs. "One of the worst ideas ever." He grinds against me, his hardness feeling incredible against my softness. "But I don't care. Even if this whole thing goes down in flames, you're already the best bad decision I've ever made."

I pull him closer. Our noses are touching now. "Last chance

to change your mind."

He searches my eyes. "Never going to happen. Ever."

For a moment, we both stop and stare at each other, and there's a whole other conversation that happens in the silence. One in which an imaginary doctor shakes his head in sympathy as he says, "I'm sorry. They're too far gone. There's nothing I can do."

I hold my breath as Max leans down and kisses me gently, and I don't want to move in case I ruin the moment. His lips are so soft and warm, I could live in this moment forever and be a happy woman. He adds a little suction before pulling back, and then he angles his head and kisses me again, a little more pressure this time, my top lip caught between his. Though his body is tense and hard, this – the gentle press and suck of his lips and the delicate way he moves his mouth over mine – it demonstrates supreme restraint. The need to discover me for the first time instead of just giving into the hormones that are demanding we get naked as soon as possible.

His kisses slowly become more passionate, and when our tongues touch, we both make noises that speak of the slow, sweet torture of taking our time. I give up trying to think and just feel, letting my muscles melt into the mattress as he adjusts his position to wrap his arms more firmly around me.

He once told me that you could live and die within the lifetime of a good kiss, and that's what this feels like. As if I've always known the shape of his mouth but never experienced it before. Like all of our interlocking parts have been biding their time, watching people come and go from our lives, until we found each other.

The longer and deeper he kisses me, the more the air catches in my chest. My blood rushes, my limbs tremble, and I feel like I'm falling in slow motion, but every second, I speed up a little.

His tongue is more insistent. He grips me harder. I go from caressing him to gripping him. Pulling at him. Walking the line from civilized to feral and back again.

"Max?"

"Hmmmm." He kisses around my words.

"You once told me that a kiss is most effective when it doesn't lead to sex."

"Yes." His hand is wrapped around my hip now, squeezing and releasing in time with his pelvis pressing against me.

"This kiss is beyond spectacular, but I just wanted to make sure that you're planning on having sex with me, right?"

He pushes his hand under my shirt and brushes it up against my ribcage, then the curve of my breast.

"No. No sex this morning." He looks down at me as his giant hand closes around my breast, the rough pad of his thumb teasing my nipple. "I'm going to fuck you now, then later when my body isn't calling all the shots, we'll get around to various forms of making love. But definitely no plain, boring sex will be happening. Not with you. Not ever."

He kisses me again, and this time he starts grinding against me in time with the sweep of his tongue. I groan and press up to meet him, and within seconds, my need for him transforms from hazy and delicate to raw and brutal as we both let the lusty beasts that have been grazing on our suppressed passion for the past few weeks, well and truly out of their cages.

He lowers his full weight onto me, and when I grab his ass with both hands and squeeze, he growls against my mouth and pushes his hand between us, using strong pianist's fingers to make me arch even more. The rush of sensation is so fast and powerful, the room spins around me. Low grunts and long moans fill the air as we work our way around each other's bodies, exploring all of the places we've been dreaming about.

As he grinds against me, his muscles ripple beneath my hands, and I can feel the shape of him beneath his underwear sliding hard against me. He's a big guy, and his weight makes me struggle for breath, but I love the feeling. He circles his pelvis. and I wrap my legs around his hips to urge him closer. He's so hard that every pass of him over my clit makes me gasp and plead for more.

"Eden." There's a world of need in his voice as he pulls off my T-shirt and starts on my bra. "Put your hands on me. Now."

I reach between us and slide my hand into his underwear. He stops dead the moment I palm him and curl my fingers around his erection. "Like this?"

He holds himself off the bed, and as I stroke him and revel in the feel of him, the expression on his face screams of pleasure so extreme, it's almost painful to experience. "Exactly like that." He squeezes his eyes shut and hisses out a breath. "This is you first warning that I'm going to need to be inside of you soon, or I'm going to lose my mind."

"That works for me."

He makes a dark noise before yanking off my panties. And then when I'm totally naked and exposed to him more than I've ever been to any man, he kneels above me and looks down in such wonder, it makes my heart ache.

"You are ... God, Eden. I don't have the words. And I've been fantasizing about doing this for way too long."

Without giving me any time to respond, he pushes my knees open and sinks his head down between my legs. Then there's no way I can stay lucid, because his mouth is on me, and all I can do is throw my head back and groan as he gives me pleasure like I've never known.

Some men treat going down on a woman like it's a chore. They'll do it if they have to, but it's not the first choice in their sexual toolkit. However, the way Max is moving his mouth across me? It's like he's starving to death, and I'm the first decent meal he's had in years. Every time I don't think he can make more pleasure jolt through to my spine, he does.

I reach behind me and curl my fingers around the cast iron headboard as I stare up at the ceiling. And when it's all too much for even that, I squeeze my eyes shut as he closes his hands over my hips and pulls me more firmly onto his face.

Oh, sweet holy Hercules.

I can't. I can't deal with anymore. I think I start pleading with him, but whatever I'm saying is a blur.

My rambling seems to spur him on, and when he groans against me, the first tendrils of my orgasm curl and twist low and deep. I squeeze my eyes shut as the pulses come faster, gaining power as they go.

"Jesus ... Max."

I'm flying so close to the edge, it would be easy to fall apart on his mouth, but I don't want that. This is the first time I've ever slept with someone I love, and I want him to be a part of me when he makes me come for the first time.

"Max ..." When the pleading tone in my voice doesn't stop him, I reach down and slide my fingers into his hair before pulling his head up until he looks at me. "I need you inside. Please."

He climbs back up the bed, and I push him onto his back, so I can pull off his underwear. After I tug them down and throw them onto the floor, I see him for the first time, and dear God ... he's beautiful. I touch the silken skin, tracing the long, thick shape of him. He makes tight noises in his throat but doesn't stop me.

This isn't something I do. I barely look at the men I sleep with, because they're a means to an end. I don't really care what they look like or whether they're hung like a horse or not. But with Max, everything matters, because every part of him turns me on. Yes, his cock is beautiful, but so is his heart and mind. Who he is matters to me more than what he looks like, and that's why he's the sexiest man I've ever known. His incredible body is just a bonus.

I want to taste every sweet inch of him. I want to discover which parts will make him groan and which will make him swear when I suck on them. I want to taste his pecs and abs, and sink my teeth into tight bands of muscles around his arms.

But right now, I'm savoring the hard shape of him inside my mouth, the taste of him on the back of my tongue, the sweet, tortured sounds he makes as I take him as deep as I can, time and again.

"Fuck ... Eden." I add my hand, twisting in tandem with my mouth. He fists his fingers in my hair, forcing me to slow down. "Wait. Please ... just ... Dammit. Get up here."

With a low growl, he pulls me up until I'm straddling him, and he kisses me deeply before reaching into the nightstand for a condom. I take it from him, and he caresses my thighs as I make quick work of rolling it on.

When I'm done, I kiss him and reach down to align us.

He takes hold of my hips as I press against him, waiting for me to be ready. Letting me take the lead despite how much I can feel him wanting to take control.

"This is new for me," he says, reaching up to cup my breasts. "Every single thing I've done with you over the past few days has been new. I've never felt this way before."

"Me, neither."

I hover above him for a few seconds as I realize there's no going back from this. Once we've taken this final step, I'll be ruined for all other men. He knows it, too, and he gazes up at me with raw adoration.

"I won't hurt you, Eden. I promise. I want this more than you can possibly know."

Even if I had second thoughts, that would haven banished them. I watch his face when I slowly sink down, taking inch by delicious inch. The pressure of him filling me is so exquisite, it makes my mouth drop open. His jaw drops too, but his eyes stay locked onto mine. And then, as I settle onto his hips and fully surround him, a look of immense awe blooms on his face. I have no idea what my expression is, because I can't make sense of what I'm feeling; relief, arousal, gratitude, wonder–all of it twists inside of me as I pull up and then sink down again.

Dear God. Yes.

This is a feeling I never knew existed. The pleasure is amplified and powered by something deeper. Something that infuses my soul as well as my body.

Max pushes his head back into the pillow and holds onto my hips while I ride him, and I've never seen a more glorious man in all my life. I pick up speed, following the rhythm of my pounding blood, and as Max winds tighter and tighter, his face changes. All of a sudden, he's looking at me with raw hunger, and lightning fast, he flips me onto my back and takes over.

"You feel goddamn incredible," he says, thrusting deep and hard, exactly how I need it right now. "Christ, Eden ... how can you feel this good?"

He kisses me, and we moan into each other's mouths as he increases the pace. When I feel myself building, winding tighter with each thrust, I reach between us and circle my fingers. Max stares down at me, unfiltered emotion on his face.

"I love you," he says and grips the back of my neck before increasing his pace. "I've loved you from the start. I couldn't help it. Everything would have been so much simpler if you hadn't made me fall in love with you."

I circle my fingers faster, unable to breathe when the first flashes of my orgasm begin to spark.

"Max ..." It's barely audible. I have no air. Everything is contracting, tighter and tighter, and he looks down at me like I'm a supernova exploding in front of him.

"Yes, Eden ... fuck, yes ..."

And then I come, and I try to keep my eyes open because this is the first orgasm with the man I love, but I can't. Wave after wave hits me, and all I can do is moan Max's name as he keeps thrusting, prolonging the experience for as long as he can.

Then, with a tortured cry, he wraps around me and squeezes. Every muscle goes tight, and my name spills from his mouth over and over again. He presses fully into me one, twice, three times, each accompanied by a sound of debilitating pleasure, and then he collapses onto me, thick arms and legs tangling with mine, melting into relaxation, and we sink into the mattress.

As we lie there, panting and boneless, chests pressed together and hearts beating in shocked, staccato time, I have no clue where he ends and I begin, and against all odds and a lifetime being terrified of this exact feeling, I think I'm okay with that.

Twenty — One
Afterglow

It took a heartbroken mother, an asshole father, and over a decade of conscientious numbing to build a fortress around my heart. And it takes Max one day to demolish it.

For so many years I've thought love would weaken me; make me shapeless and weak in a jagged, unforgiving world. But after truly letting Max in and owning up to how I feel about him, it seems the opposite is true. Being with him makes me feel like a goddamn superhero. Every sweet touch and tender look, every time he smiles at me like he can't believe I'm real, every whispered curse as I pleasure him, fills me with so much adrenaline I could probably outrun a train.

Part of me feels idiotic for being so afraid of this feeling for so long, but there's still a stubborn thorn of cynicism that needles me, whispering that I've stupidly climbed onboard the Love Express, even though I know all too well where it's going to end up. In these moments my brain gets loud and aggressive, like a drunk squaring up for a knock-down, drag-out bar fight with my heart. In the utopia of Max's arms, the drunk passes out before doing any real damage. But honestly, I wonder who would end up winning if Max wasn't with me, constantly reminding me he's in my heart's corner.

Maybe it's this fear that makes me decide to selfishly spend the whole day with him. In between phone calls to the hospital to check on Nan, he cooks for me, showers with me, and keeps me safe and warm. But most of all, he spends a great deal of time entwined with me, showing me time and again how much he loves and needs me.

Apparently, we have lot of sexual frustration to work through, because just when I think we can't possibly fuck anymore, he'll give me a look, or kiss me, or walk around half naked, and the smoldering embers of our lust burst into flame again. Yes, I'm getting sore, but the discomfort is nothing compared to how I feel when he's moving inside me. Connecting that deeply with him is euphoric every time, and a little chafing can't dampen my passion.

So now, I'm lying in bed staring at him as the early-morning sun peeks over the Manhattan skyline. He's sprawled on his stomach, his arms wrapped around a pillow; the sheet barely covering the curve of his ass. Too full of thoughts and feelings to sleep, I gently run my fingers over the muscles in his back before pushing some hair away from his forehead. Then I do something I never thought I would with a man: I sigh. As girly and romantic as it is, it's the only reaction that seems appropriate right now. This beautiful man is mine. How bizarre is that?

My first instinct is to call Asha to download my epic emotions, but right now she's probably tongue deep in a gorgeous Frenchman, to that's not an option. However, I still need an outlet, and there's one sure way for me to purge all of these thoughts that will also help my professional situation.

I lean over and press a soft kiss against Max's head before climbing out of bed, pulling on one of his giant tees, and going into the living room to take a seat at his desk. There's a huge iMac front and center, and when I touch a key, it blinks to life.

I open up a blank document and begin typing. The things I've learned from Max need to be known by others, and right now, writing them down seems the best way to do that. As with any writing, the best stuff comes directly from the heart, and that's what happens as I fill the pages detailing my experiences with Mister Romance. It's not the story I set out to write, and it's nothing like what Derek will be expecting, but it's the truth, and it feels good to speak of something so pure in a world that seems to thrive on mockery and criticism. I write about my pre-conceptions of Max's motives and how wrong they were, I write about his clients and how I misjudged them, but most of all, I write about Max and how he left behind the person he was raised to be and transformed himself into the man so many people needed him to be.

By the time I finish my final paragraph, the sun is fully over the horizon. When I hear Max yawning in the bedroom, I quickly save the document and put the monitor to sleep. I figure I should discuss what I intend to do with it before he reads it, just in case he gets the wrong idea.

When I get back to the bedroom, Max is mid-stretch, and I don't miss that the sheet is barely covering his epic morning wood.

"Good morning," he says, his voice muffled with sleep as I climb under the sheet and curl into his side.

"Morning." I glance down at his erection. "Seriously? Doesn't he ever get fatigued?"

He pulls the sheet up a little, but the outline is still clear as day. "Not around you, that's for damn sure. Believe me, I had no idea he had this kind of stamina until you came along."

I prop myself up on my elbow and look down on him. "Well, don't get any ideas. I have to go be with Nan first thing this morning, and if you start putting that thing anywhere near me, we both know I'll be here for hours."

He pulls me down for a kiss then pulls back to study my face. "Just promise that if you leave today, you're not going to freak out while you're gone and second guess us."

"I can promise I'll try not to." I give him a soft kiss and hope there are no freak-outs in my future, considering I'm an official member of the Love Cult. Right now I could write volumes of poetry about the tenderness of his eyes, the luscious curl of his lips, and the masculine perfection of his body. I'm so full of love for him, Eden from a month ago is in an alternate timeline rolling her eyes so hard, she glimpses brain.

As for Max, he just breathes deeply and stares at me, serene and vindicated. As usual, he can tell what I'm thinking, and he's patting himself on the back for turning the hardened cynic into a lovesick fool.

"You hate how much you're feeling for me, don't you?" he asks, his smile spreading.

"God, so much! It was just never in my life plan to feel like this."

"Same." He traces his fingers around my face. "You disrupted my entire world, Eden Tate. I'm used to being the one in control. The one people fall in love with. I'm not supposed to fall in love."

"Still, you must feel good that I fell for your antics hook, line, and sinker."

He watches his hand as he runs it down my neck and onto my chest. "I didn't have any antics with you, but I did go above and beyond what I'd usually do on dates. Everything was more real with you."

"Because you were trying to kill the story?"

He frowns a little. "In part. I needed you to understand what

I do and why I do it so you'd stop thinking I was an asshole, but more than that, I wanted you to see me. *Know* me. Do you think I can write a song for just anyone? Only for you, and only as Caleb.

I run my fingers through his hair, and when I graze my fingernails across his scalp, he hums his approval. "You couldn't just be yourself?"

His smile falls. "No, because I've spent so many years trying to change the man I used to be, I had no clue who I was anymore." He sits up, so now he's the one looking down at me. "And yet, no matter what character I was playing, I always felt like a better person when I was with you. For so long I've felt like no one, and you made me feel like someone again. Someone who didn't need to hide behind fake personalities to be a good man."

He leans down and kisses me, and after several minutes of slow, passionate making out, things get way more heated than I have time for.

I push him off and laugh when he groans in disappointment.

"Eden, come on. I'm in pain, here."

"Me, too. So you keep that giant dick in your pants until later, and by then Regina may have recovered enough to accommodate him again."

He flips onto his back and covers himself with a pillow. "Damn, being this attracted to you is torture."

I smile and climb out of bed. "Ditto." I walk into the bathroom and turn on the shower. "So, want to meet up for dinner tonight? If we do, I'd like to go back to the hospital afterward. I feel guilty as hell I've had nearly a dozen orgasms instead of sitting by Nan's side, but still ..." I glance out the door at him as I wait for the water to heat up. "We could hang out for a couple of hours."

It's ridiculous that after the amount of sex we've had, I still feel nervous asking him to dinner. My heart is hammering like I just invited the quarterback to prom.

He sits up and stares at me for a few seconds. The tiny silence that follows feels like a lifetime. My brain concocts dozens of reasons for his hesitation, and not one of them is good. Still, I hold my breath and wait for his reply.

"Eden, I'd love to, but tonight ... I'm working."

"Oh. Working as in ...?"

"I have a date."

My stomach turns to lead. "Right. But I thought you weren't seeing clients while we were ... well ... whatever we're doing."

"I wasn't, but I have bills that are past due. Plus, a few of my clients are having a hard time recently, and they could really use my support."

I want to say that I'm sure none of their grandmothers is comatose, but that would be petty, not to mention unfair. He hasn't worked for weeks because of me. I can't begrudge him making a living, even if it does hurt to think of other women getting his affection.

"Of course. No problem at all."

"We can see each other tomorrow night. I'll take you to dinner."

I smile. "Yeah, sure. Sounds great."

"Eden ..."

I know he's going to apologize, and I really don't want him to. "Max, please don't worry. I'm fine. You have bills to pay. I totally understand."

I strip off before climbing into the shower. The water is too hot, but it feels good right now. I let it run over my skin as I try to release the tension in my muscles.

Realistically, I was prepared for this. I've always thought a relationship would contain some degree of disappointment and compromise. Max's work is important to him, and rightly so, but that doesn't make it easier to accept that if I go all-in with him, I'll be a possibly unemployed journalist whose boyfriend services a large percentage of New York's gorgeous socialites. I need to find a way to be okay with that.

When I turn around to wet my hair, I jump when I see a shadow on the other side of the shower curtain. I pull it aside to see Max there wearing a troubled expression.

"Dates are just work," he says. "They don't change how I feel about you." He steps closer. "With everything coming out in the article, I don't know how long this ride is going to last, and I need the money. I'm a college dropout buried under massive debt. I'm never going to be able to earn this much doing something else."

"I know. And I don't want you to quit. You're amazing at what you do, and those ladies need you."

"But it bothers you, doesn't it?"

I turn off the water. When he hands me a towel, I step out and wrap it around me. "Max, if the thought of you romancing and kissing other women didn't drive me insane with jealousy, then you should be concerned about the depth of my feelings." I stretch up to kiss him. "Listen, I knew what you did for a living and fell in love with you anyway. I'll figure out a way to deal with it, okay?"

He stares at me, unblinking for a full three seconds, and I wonder if I've just committed some sort of relationship taboo I wasn't aware of.

"Max? Are you okay?"

He swallows and nods, and I see the muscles in his jaw working overtime. "Yeah, you just ..." He looks like he's struggling to keep himself together. "You just told me you love me for the first time, and I thought I was prepared for it, but it turns out I'm really not."

He pulls me into his arms and buries his face in my neck. "Say it again."

I laugh and squeeze him tighter. "I'm in love with you, Max Riley. Stupidly, sickeningly, revoltingly in love. Does that make you happy?"

I can feel him smiling against my skin. "More than you can possibly fathom." He pulls back and looks down at me. "For the record, I'm also revoltingly in love with you, so I guess we're doing this."

I smile. "I guess we are."

We've been so wrapped up in the bubble of pleasure in which we've been living, we haven't thought about what will happen when we leave this apartment. But now that our feelings are out there, larger than life and scary as hell, we have to find a way to make this thing work in the real world.

"And you're sure you'll be okay with me going back to work?"

He studies my face for a reaction, and I strive to keep my smile sincere.

"Definitely. Now, get out of here before I do things to you that will require me to take another shower."

He gives me a quick kiss and a swat on the ass, but as he walks out into the bedroom, I get a twisting feeling in my stomach that this fresh, shiny relationship we're building is being constructed on shaky ground.

🍒

By the time I've blow-dried my hair and slipped into Max's robe, I can already smell he has breakfast underway. When I get to the kitchen, there's a plate of food on the counter that looks like it was made in a restaurant. Max is bustling around in just his jeans, making real coffee from the vintage espresso machine. I take the moment to gaze at him in awe.

He catches me staring. "What?"

"Just wondering if there are things you suck at."

"Of course. Too many to mention."

I sit on one of the metal stools in front of the stainless-steel-topped island. "Hit me with a few, just so I know you're not lying."

"Okay. Accounting. I'm terrible at it, and it bores me out of my mind."

I scoop some eggs into my mouth. Predictably, they're delicious. "Welcome to the club. And ...?"

"Bowling. I'm king of the gutter balls."

"Yeah, yeah. That's all small potatoes. Anything major?"

He brings over a perfectly made cappuccino and places it in front of me before sliding his arm around my waist and pulling me against him.

"Yes. Staying away from the woman who makes me harder than steel. I'm freaking terrible at that." He leans down and claims my lips, and despite there being minimal pressure and zero tongue, the wave of desire that rushes through me has so much power, it could launch a city-sized satellite into space.

I touch his face as we both just stand there, lips pressed together, breathing rapidly.

When we pull apart, I stare up at him. "I have to finish getting ready, evil man."

"Not yet." He kisses me again, deeper this time, definite tongue, and if his intention was to make me forget what I was about to say or do, he's successful. When he pulls back, his breathing is just as screwed up as mine. He cups my breasts though the soft fabric then grunts in frustration and steps back. "Eat your breakfast. Maybe if your mouth is busy, I'll forget about all the things I want it to do to me."

I make quick work of my plate of food as he cleans up, and I gaze at the wonder of his back. He's gone quiet and seems deep in thought, so I head off to finish getting ready.

When I finally emerge fully dressed to face the day, I'm shocked to find Max sitting in front of the computer. His forearms are on the desk, and he's leaning forward, his face illuminated by the giant screen.

He looks over when he hears me approaching. His expression is a little guilty, but there's something else I can't define.

"You wrote the story this morning?"

I nod. "I couldn't sleep. Too many thoughts."

"This is what you think of me?"

His tone is impossible to read, so I bite the bullet and go with honesty.

"Yes."

He points to the final paragraph then reads it aloud. "Everything is ordinary until someone loves it, then it transforms. Suddenly it's beautiful. Incredible. *Priceless.* Everyone deserves to feel priceless at least once in their lives. Despite his troubled past, Max Riley has created a business out of making women feel that way, and it says something about the state of our image-obsessed society that his business is booming. Maybe if there were more people like Mr. Riley to spread the soul food of romance, the world would be a better place."

He goes quiet then turns to me. "Eden ... this article is ..." He shakes his head. "I'm not worthy of it."

"Yes, you are. I wouldn't have written it otherwise."

He leans back in the chair. "When will it be published?"

I step closer, nervous about how tense he is. "It won't. I've decided to tell Derek I'm pulling it."

I expect to see relief on his face, but instead, he seems conflicted. "This piece is ... brilliant, Eden. Seriously. I couldn't have dreamed you'd write something so beautiful about me. Philosophical, even. This article could make your career."

"Yes, but at the expense of yours, and I'm not willing to do that. I feel better for writing it all down, but Max, you know as well as I do that if I publish this, your business goes up in flames."

He reaches over and takes my hand, and I stand between his legs as he looks down at our fingers. "In the beginning, this decision was so simple. It was either you or me. A fight for survival, but now ..."

I stroke his hair. "I know what you mean."

He leans back in the chair, and we stare at each other. There's no easy answer here. No matter which way we turn, someone is going to be ruined. My stubborn, selfish side doesn't want it to be me, but then I think about hurting him, and it makes me feel sick. Is this what love has reduced me to? Giving up my dreams to protect the man I love?

Maybe Derek will be merciful and not fire me. And maybe I'll be wrong about Max's work tearing us apart.

I don't think either of those things is likely, but I at least have to try.

"This is what relationships are about, right?" I say, sitting on his lap. "Sacrificing what you want for the person you love?"

I lean over and close the document, and Max puts his hand on top of mine on the mouse.

"I wish there was another way."

I sigh. "In a perfect world we could both get what we want, but I know that's not possible, so ..." I give him a smile before sending the document to myself as an email attachment. "I promise, this is for my eyes only. I just want a copy, so whenever I feel like a talentless hack, I can remind myself I once wrote something decent and profound."

When a whooshing sound announces the email has been sent, I delete the document, and then to make it extra painful, I empty the trash.

"Derek's away in Europe for two weeks, but when he gets back, I'll tell him I'm dropping the story. If I beg hard enough, he might let me go back to writing memes."

When Max looks at me in sympathy, I run my fingers over his furrowed brow. "I don't want this to come between us."

"I just hate that you had to do this," he says. "*Thank you* doesn't even start to cover how grateful I am. Will you be okay?"

"Sure. Have you forgotten that I now have a superfine boyfriend for emotional support?" I shudder a little. "Wow, it feels bizarre to say that."

He makes a noise in his chest and pulls me tighter against him. "Maybe you need to say it again, just to get used to it."

"Hmmm. My superfine boyfriend seems to like it when I call him that."

"Fuck yes, he does."

He pulls me in for a kiss, and it's just what I need before I leave our love-bubble to face the real world. Maybe everything will be okay with him by my side. If anyone can make me believe that, Max can.

Twenty — Two
Reality Bites

"Well, that's about all the news today, Nan," I say as I close the paper. "Some big dudes played some other big dudes in sports involving balls, but I know that bores the hell out of you, so I'll sum it all up by saying someone lost, someone won, and lots of people were happy and sad over it."

I fold up the paper and put it on the floor. There's zero space on her nightstand, since they moved her out of the ICU and into her own room a few days ago. If I ever doubted that other people loved Nan as much as Ash and I do, the plethora of vases filling every inch of spare space would prove me wrong.

There's even a bunch of roses from Derek. When they arrived, they reminded me how much I'm not looking forward to telling him I'm shelving my article. After how kind he's been about giving me more time, it almost feels like I'm betraying him.

I grab my phone and look at the text he sent me earlier: <*Hey, Tate. Hope your grandma's doing okay. Looking forward to reading your FINISHED article when I get back. Don't let me down. I'm expecting big things from you. Our bottom line needs this.*>

I know that *Pulse* has been struggling financially, and my

article would have generated some much-needed income, so thinking about delivering the bad news makes me break out in a cold sweat.

Still, it has to be done. What choice do I have?

I put my phone away and stow my guilt as I rub some moisturizer into Nan's arms.

"In other news, Asha called last night to tell me she's met a man in France and is taking some of her vacation time to spend it with him before she comes home, so, phew."

Even though Nan stays completely still, I can feel her implied judgement. "Nan, you didn't hear how happy she was. If I'd ruined her euphoric mood with tragic news about you, it would have been like smashing a butterfly with a tennis racquet. Plus, she was so over the moon to hear about me and Max she squealed 'I knew it!' at least five times, and I didn't want her to then turn around and yell at me. There'll be plenty of time for that when she gets home."

As I finish up and rub the excess lotion on my own arms, my phone buzzes with a text from Max.

<On my way. See you soon.>

My whole body lights up in anticipation. With me spending the past two days at Nan's bedside and him working at night, our quality time has been minimal, so I'm hankering for a good, hard dose of Mr. Riley. We're going to grab dinner tonight and, if there is a God, get naked together. Honestly, the food isn't the star in this scenario. I'd go hungry if it means more time with Max between my legs.

I quickly check my appearance in the bathroom then grab Nan's hairbrush, so I can pretty her up for our visitor. She loves all of the new-age braid styles, and when I do her hair in an intricate way, she looks more like herself.

"So," I say as I pull her hair to the side and detangle it. "I've officially been dating Max for two days now, but ..." I divide her hair into three sections and start braiding. "We're already facing a major hurdle. I mean, can you imagine dating a man who melts panties for a living? Because I'm not going to lie, it's a struggle. I know I should be able to separate fantasy from reality, but when the fantasy includes him making out with other women on the regular, it's tough. I just hope it gets easier to deal with over time, because otherwise ..." Dammit, I don't want to dwell on 'otherwise' It hurts too much.

I curl the braid up to the top of her head and secure it with some pins, then pop in a couple of her favorite daisy clips.

"There," I say as I step back to assess my work. "You're the prettiest elderly teenager in this place." I lean over and kiss her forehead. "Of course, you'd tell me a man as amazing as Max is worth any amount of angst, wouldn't you?" I sit and take her hand. "And you'd probably be right."

I hear a noise, and when I look up, I see Max is in the doorway, watching me with a contemplative smile. "What would Nan be right about?"

My chest lights up with tingles, and I wonder if that's a normal thing. "Everything. As usual."

I stand and wipe my sweaty palms on my jeans. "Look, Nan. Max is here." Even saying his name makes butterflies take flight in my stomach.

He smiles. "Happy to report that Moby and I watched a couple of hours of *Animal Planet* together today. You know, he loves seeing how the common animals live."

Max has been visiting Moby every morning to make sure he doesn't get depressed, and Moby has taken to him like a duck to ... well, you know.

He looks at me and shakes his head. "I'm not saying that you've gotten even more beautiful since I saw you last, but ..."

He takes a deep breath and lets it out. "God, I've missed you."

"It's been forty-eight hours."

"And that's forty-eight hours too long." He comes over and pulls me into a hug, and these days I don't tense up. I hug him back fiercely and let him take away some of my tension.

He pulls pack to look at me. "Would it be disrespectful to kiss you in front of your Nan?"

"No. In fact, the shock of me being affectionate with a man might actually wake her up. Go for your life."

He kisses me, and within seconds we're deeply invested in each other's mouths. Lord, this is strange. Feeling all of this. Letting myself enjoy it. Having a heart so full it seems too big for my body.

We pull apart and step away from each other when a black nurse with unicorns on her scrubs comes in to check on Nan. Her name is Shirley, and she's my favorite.

"Don't let me stop you," she says. "I never bought the story that you two were brother and sister anyway."

Max wipes my lip gloss off his mouth and hides a smile. Then he grabs another chair, and we both sit beside the bed.

"So," Max says as Shirley takes Nan's readings and straps on a blood-pressure cuff. "I know we had plans tonight, but I have to work."

"Another date?" I say, unable to hide my disappointment. "That's the fourth one this week."

Shirley finishes up notating Nan's vitals and shoots us a look. "Oh, Lord. I'm outta here. You two have things to sort out."

I can't say she's wrong.

When she's gone, Max takes my hands. "I'm sorry. I have a backlog from the dates I canceled while I was trying to win you over. I'm just as disappointed as you are." He links his fingers through mine. "The next couple of weeks are going to be hell, but then ... I'm doing everything I can to make sure we'll have more time together. I promise."

I'm feeling mildly resentful that a duck is seeing my man more than I am. "I could come over to the loft in the morning. Give you a special wakeup call."

He looks down when I put my hand on his thigh, and I can practically hear the frantic rush of blood to his groin. "God, I'd love that, but tomorrow's not great. Late night tonight, early start tomorrow. Maybe Friday?"

I lean away from him. For all of his acting prowess, right now it's as clear as the boner in his pants that he's hiding something. My brain says to call him out and try to get to the truth, but my heart whispers that the truth is probably the last thing I want to hear. There's something going on with Max, and if he's keeping it a secret, it must be something that will hurt me.

"Okay, then," I say and do my best to act like anxiety isn't turning my stomach into acid. "I'll wait for you to call. Let me know when things slow down a little."

He stands and pulls me to my feet, and then he cups my face with both hands and kisses me so deeply, I almost believe everything will be okay.

"I love you," he says then kisses me again. "I promise, things will be less crazy soon. I'll see you in a few days."

He holds me for a few seconds, and then with effort, he pulls away and heads to the door.

When he leaves, I sigh and sit back in my chair. "I think you had the right idea, Nan. Ducks are way less stressful than men."

CƷ

As I step into Nannabeth's apartment, I'm suspicious of how

quiet it is. Usually as soon as Moby hears a key slide into the door he comes running to see who it is, but there's no duck to be found.

"Max? Moby?" I walk into the living room and find Max's leather duffle there, but the apartment's empty. Figuring they must be up on roof, I head toward the back stairs.

It's been two days since Max came to the hospital, and I've snuck away from Nan's side in the hope of surprising him and convincing him to have lunch with me before he disappears for a date. It's crazy that now that I'm officially his girlfriend, I'm seeing less of him than when he was just the subject of my story. How is that fair?

We talk on the phone, but it doesn't make being separated any easier. I just need to see him for a few minutes to quiet my natural paranoia that whispers he could still be playing me. Now that I've agreed to kill the story, it seems like he's going back to business as usual and keeping me interested enough not to make trouble. I don't truly believe that, but my illogical, distrustful side does. When I look into his eyes, it makes that part shut up for a while. Being in his arms doesn't hurt, either.

When I get up to roof, I curse that I've left my phone in the apartment, because the sight that greets me needs to be recorded for generations to come. Max is next to the pond wearing just shorts and running shoes, doing shirtless pushups, and Moby is sitting on his butt. Every time Max goes down then up again, Moby quacks, like some sort of feathery personal trainer.

I stay where I am and just watch, stifling my laughter. There's something about the hotness of Max mixed with the adorableness of Moby that makes my heart, as well as locations lower on my body, go into overdrive.

I take my time to ogle Max and all of his sweaty, bulging glory as he does more pushups than I care to count. Dear God, those muscles. I've never really thought about how many places there are to fuck on Nannabeth's roof before, but I'm sure as hell scoping them out now. He's covered in tattoos today, and I wonder which fantasy they're for. Then I stop wondering, because every scenario I come up with is way too sexy to contemplate, and I don't want to think of him oozing all of that sexiness over someone else.

When Max finishes, he stands up slowly to give Moby a chance to flap to the ground.

"Okay," he says, pointing to the pool. "Three times around it, and then you can have a swim." Moby looks up at him and quacks. "Hey, don't do the crime if you can't do the time, buddy. Maybe in the future you'll think more carefully before knocking over an entire box of oats and then spreading them all over the kitchen. Let's go. Move that little feathery ass." Max takes off at a slow jog, and Moby waddles to keep up, quacking angrily as he goes. "Complaining isn't going to help. Come on. Pick up the pace."

I smile as they do their laps, and when they're done, I emerge from the shadows of the stairwell doorway just as Moby jumps up into the pond and splashes around.

Max flinches a little as I approach, clearly not expecting company.

"Oh, hey." His shock melts into a smile, and he jogs over to meet me. "I didn't expect to see you here." He leans down and gives me a soft kiss, but when I try for more, he steps back. "Trust me, you don't want to go there. I'm disgusting."

I step into him and put my hands on his chest. "I don't care. Kiss me."

Lust flashes in his eyes, and he takes my head and angles it to the side before kissing me, slow and intense. He hasn't shaved in a few days, and the roughness of his scruff is sexy as hell. He angles me the other way and groans against my lips. When he pulls back, he looks down at himself and sighs.

"See what you do to me? One kiss, and I'm rock hard. No other woman has ever had this effect on me before."

I look down at the shape of him, jutting out and stretching the front of his shorts. "You know, it would really be a pity to see all of that go to waste. I could take care of it, if you want."

I palm him gently, and he groans again. "You have no idea how much I'd like that, but I have to shower and get dressed. I have a date downtown in forty minutes, so I'm already in danger of running late. Are you okay to stay up here with Moby for a while?"

"Yeah. Of course. I'll come down and see you before you go." I hide my disappointment and try not to pout as he jogs over to the stairs and disappears.

Welp, best laid plans and all that. At least I got a kiss.

I go over to the pond and squat near the edge, so I can pick some leaves out of the water, and when I glance over at Moby, he looks toward the stairwell and quacks.

"Yeah, buddy. He's left us." He quacks again. "Well, he has a very important job that helps people feel good about themselves. It shouldn't make me jealous, right?" Moby swims over to me and nuzzles my hand, and I take the cue to stroke his head. "Oh, you're jealous, too? Thank God. Nice to know I'm not alone."

He swims for a few more minutes but keeps looking over at the stairwell.

"Okay, fine. We'll go down and see him. Come on."

Moby jumps out of the pond and shakes off some water. Then I pick him up and carry him downstairs.

When we get back to the apartment, Max is freshly showered and smelling all citrusy and edible. I turn on the TV and put Moby in his spot on the couch then watch Max get ready. He's wearing beat-up black jeans and black boots, and I watch his muscles ripple under his tattoos as he rubs some sort of gel into his hair to make it chaotic and messy.

"Playing Caleb today?" I ask, even though I hate the idea. No one should be allowed to swoon over that sexy musician except for me.

"Uh ... no." He finishes his hair and pulls a black T-shirt from his bag. "I'm locked in to something a little rougher today." After he pulls on the shirt, he digs into the bag again and removes a grungy leather jacket that has *Sons of Diablo* embroidered on the back.

"A biker?"

He nods and says, "Yep," then shoves his dirty clothes and toiletries back into the duffle.

"So, how does this scenario work?"

He frowns as he zips the bag. "Oh, you know. Rough guy just needs the love of a good woman to tame him." He sits in Nan's favorite chair and laces up his boots.

"Has this client done this scenario before?"

"No."

"Is it an existing client or someone new? Is she playing a role as well?"

He glances up at me then back to his boots. "Eden, I don't think talking about work stuff is useful. I know you have a hard time with it."

"Maybe if I know more about what's going on, it will be easier."

He stands and looks at me. "And maybe it won't. If you were playacting with other guys, I know damn well I wouldn't want to hear about it." He walks into the kitchen, and returns with a fresh bowl of food for Moby, which he puts next to him. "Don't eat that all at once, okay? It has to last until Mrs. Schott comes to see you in the morning."

"Max ..." He turns to me, and I take his hand, trying to hide how my stomach is churning with anxiety. "I can guarantee nothing you tell me will be worse than what I'm imagining. Have you forgotten I've been on dates with you? I know how sexy they are."

He brings my hand up and kisses the back of it. "Well, for a start, my regular dates are nowhere near as sexy as what I experienced with you. Our chemistry was off the charts. Today's date is no big deal. My client is playing Dyson's girlfriend. He's an abusive asshole. Dyson has found out I like her, we fight, and then I romance the client for the rest of the night."

"Uh huh." I sidle up to him. "Okay, so ... give me a little taste of this sexy bad boy." I run my fingers up the strong muscles in his neck.

"Eden ..." He tenses his jaw. "I really don't think this a good idea."

"Please? I could help you get into character." I don't know what the hell I'm doing right now, but I feel like I'm on the outside looking in, and I hate it.

He searches my face for a few seconds and must read how I'm feeling, because the next thing I know he grabs me roughly by my shoulders and shoves me back into the wall. "Is this what you want? To see me lose it, because I can't fucking stay away from you? Is this why you came here?"

The personality change is so sudden, he catches me off guard, but when I realize he's just slipping into character, I try to follow his lead.

"I came here to be with you," I say, pushing him in the chest. "I don't have your self-control. I can't just feel this way and ignore it."

His expression becomes hard and incredulous. "You think I

can *ignore* how I feel about you? Are you fucking kidding me?" He searches my face, his anger fading the longer he stares at me. "Every day it kills me to not be with you, but what choice do I have? When I look at you, how I feel is written all over my face. This is why you can't come around. Because every damn person I come across can tell I'm out of my mind in love with you. "

He cups my face with both hands then kisses me, hard and needy. I kiss him back in the same way. It's rough and accompanied by desperate noises, because we both know we're not going to get the satisfaction we crave right now. His date is waiting, and unlike me, she's paid for the pleasure of his company.

"I have no more time," he says, as he kisses me once more.

"I know." He pulls back and leans his forehead against mine, and we're both panting when we take one last look at each other.

"Just out of interest," I say, still regaining my breath. "Do you kiss your clients like that?" It's out of my mouth before I have a chance to stop it.

Dammit, Eden. Stupid.

Predictably, Max tenses, and it feels like a bucket of water has been poured over us.

He steps back and adjusts his erection before putting his hands on his hips and sighing. "Eden ..."

"I'm sorry. Don't answer that. I don't want to know."

He turns and grabs his bag. "I have to go. I'll call you later, okay?"

I lean back against the wall, feeling foolish and petty. "Sure. Later."

"Bye, Moby." He opens the door and turns to look at me. "For the record, I don't kiss *anyone* the same way I kiss you. Never have, never will. And in the future, I think it would be best if we don't discuss work."

I nod, and he gently closes the door behind him.

I cover my face with my hands and grunt in frustration. *Well, that could have gone better.*

I walk over and flop next to Moby on the couch, and notice he's watching me with narrowed eyes.

"Don't judge me. I know, okay?" He continues to stare. "Moby, you don't know what it's like. This is my first relationship, and I can't deal with how much I love him most days. But the irony of our situation is that when we're together, I can't imagine life without him. And when we're not, part of me thinks we're both better off that way. And I don't know if this is just how relationships work."

Moby makes a soft noise and comes and sits on my lap. I stroke his feathers and try to let go of my tension.

"He knows how much I hate sharing him, Mobester. That's why he doesn't want to talk about it. But is this what our life is going to be like now? Me raging on the inside and him trying to sweep the issue under the rug?" Moby snuggles into my arm, and I can't believe I'm so disoriented by this situation, I'm asking for advice from a duck.

I almost miss the days when I didn't give two squats about Max Riley. It was an easier, simpler time.

CR

I finish reading the final paragraph of *Great Expectations* and close the cover. "See, Nan? This is why I'm always nice to homeless people. You never know when they might turn their lives around and become grateful rich people who want to give you heaps of money."

I put the book on the floor with the growing pile that have

already been read and yawn. I've slept here for the past few nights. I figure if I can't be with Max, I'll be with Nan. I just wished that when I talked to her about how my life seems to be spiraling into areas I can't seem to navigate, she spoke back. Maybe then I wouldn't feel so lost.

"Nan," I say and brush a stray piece of hair away from her face. "I haven't said it for a few days, but ... could you wake up now? I miss you." My throat tightens and my eyes well up. "God, how I miss you. I swear, if you just wake up you can lecture me all you like about my love life. In fact, I'd welcome you meddling right about now." I wipe away a stray tear. "I have an amazing man, but there's this terrible feeling I'm losing him, and I don't know why."

I take her hand, and for a brief second I think I feel her fingers tighten around mine. But as I hold my breath to see if it happens again, I realize it must have been wishful thinking.

Feeling frustrated and way too emotional, I wipe my face dry and hug her arm. "Please wake up. Please." I close my eyes to stop the tears. "I've tried life without you, and I hate it. Come back to me. Please."

I pray silently for a while, and I must eventually doze off, because I have a dream in which Nan lectures me about how wonderful Max is. As I come to, I hold onto the last vestiges of it. I've missed the sound of her voice so much, even hearing it in a fantasy makes me smile.

"I mean, really, Eden. It's probably all in your head. You clearly love him. Why are you trying to sabotage things before you've even tried?"

God, that's so realistic, it's scary.

I snap my eyes open to see Nan staring down at me, eyes blue and bright.

"Oh, so you are awake? And here I was thinking you were

pretending to sleep just to avoid the conversation."

I sit up so fast, my head spins. "Nan?"

She looks down at her arm. "Oh, thank God. You've been leaning on that thing for so long, I can barely feel it."

I stare at her in shock for a full three seconds, until the reality of what's happening slams into me like a Mack truck, and then I lunge for the remote and hit the nurse button at the same time I yell at the top of my lungs.

Nan recoils. "Good God, Eden, keep your voice down! You'll wake the dead with that caterwauling."

Shirley hurries into the room, and when she spies a conscious Nan, her mouth drops open in disbelief.

"You see it too, right?" I whisper, terrified I'm actually still asleep.

"Oh, yes, honey," Shirley says. "She's most definitely awake." Another nurse comes in, and Shirley instructs her to page the doctor immediately.

Nan looks at each of us in turn as if we've lost our minds. "Of course I'm awake, and what's more, I'm starving. What's a girl have to do to get a sandwich around here?"

High, hysterical laughter bubbles out of me, and then I'm bawling like a baby as I sprawl across Nannabeth's chest and hug her as hard as I can without hurting her.

"Oh, sweetie," she says as she pats my back. "It's okay. I was only joking about the sandwich. But seriously, I'd murder someone for a coffee. And an explanation as to why I'm wearing this hideous gown. I look like an old woman."

ೞ

An hour later, Nan has been thoroughly x-rayed and examined, and the reality of what's she's been through finally sinks in when the doctor announces her left arm is partially paralyzed.

"It's quite normal to have something like this after a head injury," he tells Nan, "but I can't guarantee it's not permanent."

Nan waves him off with her good hand. "I'll be fine. Do you think I'm going to let a coma slow me down? Please."

I laugh, because if anyone can beat a little pesky brain damage, it's my nan.

"Now," Nan says. "When can I get out of here? And don't tell me a few days, young man, because I'm not having it. I have a duck to get home to."

He glances over at me. "Uh ... it's normal for patients to be disoriented. I wouldn't worry too much about minor delusions."

"Oh, I'm not worried," I say. "And that's not a delusion. She really does have a pet duck."

Nan looks at the doctor with a smug smile. "Now, about you getting me a speedy discharge ..."

As Nan browbeats the doctor about leaving, I'm floating on cloud nine. She's back. Thank you, Lord!

I pull out my phone to call Max, but then I realize he'll be in the middle of a date, and I really don't want to break such happy news in a voice mail. It's weird that not being able to share my happiness with him takes the shine off it a little. Like nothing is truly real until he knows about it.

"Eden?" I look over to see Nan staring at me. Apparently, she's chased the doctor away. "Everything okay, sweetheart?"

"God, Nan, I should be the one asking you that. You're the one who's been comatose."

She smiles. "I'm fine. I'm just cranky they want to keep me here for the rest of the week. Poor Moby must be out of his mind with worry, even if Max has been visiting him."

I go over to her. "How do you know that?"

"Oh, I heard lots of things over the past two weeks." She gestures to the chair beside the bed. "I can't believe you waited until I was unconscious before getting yourself a boyfriend. Really, Eden. You deprived me of all of the juicy details. So just in case I missed anything, I want you to tell me the whole story from the beginning, and don't leave anything out. I want to know everything about your handsome Max Riley."

Twenty — Three
Morning Delight

It's all Nan's fault that I'm on my way to Max's apartment at seven a.m. wearing only sexy underwear beneath a trench coat. She grilled me for hours about Max and what's happened between us, and when I mentioned his work was causing tension, she told me I had to be proactive in addressing our issues. Last night she practically shooed me out of her room and told me that if I was worried about losing our connection, I should show up unannounced this morning and 'blow his socks off'. I don't think she meant 'blow' as in suck his dick, but with Nan, I'm never sure. She can be filthy when she wants to be.

As I climb the stairs to his apartment, I'm surprised to hear voices. From what he's told me about the hours he's been working, I expected him to be fast asleep after a long night with multiple clients, but it sounds like he's having breakfast with Dyson.

Dammit. I'm wearing thigh-high stockings and stilettos with a super-short trench coat. I don't think it will take too much imagination for Dyson to figure out why I'm here. I wonder how embarrassed Max will be to have his friend witness my blatant booty-call.

Oh, well, I guess we'll find out.

When I knock, everything goes silent for a moment. Then I hear heavy footfalls before Max pulls open the door. He's wearing a white tank under a plaid shirt, with faded jeans and work boots.

Dear God, that's a good look on him.

His eyes widen when he sees me, but I'm not sure it's in a good way.

"Hey. Hi."

"Hey." He does a full sweep of my outfit, and then his mouth drops open. "Jesus, am I still asleep? Because I swear to God I had a dream the other night that started just like this." I can see Dyson moving around in the background, and despite how turned on Max seems, he's also nervous.

"Uh ... I just thought ..." God, I feel ridiculous. "I wanted to come and let you know the good news in person. Nan woke up."

"Holy shit, Eden! That's fantastic news!" He pulls me into his arms and lifts me off the floor. "Is she okay?"

I cling to him as my legs dangle. "She's great. A little paralysis in her left arm, but it's already getting better."

He puts me down but keeps his arms around me. "I can't tell you how happy that makes me. I'll stop by this afternoon after we wrap up our job." He looks over his shoulder then back at me. "Do you want to come in? I was just about to head out to work, but ..."

"I'm sorry. I should go."

As I turn away, he grabs my wrist and pulls me toward him. "I have a few minutes. Come in."

He takes my hand and leads me inside where Dyson is also dressed in work gear and clutching what looks like a collection of architect's drawings. There are two hard hats on the kitchen bench.

Dyson gives me a wave and does a double take at my outfit before playing it casual. "Hey, Eden. Good to see you. I couldn't help overhearing. So great about your Nan."

I give him a smile. "She said she loved your Mr. Darcy. Thanks so much for doing that."

He waves his hand in an 'it was nothing' gesture. "Just happy to hear she's on the mend."

I look at Max, then at Dyson. "Construction worker fantasy?"

Dyson nods. "Yeah. Rich client has booked us for an extended role-play. Long hours. Lots of extra actors. It's pretty intense."

He shoots Max a look then grabs one of the hard hats and heads toward to the door. "Anyway, better go. The guys will be waiting."

He hurries out and closes the door behind him. Then there's silence as Max stares at me.

"So, this outfit ..."

"I feel stupid."

"You shouldn't, because, damn ... I almost had a heart attack when I opened the door. Dyson is a friend and all, but getting aroused in front of him isn't something I'm cool with." He steps forward and grabs the belt. "May I?"

The way he's looking at me makes all of my saliva dry up, so I just nod.

He unties the belt, and when the coat falls open to reveal the smallest black lace lingerie I could find, I think his saliva dries up, too.

"God ... *damn*."

Slowly, he pushes the coat off my shoulders, and it drops to the floor with a soft whoosh. He runs his fingers over my breasts, his eyes getting hungrier every second. The need I feel in him when he looks at me like that makes me happy. It gives me hope that if he ever had to decide between me and his work,

I'd have a fighting chance of coming out on top.

He walks me back until the cold metal of the door is pressing against my butt, and then he cages me between his arms. "You look ... edible. But, I really should go."

"Should you?" I reach behind me and flick open the catch on my bra. He swallows as I slide it off, his gaze searing my skin. *Choose me, Max. Please. Not your job.*

"Eden ..." He cups my right breast and brushes his thumb over the nipple. I shiver and put my hand over his, urging him to squeeze harder. "If I could, I'd make love to you all day. You know that, don't you?"

"Then stay." *Choose me.* "Please, stay." I pull him forward by his waistband and unbuckle his belt, then I start on his jeans. "Even if it's only for a while longer."

He stares at me, and I don't know if he can read my deeper meaning, but his expression becomes more serious.

"I'm working really hard to try and make sure we can be together more. I hope you know that."

"I do. I just ... I don't know if I can go on like this. I feel like everyone else is getting more of you than I am."

"Eden ..." He kisses my cheek, then my neck. "This isn't how I want it to be."

"But this is how it is. And I thought I could handle it, by maybe I can't."

He pulls back and gazes into my eyes. "Don't give up on me. I know it's difficult right now, but I just need some time."

I pull off his plaid shirt, and run my hands over the tight muscles in his arms. "To do what?"

"I'm still figuring that out." He bends to kiss my breast, teasing my nipple just enough to have me squirming against him, desperate for more. "Just trust that I love you, and will move heaven and earth to make you happy."

I grip his head as he sucks a nipple into his mouth and anchor my hands in his hair to stop my legs from buckling.

"You know what would make me the happiest woman on the planet right now?" I slide my hand into his underwear, and he groans as I close my fingers around him, already rock hard. "Having you inside me."

"Fuck ... Eden ..."

"Please, Max. I need you."

I see the moment his resolve melts. His eyes become fiery, as if the pressure of having to always disappoint me is too much.

He shoves me back against the door and kisses me, hard.

"How the hell am I supposed to resist you? All day long I dream about being inside you, even when I'm with clients. It's freaking ridiculous."

Then he's ripping off his tank and yanking down my panties, and as soon as his jeans and underwear are out of the way, he pulls my leg up to his hip and thrusts deep inside of me.

I gasp as he fills me, and he does the same, our voices echoing in the empty apartment.

"God ..." He freezes, then withdraws slowly before pushing back in. "Whenever I'm inside you, I don't ever want to leave."

"Then stay."

When he starts to thrust, our conversation ends, because the only sounds we're capable of making are long, extended moans and needy grunts. But I'm not sure the desperation that drives us is a good thing. It feels like we're both hanging on to the present to avoid thinking about our uncertain future.

Twenty — Four

Survival of the Hottest

Another week goes by with me trying to ignore my growing sense of dread about Max and my inability to deal with his job. I feel like I have a countdown clock running in the background of my life. I just have no idea what will happen when it reaches zero. Will that be it for me and Max? Game over?

I sigh and dig weeds out of Nan's garden beds. My mood isn't helped by the knowledge I'm turning into one of those women I used to think about with disdain. The ones who go out of their minds obsessing about a man and what they'd do if they lost him. The ones who are lovesick and pathetic.

Nearby, Nan kneels beside Moby's pond and fusses with him. "I think he's limping."

"Nan, he's swimming. He can't limp while he swims."

"He can and he is. I think he sprained something flapping around when Max came over yesterday. I swear he's imprinted on that man. He gets way too excited whenever he sees him. Maybe he needs an X-ray."

I shake my head and go back to pulling weeds. It's good to see that Nan's near-death experience hasn't changed her. She's been home for a week now, and everything's almost back to normal. Her left arm still doesn't have much strength in it, but at least she can move it.

Even though Max is still working day and night, he's dropped over a few times. I know he's coming to see me, but he spends most of his time chatting with Nan and charming her into a stupor. He still throws me glances that make me wish we were alone and naked, but I've been trying not to pressure him regarding sleepovers, because honestly, he looks exhausted. No wonder he's never had a successful relationship. The man's a workaholic. Just one more thing that doesn't bode well for our future.

He's asked me to give him time and trust him, and I'm trying to do that, even though patience and trust are two things I have in short supply.

"Not seeing Max again today?" Nan asks as she throws some bread into the water for Moby.

"Nope. Apparently, there are a whole bunch of other women he'd rather spend time with." Jealousy, however, I have by the bucketful.

"Aw, sweetie, you know that's not true. He's a freelancer. He needs to take the work when it's there."

"I know, Nan. I just can't help feeling ... we're the right people who met at the wrong time. The odds are stacked against us."

"He loves you. I know that much."

"Maybe. But sometimes, that's not enough." I always swore I wouldn't buy into the lie of 'the one' and the whole 'love can overcome anything' malarkey, but now that I have, it hurts like hell to find out I've been right to be cynical all these years.

I dust off my hands and walk over to her. "Anyway, I'm trying not to think about my issues with Max. I have to get ready for my final meeting with Derek. I'm going to beg him for my old job back and hope he's in a good mood. If he's not, Asha and I might have to come and crash here when we get evicted."

Nan pulls me down into a hug. "I'm sad you can't publish that beautiful article about Max, honey, but do you really want to hold onto that job? You hate it."

"True, but I'm pretty sure I'd hate being unemployed even more." I kiss her on the cheek. "So, tell me honestly, will you be okay here by yourself?"

She pulls back and scowls at me. "Now what have I told you about treating me like I'm an old woman? I won't have it, Eden. One little coma, and you tiptoe around like I'm made of eggshells. I'll be *fine*. Plus, your sister is getting back today, and I promised her we'd spend the afternoon making voodoo dolls of you and sticking them with pins."

"She's not going to forgive me any time soon for not telling her about your accident, is she?"

I hear a noise behind me before a familiar voice says, "No, she's really not."

I spin around, and then Nan and I both let out noises of delight when we see Asha standing there, looking even more radiant than she was before she left.

"Oh, my God!" I say as she runs over to us and wraps us in her arms. "Ash, I've missed you so damn much."

She squeezes me as we all cling to each other in a three-way hug, and I don't even care that I'm crying right now. My sister is home, and she couldn't have come at a better time.

She pulls back, tears glinting on her lashes. "I got in early, so I came straight here." She turns to Nan and gives her a thorough examination. "Are you okay?"

Nan rolls he eyes. "Don't *you* start with me. This is why I choose to never get sick. People start to treat you like you're an invalid."

I hug both of them again, happy that at least this part of my life is holding together.

"I need to hear all about France, Ash, but right now I have to go get ready for my meeting with Derek."

Ash takes my hand. "I'm so sorry about the article, Edie. I know how much you wanted that promotion."

I shrug. "*C'est la vie*, right?"

She hugs me again. "At least you have an amazing man to console you."

"Yeah," I say, pushing down my emotions. "At least I have that."

Ash says she'll help me get ready, and then turns to Nan. "Will you be okay by yourself, old girl?"

Nan stares at her, unimpressed. "Get out of here before I forget why I love you two so much."

We laughs as we head downstairs, and by the time Asha is finished with me, I look like a French model. She's dressed me in the prettiest floral wrap-dress I've ever seen, rationalizing that if I look like a delicate flower, Derek might be less inclined to yell at me and toss me out into the street. I can only pray she's right.

"Edie, no matter what happens today, know that I couldn't be prouder of you." She hugs me again. "But please know I will be torturing you for months as payback for not telling me about Nan."

I laugh and squeeze her. "I'd expect nothing less. See you later."

As I head toward the subway station, I take some deep breaths to calm my nerves. I wish I could talk to Max. I know he's working, but I crave his support right now.

As if I've willed it to happen, my phone lights up with his number, and a wave of relief rushes though me as I answer. "Hi. I didn't think I'd get to speak to you until later."

"I snuck away." Even through the phone, his voice soothes me. "How are you feeling?"

"Like I could win the World Barfing Championship." I just have to remember I'm doing this for him. Maybe that will stop my stomach from churning with too much acid.

He makes a sympathetic noise. "I just want you to know I'll never forget that you were willing to give up you dream for me. One day soon, I'm going to make it up to you."

"With sex?"

He chuckles. "Among other things." His voice gets softer. "You're an amazing woman, Eden Tate. I hope you know that."

I look both ways then cross the street. "I don't think Derek would agree with that assessment."

"You never know. He might surprise you."

"Sure. And I might suddenly sprout a tail."

"Is it wrong that I'd still do you with a tail?"

"Not at all. Mutant-girls need lovin' too."

He laughs, and I pause at the mouth of the subway and take in a breath and then release.

"Okay, I gotta go and meet my doom. Will you call me later?"

There's silence for a second, and then he says, "Absolutely. I love you."

I take one more deep breath as I head down the stairs. "I love you, too."

CR

Half an hour later, when I arrive at the Pulse offices, I suspect the writing's already on the wall for me. Every head turns my way the second I step in the door.

Shit. Not a good sign.

Despite his faults, Derek has a pretty good sense of people. He's probably predicted what I'm going to do and informed everyone I'm not long for this office. That suspicion unnerves me more than I'd like.

As I mutter greetings to everyone, Toby peeks his head over the top of his cubicle, but before I can say hello to him, he ducks out of sight.

I walk over and find him hunched down in his chair. "What are you doing?"

He looks around and sits up, as if he didn't know I was there. "Oh, Eden! Hi. How are you?" He stands and gives me an awkward hug. "Great to see you. Good to hear about Nan. I hear Asha's coming home today? That's fantastic. How's everything? Good?"

"Toby." He snaps his mouth closed. "What's going on?"

"Going on? Nothing. Why? Everything's fine. Why wouldn't it be?"

"You're babbling. You only do that if you're drunk or nervous, and since it's not even lunchtime, I hope you're not drunk."

He blinks a few times then glances over at Derek's office. "I can't say anything. You'll have to see Derek."

"Is he suing me or something? I haven't even told him about the story yet."

"You'll have to talk to him." He's like a damn chicken, looking everywhere but at me.

"Do you want to catch a bite afterward? Help me drown my blues? I'm buying."

"Yeah, maybe. I have a lot of work. I'll see."

Now I know there's something wrong. I've never known Toby to blow off a free lunch before.

"Tobes, please promise me that if I get fired, we'll still be friends. Just because I no longer work here doesn't mean we can't hang out, right?"

That makes him focus on me, and he gives me a reassuring smile. "As if you could get rid of me that easily. I'll always be there for you."

"TATE!" I look over to see Derek standing in his doorway. "Let's go. I don't have all day."

I give him a nod before turning back to Toby. "Okay. I'll see you later, yes?"

He pats my shoulder. "Absolutely. Good luck." I'm a little hurt Toby isn't more distressed. Doesn't he understand what's at stake here? I'm about to beg a man who has the temperament of a cranky Rottweiler to allow me to go back to churning out memes, a job I'm terrible at and despise. And if I'm not successful, which I doubt I will be, Toby will lose his cubicle buddy forever. How is he okay with this?

As I walk into Derek's office, everything seems to go into slow motion, and I swear I hear gallows drums. If he's feeling generous, maybe Derek will allow me a last cigarette. Despite everything, if this ends up being my last day here, I'm going to miss this place. I really liked the people, not to mention a steady paycheck.

As I approach the door, I pull my shoulders back. I've been trying to prep myself all morning for Derek's reaction to what I'm about to tell him. Maybe I should have worn a rain poncho just in case his head explodes with rage. I've heard brains are a bitch to get out of silk.

After closing the door behind me, I sit in the chair in front of his desk, and for once he's not typing away on his tablet. He's sitting calmly with his fingers steepled in front of his mouth, and he's staring at me with those cold, gray eyes. I cross my legs and clear my throat, and I'm about to lay everything on the line when Derek says, "Nice dress."

I look for the sarcasm in his tone but can't find it. "Uh ... thanks. Nice ... uh ... haircut." I'm not lying. For once his hair doesn't look like he's been pulling it out by the roots all day.

"I hear your grandmother is recovering well."

"Uh, yes. Thanks. She loved your flowers." I clear my throat. "So, Derek ..."

He leans back in his chair and crosses his arms over his chest, a small smile curling the edges of his mouth. "You're a sly one, Tate, I'll give you that. You kick and scream for me to give you this assignment, then you bitch about protecting your sources, you tell me that you're going to write a ball-shriveling scandal that will have New York's social elite scrambling under the nearest rock, and then after I give you an extension on your deadline ... well, then you don't deliver on any of it."

Okay, so he already knows. I wonder if Toby told him, and that's why he was acting so strangely. "I'm sorry, Derek. I really am. I know I haven't given you what I promised."

"No, you haven't. But goddammit, woman, you've given me something better, and I wanted you to be here to see the reaction when it went up on the site. Honestly, I think it's going to break records, Tate. My ass is tingling just thinking about it."

I roll his words around in my brain for a second, hoping they'll re-form into a different pattern that makes more sense, but they don't.

"I'm sorry, what?"

He holds up his finger and looks at his watch. "Just be patient. It went live a few minutes ago, so any second now ..." He seems to hold his breath for a full five seconds, and then, as if on cue, every phone in the entire place starts ringing at once, including his.

He smiles, and it's such a foreign expression on his face, it looks all wrong. "I knew it."

He taps some keys on his computer then turns it around so I can see. Staring back at me, front and center on the *Pulse* Features page, is my story, and beneath it is a counter showing the number of clicks it's receiving, as well as incoming traffic to the site.

"Jesus. It's even better than I predicted. Look at this." He brings up his inbox. "We're already getting requests to use it on subsidiary sites. There's one from the *New York Times*. This is insane."

He continues tapping on keys and mumbling excitedly as I sit there in shock, my blood pressure getting higher every second. This can't be happening. How is this happening?

In my purse, my phone starts vibrating, but I ignore it.

"Derek, how did you get that story?"

He keeps his eyes on the screen as he lets out a short laugh. "Oh, you really want me to eat crow and say you were right to browbeat me into giving you a chance? Fine. The story was your idea. Mind you, when you emailed it through to me this morning, I didn't think it would be so fucking good. Sorry I doubted you. There. Happy now? Because I only throw out two *sorry*s per year, and you've just used up your quota."

People start knocking at the office door and come in bearing messages about other news outlets wanting details about Mister Romance so they can run their own features, but I barely hear them. All I can think about is that someone sent him that story, and now, in the space of a few minutes, Max is out of business.

Goddammit.

"Derek, this came from *my* email account?"

He stays glued to his screen. "Yeah. Why?"

No matter how much I deny that this is my fault, Max won't believe me, and I could hardly blame him. After all of those noble sentiments about me giving up my dream for him, it's going to look like I turned around and betrayed him.

I get up and walk out of Derek's office in a daze. He's so busy, he barely notices. People congratulate me as I pass, but it all rings hollow. I feel like throwing up.

When I reach Toby, a light bulb goes off in my brain.

I poke him in the chest. "What the hell, Toby? You hacked into my email? *You* sent Derek the story?"

Toby stands and holds up his hands. "Okay, just wait a second before you murder me. Yes, I didn't want you to get fired, so passing along the story was the best way of preventing that."

"I can't believe this! You've ruined everything! Max's business ... his trust in me."

"Wait, stop. I'm just the tech genius in this scenario, not the mastermind." He holds his phone out to me. "There's someone you need to speak with."

I take the phone, my face burning with anger and embarrassment. "Who is this?"

"Eden."

I squeeze my eyes shut. "Max, I have no idea what's going on. I'm so sorry. I never wanted this to happen. I promise, I intended on coming here and killing the story. You have to believe –"

"Eden, stop. I know it wasn't you."

"You do?"

"Yes. Because it was me." I turn to Toby, who's now smiling from ear to ear. "I couldn't let you throw your career away for me, and seriously, that story was so damn good, everyone needed to read it. I'm so proud of you, I can't put it into words."

"But ... your business."

"We have a lot to talk about. Can you come to the warehouse?"

"Now?"

"Well, as soon as Derek pulls his head out of his ass long enough to give you a huge promotion and a substantial raise, yes."

I sit down in Toby's chair. I don't trust my legs to hold me up anymore. Now I know how Alice must have felt the day she fell through the rabbit hole.

"Max, what the hell is happening?"

"It will all become clear soon. I'll text you the code for the warehouse door. Come straight in when you arrive. I'll be waiting."

Then he hangs up, and I feel like all the air has been knocked out of my lungs. I sit there and stare off into space as a cyclone of activity swirls around me. Just when I think I have a handle on everything, this happens. I'm so confused, I don't know whether to laugh or cry.

℘

By the time I make it to the alley behind Max's warehouse it's midafternoon, and I'm hoping that whatever I'm walking into is good news. I still can't believe he exploded his career in order to save mine, but I don't know what that means for us. Being made the new Head of Features at *Pulse*, and the sizable raise that came with it, means nothing if I can't keep Max in my life.

When I get to the stairs, I notice the mural is different. Instead of a man half hidden in shadows, there's a couple embracing, and they look remarkably like Max and me. The motto on the door is different, too. It used to read, *Abandon hope, all ye who enter.* Now, it reads, *All you need is love.*

A rush of flutters takes flight in my stomach as I pull open the door and step inside.

When the door closes behind me, I'm engulfed by darkness. There's a dull glow from the exit sign above the door, but otherwise all I can see is inky blackness.

"Max?" My voice echoes, but not as much as I expect considering how big and empty the space is. I grab my phone to use the flashlight, but then I remember it ran out of juice about thirty emails ago, so I drop it back into my purse and take a tentative step forward.

"Max? Are you here?"

"Eden." His voice wraps around me, deep and resonant. "How are you feeling?"

"Confused." I squint when I think I see something glint a few yards in front of me, but there's not enough light to make it out. "What am I doing here? And what happened today? You asked Toby to hack me and send that article to Derek? Knowing what it would do to your business? Is this ..." I clench my hands against the tightening in my throat. "Are we done? Is that what this is all about?"

There's silence, then he says, "You tell me. Am I too late?"

"Too late for what?"

"Proving that you're the most important thing in the world to me."

I hear a click, and then a path of light illuminates the floor from where I'm standing to where Max is, a dozen yards away. He looks slick and sharp in a grey suit, but his expression is troubled. "I know you hated thinking about me with other women, and ... I should have told you what I was planning earlier, but I didn't want to get your hopes up before I knew I could pull it off. I signed the final contracts a couple of hours ago."

"Max ... I still don't understand what's happening."

"You will. But first, I have to know ... do you love me?"

I step forward, hating the distance between us like it's a living being. "How do you not know by now that I love you more than

I thought I could love anyone? It's sad and pathetic and wrong how much I love you, and most days I'm so desperate to see you and touch you, I want to punch myself in the face."

He tries not to smile. "That's the sweetest thing anyone's ever said to me. And believe me, the feeling is entirely mutual. But loving me shouldn't have a price tag, and if you hadn't published that story, you would have been sacrificing your career for me, and I couldn't live with that."

"So you decided to sacrifice yours? I thought we'd settled this. You need the money. Your debt ..."

He walks forward, slowly. "Eden, the second I fell in love with you, I knew my career was over. As much as I tried to continue on, I couldn't do it anymore. Not in the same way. I didn't want to touch anyone but you, or kiss anyone but you. I was doing my clients a disservice, because when I was with them, I was counting down the hours until I could be with you again, and that's not fair to them, or you, or me."

He stops a few feet away, but I force myself not to touch him, until I can comprehend where we stand. His words make my heart expand in my chest to the point of pain, but I'm still confused. "So ... you're telling me you're retiring?"

"In a way. In nature, you either evolve or die. I decided to evolve."

He clicks something in his hand, and I hear a beeping sound. Then, all of the lights come on at once, momentarily blinding me, and I shield my eyes. When I lower my arm, I see the vast warehouse space has been transformed into a trendy, urban office space. On the wall behind the front desk is a stainless-steel logo.

"Romance Central?"

Max steps forward and takes my hands. "In your article, you said that everyone deserves to feel priceless at least once in their life, and I couldn't agree more. By myself, I could only service a dozen clients, but if I pass my skills along to others ... I can make a whole army of Mister Romances. And Miss Romances. I think there are a lot of guys out there who could also use some self-esteem therapy, too."

"Wait, you're ... franchising?"

He smiles. "In a way. I'm going from a one-man operation to a corporation. Taking tailor-made romance to the masses."

The relief I feel is so powerful, tears prickle my eyes. "For weeks I thought we were heading toward this terrible apocalypse where you'd have to choose between me and your work, and I didn't stand a chance."

He stares at me like I'm insane. "Eden, if it comes down to choosing between you and anything else on this planet, I'd choose you ... every single time." He comes over and takes my hands, and all of a sudden I feel stupid for having ever doubted him. "Everything else in my life is optional, *except* you. You're essential."

I look at our intertwined hands. "Well, now you're just trying to make me cry."

He pulls me into his arms and hugs me and after I've pulled myself together he says, "Would you like a tour?"

"I thought you'd never ask."

He leads me into the office area where the whole space has been fitted out with an eclectic mix of secondhand furniture, and I'm positive I'm not nearly hip enough to be here. The design has made use of the original brickwork, and the rest of the spaces have been defined by tall glass walls.

"How on earth did you do all of this so fast?"

"We had a lot of help. Remember Vivian from Valentine's Foundation?"

"Of course."

"She's the head of a multi-million-dollar construction and

property development company. She brought in her whole crew. Come look."

He shows me around, and apart from several large offices, there's a central kitchen, a spacious training room, and at the back, beneath the huge paneled windows is a giant conference room complete with a long wooden table, at the end of which is something underneath a black cloth. The rest of the table is covered in headshots of a huge range of men and women, all different ethnicities and ages, and judging by some of the bios, sexualities.

Max gestures to them. "This is our first batch of *Romance Central* candidates. All experienced actors. All decent people. Training starts next week. Dyson will take over all of my existing clients. And with so many more people being available for dates, we can charge less and still stay financially viable."

He clicks the control in his hand again, and a large screen on the wall lights up with a slick-looking website. "Toby did the site for us and then sneakily inserted the link to it on the bottom of your article. We've had over three-hundred inquiries since it went live."

I feel myself gaping. What he's achieved is astonishing. "Where did you get the money to do this?"

He pulls away the black cloth. Underneath is a scale model of the warehouse, fully developed into a trendy apartment complex, with Romance Central taking pride of place in the ground floor. "Presenting New York's latest apartment-warehouse development. Vivian and I are now partners. I've signed over fifty percent ownership of the warehouse, and she's taking care of all construction costs, as well as giving me a healthy chunk of the profits. It's going to take about a year for all the construction, and we'll have to relocate the offices for part of that time, but the bottom line is still impressive. When all of the apartments are sold, I should be able to clear my family's debts and even have a little left over."

He stares at me as he waits for my reaction, and it's clear how nervous he is. I don't know why, because surely he knows I thought he was brilliant before all of this. Now, I'm convinced he's an actual genius.

I walk over and put my arms around his neck. "Max, this is ... unbelievable."

He wraps his arms around my waist and pulls me close. "So, you approve?"

I stretch up on my toes and kiss him gently, beyond grateful he found a way for us both to get what we want.

When I pull back, he lets out a shaky breath. "Okay ... I'm going to take that as a yes." He slides his hand along my neck as he kisses me again, more intense this time. It's so thrilling, it feels as if it's the first time all over again, and in a way, it is. This is us with nothing to hide. No secrets, or agendas, or characters. Just the relentless need to be together.

"So, we're alone here?" I ask as I push his jacket off his shoulders.

He tugs his tie free and throws it on the floor. "Totally alone."

"Was this by design?"

"Maybe. This is a beautiful table. It would be a shame not to christen it and celebrate this new chapter in our lives."

"I couldn't agree more."

We both moan when he kisses me hard and lifts me to sit on the edge of the table. Then, he cups my cheek and kisses down my neck, and I lean back, pushing up to meet him.

"So," I say, my voice tight as my body explodes with sensation. "Your official title will be, what? Mister Boss-Man? Big Daddy Romance?"

"I don't really care, but feel free to call me *sir* any time." He finds the tie of my wrap-dress and tugs at it. "The main thing is that the only woman I'll be dating will be you." He pulls open the dress and makes an animalistic noise as he stares at my body. "Dammit, you're too gorgeous to be real." He kisses down my neck, nipping and sucking as he goes.

"One more very important question," I say, barely able to breathe as he kisses my breasts, then down to my stomach. "Will you have free and easy access to the costumes?"

He stops and looks up at me. "Do you have something particular in mind?"

I shrug. "Well, we could start with the *Officer and a Gentleman* uniform and work our way through the rack."

"I knew I should have used that on one of our dates."

I urge him to straighten up, then start on the buttons of his shirt. He watches me with barely restrained energy, like a panther waiting to pounce.

"Just out of interest," he says. "Which of my characters was you favor –"

"Kieran." I pull his shirt open and run my fingers over his broad chest, then trail down to the ridges of his abs. God, he feels amazing.

"Wait a second." He grabs my hands and stops me. "Don't you want think about that for more than half a second?"

"Okay." I pause and pretend to think. "Kieran."

He glares, and it's sexy as hell. "You're supposed to say that you found me sexiest when I was being *myself.* C'mon, Eden."

"Oh. Well, sure. But the accent, Max. That freaking, goddamn sexy *accent.*"

His face darkens, and he advances on me until I'm scooting my butt back on the table. Then he's climbing up, crawling after me with an expression that screams of all the things he's about to do. I'm certain there could be spanking involved.

"Oh, yeh like the accent, do yeh, lass?"

"God, yes. Keep talking."

He kneels between my legs and unbuckles his belt, and my gaze falls to where his long erection is straining the fabric of his suit pants. "Oh, I'll keep talkin' alright. Top 'o the mornin' to yeh, Miss Tate. Now, get yer feckin' panties off."

There's a rush of activity as we get clothing off and out of the way, and when there's only skin pressing against skin, we both groan in relief as he pushes into me.

He looks down at me in awe, and cradles my head as his hips connect with mine. He fills me so completely, I don't want him to move.

"Max ... I love you."

He leans his forehead against mine. "I love you, too." His voice is soft. "God, Eden, how I love you."

As he starts to thrust, slow and deep, all of a sudden, nothing else exists for me outside the circle of his arms. For so many years I thought I knew about pleasure. I thought it was defined by the empty, soulless encounters I engaged in after I'd had enough alcohol to dull my expectations. But *this* ... having a man who looks at me like I'm the reason the sun rises is a powerful reminder that I knew nothing, and I'm more than happy for Max to educate me as he slides home, time and again, proving without a doubt that pleasure with him is in a whole other universe compared with other men.

As a testament to that pleasure, the warehouse echoes with muttered curses and strained moans as we give the conference table the most mind-blowing christening possible. Twice.

In fact, we christen a lot of the new offices over the next several hours. *Romance Central* well and truly earns its name.

When our bodies are heavy and satisfied, and we're wrapped in a rug on Max's oversized leather couch, he leans down and kisses me, and I think it's the sweetest, most loving kiss I've ever experienced. It tells me how happy he is. How grateful. And I kiss him back, doing my best to tell him I feel exactly the same way.

"Do you still think that happy endings are a myth?" he asks, running his fingertips up and down my arm.

I stroke his beautiful face, more content than I've ever been. "I may not believe in happy endings, but happy beginnings are another story."

He smiles, and as we adjust to a more comfortable position, I snuggle into his chest and close my eyes.

Even though I teased him about finding Kieran the most attractive, the truth is, I fell in love with every single one of his characters, because they were all different versions of him. Each was sexy, and sweet, and intelligent as hell. Each mesmerized and aroused me. But the real Max, the man he is every day, when no one but me is looking, is my one true love. He took a distrustful cynic and turned her into a woman who totally believes in the healing power of love. He opened my eyes to the reality that a kind touch and loving glance can make people feel more special than all the money in the world. And even if he never goes near another costume for the rest of his life, I'll always think of him as a superhero and a rock star, all wrapped up in one.

But perhaps his most impressive achievement is helping me to finally understand that romance rules, and anyone who tries to tell you otherwise is fooling themselves.

The greatest thing you'll ever learn
Is just to love
And be loved in return.

NAT KING COLE

Also by Leisa Rayven

THE STARCROSSED SERIES
BAD ROMEO
BROKEN JULIET
WICKED HEART
BAD ROMEO CHRISTMAS

Coming in September 2017
Book 2 in the Masters of Love series
PROFESSOR FEELGOOD

For more information, please visit
WWW.LEISARAYVEN.COM

Acknowledgements

Whenever I finish a book, I feel a strange sense of loss, and that's especially true with this one. I've had Max and Eden's story rolling around in my brain for a while now, and for the four months that I've been writing it, I've lived them, breathed them, and thought about their journey for most of my waking hours, especially in the shower. (This is an author thing. Don't ask me why, but we all do it.)

So, now that I've typed 'the end' on their story, I feel like I'm saying goodbye to close friends; ones I won't get to spend time with in quite the same way ever again. However, whatever sadness I feel is lightened by the knowledge that I'm only saying goodbye so I can send them to you, and I have no doubt you'll take good care of them.

I couldn't have completed this journey without some truly spectacular people in my life.

Firstly, my agent Christina, who is always incredibly supportive and lends me her brilliance whenever I need it – I'll never forget that time one of your editorial notes was just a shouty-caps expletive with several exclamation marks after it. That will forever make me smile. I'm so grateful you and the whole team at the Jane Rotrosen Agency always have my back.

To my rock of a husband, who holds everything together when I'm late on a deadline and falling apart – Jason, I couldn't do *any* of this without you. Thank you for listening to my frantic brainstorming, for reading the same scenes over and over again and convincing me they're not trash, and for constantly telling me how proud you are, even when I'm cranky and stressed and absolutely don't deserve it. You're the best person I've ever known, and if our sons grow up to be half the man you are, I'll be the proudest mum ever.

To my amazing editor, Caryn – Catty-Wan, you complete me. I can always rely on you to hold my hand and kick my ass in equal measure, as well as leave hilarious notes in the margins about all the support groups I need to join for grammar abuse. Thank you for being the yin to my yang.

To my best friend, Andrea, who always reads the first draft of everything I write, and is so damn enthusiastic and supportive she gives me the energy to slog through the second, third, and fourth drafts. You're my sunshine, sweetie, and the sister I choose for myself. I love you.

To my PR Goddess, the gorgeous Nina Bocci – lady, you are a freaking rock star. Thank you for forcing me and my books onto people. Working with you is always a total pleasure, and not just because you have an awesome rack. You're also pretty. And kickass.

To Regina Wamba, who brought Max to life with her gorgeous cover design – you're a true artist, lovely lady. Thank you for your talent.

To my wonderful proofreaders, Celine and Anne – you guys save my life when I can't stand to look at my own words anymore to root out the inevitable typos. Thank you so much for your time and eagle eyes.

To all my beautiful Babes in Romeo's Dressing Room – *waves* Hi, lovelies! Thank you so much for enabling my craziness and brightening my life. I adore all of you.

To all of the unbelievably supportive bloggers and readers who go above-and-beyond to promote authors they love – you guys are the bedrock of the whole industry. Without you, authors would just be crazy people acting out scenes in their showers and writing books no one will ever read.

Finally, I'd like to say something to all the romantics out there; those of you who spend your lives dreaming and living out thousands of lives through books; those who find wonder in the mundane and magic in the everyday – to you I say *thank you.* Thank you for your passion and imagination, and most of all, thank you for your love. You're more precious than you'll ever know, and the world is a better place for having you in it.

Much love to you all,

Leisa x

Made in the USA
Middletown, DE
11 May 2017